The
Ninth Man

The
Ninth Man

A Russ Berard Charleston Mystery

by Brad Crowther

INGALLS PUBLISHING GROUP, INC

INGALLS PUBLISHING GROUP, INC
PO Box 2500
Banner Elk, NC 28604
www.ingallspublishinggroup.com

Copyright © 2011 by Brad Crowther
Text design by Luci Mott
Cover photo of the Arthur Ravenel Jr. Bridge
by Karen Julian Smith, simplylifephoto.com
Cover design by Aaron Burleson

This book is a work of fiction. All characters, places and incidents are either the product of the author's imagination or are used fictitiously, and any resemblance to persons living or dead, business establishments, events or locales is entirely coincidental.

Without limiting the rights reserved under copyright above, no part of this publication may be reproduced, stored or entered into a retrieval system or transmitted, in any form or by any means (electronic, mechanical, photocopying, recording or otherwise), without the prior written permission of both the copyright owner and the above publisher of this book. Exception to this prohibition is permitted for limited quotations included within a published review of the book.

The scanning, uploading and distribution of this book via the internet or via any other means without the permission of the publisher is illegal and punishable by law. Please purchase only authorized editions and do not participate in or encourage piracy of copyrighted materials. Your support of author rights is appreciated.

Library of Congress Cataloging-in-Publication Data

Crowther, Brad.
The ninth man : a Russ Berard Charleston mystery / by Brad Crowther.
p. cm.
ISBN 978-1-932158-92-2 (trade pbk. : alk. paper)
1. Diaries--Fiction. 2. Murder--Investigation--Fiction. 3. Charleston (S.C.)--Fiction. I. Title.
PS3603.R79N56 2011
813'.6--dc22
2011013558

First printing: November 2011

ACKNOWLEDGMENTS

I will be eternally grateful to the wonderful people at Ingalls Publishing Group who turned a sow's ear into a silk purse. In particular, I couldn't be more appreciative of the efforts of my editors, Judy Geary and schuyler kaufman, both accomplished writers who understand the agony and the ecstasy of the process. Judy was the first at Ingalls to read the manuscript, and her encouragement, patience, sense of humor, and tactful suggestions guided me from start to finish. Schuyler's insights about plot construction and character development, her attention to detail, and her relentless but gentle insistence on excellence made this a far better book than the manuscript I submitted. And there would be no book had Bob and Barbara Ingalls not been willing to take a chance and invest the resources necessary for publication.

DEDICATION

To my wife, Chris, truly my better half, who has walked with me in all kinds of weather. Without her love, support, and tolerance for flaws such as my writing addiction, neither this book nor any other accomplishment would have been possible.

And to my father, Walt, who never lost faith in my writing potential. I wish he could have remained in this world long enough to celebrate publication with me, but I believe that somewhere he is reading *The Ninth Man* and smiling.

In February 1864, the Confederate 'fishboat' *H.L. Hunley* became the world's first successful combat submarine when it sank a Union ship blockading the Charleston, South Carolina harbor. The Hunley and its crew vanished that night and did not emerge for 136 years. The Hunley was raised from the ocean in 2000 and is being restored, but at this writing, the cause of its sinking has yet to be determined.

Prologue

Blood dripped from the knife blade, staining the ground at Moze Cheddar's feet near where he'd set the Hunley diary and other items for his trip. Deer blood from venison steaks Moze was slicing, not human blood. Moze had covered the blood where the boy fell last week. Raked and turned over the soil, spread grass, leaves, and twigs on top before he'd drug the body deeper into the woods for burial.

Been four boys last week, but Moze'd killed just the one. How it had happened, Moze returned to the cabin from fishing, and standing on the front porch was someone didn't belong there. Fella caught sight of Moze and stepped quick into the cabin shouting a warning. Moze dropped his fishing gear, yanked the Sig Sauer pistol from his pocket, crouched low and advanced real cautious-like. Near to the cabin, he heard noises in back and went that way hisself. Coming around the cabin corner, he saw four boys wearing masks and carrying weapons. They was rushing toward tree cover, and Moze hollered at 'em to stop. 'Course they didn't.

They'd led Moze a merry chase through the woods. He heard one giving commands to the others, a strong, deep, confident-sounding voice with authority in it that reminded Moze of somebody, maybe an actor or politician. Or maybe a memory of the voice of another enemy Moze had chased through woods or jungles when he'd done battle for his country.

Eventually Moze had closed in on the slowest, who turned and raised his weapon, giving Moze no choice but to fire. Moze shot to wound, but the bullet struck wrong when the boy slipped and went down. Moze left him and followed the other three. They made it to a silver sports utility vehicle and rumbled away, but Moze got hisself a glimpse of the license plate and remembered the number.

Boy Moze had shot was lying on his side making wheezing noises when Moze got back to him. Skinny, scrawny-armed boy wearing olive wind pants, gold and white running shoes, black short-sleeved tee-shirt and navy blue face mask. Moze slipped off the face mask gentle as he could, uncovered wispy blond hair and teary brown eyes full of the fear of dying. A look Moze had seen too many times in too many places. Boy hadn't expected his life to end that day. They never did.

"I maybe can help," Moze had said, though he knew he couldn't. "Need things from you first, though. Need to know why you came, who the others are."

Skinny boy's lips had moved, and for a moment Moze thought he'd talk. But the moment died, along with the boy.

After burying the boy, Moze had inspected his cabin, brewed coffee and studied what was in the boy's wallet. Name was Dewey Welch according to his South Carolina driver's license. Date of birth would make him twenty-five. Lived in Mt. Pleasant, near Charleston. A hundred and nineteen dollars in the wallet, credit cards, pictures. Nothing accounting for why Welch and the others had come.

Could be the four was robbing lake front cabins, but it hadn't felt right to Moze that they'd traveled from Charleston to upstate South Carolina for that. Then too there was what the boys had and hadn't done. They'd ransacked Moze's desk, table drawers and file cabinet, spilled papers to hell and gone. But they hadn't taken nothing of value. Not the collection of timepieces nor the stamp collection. Not the silver left to him by his mother. Not the foreign coins he'd brung home from the places where he'd done his country's killing.

No, it wasn't chance they'd hit Moze's cabin. They'd been after something in particular. And sipping coffee and staring out his kitchen window at the evening gloom, Moze's gut had told him that the something in particular was the diary his great-great-great-granddaddy had wrote explaining what happened to the Confederate submarine *Hunley*.

Been a big mistake to let that Gavin Berard fella come to the cabin to talk, Moze realized. Been a surprise when Berard had phoned, said he was a minister from down in Mt. Pleasant outside Charleston near where the *Hunley* was undergoing restoration. Said he'd done a lot of study on the *Hunley*, come across a letter wrote by a fella named Stanton who'd been Secretary of War under President Lincoln. Letter mentioned the name Ezra Cheddar, said Ezra had been a Union spy sent by Stanton to Charleston on a secret mission involving sabotage to a Confederate vessel. Wasn't many details, but this Gavin Berard fella had wondered could the Confederate vessel have been the *Hunley*. So Berard had done more reading, more tracing and facts he'd come up with gave the impression Moze was a descendant of Ezra Cheddar.

Moze had allowed that this was true, an allowance he reckoned now had been his first step toward trouble. Next the Berard fella had asked could he come to see Moze at his cabin, talk about Ezra's spy work in Charleston, talk about whether that spy work had anything to do with the *Hunley*. Moze had said no, said he was a quiet man leading a quiet life who didn't have no desire to make private family matters public. Berard wouldn't let it go, though, and he had hisself a real persuasive manner. Said he didn't have no wish to embarrass Moze or Moze's family name, said he just wanted to learn, said nothing that was told to him during their conversation would go no further.

So Moze had said all right, and the Gavin Berard fella came to the cabin, and Moze gave him sweet tea and homemade oatmeal cookies, and they sat on the deck and had theirselves a conversation. Berard told Moze it was nice to be up here in the woods looking out at the lake and drawing good clean breaths. Berard had a calming voice, an open face and kindly blue eyes, no trace of deviousness about him. And Moze, who'd stayed alive by not trusting nobody in all the time he'd done violent work for his country, found hisself trusting Berard.

Eventually, as the sun sauntered west and gray shadows spread over the lake, Moze had told the Berard fella about Ezra's diary. Moze had his reasons for telling. He wanted Gavin Berard's help. There was a relative of Moze's living in Charleston who Moze had never met on account of trouble between two sides of the family that went all the way back to Ezra Cheddar's daughter and son. Moze figured this relative, his only living kin, oughta know about the *Hunley* diary, being descended from Ezra. But Moze wasn't sure how best to make the approach, earn hisself the relative's confidence and tell what needed to be told. A minister fella like Gavin Berard who was practiced in handling delicate matters might could advise him.

Gavin Berard had leaned forward in his chair with palms on his knees and listened real attentive to Moze's tale about the *Hunley* diary, mouth ajar and eyes wide like a small boy hearing a ghost story. Of course, in a way the diary was a story about ghosts—eight ghosts, or nine depending on how you counted.

Moze hadn't told many details about the diary, just painted the general picture. When he was done, the Berard fella asked a mess of questions, most of which Moze wouldn't give no answers to. Caution kept a check on Moze's trust. Finally the minister asked the big question Moze had knowed was coming. Could he see the diary? Moze said no, said it quick and firm. Could he just see sample pages Berard wondered, read 'em at the cabin, not take none with him.

Moze had give it thought, then he asked would the minister help him with his relative in Charleston in return for Moze showing pages of the diary. The Gavin Berard fella said he'd help bring Moze together with his relative on account of it being the right thing to do, he wouldn't put no conditions on it such as Moze showing him diary pages.

Moze had liked it that Berard was willing to help without requiring nothing in return. Caused Moze to trust the minister even more. So Moze brought out copies of a few diary pages and watched the Berard fella read 'em. Saw the excitement grow in his eyes, saw the joy on his face. When Berard was done reading, he shook his head in wonder, told Moze this was a story that oughta be told.

What the minister fella had wondered, would Moze consider using the diary to raise money to honor the *Hunley* crew and help with restoration of the submarine. Maybe could have fund raising events where sections of the diary was revealed and actors played out the scenes being read. A contract could be negotiated so Moze shared in the profits.

Moze had told the minister he'd give thought to the idea, but first needed to take care of this business with his relative. Back in time Moze had made a promise to another on that side of the family about keeping the diary secret. That man was dead now, but Moze owed it to his memory to let the living relative know what was what before anything got told to the public. He didn't have no interest in making money for hisself, but would let the other decide.

Gavin Berard fella had said he understood, and when he got back home to Mt. Pleasant he'd study on how to put Moze in touch with his relative, maybe arrange a meeting at Berard's church, where Moze and the relative would feel at ease.

The two men had shook on what was decided, and Moze had believed the Berard fella's word was good. There'd been something about the minister caused you to put faith in him.

But that was five weeks ago, and there hadn't been no word from Berard since. No word unless you counted the four boys, who could have been sent by Berard to do his dirty work. Didn't take no stretch of the imagination to believe Moze had been suckered by the minister, who'd gone home from the cabin and laid plans to steal the diary.

Moze had remained on alert after the boys' visit, slept outside the cabin several nights. Waited to see if somebody would show up to ask about the dead boy, but nobody did. Waited to see if more would be dispatched by the Berard fella or whoever had sent the others. Moze could kill all that was sent, but killing tuckered a body out. It was why he'd come back home to live a peaceful life in the lakefront cabin. All the killing for his country had wore him down.

Funny about that though, because in a way the cabin was responsible for this trouble. Cabin had been built as a getaway place by Moze's ancestor, Ezra, the one who'd wrote the *Hunley* diary. But the place had fallen into disrepair over the years, didn't get no use until Moze had started to fix it up in between the jobs for his country. Moze had found that sawing, hammering, and performing other such simple tasks in pure solitude soothed his soul after godawful work whose memories shook him awake screaming in the night.

Fixing up the cabin was how Moze had discovered the diary, which was preserved real careful like in silk oilskin and hid behind a rotting wall Moze took down. Surprised Moze no end when he read through the pages. He hadn't had the faintest damn notion of what Ol' Ezra did during the Civil War till the diary gave up its secrets.

If Moze hadn't found the diary, there wouldn't have been nothing to tell the Gavin Berard fella, the four boys wouldn't have come, and the Dewey Welch boy wouldn't be dead. But that was all water passed under the bridge, no way of getting it back.

Question was what to do now. Moze had just about decided to go down to Mt. Pleasant and have hisself a few words with Gavin Berard when a letter showed up the other day that confused matters to hell and gone. Letter from somebody didn't give their name said Gavin Berard had been murdered. Said the letter writer knowed Gavin had talked to Moze about his *Hunley* diary, and said the writer had interest in obtaining the diary from Moze. Gave a phone number that was an indirect way for Moze to get in touch with the writer.

Letter also said Gavin Berard had hisself a son named Russell Berard who'd been a police detective up in Newport, Rhode Island, but was back home to investigate his daddy's killing. Said this Russell Berard might could be a good fella for Moze to talk to about what had happened to Berard's daddy.

Letter created a whole lot of worries for Moze. Only way the writer could have knowed that the minister Gavin Berard had talked to Moze about the *Hunley* diary was from Gavin Berard hisself. Which caused Moze to think the minister fella hadn't been so trustworthy as Moze had believed. Also caused Moze to wonder if the minister had told others about the diary.

Moze's head hurt trying to think it through, but when it was all added up, there didn't seem to be no way around Moze going down to Mt. Pleasant to try to find out who was doing what and why they was doing it. Moze didn't figure he'd call the phone number the anonymous letter writer had given right away. He'd get the lay of the land first, prob'ly have a friend of his in the government check into this Russell Berard fella. Depending on what the check showed, might could be Moze'd talk to Russell Berard, see if the minister's murder had something to do with the *Hunley* diary. But if Moze talked to the Russell Berard fella, he'd do it real careful. Wouldn't walk up to Russell Berard's front door, ring the bell and announce hisself.

Also, Moze still wanted to get hold of his Charleston relative and pass along information about their ancestor, Ezra and his *Hunley* diary. With Gavin Berard not able to help on account of being dead, it was all on Moze's shoulders now to locate the relative and make his approach.

So Moze'd finish slicing and wrapping the venison steaks, lay them in the freezer and clean the knife. Then he'd pack. Wouldn't pack much, he was experienced at traveling light. A few clothes, rain gear, sleeping bag, knife, guns. For guns he was thinking the Kalashnikov assault rifle, Galil sniping rifle, S&W 686 revolver and Sig Sauer automatic. Might take free weights, but they'd be heavy in the truck, and he could lift rocks and do pushups instead.

A question Moze had stewed over was whether to bring the diary along. Truck had secret compartments, but leaving the original diary in the hiding place he'd made in the woods seemed safer. Wasn't nothing bad could happen to it in the hiding place, and wasn't nobody going to find it there. Moze would carry copies though. Might be he'd need pages to bait folks out of the darkness and into the light.

Among those in need of baiting was the three surviving boys who'd broke into Moze's cabin. Moze had run the license plate number of the silver SUV belonged to those boys through his government database, and he had a name and address. He'd look the boys up, and the rest would come natural. Moze especially desired words with the leader boy who'd been directing the others through the woods. Moze'd recognize that confident-sounding voice when he heard it again, and when Moze was done, the voice wouldn't be no more than a blubber.

Chapter One

I crossed out of Charleston above the Cooper River on the bleak side of midnight. Crossed on the Ravenel Bridge, its cable lights snuffed to give egg-laying turtles a modicum of privacy. The Ravenel had replaced the Grace and Pearman Bridges, now demolished. Other elements of my past were absent also. My father, Gavin Joseph Berard, four weeks dead—murdered in his office at the Mt. Pleasant church where he'd ministered. My mother, Agatha Tynes Berard, three weeks missing—disappeared during her swim to eternity.

Mom had left her suicide letter in a white envelope on the kitchen counter. Hand written in blue ink on twenty-four pound, watermarked stationery, lovely flowing script. Lengthier than most suicide notes I'd seen as a police officer, because she'd wanted people to understand why and how. Why was grief over my father's murder. How was a swim that replicated the final journey of the Confederate submarine *H.L. Hunley*.

I'd known the story since before I could talk ...

On a February night in 1864, the Hunley *pushed off from Breach Inlet on Sullivan's Island, its crew wedged into a compartment less than four feet high and forty feet long. The men used hand cranks to propel the submarine about four miles out into the South Carolina waters, where they rammed a torpedo through the starboard side of the* Housatonic, *one of the Union ships blockading Charleston Harbor.*

The Hunley *reversed course, played out the line attaching the sub to the torpedo and detonated the explosive. The blast blew a hole in the side of the* Housatonic *and sank the ship in less than five* minutes. But the *Housatonic's masts remained above water because of the shallow ocean bottom, and other Union ships were quick to respond. For better or worse, only five* Housatonic *crew members perished. The* Hunley's *fate was harsher. The submarine vanished and didn't emerge for 136 years.*

On a July night, my mother had stepped into the Breach Inlet surf and begun swimming toward the spot where the *Hunley* torpedoed the *Housatonic*. She'd waited until a few days after Dad's funeral, when I'd gone up to Rhode Island to make final plans for relocating back home. Nobody knew how far she had made it before she vanished. Her body had yet to be found, but three weeks was a short time in comparison with how long it had taken to locate the *Hunley*.

Mom's swim had been symbolic of her intention to rejoin my father, whose passion for the *Hunley* and its story had been one of his few interests outside the ministry and his crusades for social justice. I recalled the excitement in Dad's voice when he'd described watching the sub come out of the water; he'd been an active member of Friends of the *Hunley* and conducted his own extensive research about the Confederate "fish-boat."

I stopped at a 24-hour Griddle Grill off Johnnie Dodds Highway on the Mt. Pleasant side of the Ravenel. Diner food held more appeal than going home. Not home really—my parents' house. The ownership papers said Russell Q. Berard now, but that was a legal formality, not an emotional attachment. My parents had moved to the house after I was grown and gone.

I parked and stepped out. August humidity clung to my skin like shower mist, and odors of gasoline and food grease fouled the air. Lights winked in a compound of tourist economy motels across the highway. My eyes stung with fatigue, and my heart ached after two days in Savannah discussing estate issues with my sister.

I bought yesterday's *Charleston Post and Courier* from an outdoor rack by the Griddle Grill door and went in. Just me, a waitress, a cook and a brisk jolt of air conditioning. I took a booth. The waitress, thick-bodied and sad-eyed with a name tag that read "Sylvia," moved toward me with a coffee pot and an air of hopeless resignation. I wondered what unfortunate life events had brought her to the graveyard shift of a Griddle Grill. She might have been wondering the same about me. I ordered scrambled eggs, wheat toast and coffee.

Sipping coffee, I leafed through the *Post and Courier*, and an article about a high school classmate caught my eye.

Opposition is growing toward the creation of a reality television show based on the sinking of the Union warship *Housatonic* in Charleston Harbor by the Confederate submarine *H.L. Hunley* during the Civil War. The *Hunley* was raised from the ocean near Sullivan's Island in 2000 and placed in a specially designed tank in what is now called the Warren Lasch Conservation Center on the old Navy Base in North Charleston. Conservation efforts continue, and the nonprofit organization, Friends of the Hunley, sponsors weekend public tours.

Entrepreneur Arnold T. St. John, a Charleston area native and resident of I'On in Mt. Pleasant, confirmed that a *Hunley* reality show to be filmed in the Charleston area is under development, but St. John would not disclose details. Jubal Jeff Longstreet, president of Guardians of the Confederate Truth, said his organization will, "take all necessary actions to ensure that Mr. St. John does not attempt to capitalize on the wonderful story of the Hunley and mock or dishonor its crew." Business leaders, elected officials, and groups like Friends of the Hunley have expressed concern as well.

There have also been rumors that St. John is pursuing a heretofore unknown diary indicating that there was a ninth crew member aboard the *Hunley* during the attack against the *Housatonic*. It had long been thought that the submarine carried a crew of nine, but when the boat was recovered, excavation found the skulls and other remains of only eight persons. St. John would not comment on the existence of a secret diary.

I smiled. No great surprise. In high school Arnie had been unsurpassed at tracking alligator dung into the parlor. Many had written him off as a prankster, but I'd always suspected that there was a darker, more malicious motive for his behavior. His father had risen out of poverty to become a successful businessman, but for reasons including lack of social graces, he had been constantly rebuffed in his efforts to join Charleston's elite. These rejections—denials of admission to exclusive clubs, lack of invitations to prominent social events—had made Arnie's family a source of derision. Unable to strike back directly at the persons responsible, Arnie had instead humiliated people within his reach. Now that he had wealth and influence, no one was beyond Arnie's reach, including civic leaders who took pride in the *Hunley*, and did not tolerate public embarrassment.

But I had more important things to do than psychoanalyze Arnie St. John and speculate about his intentions. My own issues would keep me busy well into the future.

I was on a second cup of Griddle Grill coffee and the sports section when trouble arrived. Three counts of trouble. Mid-twenties males wearing tee-shirts, jean shorts and work boots. Tattoos on their tanned arms. They banged through the door like an occupying force, loudly profane and sky high. Standing near me, Sylvia murmured, "Shit."

A muscular blond led the pack my way. He paused briefly at my side, and I could feel his glare. I yawned and studied the baseball scores. He continued past and thumped down in the next booth, rattling the partition between us. Tubby-brown-hair came next and took the opposite side, with sinewy-black-hair following and sitting beside Tubby-brown-hair. The air soured from their odors of perspiration, marijuana and beer. The blond at my back added to the stench by lighting a cigarette.

"You can't do that in here," Sylvia told him, hovering with her coffee pot. "There's no smoking." She didn't say it shyly.

The blond laughed. "No smoking! Damn if you ain't a hot sketch. Remember what I told you before, sweet cakes? You come down from New York or wherever, you got to learn the ways of the South. We smoke, and we don't go crazy over dumb-ass laws. So pour the coffee and shut that filthy mouth you use to make other girlies feel good."

"That was a cute routine the first time you came in here and used it on me," Sylvia said. "It's tired now. Extinguish the butt or take the party elsewhere."

There was tense silence before black-hair spoke sotto voce, "Easy, Ronnie. There's later to think about. We don't want to get jammed up now."

More silence, then Ronnie laughed again. "Okay sweet cakes, maybe I was hasty with my attitude. I'll finish the butt outside. Bring me a cheeseburger well done with onion rings."

Ronnie rose and departed the booth. As he passed by, he glanced down at me. "What you staring at, bud? This conversation disturbing you in any way?"

"Not at all," I said. "I enjoy a floor show with my meal."

He chuckled. "Floor show, huh? That's a good one. Maybe we got a spot in our act for a comedian like you." His hand wrapped around my shoulder, fingers squeezing lightly. "I'll go outside, take care of this cig. When I come back we'll talk."

"I'll wait with breathless anticipation," I told him.

He bent toward me, eyes glittering, mouth a mean slit. "I'm not a guy you want to try and have the last word with, bud. The last word's always mine—one way or another." He squeezed my shoulder harder.

"Damnit, Ronnie, knock it off!" Black-hair commanded.

Ronnie scowled, glowered at me a moment longer, then released my shoulder and swaggered away.

Sylvia paused beside me after pouring the pack's coffee. "You want to pay your tab while he's outside, there's a rear door you can use."

"I'll be fine, but thanks," I said.

When Ronnie returned, black-hair was using the rest room. Free of constraints, Ronnie plopped down across from me. "That your Avalon out there with Rhode Island plates?"

"It is."

"A Yankee, huh? What you doing in low country?"

"I recently retired from my job and relocated here. Mostly because I'd heard how friendly the people are. I'm willing to allow for exceptions."

Ronnie cocked his head. "You got a quick wit, bud, but don't push it too far. You piss me off, we'll go out in the parking lot, and

I'll beat the shit out of you."

Ronnie had a point. If we kept needling each other we probably would end up in the parking lot. He was a bully with a hair-trigger temper spoiling for a brawl. My insides were churning with rancor about loss of loved ones and other life circumstances. Why not make Ronnie the outlet for my rancor? There were a couple of 'why nots'. I fancied myself the more mature one in our nascent and hopefully short-lived relationship. I'd been a long-time cop until a short time ago and ought to have greater regard for law and humanity than to provoke a fight.

"Let's both of us quit pushing and you rejoin your friends," I suggested.

Ronnie pursed his lips. "Yeah, we can do that." He leaned across the table to get in my face. "Long as we're clear about ... whadda they call it? ... The balance of power."

"I'm clear," I said.

He frowned, possibly sensing that my clarity of vision diverged from his. But he let it go, no doubt bored with the game. Ronnie appeared to be a guy who grew bored quickly and moved on. He stood and slapped me on the shoulder. "Well that's good then, bud. That's real fine."

Ronnie and I were best pals now, brimming with bonhomie. There wouldn't be any blood spilled here this early AM, nosiree. That pleasant daydream survived less than a minute.

Wobbly from beer and weed, Ronnie lost his balance. He threw his arms up, staggered backward and slammed into Sylvia. The tray of food she was bearing flew from her hands and crashed against an empty table. Plates shattered, cutlery clanged, burgers came apart, and slaw and onion rings spilled on the linoleum.

"Stupid bitch!" Ronnie snarled. He pushed Sylvia, and she banged into a chair. He seized her shoulders and shook hard, bouncing her head back and forth.

Here we go, I thought, coming fast from my booth.

Ronnie raised his left hand to slap Sylvia, and I grasped his elbow and twisted the arm behind his back in a hammerlock. Swinging my hip in front of his elbow, I increased my leverage and bent him forward and gripped his greasy blond forelock for additional control.

"Take a stroll with me, Ronnie," I said. "We'll chat about things."

"You just made the biggest mistake of your life," he hissed.

"You're speaking out of ignorance," I said. "You have no idea what big mistakes I've made." I propelled him through the door and out into the muggy black morning.

Clear of the restaurant, I released his arm and pushed him away. He stumbled, righted himself and pivoted. He was an inch or so shorter than my six feet two, but he had ten or fifteen pounds on my one-eighty-five. His eyes were feral in the hazy neon light, his face taut with fury. He massaged his shoulder and bared his teeth like a mongrel. "You're truly screwed now, bud."

I'd been in this situation often enough to know it was a waste of time to reason, so I waited. He advanced in a crouch, fists clenched, veins bulging in his biceps and forearms. I rolled away from a lunging roundhouse left and kicked him just below the kneecap. He yelped, dropped his guard and grabbed his leg. I jabbed stiffened fingers into his kidney, stomped on his instep and slammed his chin with the heel of my hand. He tottered backward and I kicked him in the groin, hard enough but not too hard. He toppled to his hands and knees, gagging.

The Griddle Grill door banged as Sinewy-black-hair and Tubby-brown-hair came out to join the fray. "Jesus, Ronnie, I can't leave you alone for one goddamn minute!" Black-hair said.

"Are we done?" I asked, adrenaline surging.

"I'll show you who's frigging done!" Tubby said, stepping toward me.

Black-hair grasped Tubby's arm to hold him back, and Tubby didn't resist. Black-hair studied me speculatively as if he were making mental notes. "Yeah, we're done."

I walked past them and reentered the Griddle Grill. Sylvia and the cook were cleaning the mess from the spilled tray. Sylvia looked up from the floor, where she was using a whisk broom to sweep food and plate fragments into a dust pan. "Thanks," she said. "Those guys should be locked up somewhere. Especially that Ronnie."

"You want to file a police report, I'll hang around and make a witness statement."

She sighed and shook her head. "Those punks are connected, and me, well, I've got some baggage as far as the cops are concerned."

I nodded. It was a story I'd heard hundreds of times when I was a cop. I helped finish the cleanup, took some bills from my wallet and handed them to Sylvia.

"This is way too much," she said.

"It's not likely Ronnie and the boys will be paying for their meals. This is for them also."

She tilted her head and regarded me as if I were from another planet. "There's no reason for you to do that."

"It feels right," I told her.

She rang it up in the register and gave me change and a receipt. I told her to keep the change and wrote my name and number on the back of the receipt and returned it to her. "If you have second thoughts about the police report and want a witness statement, call me."

She glanced at what I'd written and studied me more carefully. "Russ Berard. Not related to Gavin Berard? There's a resemblance. The long arms, shape of your face, blue eyes ..."

"My father."

She grimaced. "I'm really sorry. Your father was a wonderful man. I volunteered to help with a gay rights event he was organizing. It's terrible his killer hasn't been caught." She hesitated. "Some people wonder how hard the police are looking."

I nodded. I was one of those people.

"Anyway," Sylvia said, "your kindnesses make perfect sense to me now. You're a good man like your father. Thank you again."

That caught me by surprise. I'd always thought of myself as the polar opposite of my father. He'd chosen the ministry, I'd chosen law enforcement. He'd seen good everywhere, I'd waded hip deep through every form of depravity woman and man could conceive.

I said good night and suggested Sylvia lock the door behind me. But outside I learned my nocturnal tribulations had an epilogue. Ronnie and the Ronettes were waiting.

Chapter Two

"**How they** hanging, bud?" Ronnie asked. I had a hunch it was a rhetorical question.

He was sitting on the hood of my Avalon smoking a cigarette. Tubby-brown-hair sipped from a beer can with a work boot propped on the Avalon's front bumper. Black-hair stood apart with his arms crossed and an amused expression on his face. The occasional vehicle swooshed along Johnnie Dodds, and an eighteen wheeler's brakes squealed as a traffic light changed red. A soft breeze carried the putrid odor of rotting garbage from the Griddle Grill dumpster.

I looked at black-hair. "I thought exercise period was over."

He shrugged. "We have time to kill, and when Ronnie gets like this the easiest thing to do is let the mood run its course. I blame a lifetime diet of Southern fried food for his moods."

"Could be the tobacco also," I suggested.

"Nah. I smoke, and I don't act like a six-year old."

Something was familiar about Black-hair, but I couldn't make the connection. Something about his bearing and mannerisms.

"Hey, guys, over here," Ronnie said. "This is about me. And about you too, bud. But don't get me wrong, I ain't after more trouble. You kicked my ass fair and square. You're a tough ol' boy, yes you are. What it is, a friend of ours wants to meet you. Figured we'd stick around till he gets here, you know, make the introductions."

Ronnie was in fine fettle, once again in control, at least in his mind. Which caused me concern. I wondered if his 'friend' might be a small army carrying lead pipes. I couldn't see much percentage in hanging around to find out. "It's swell of your friend to come out this late," I said. "And I'm certainly flattered. But I'm going to have to take a rain check. Why don't you have his people call my people and we'll schedule something for another time."

Ronnie chuckled. "A rain check. Have his people call your people." He smacked Tubby-brown-hair on the shoulder "This guy cracks me up. Don't he crack you up?"

"Damn, Ronnie!" Tubby whined. "You made me spill my beer!"

Ronnie ignored that crisis and returned his attention to me. "I gotta caution you, though. This friend of ours, he don't got him a good sense of humor like me, so you might want to gear that wit of yours down a few speeds."

Headlights flashed across us as a car entered the lot from McGrath Darby Boulevard.

"Your friend?" I asked.

"Sure is," Ronnie said.

A Mt. Pleasant police car. There was no end to the twists in this improvisational drama. The car slid to a halt a few yards from our gathering. The driver's door swung open and a man stepped out. Hatless, he ran a palm over his close-cropped hair. A quick appraisal satisfied him there was no imminent danger, so he shut the door and sauntered forward. He was about 5'9", but with erect posture and shoulders pushed back he appeared taller. Slim and fit, he moved lightly on his feet like a point guard.

"This the Yankee?" he asked Ronnie in a Carolina drawl.

"In living color," Ronnie told him.

The patrolman tilted his head and gave me the once over. His eyes were close set and piercing beneath thick brows. His uniform was clean and crisp, his shoes shined. He stood near enough that I could smell his cologne, a popular manly, musky scent. He played with a toothpick in the corner of his mouth and rubbed his fingers across the leather of his holster. "Officer Durrell Pritchard, bo. What's your story? Hear you worked these boys over pretty fierce."

"Ronnie was pushing the waitress around inside," I said. "I walked him out and he took a swing at me, so I immobilized him with as little force as possible."

Pritchard removed the toothpick and puffed a cheek with his tongue. "Immobilized him with as little force as possible," he repeated. "You a cop or military?"

"Recently retired cop. Military a long time ago."

"Should have known," Ronnie said. "A goddamn cop."

"Shut up, Ronnie," Pritchard told him. "What say we see some ID, bo."

I took my wallet from my pocket, removed the driver's license and passed it to him. His hands were square and callused, the fingernails chewed. He looked at my license, blinked and looked again. His head came up, the corners of his mouth curled down, and a nasty light glinted in his eyes. "Well, well. Russell Q. Berard, son of the preacher man had his candle snuffed awhile back. Preacher man who loved queers, niggers, spics, druggies, you name it. Anybody but straight thinking, procreating white folk. Your daddy didn't much care for the po-lice either, did he, Mr. Berard? Forever screeching about how we abuse the rights of scumbags and dirtballs."

Blood roiled through my body and a vein pulsed in my forehead. I knew he was goading me, but it was working. I was exhausted, edgy, mad at the world, mad at me, bitter and feeling reckless. Roughing up Ronnie hadn't sated my hostility. Punching a patrolman might do that—if I didn't mind the consequences. I focused beyond Pritchard's right shoulder and drew and released two slow breaths.

Swinging my eyes back to meet his, I said, "You have an interesting notion of respect for the dead, Officer."

Pritchard broke eye contact and flicked a forefinger at a mosquito on his forearm. "No disrespect intended, but your daddy was a man got people's emotions riled up. Kinda surprising you went into law enforcement considering his attitudes about the profession and all."

He shuffled his feet and stared out at Johnnie Dodds. "'Course you ain't exactly loyal to the breed, are you? I read what you said in the *Post and Courier*. How the Mt. Pleasant Police Department don't seem to be trying very hard to catch your daddy's killer. How Mt. Pleasant detectives don't know jack shit about conducting a murder investigation. How things'd be done different up in fancy Newport, Rhode Island, where you was a detective."

That was an exaggerated interpretation of my comments, but there was no denying I'd said things in the heat of the moment that would have been better left unsaid. "I apologize for any offense I gave," I told him.

Pritchard made a face like he'd swallowed sour milk and spat on the pavement. The windows of his patrol car were down, and the radio crackled with unintelligible static. Tubby-brown-hair snapped the tab of another beer can, air hissing free. Pritchard paid no heed. Apparently public drinking wasn't one of his current enforcement priorities.

"What I'm thinking," he said. "Maybe you come down here from the North to show us country boys how a real detective works. And maybe you got the idea Southern folk ain't nothin' but shit stuck to the bottom of your shoe. So maybe you went out prowling for trouble, and these three boys had the bad luck to get stuck in your sights. That what happened, Mr. Berard?"

Pritchard had a knack for slurring 'Mr. Berard' as if it were an obscenity. I wondered if he'd honed the skill during interactions with my father.

"Why don't we go inside and hear what the waitress has to say," I suggested.

A muscle twitched in his cheek, and he spat again, this time nearer my feet. "That bull dyke don't got nothing to say interests me. These boys want to file an assault charge, I can take you over to the detention center, let you spend a cozy night. Witness stories and such'll get sorted out tomorrow or later."

Both of us knew he wasn't taking me to the detention center. Pritchard had some connection to Ronnie and was harassing me as a favor. But he didn't have any kind of case, and if he locked me up it would come back to bite him. In addition, Pritchard's supervisors might not appreciate the fact that he was close enough to a guy like Ronnie to respond to his personal appeal for help.

I put my arms behind my back and drew my hands together. "I'm ready."

"Ready for what?" he asked.

"To be cuffed. I assume it's department policy to cuff any arrestee you transport."

"Nobody said nothing for certain about you being arrested, smart ass."

"Told you he's a comedian, Durrell," Ronnie said.

Pritchard scowled. "I'm sick of the bunch of you. I never should have come down here. Let's get this shit done. You wanna file an assault complaint or not, Ronnie?"

"He's not filing a complaint, Durrell," Black-hair said, glancing at his watch. "We have a pressing engagement."

Ronnie stroked his chin and frowned pensively. Not that he'd ever be confused with The Thinker. "Guess I'll have to let this vicious attack on my person go unpunished, but it'd be nice to know where Mr. Berard's staying. He told me he ain't just passing through seeing the sights, he's relocating down here permanent. If I wake up with whiplash from the pounding he gave me and wanna take legal action, his address'll come in handy."

Pritchard looked at me like I was the skunk who wouldn't leave the garden party. "Relocating here permanent, huh? That's cause for jubilation. Got yourself a local address yet, Mr. Berard? For my report I mean. Not for Ronnie's whiplash."

I gave him the address, and he wrote it in a small notebook. Then he frowned and ran a forefinger along the black stubble beneath his nose. "That in Snee Farm?"

"It is."

"Where your folks lived?"

"Yes," I said again, wondering how he knew where my parents lived.

"Setting up a base of operations there?"

"I'm living there."

"Not planning on doing any private investigating are you? Investigate your daddy's killing and such?"

"My plans are still percolating. I may take a job at Piggly Wiggly."

Pritchard stepped closer. His shoulder muscles were bunched, his fists clenched at his sides. Malevolence burned in his eyes like red coals. "My advice is go back to Rhode Island and take a job there. Be a lot safer." He brandished the veiled threat like a razor-honed blade.

"I'll give that advice careful consideration," I said, meeting his glare.

"Yeah, you do that. Now all of y'all get to hell out of here."

Ronnie slid off the Avalon hood, and Tubby removed his work boot from the front bumper. I got in the car and started the engine. Ronnie came over, braced his hands on the roof and bent at the knees until we were at eye level through the open window. There was a pimple below his lip and a streak of dirt on his cheek. Odors of tobacco and dried sweat invaded my window like a chemical bomb. "It's been fun, bud," he said. "See you next time. Got your address stored right here." He tapped his forehead, winked and be-bopped away.

He didn't be-bop far. Pritchard was waiting for him by the patrol car. The patrolman gestured toward me, thrust his chin at Ronnie like a bantam rooster and began to squawk. I couldn't hear the conversation, but it wasn't making Ronnie happy. His face contorted, and he waved an arm and shook his head. The byplay continued for a couple of minutes until Pritchard put in a final word, Ronnie shrugged, and they separated.

Pritchard got back in his patrol car, and Ronnie took the shotgun seat of a silver Jeep Cherokee, with Black-hair driving and Tubby-brown-hair in the rear. Pritchard swung the patrol car right onto McGrath Darby toward Coleman Boulevard and Patriots Point. Black-hair steered left out of the lot and was halted by a red light on Johnnie Dodds. A dark-colored truck, possibly green, that had come along McGrath Darby stopped behind them. The traffic light changed, and the Cherokee and the green truck went straight across.

I thought about following. The three amigos weren't heading for a church dance at 2:00 AM. But I wasn't a detective anymore, and I'd never been a detective in Mt. Pleasant. The Cherokee gang's marauding approach to life was no longer my problem.

Chapter Three

My missing wife, Kam Lim, had tried to teach me to meditate, dragging me into it kicking and screaming. In my Marine Corps and police worlds, meditating hadn't seemed macho enough, not like pumping iron and running to exhaustion. But eventually Lim had convinced me that meditation was made to order for coping with life's stressful moments. This morning qualified as one of those moments. Stress gripped me by the eyelids and dangled me upside down.

Booming pre-dawn thunder had slammed me awake disoriented and trembling, as if I'd been reclaimed from the dead by a nerve-jangling jolt of electricity. Residual from the Griddle Grill confrontation with Ronnie were a sprained finger and throbbing pain in my arthritic knee. At my age I couldn't stay out late brawling and expect to face the morning refreshed. I was an aching, hobbling poster child for the first of Buddhism's Four Noble Truths: suffering is the central fact of life.

I found my mother's yoga mat in the attic and carried it out to the deck of the indoor pool, a rectangular room on the rear of the house with sliding glass doors and screens and a cathedral pine ceiling with skylights. The pool was only about ten yards long; mom had done her serious swimming with the Palmetto Masters team at Martin Luther King pool in Charleston.

I unrolled the yoga mat, sat with my spine straight and shoulders relaxed and put my hands in my lap, left palm upward on my right palm. I wondered if Lim could see me. After we'd married and settled in Rhode Island, she'd returned to Cambodia for a visit with family and friends. Then word came that she'd joined a rebel group fighting the Vietnamese invaders who controlled Cambodia. I shouldn't have been surprised. Lim and some of her family had fled Cambodia after other family members were murdered by the Vietnamese. Nothing, not even innumerable meditation sessions, had calmed Lim's turbulent soul, and it wouldn't have taken much for her to be drawn into the war. I'd wanted her back though, and I'd been preparing to go to Cambodia to get her when word came that she'd disappeared.

I had so far made four trips to Cambodia to search for Lim. I'd uncovered countless leads, followed every one to the end, and every ending had been bitter and cold. I still meditated regularly, but I couldn't fill the hollowness of my soul if I repeated my mantra from now until doomsday. I began breathing deeply through my nose, counted one as I inhaled, two as I exhaled, went to ten and repeated the sequence. My focus was on following the breaths. Then I began my mantra: liiimmm ... liiimmm ... liiimmm ...

I was sifting through my parents' files in the downstairs office when a midnight blue sedan came down Casseque and turned into Covenant Square. The sedan caught the attention of a neighbor's dog, and the dog's barking caught my attention. From windows overlooking the driveway I watched the car park and saw an athletically built woman wearing a lime green summer suit emerge. Her caramel colored hair gleamed in the sunlight like polished wood. She squared her shoulders and started up the walk.

Uh oh, I thought. I'd last seen Ellen Talley, captain of the Mt. Pleasant Police Department's criminal investigations division, a couple of weeks ago. Her parting remark then, actually a parting scream, had been that she'd rather walk barefoot through a field of rattlesnakes than talk to me again.

She said Russ when I opened the door, and I said Ellen. Immediate dialogue depleted, silence chilled the foyer like an Alaskan wind. Eventually I drew on my reserve of good manners, invited her in, and asked if she wanted to sit by the pool. She said fine.

We sat at the teak table against the rear sliders. The doors were open, and humidity dripped through the screens. The ceiling fan whirring above the pool provided marginal relief. Beyond the back fence a golf cart rested beneath trees off the fourteenth fairway, and a lumpy man wearing khaki shorts and a yellow shirt took practice swings in the rough.

"You play?" I asked, searching for an icebreaker.

"Once or twice a week when my schedule allows."

"You should give me lessons."

"The pro here is excellent," she said.

"But I didn't teach the pro how to throw a football, swing a baseball bat and bait a fishing line. I did teach Jimmy's bratty little sister how to do all those things."

"You taught me the butterfly and breaststroke too. But last time we saw each other you didn't give the impression you wanted to be friends anymore." She looked away and rubbed her fingertips across the teak.

"That conversation didn't have anything to do with being friends," I said.

"And this visit doesn't have anything to do with your father, Russ. I'm sorry."

Hope drained in a rush, leaving me empty. I didn't know what I'd been hoping for, though. My father was dead. No words Ellen could have brought would change that. I'd been on the other side of this conversation too many times. Too many times told families of murder victims it was no good being consumed by thoughts of revenge, blah, blah, blah.

"What I wanted to ask about," Ellen said. "You were involved in an altercation early this morning at the Griddle Grill. Officer Durrell Pritchard responded."

So the Griddle Grill festivities were going to be more than just a memory. I nodded.

"I got an earful about the incident from Sylvia, the waitress," Ellen said. "She had a lot of nice things to say about you and nothing nice to say about anyone else involved, including Pritchard. His supervisor will be having a conversation with him later."

I appreciated Ellen's courtesy, but it didn't add up that a CID captain would be investigating something so minor. "So you came to tell me I have nothing more to fear from Pritchard and I can sleep peacefully again?"

She ran her tongue around the edges of her teeth. "I came to tell you that one of the boys who hassled you at the Griddle Grill was killed several hours later."

That brought us down to brass tacks. We stared at each other for a moment. "Not Ronnie?" I asked.

"No, Jason Grimes."

"Tubby with brown hair?"

Her eyes narrowed. "Lucky guess?"

"He seemed like the weak link."

"I suppose that's one way to describe him. Jason was a follower. We've collared him before, but just minor stuff."

"Where was he killed?"

"Near the clubhouse of the Etiwan Pointe townhouses. Know where they are?"

"No."

"At the end of Wando Park Boulevard off Long Point Road."

"Not far from here," I said.

"Indeed."

"How was it done?"

"He was shot."

"What with?"

"Thirty-eight caliber bullets. We didn't find a gun."

"I have a .38 Special."

"I know," she said. "A PI license, too. You got that really fast."

"I have some law enforcement friends down here, hard as that may be to believe. People from SLED I became acquainted with when I was a Newport cop. Want to run ballistics tests on my .38 to see if it's the murder weapon?"

"Maybe later. Right now I want to ask you some questions." She took a notebook and pen from her handbag. "There were only three at the Griddle Grill? Not a fourth, possibly in a car outside who didn't go in?"

"I don't think so. There definitely wasn't a fourth in their vehicle, and except for Pritchard nobody else left the lot when they did. Why?"

"A kid named Dewey Welch is usually the fourth wheel. Nobody's seen him recently, and we can't locate him. Of course, we can't locate Ronnie and DuBois either."

"DuBois is dark-haired, sinewy, looks multiracial?" I asked.

An inscrutable look briefly darkened Ellen's eyes like clouds crossing beneath the sun. "He is multiracial. Did they give you any idea where they were going after they left the Griddle Grill, what they were planning to do?"

I replayed the events in my mind and then verbalized them. "Inside the restaurant, when Ronnie was harassing the waitress, DuBois warned him that they couldn't get jammed up because they had to think about later. Then when things were wrapping up in the parking lot, DuBois told Pritchard they had a pressing engagement. But there wasn't any mention of exactly where they were going."

Ellen scribbled in the notebook. "Did you leave before or after them?"

"After. I was the last man out."

"What were they driving?"

"A silver Jeep Cherokee." I gave her the plate number, which I'd memorized out of habit. She didn't seem excited about the information; probably she already had it.

"Did you see which way they headed?"

"Across Johnnie Dodds."

"What about Pritchard?"

"Different direction. A right out of the parking lot toward Coleman or Patriots Point."

"And what did you do when everyone else was gone?"

"Drove home, drank a glass of water and went to bed."

"Any witnesses?"

"None. I haven't been back long enough to make cuddly bedtime friends."

She capped the pen and shut the notebook. "I'm sure you'll find someone. There are always online dating services."

"You forgot a question," I said.

"What question?" Her tone was brusque. She didn't seem grateful to have a person of my stature mentor her interrogatory technique.

"The question about whether I saw anything else worth reporting."

"Did you?"

"A dark colored truck, green maybe, came up McGrath Darby and crossed Johnnie Dodds behind the Cherokee."

"You think the truck was following the Cherokee?"

"I don't know, but that time of night there'd been almost no traffic on McGrath Darby."

"Did you see the truck's plate number?"

I shook my head. "Too far away in the dark."

She uncapped her pen and wrote more notes.

"Have any leads?" I asked.

"I can't comment on that. We're not releasing certain details of the case to the public."

"So I'm the public?"

"Who do you think you are?"

I couldn't restrain my mouth's next impulse. My irrational rage at the universe continued, and Ellen was the new closest target. "No one of importance. Just a guy whose father was murdered and who doesn't understand why the police can't get off their butts and find the killer."

Her eyes flashed. "I don't want to get into this, Russ. I really don't."

"I bet you don't."

She stood quickly, face flushed. "Your parents were my friends! I used to stop by and see your father at his church, and your mother would invite me over for tea and a chat, especially after my divorce! I think she thought … Never mind what she thought! The point is I really cared about them, and I want to solve your father's murder almost as much as you do! So you can go to hell, and on the way there you can fall off your high horse!"

She arched her neck, stared up at the pine ceiling, ran her hands through her caramel hair and swallowed. When she regained control she brought her eyes back down to meet mine. "What's happened to you, Russ? You used to be such a nice guy."

What had happened was I'd lost both parents and made a career miscalculation that caused me to retire impulsively and churlishly from a job I loved. I could have told Ellen all that, but I was pretty sure her question was rhetorical and she wasn't interested in providing therapy. "Can you fill me in on any progress investigating my father's death?" I asked in a calming voice.

But the time for calming had passed. "I'm not filling you in on anything!" She slung her handbag over her shoulder and stomped across the pool deck, wide hips swaying and straining the fabric of the snug skirt. I doubted she was expecting to be shown out, so I didn't offer.

She paused at the sunroom door and looked back. "I misspoke. There is one thing I want to fill you in on. Cherisse Dane is back in town, remarried to Arnie St. John and living in I'On. DuBois, the multiracial kid from the Griddle Grill, is her son. When I interviewed Cherisse earlier, she said she'd heard you were back too, and maybe she'd hire you to find DuBois and help her with this situation. That would be cozy given the history between you and Cherisse. But I advise against it. You muck around in a police investigation and I'll gut you like a catfish."

I sat at the table stunned, not by the threat but by the revelation that Cherisse was living a few miles away and DuBois was her son. Something about DuBois had seemed familiar, and now I knew why. He had Cherisse's nonchalance, self-confidence and air of superiority.

Eventually I got up and wandered into the office. Through the window I saw Ellen settle into her car. She sat unmoving for several seconds, then smacked the steering wheel with her palm, grimaced and shook her hand. *Well done, Russell,* I thought. *You made her mad. You win.*

She started the car, blasted backward out of the driveway, ground gears and screeched away.

Chapter Four

Moze Cheddar gassed his truck at a Kangaroo station on Coleman Boulevard in Mt. Pleasant, also bought black coffee and two glazed donuts. Cashier gave him three singles with his change. He left the bills on the counter, asked for three Powerball quick-picks.

Didn't have no idea what he'd do if he won. Most likely rip up the ticket. Some folks in his past wasn't favorably disposed toward him, had their grievances. Likely to search him out if he was to show up on the news. But there was more immediate matters to stew over just now. He put the lottery ticket in his glove compartment and guided the truck out of the station.

Moze followed Coleman to where it changed to Ben Sawyer and crossed over the Inland Waterway onto Sullivan's Island. Turned right towards the southeast end of the island and found a parking slot near Fort Moultrie. Rain was heading north, and the sun was climbing fast and shimmering bright. Cloud swatches puffing around the powder blue sky looked like stringless white kites.

Moze stepped out of the truck with his coffee and donut sack and looked at the red brick wall ringing Fort Moultrie's grassy embankments. Atop the embankments was cannon and other armaments, a tower, and fluttery American flags.

Moze sipped the coffee and grimaced. Convenience store crap. Donuts was good anyhow. No nutrition, but he'd buy vegetables and fruit at a market later. Right now he needed the come-awake rush from caffeine and sugar. Hadn't been much sleep.

Moze had arrived in Mt. Pleasant yesterday, cruised the area to get his bearings, then located the address attached to the license plate number of the silver SUV belonged to the boys who'd broke into his cabin. SUV was registered to a fella name of Ronald Hodge according to information from Moze's government database.

Moze had waited and watched until a couple of boys had come out of the address, got into the silver SUV, and drove to a big ol' house in a ritzy development called I'On. While the boys was inside, Moze'd done Internet research on his truck computer and learned some interesting facts. House belonged to a fella name of Arnold St. John. That led Moze to an article in the *Charleston Post and Courier* told of a reality show St. John was developing based on the *Hunley*. Article also mentioned that St. John had interest in a secret diary about a ninth man who'd been on the *Hunley*. Moze'd shook his head in frustration. Seemed like now the whole damn world knew of that diary.

Eventually, the two boys had left the I'On house and drove off, and Moze followed. Boys went here and there, picked up a third boy and stopped at a Griddle Grill restaurant.

That's when the proceedings had become real interesting. Wasn't long before one of the boys got pushed through the door by an older fella held the boy in a hammerlock. Older fella and the boy tussled, but there wasn't much to it. Older fella handled hisself nice, put the boy down quick. Then a Mt. Pleasant police officer showed up, jawed with the older fella, jawed with the boys. When the jawing was done and everybody was in their cars, Moze had used his night vision scope to read the older fella's license plate and run it through the government database on his truck computer. Came back Russell Berard, which was the name of the person the anonymous letter had said could help Moze. Son of Gavin Berard, the minister who'd come to Moze's cabin, taken a strong interest in the diary, gone back home and got hisself killed.

Could be that Russell Berard fighting with the boy in the Griddle Grill parking lot meant Berard was on the opposite side from Arnold St. John. But there hadn't been no chance for Moze to think on that, 'cause all the people in the parking lot had climbed into cars and skeedaddled. Moze had decided to keep following the boys, thinking he could look the Russell Berard fella up another time. Boys had gone to a place called Etiwan Pointe, and events there had turned mean and ugly with real unhappy results.

Moze shook his head to clear it of Etiwan Pointe thoughts for now and strolled a sidewalk with plaques that told some history about Fort Moultrie. Fort was named after Colonel William Moultrie, who'd commanded when British ships was turned back in 1776, saving Charleston from occupation for a time. Federal troops had manned the fort till the Civil War, when Confederates moved in. Union cannon shells had beat the fort's brick walls to hell by the time the Confederates evacuated Charleston in 1865.

Moze walked across a band of mowed grass to jagged rocks at the water's edge. Water was vile green like a serpent's skin. Straight out was Fort Sumter where the Civil War had got underway when Confederates fired on the Union garrison there. Just to the right was a patch of beach, and farther right was the bridge between Mt. Pleasant and downtown Charleston. To the left the Atlantic Ocean ran as far as the eye could see and bumped against the horizon.

Moze didn't care for the ocean, never had. Too much water in one place. Stretched forever. A wrong wind caught you out there, you wasn't coming back. Get blown off the side of the earth maybe. Moze preferred forests with lakes for fishing, but no lake so large you ever feared not finding your way home. It was safe in them kind of areas, not like down here on the coast where a man stood exposed. Not much woods for cover. Most everything developed and open, and the ocean blocking an eastern escape. Made a fella jittery.

Moze chewed on a donut and thought about boys dead in the Revolution and Civil War, which brought to mind the boy who'd died last night. That weighed heavy in Moze's heart. Damn waste. Always was. The boy had looked almost peaceful sprawled in the grass. Peaceful baby-faced boy if you didn't pay no heed to the bullet holes and the blood. Just like the peaceful baby-faced boy Moze had killed in the woods outside his cabin. Two down now.

Moze sighed. Bad feeling he had about this business was getting worse. The two down wasn't going to be the final ones to meet their maker.

Damn shame he hadn't been able to put his hands on the two remaining live boys at Etiwan Pointe last night. Moze had heard the boys' voices at Etiwan Pointe, and one of the voices belonged to the leader of them that had raided his cabin, wasn't no doubt about it. Could have learned a lot had he grabbed the leader and the other live boy, but he'd bungled, no point pretending different. No point crying over spilt milk neither. There'd be another chance, and Moze wouldn't bungle the next time.

Chapter Five

I returned with groceries mid-afternoon and found a mud-splattered red pickup truck defiling my driveway. The pickup smelled of fish and sun-baked metal. A sticker plastered to the rear bumper read, *I was born in the South, but I had an ACLU card smuggled in.* The pickup belonged to Gary Nagle, my sometime best friend. Sixty-three days ago on my Newport deck he'd flicked a knife that stuck in a post eighteen inches from my groin. Gary had been up from Charleston for a visit, and I'd suggested he do something about his drug habit. He'd thought the part where I said "… or else get out of my life" was a trifle harsh and insensitive. So he'd flicked the knife and gotten out of my life.

Now I found him in a chair by the edge of the pool, bare feet and ankles submerged in the water. He was wearing shorts and a sleeveless tee-shirt, reading an Archie comic book and drinking Dr. Pepper from a can.

"Russell Quentin Berard," he said. "How the pins dropping, Q? All strikes and spares?"

"Splits and gutter balls," I told him.

He laughed. "You never could bowl for shit. So you bought your military time, cashed out of the Newport PD with twenty-five years of service, and here you are a retired man of leisure at forty-seven. And here I am the same age still trying to decide what to be when I grow up."

His receding dirty blond hair was brushed back and bound in a ponytail, and he'd grown a goatee. Jowls spread over his throat, and the sleeveless tee-shirt exposed muscled arms and shoulders coated with flab. "I opened the sliders to get some air," he said. "Hope you don't mind. It was brutal damn hot when I came in."

"You got in how?" I asked.

"Key. Your dad gave me one. I used to crash here on occasion when making it home looked like a tall hurdle." My father had given Gary a key. Ellen Talley used to stop by for tea and chit chat with my mother. What had my parents been running, a drop-in center for my old high school friends?

"By tall hurdle you mean when you were drunk or drugged?"

Gary chewed his lip and stared at the lettering on the Dr. Pepper can. "I come in peace, Kemo Sabe. What say you ratchet down a notch? I did a little rehab after that misunderstanding in Rhode Island. And I'm going to AA and NA meetings. You still got my knife, by the way?"

"I've got it." I pulled a chair near his, kicked off my sandals and dipped my feet in the water. "Are you working?"

"Same ol' same ol'. Fishing, landscaping, music. Nothing to make you proud. But I am interviewing next week for chief of pulmonary surgery at the Medical University."

"Touché," I said. "Pass me one of those Dr. Peppers."

He opened a green cooler beside his chair, lifted a can and flipped it to me.

"No work today?" I asked.

He shook his head. "Why is it every time I talk to you I feel like I'm being grilled by a probation officer?"

"You should be flattered I'm so interested in your well-being."

"That's why I keep coming back for more. And I do have work. Night work. My band's playing downtown." He dug a pack of cigarettes from a pocket of his shorts, gazed at the pack longingly, then looked at me. "A man can't quit all his drugs at once."

I could have showed him my sour, disapproving face, but he'd seen it a million times. "No ashes in the pool," I said.

He located matches, lit a cigarette, inhaled and sighed as if pain medication had kicked in. "I hear you beat the shit out of Ronnie Hodge last night. That'll catch folks' attention."

"That was my goal, establish street creds as a fighter. And you're the second person to come by here today and mention the tussle with Ronnie."

"Who was first?"

"Ellen Talley."

He whistled. "Hot little Ellen. Wish I'd been smart like you and recognized her babe potential when she was a snot-nosed kid. She's divorced now, you know. Did she offer up that pretty body for your personal pleasure?"

"She offered to gut me like a catfish if I mess up her murder investigation."

Gary laughed. "That's Ellen. Jason Grimes' murder she was talking about?"

"You still get around, don't you?"

He shrugged. "I know people, hear things." He blew a smoke ring. "Saw another of your old girlfriends earlier. Cherisse Dane is back in town."

"You're second with that news flash too," I said.

"Ellen again?"

"Uh-huh."

"She tell you Cherisse's boy, DuBois, disappeared with Ronnie Hodge after Jason Grimes went down last night?"

"Uh-huh."

"Damn. She scooped me on everything."

"You need to begin your day earlier. Where did you see Cherisse?"

Gary dropped his cigarette in the open tab of the Dr. Pepper can and scratched his goatee. "The joint my band's playing at downtown? Cherisse owns it. Previous owner called it Secessionville. Cherisse changed that to Denmark Vesey. Name change got her a shitload of publicity and a shitload of threats. Place is rocking, though. I stopped by her house earlier to talk about our schedule and pick up a check."

Denmark Vesey ... Only Cherisse would name a Charleston club after a slave who'd organized a revolt in Charleston in the 1820s. I bet there'd been ugliness and threats in a city that still referred to the Civil War as the War of Northern Aggression.

Gary stood. Sun beaming through the screens wrapped him in a false halo. The white hairs on his thick arms were slick with sweat. His body odor consorted with the rancid smell of cigarette smoke and the pungent scent of marigolds blooming out back.

"Cherry got all dreamy-eyed when she spoke your name, Q. It's still there for her."

"That dream died a long time ago," I said, bitterness in my throat thick like bile.

I silently debated whether to ask my next question, decided

not to and was astonished to hear someone with a voice exactly like mine ask it anyway. "What's the situation with Cherisse and Arnie?"

Gary smirked "Now we're getting down to it, huh?"

"We're not getting down to anything," I insisted, noting that my voice sounded way more annoyed than it should have sounded if I weren't getting down to something. "If I'm walking into a mine field here, a rough sketch of the location of the mines could be helpful."

"Uh-huh," he repeated.

"Wipe that mockery out of your voice, damnit!"

He chuckled, pleased to have cut under my skin. "Cherisse and Arnie are using each other, probably have been since the day they got hitched. They both know it, and they both know it's coming to an end."

"Using each other how?"

"Cherry's just continuing a lifelong pattern of partnering with whoever can do the most for her at the moment. You were the best guy in high school, so she partnered with you till she decided to broaden her horizons. Then she dumped you and jumped a bunch of levels and hooked up with somebody else. He took her out in the world and showed her new things, and when he'd run out of things to show her, she moved on to somebody else. She's been doing the same shit ever since."

"Thanks for that part about her jumping a bunch of levels when she dumped me," I said.

"You know what I mean. He was an older business guy, had a lot of experience with life, not to mention a lot of cash he didn't mind showering on Cherry. She's a sexual magnet for men, gives us all ideas, so she takes the best offer. Hard to blame her for that."

"Unless you're the one with her when she decides to accept another offer."

"Well, yeah, except for that."

"What exactly is she using Arnie for?" I asked. "From what I understand, her previous husbands took her into the upper tiers of society. And, from what I also understand, the divorces left her flush with cash. Plus she seems to be doing just fine making money on her own."

"You're half right," Gary said. "The part that's wrong is the part about money. The way I hear it, Cherisse is a shitty businesswoman. Supposedly she made a bunch of dumb-ass investments in New York and was a half-step from bankruptcy when Arnie bailed her out. And supposedly she's right on the edge again, only this time Arnie's not helping."

I thought it over. "All right, Cherisse has been using Arnie for money, and his largesse is drying up. What's Arnie been using Cherisse for?"

"A check-off."

"What does that mean?"

"Cherry's on the wish list of most guys who've ever known her. Now when Arnie reaches a ripe old age and he's sitting in a comfortable arm chair beside the fire on a cold winter night sipping brandy and reviewing his wish list, he can check off *Marry and/ or fornicate with Cherisse Dane*. He can take a crapload of points for that, too."

"That's a swell view of human nature," I said.

Gary grunted. "As many years as you were a cop and the shit you saw, I don't see how your view can be much better."

He had a point.

"Anyhow, Cherry'll be at the Vesey tonight," Gary said. "And she asked me to ask you to drop by, get caught up with each other's lives. Talk about whether you can help find DuBois. Hear my music too. I got a girl singer with a voice will buckle your knees. I'm in love."

This would be approximately the eleven hundred and seventy fourth time Gary had fallen in love. "If you need a best man, there's nothing I'd rather do than give you away," I said.

Gary's eyes clouded. "Yeah, best man ..." He'd been best man at my wedding to Kam Lim, and he'd been by my side on all four trips I'd made to search for her.

Gary slipped on his sandals and hefted his green cooler. "So I can tell Cherisse you'll come by the club tonight, have a chat?"

"I'm retired."

He grinned. "You might be retired from being a cop, but ain't nobody retires from Cherry. You've been in hibernation from her all these years, but she'll snap you out of your deep sleep real quick."

Chapter Six

History bleeds through Charleston from the collective wounds of fallen Revolutionary and Civil War soldiers and flogged slaves, lending irony to the nickname of Holy City, attributable to an abundance of churches.

I entered the city and its bloody history off the Ravenel Bridge and drove down East Bay Street toward the bottom of the peninsula. To my left were railroad cars and container cranes at the Columbus Street Terminal. Across the Cooper River from the terminal was Patriots Point, home to military museums and the USS Yorktown, a decommissioned World War II aircraft carrier that had picked up the Apollo 8 crew in 1968.

Below Calhoun Street I passed the Old City Market, three open-air structures and a main building modeled after a Greek temple. In the 1800s City Market had sold meat, fish and local produce. Today it sold jewelry, tee-shirts, sunglasses, art work, sweet-grass baskets, candy, souvenirs and more, much of which was schlocky and non-local. But a new property management firm had plans for an upscale makeover.

Cherisse Dane's club, Denmark Vesey, was west of East Bay Street in the French Quarter. I parked east of East Bay in a public garage near Waterfront Park. The night sidewalks were strewn with cheery folk stuffed full of fine cuisine from restaurants such as Magnolias, Blossom, Cypress and High Cotton. It was uplifting to intermingle with cheery folk, but I was on the periphery. Why not sidle up to one of the happy groups and try to attach myself? Step out of my current life into a new one. I gave that notion short shrift. Stepping out of an old life into a new one was how I'd ended up back in South Carolina, and the early results of that metamorphosis weren't promising.

Walking to the club I asked myself why I was walking to the club. The trip wasn't long enough to generate a satisfactory answer. A walk from Charleston to Missoula wouldn't have been long enough to generate a satisfactory answer. I played with the idea that seeing Cherisse would prove Gary was wrong about her still being in my blood, but that idea didn't digest smoothly. Reopening the door to Cherisse married to Arnie St. John was inviting trouble as surely as if I sent Arnie an engraved invitation to remove my tonsils with a screwdriver.

Denmark Vesey was near the Old Slave Mart Museum on Chalmers Street, a building that had been part of a complex known as Ryan's Mart, where slave auctions occurred until 1863. Proximity of the club to the museum was à propos, because Denmark Vesey had been a brilliant and accomplished slave who bought his freedom and then was hanged when he allegedly planned an insurrection of other Charleston slaves.

I pulled open the Vesey's oak door and stepped into modernism, not history: creamy floor tile, plum painted walls, horseshoe bar, band stage, dance area and comfortable chairs in conversational circles. Business was brisk for a week night, but August was prime tourist season, and Charleston was a get-out-and-boogie city for locals as well. The customers were a mix of ages, races and attitudes. Early-twenties College of Charleston students, older nattily-dressed professionals, and lean and hungry community activists.

I took a stool at a red oak bar so brightly burnished I could see my reflection. A TV above an island of liquor bottles was showing a documentary about Sherman's march through the South. Denmark Vesey wouldn't be confused with a sports bar. There were two bartenders. I surmised that the Asian female tended because she was too beautiful to model, and that the African American male tended because he was too large to play defensive tackle in the NFL. Just my luck the oversized tackle was serving my area. I bought a beer and watched Gary Nagle setting up on stage with his band. Gary on bass guitar, another guitar player, a drummer, a keyboarder and an early-thirties female vocalist.

In a poetic moment Gary had branded the band the River City Soul Cutters because, he said, the voice of the vocalist, whose name was Lina Pinheiro, "sliced into the dark recesses of a man's soul." I didn't yet have an opinion about her voice, but her looks did things to a man. About 5'3", plump face and curves, short black hair, porcelain skin, lush red mouth and eyes like smoldering obsidian. Gary hovered around her pointlessly, his yearning as obvious as a child staring at a puppy through a pet shop window.

Gary twanged a guitar string to test the sound system. As if that were a signal, the Vesey's front door opened and Cherisse Dane appeared in the halo of entrance light like a Nubian princess. An ankle-length dress patterned with pink and blue flowers furled around her slender body. Waves of dark hair shone in the light. Déjà vu made my stomach churn. Once upon a time a wavy-haired Cherisse wearing a flowery blouse and short skirt had entered a high school English class and I'd lost my heart. And once upon a later time a woman named Kam Lim with silky black hair and a floral-printed dress had entered a Providence, Rhode Island bar where Gary Nagle was jamming with local musicians, and I'd lost my heart again.

Cherisse glided between tables with a hip-rolling sway that drew eyes. In high school she'd been a middle distance runner who floated around the track, and she hadn't lost any grace in the intervening years. She paused at one side of the horseshoe bar a distance from where I was sitting and spoke to the male tender. The bar was crowded, not likely she'd notice or recognize me. It had been more than two and a half decades since we'd been together. I'd grown an inch since then and added fifteen pounds. My blue eyes were hopefully wiser, my russet hair dulled by the years, my nose broken twice.

Conversation with the tender completed, Cherisse continued down the side of the bar to a hallway. The tender moved along the center of the horseshoe, refilling drinks. On stage, Gary Nagle touched Lina Pinheiro's arm, leaned close, and whispered words that made her laugh.

The tender reached me, said, "You care for another, suh?"

I said yes. He filled a clean glass from a draft beer spigot and set the glass before me on the red oak. I took out my wallet. The big man shook his head. "Ms. Cherisse say to me, she say Lewis, that fella sitting down there, he an old friend, Mr. Russell Berard. You give me a couple of minutes, pour Mr. Russ a fresh drink on the house. Ask him he care to join me in my office to drink his drink." The tender pointed a forefinger the size of a table leg in the direction Cherisse had sashayed. "You go along that hallway, Ms. Cherisse's office be the second door on the left. You have yourself a pleasant evening, suh. It been my pleasure to serve you."

The hallway had been sprayed with a pine-scented freshener that was no match for the odors of pipe tobacco, perfume, and a musky cologne that reminded me unpleasantly of the way the Mt. Pleasant cop, Durrell Pritchard, had smelled during our clash in the Griddle Grill parking lot.

Halfway down the hall I fought the urge to turn and run. But it was too late for running. I knocked on Cherisse's door. She called, "Come in."

I took a deep breath and went in.

Cherisse was on the phone. She flashed a smile and motioned to a tan leather sofa. I put my beer glass on a table and remained standing. Through wall speakers I heard Gary and the other guitar player open with gentle chords. The keyboarder and drummer slid in smoothly, and Lina Pinheiro began to sing. A ballad, but the lyrics were irrelevant. Her throaty, raspy voice did indeed slice into my soul.

"She's incredible isn't she?" Cherisse said, finished on the phone and approaching in a swirl. Milk chocolate skin tight around her chin and throat, wide-spaced almond eyes glowing with vitality, teeth brilliantly white. "Gary did me an enormous favor bringing her around. I'm going to help them cut a CD."

She used a remote control to mute the speaker sound and stopped an arm's length away, as if there were invisible barriers between us. There were barriers—time and memory—but they weren't physical.

Cherisse reached out and took my hands. Her fingers and palms were warm. She cocked her head. "Russ, this is … it's just … I can't put into words how wonderful it is to see you."

She wrapped her arms around me, pressing our chests and thighs together. When she pushed back her breathing was ragged, as if she'd run forty yards. "Let's sit," she said.

She folded herself down on the sofa with a one-piece motion as sinuous as a snake's coil. My sitting earned considerably fewer style points.

She smiled. "Dr. Cherisse prescribes yoga for that balky knee."

"That's what my mother prescribed."

She winced. "Russ. Your mother, your father. I'm so terribly sorry. They were such wonderful people."

I nodded.

"I should have come to their funerals. I was in Europe at an international civil rights conference, but I heard about their deaths, and I should have returned home."

"It wasn't necessary."

She looked down at the floor. "Only doing what's necessary isn't ... it's not enough. By my age I should have learned to do the right thing."

Cherisse's age was my age, and about all I'd learned was that it was remarkably easy to find good reasons for not doing the right thing.

"What was it you used to tell me?" I said. "Guilt is a worthless emotion. It slows you down, makes you look backward when you should be moving on."

She sighed. "That was a long time ago. I was totally self-centered, no one knows that better than you. My attitudes are different now." She adjusted her legs and brushed my ankle with her shoe. "For example, have you heard that Arnie St. John is my current husband?"

I nodded.

"You're probably wondering why I married the class buffoon."

I shrugged. "It's not a match anyone predicted in the senior yearbook. Of course, no one predicted Gwen Kiely would drop out of Georgia Tech and make porn movies either."

Cherisse opened the drawer of an end table, withdrew a pack of cigarettes, studied the pack and threw it down on the table. "Why does everyone in South Carolina smoke? How am I going to give these damn things up with that sort of peer pressure?"

"Look on the bright side. Fried catfish and grits with brown gravy might kill you before lung cancer does."

She smiled. "You always could make me laugh. Maybe I should have married for laughter. All three of my marriages have been for financial and social advantage." I didn't recall Cherisse spending much time finding fault with herself in high school. She had been, as she'd said, self-centered, able to rationalize any action that got her something she wanted, regardless of who got hurt in the process. I wondered if this self-criticism was a mood, a result of dashed dreams, or a routine for my benefit.

She modulated her voice, made it softer with a heavy-hearted catch. "I need help, Russ. I need it desperately. I know Gary told you."

"Your son."

"DuBois. Please help me find him."

"I'm not sure I have the ability to help, or even if you need me. Ellen Talley came by today. It sounds like the police are making a serious search for DuBois and his pal, Ronnie."

Cherisse's eyes glittered malevolently. "Ellen Talley would just as soon shoot DuBois as run him over with a bulldozer."

"Ellen has a murder to solve, Cherry. DuBois and Ronnie ought to be prime sources of information about what happened. It won't be in the cops' best interests to get trigger happy. You haven't heard from DuBois?"

She shook her head. "I've been calling his cell phone constantly. No answer. And I went to his condo, but he wasn't there."

"You have no idea where he might have gone?"

She shook her head.

"What would you expect me to do?" I asked.

"I don't ... I'm not sure. I just feel like I need your support. I trust you, but I don't trust the Mt. Pleasant Police. You were a detective, so you know how to handle situations like this. You might be able to find DuBois. Even if you can't, if DuBois contacts me I'd like you to talk to him, give him advice. He ... it's all complicated. His relationship with me, his relationship with Arnie. DuBois is from my first marriage, he's not Arnie's son, obviously."

"I had a run-in with DuBois and his friends last night," I said. "I doubt if he'll want to talk to me."

She leaned toward me and put her hand on my knee. "He'll talk to you. I'll convince him. Please say you'll help, Russ."

It was impossible to think clearly with that damn hand on my knee. "If you haven't heard from him by tomorrow afternoon, call me and I'll see what I can do."

Chapter Seven

Halfway down the corridor from Cherisse's office I realized I'd left my unfinished beer behind. I wasn't going back for it though; no telling what she'd convince me to do next.

I ordered another beer from Lewis, the human office building. "You have a nice talk with Ms. Cherisse, suh?" he asked.

"Very nice. We talked a little about her son, DuBois. You know him?"

Lewis wrinkled his brow. "We acquainted."

"Does he ever come in here, sit at the bar, chat with you about things?"

Lewis' eyes flickered like warning lights. "I get you that beer, suh. You excuse me, but Ms. Cherisse don't care fo' me making small talk when we busy like this."

"Sure. Think we can talk another time?"

"Might could happen." He made it sound like a threat.

Lewis returned quickly to deliver my beer. He departed just as quickly. He didn't say anything about this beer being on the house. I'd handled him masterfully. One minute he was a cuddly teddy bear, the next minute he wanted to be separated from me by several universes. It was comforting to know I hadn't lost my interrogative skills.

Lina Pinheiro's voice carried through Denmark Vesey like a mournful wail. She told a familiar story of ill-fated love. But she told it with a mellifluous ache that made it sound new. People listening had lived the story. In fact some of them were probably here to try and forget they'd lived it. But Lina was determined to make them remember. She chipped away at their alcoholic glaze and reopened old wounds.

If Gary didn't marry Lina, maybe I would. Or maybe Cherisse would divorce Arnie and I'd marry her. Or maybe I'd marry Ellen Talley and she'd quit the police department and we'd start a private detective agency in Aruba. Or maybe I'd just been celibate far too long.

Clinging to the microphone with both hands, plump body pulsating to the beat, Lina finished her sad, sad song. And the Soul Cutters took a break.

Gary motioned, and I followed him through the kitchen and out a rear door. He slumped down on a wooden crate and leaned his back against the Vesey's blue-gray exterior. The armpits of his short-sleeved lemon shirt were stained, and he reeked of sweat and Lina's lavender perfume. She'd used him as a stage set, swirling close and vamping. He lit a cigarette and hand-brushed damp hair off his forehead. "I'm getting too old for this shit, Q. The bones are weary."

I could tell him to stop smoking, exercise, eat healthy. But there was a better chance of bottling airplane exhaust than changing Gary. And a real friend would accept him for what he was. He'd always accepted me for what I was. If I ever developed faults, I was certain he'd accept those too. "If you quit the band and pass up a chance to make something happen with that girl, you're an imbecile," I said.

"Well, this is new," he said. "Usually you complain I'm involved with sluts."

"I only told you that twice, and both times it was true."

"Yeah, maybe." He exhaled smoke and stared down the back street. "You and Cherisse get caught up on all the years gone by?"

"It was good to see her again."

He snickered. "Always careful with the words, Q. You gonna help her find DuBois?"

"I told her I'd think about it. Do you know him?"

"A little bit."

"What's he like?"

"He's okay," Gary said. "Plenty of smarts, just hasn't figured out how to use 'em. Studied economics or some other braniac shit at Columbia University when Cherisse lived in New York with her second husband, a TV exec. But Dub—that's what they call him—dropped out and bounced around doing different dead-end jobs.

Just like me when I was his age."

"When you were his age you were in the Marine Corps."

"Okay, then he's just like me now. You prob'ly remember Dub's real father was Cherisse's first husband, Bryson Capshaw. Dude who got Cherry pregnant not long after the two of 'em graduated from the University of Georgia. Pregnancy came before the marriage, which surprised me and a lot of others. Wouldn't have thought Cherry would make a mistake like that. A kid and a husband just slowed her down."

I did remember now. Cherisse and I were a long time split up, and I was at college in Ohio, but I'd heard the stories from Gary and other friends. Bryson Capshaw had come from a wealthy and influential South Carolina family. The family was extremely conservative, with political aspirations for Bryson and not enamored of interracial marriage. Bryson himself had misgivings about a black wife and a mixed-race son; he'd married Cherisse because he'd been dazzled by her magic, and because he felt obligation for having impregnated her.

In addition to racial hangups, the Capshaw family, including Bryson, had traditional views of gender roles in marriage, which Cherisse refused to accept. She had, for example, continued to use her own last name, and she'd hyphenated DuBois' name as Dane-Capshaw. Family members didn't mind so much that Cherisse wasn't identified as a Capshaw, but they'd seethed about a mixed-race baby carrying their label and the label of a liberal activist black woman.

The marriage had been doomed from the get-go. "So Cherisse and Bryson divorced fast," I said. "And Cherisse walked away with a pile of Capshaw money."

"That was the deal," Gary said. "And Bryson and the other asshole Capshaws got as far away from Cherry and Dub's lives as they could get. Bryson never was any kind of father, just sent dough, which was fine with Cherry. She legally dropped the Capshaw part of Dub's name after the divorce and made him DuBois Dane, which was fine with Bryson and the other Capshaws."

He paused and wrinkled his nose as if he'd detected a new foul odor in the air. "You know who Bryson turned into?"

I did. "He became prominent working in the family business, then he got elected to the South Carolina State legislature and became even better-known as an ultra-conservative. He went around the state making speeches about how the South's secession from the Union had been based on states' rights issues, not slavery and had been the right thing to do. And he opposed any civil rights legislation for minorities and any funding for minority programs."

Gary nodded. "Ran all over the damn place shouting about good old-fashioned Southern values and how much better the South was than the evil, liberal North. Some of the crap Bryson spouted made you think he didn't believe slavery was such a bad thing either. People ate up his bullshit with a spoon."

I'd been settled in Rhode Island by then, and my memories were fuzzy. "Didn't Bryson's marriage to a black woman and his fathering a multi-racial son ever come up?"

"Oh, it came up," Gary said. "And Bryson was ready. Claimed his personal experience had taught him the problems with letting the races get too close. Better to keep 'em apart. Don't think he ever actually used the word segregation, but it was implied. He was born again, hallelujah, he'd seen the light. His speeches were like frigging tent revival meetings with him speaking in tongues. Only things missing were snake handling and laying on of hands, though there was plenty of reports of him laying his hands on women who came to his speeches and stayed afterward for individual instruction. Different kind of preaching than your dad's, but your dad was acquainted with him."

My dad? How ..? Then I recalled. "The *Hunley*."

"Yeah," Gary said. "A shared interest by two men who couldn't have been more different. Except, your dad liking the *Hunley* was clean. Bryson did what he did with everything, turned it into a political opportunity. He was there cheering when they brought the *Hunley* out of the water, got his photo taken at anything having to do with the sub. Built it into his speeches, too. Talked about how the *Hunley* was an example of Southern supremacy, these brave men in a tiny fish-boat who outsmarted a harbor full of Yankee warships and sank one of 'em. A David and Goliath story with David sacrificing himself for the greater good of the Southern way of life. Worked God in there somehow, too."

"What happened to him?" I asked. "Didn't he die in a car accident or something?"

Gary laughed. "Poetic justice they call it. He was all set to be the Republican candidate for governor, but it turned out his appetite for black women hadn't shut off when he and Cherisse divorced. He had a few drinks at a private club in Summerville after an event one night, picked up a black chick who was waitressing and whisked her away toward his condo on the Isle of Palms. Only he never got that far, because the drinks had gone to his head. He crashed into a concrete abutment on 526, and a jagged piece of steering wheel jabbed into his heart. Black chick walked away with just a few scratches. I say that was God's work."

I thought all this over and tried to connect events to the original subject of our conversation. "And the moral is that DuBois' head has been really messed up?"

"Big time," Gary said.

"How did he end up in Charleston?"

"Followed Cherisse and Arnie. They reconnected in New York after Cherisse divorced the TV exec. When Arnie and Cherisse got married, Arnie decided to move back here, show everybody he'd landed Cherisse and drop shit all over the city with his dumbass *Hunley* reality show. He gave Dub a job with his company creating the show, but it's not real clear to me exactly what Dub's doing. Whatever it is, he's out of the office a lot with Ronnie Hodge, a kid named Dewey Welch and Jason Grimes, the one who got killed last night."

"How did DuBois get involved with a guy like Ronnie?"

"Don't know," Gary said. "Could be they drank in the same bars."

"What's Ronnie's story?"

Gary exhaled smoke and scowled. "Ronnie's bad news. But he's connected to some guys, some cops too. Keeps him from taking a serious jolt. At least it has before."

"You think DuBois and Ronnie are dead?"

"Can't see it, Q. Why would their bodies have been moved when Jason Grimes was left sunny side up by the Etiwan Pointe clubhouse?"

"So they're hiding out?"

"Either that or whoever killed Jason took Dub and Ronnie and has them chained up someplace questioning the crap out of them."

"Questioning them about what?"

Gary yawned and shook his head. "I make a guess, you make a

guess, they're just guesses."

"If I decide to look for DuBois, I'm going to need your help and your guesses. I'm the new guy in town with no contacts, and you know everybody and walk both sides of the line."

He cocked his head. "We've known each other since we was what, five years old? You wanna name one time in all those years when I didn't help when you needed it?"

"I can't think of a time."

"Bingo." Gary took a final puff of his cigarette, dropped the butt and ground out the sparks with the sole of his high-topped red and white sneaker.

"Bingo" sounded like an accusation, or maybe I had a guilty conscience. There were plenty of times I hadn't given Gary the help he wanted under the theory that what he wanted wasn't what he really needed. Russell knew best. But these days I wasn't feeling quite so omniscient. My attitude toward Gary rang hollow now, seemed like condescending bullshit. Which was probably what it had always seemed like to him.

Moonlight leaked through the clouds and puddled the street. Car doors slammed in the distance, and an engine revved.

The rear door to Denmark Vesey creaked open, and Lina Pinheiro's round face appeared. Her dark eyes glistened in the frame of light from the kitchen. "Next set, Gary."

He told her he'd be right there. Her face withdrew and the door closed.

"You forgot to introduce me," I said.

"I didn't forget. Don't want the competition."

"Then I'm going home to bed."

He saluted. "Sleep tight."

I was ten yards down the street when I heard, "Q!" I turned.

"There's a guy might come to see you."

I stared at Gary's shadowy figure. "Who and why?"

"Just a guy who's got something somebody's after."

"Put in your real teeth and start over."

"I gotta get back. Be in touch tomorrow, tell you more then." He opened the door, illuminating his beefy frame.

"What's this guy's name?" I called as the door swung shut.

"Moze Cheddar," carried faintly back to me on the breeze.

Chapter Eight

Moze approached Berard's house from the rear off the golf course, path lit by a fat glop of a moon and haze-dimmed stars. He'd dressed hisself for night work: dark cotton pants, long-sleeve tee-shirt, baseball cap and running shoes. Sweat splotched his brow; smells of mowed grass, jasmine and pine sweetened the breeze; lightning bugs flashed.

Moze had drove past Berard's, saw no lights, garage doors shut, empty driveway. Wasn't the sort of neighborhood where folks left cars on the street overnight, so he'd parked the truck at condos a couple of miles away, entered the golf course near there. Golf course was safer than streets this time of night. Besides which, walking open in the streets agitated Moze's nerves. His walking experience was mostly through fields, forests and jungles.

Moze moved behind a tree across the drainage ditch from Berard's and reached into his knapsack. Knapsack held this and that: tools, handcuffs, unsalted pretzels, night vision scope, face mask, blindfold, gloves, bottled water, flashlight, binoculars, rope, wire, fig bars, Sig Sauer pistol and a section of the diary. Moze's hand came out with the Sig Sauer and face mask. Put the pistol in his pocket, took off the baseball cap and wiped his brow. Slipped on the face mask, pulled the cap over top of the mask, crouched and jumped the narrow ditch. Paused, listened, looked. Dogs caused him worry, but there wasn't no barking. Most likely folks had took their animals in for the night.

Stockade fence enclosed Berard's yard. No outside or interior lights showing. Moze went through the gate, used tree cover to position hisself where he could see the deck doors and windows.

Watched for a time, noticed no movement in the house. Loped across the grass and up the deck steps. Sticker on a window said the house was protected by a security alarm. Moze smiled. Always appreciated security alarms announcing their selves. He opened the backpack, removed the flashlight and tools. Wouldn't take long to disable the alarm. Easier back when you could just cut the phone line so no signal was sent reporting the break. Nowadays the better systems had got that covered by using wireless. Still there wasn't nothing foolproof, and Moze had familiarity with this particular system advertising itself on Berard's window.

Chapter Nine

A bang roused me. The clock beside the sofa bed in the downstairs den read 2:13AM. I lay semi-conscious wondering if I'd dreamed the noise. A second bang brought a halt to the wondering. I slid open a drawer of the end table and reached for the .38 Special I'd tucked in before I went to sleep. It wasn't there. Maybe the .38 had gotten hungry and gone to the kitchen for a tuna sandwich and a glass of milk. Maybe that was the noise I'd heard. Or maybe the .38 had been kidnapped.

    I got up, pulled a tee-shirt over my boxer shorts and went through the connecting door to the office. Street light shining in the front windows showed nothing hazardous to my health. I went out to the family room, which opened to the kitchen and sun room. All appeared clear in those areas. If there was downstairs trouble it was running out of rooms.

    Or so I thought. The man hit me from the side as I crossed the kitchen toward the dining room. He'd been crouched out of sight behind the island counter. I smashed against the door of the pantry closet. He punched my kidney, hooked my ankle with his foot and shoved hard. I staggered backward, bumped into the kitchen table and sprawled across it. Before I could recover, he had an arm locked around my throat from behind and had my left arm twisted and pressed into my spine. I rolled across the table, dragging him, and we fell and crashed on the hardwood.

    I came up fast, but he was equally quick. We squared off, and I got my first look at him: a short, sinewy, broad-shouldered man dressed in black and wearing a mask. He snapped a kick at my face, I caught the leg, twisted, and threw him down on the family room rug. He bounced to his feet and spun, knees bent. We spent a couple of minutes impressing each other with our martial arts repertoires, neither accomplishing much. I crowded him toward the fireplace, and he glanced at the metal poker but left it alone.

He was lithe and springy, difficult to contain. He feinted to the right, but I didn't fall for it. Except it wasn't a feint, and he juked past me, rolled an ottoman against my shins and broke for the sliding glass doors to the deck. I got loose of the ottoman, chased him out the door, leaped off the deck and landed on his back. His elbow jammed into my solar plexus as we hit the grass, whooshing air from my lungs.

I struggled to my feet gasping as he sprinted toward the open rear gate. He grabbed a knapsack off the fence top and closed the gate behind. I wobbled more than ran in pursuit, still fighting for breath. By the time I worked the gate open and got across the ditch to the golf course, he was long gone in who knew which direction.

I went back to the house, washed my face and hands in the kitchen sink and toweled off. Calling the police and reporting an intruder would be the right thing to do. The right thing if I were a masochist. Before I could sing all the verses of Dixie, Ellen Talley would be over here asking a thousand questions I couldn't answer.

A baseball cap my visitor had been wearing cluttered the kitchen floor. Unfortunately, there was no inside label with his name, address, telephone number and e-mail address. Break-in artists were a thoughtless bunch. How did they expect home owners to make follow-up contact?

I went to the refrigerator for juice and learned the baseball cap wasn't the only item left behind. A manila envelope lay on the bottom shelf beside a carton of eggs. A gun on top of the envelope served as a paper weight. The gun was the .38 Special I'd last seen resting comfortably in the drawer of the end table beside the sofa bed when I went to sleep.

I poured a glass of grape juice, carried the glass, gun and envelope into the family room, and slumped on the couch. I set the glass in a coaster on the coffee table, dropped the gun on the cushion next to me and contemplated the envelope. I had a feeling I'd be wise to burn it, but that would involve getting off the couch. Besides, it was too hot for a fire. I undid the clasp and pulled out several sheets of paper. The top sheet had a handwritten note.

Mr. Berard,

There's certain abilities come natural to me that the government had a use for. They gave me training and experience, but didn't no one never teach me how to write proper. So I got to make my apologies right here at the beginning in case I don't do a clear job explaining. What it boils down to, your daddy came to see me, and I told him about a family diary of mine, let him read a few pages. Then he went back home and got hisself murdered. I liked your daddy, and I'm real sorry about him dying.

Letter showed up at my cabin the other day with no name on it from somebody wants to buy my diary. Letter mentioned your daddy and you. Said you'd worked as a police detective in Rhode Island and was back home investigating your daddy's murder. Letter said you might be a good fella for me to talk to about whether your daddy's murder might have had something to do with my diary. But I haven't never heard of you, don't know why I should believe the letter writer. So I talked to a friend still works in the government, asked him could he look you up. He did that and says you had yourself a proud record in the military and police. Says it appears you're a smart, honest fella who can be trusted.

So I'll take me a chance. Not a real big chance at the start, but a chance just the same. What these other pages with this note are, they're the first part of my ancestor's diary. You read this first part, get an idea of what it's all about. Then I'll come by again and we'll talk, see if there's ways we can help each other.

Could be you're wondering why I didn't just ring your doorbell, explain myself, and hand you these pages. There's good reasons. I don't yet know exactly how you or your daddy fit into this trouble, so it's best I use caution in my approach.

Won't apologize if you and me had ourselves a little tussle when I dropped off these pages. If that happened, I didn't mean no harm by it, and I don't expect neither of us suffered any injury. My government friend who checked up on you says you're supposedly a fella who knows how to handle hisself. Thought I'd see if that's so. If you and me get paired up later on, we ought to have ourselves an idea of what the other fella can be counted on for.

The note was signed Moze Cheddar, and the pages with it were photocopies of longhand text. As I puzzled out the archaic script, the words gradually became clearer to me until I almost heard the writer's voice in my head. This is the story the pages told:

My name is Ezra Cheddar. I was born on August 4 of the year 1836 in Pittsburgh, Pennsylvania. My father was an educated man with a position of importance in an iron factory. Good fortune spared his factory during the great fire of 1845. In my teens I worked at the factory as school allowed. My parents placed much importance on education for my brothers and sisters and me, and I continued studies at Western University of Pennsylvania in Pittsburgh. After graduation, my father wished me to take a position with his factory, but there was wanderlust in my blood. I packed my belongings and the small amount of money I had saved, and boarded the Pennsylvania Railroad bound for Philadelphia.

In Philadelphia, I held various positions, being less concerned with making my fortune than with enjoying the many stimulations of a city new to me. Eventually feeling the urge to move on, I traveled to New York, and then down the east coast.

I had discovered an affinity for theater while at Western University of Pennsylvania, and in Baltimore I became involved with a troupe of actors. At first I assisted the troupe with backstage production. But when a cast member came afoul of the law, I was conscripted to replace him. The part required a Southern accent, which gave me initial challenge. I have a good ear and an ability to mimic, however, and in short order I mastered the dialect and the role.

I greatly enjoyed the opportunity, and my performance was apparently satisfactory, for the troupe asked me to accompany them as they traveled south. I agreed, and adopted Nathaniel Clary as my stage name. The other actors had a wandering spirit like mine, and we made our way through Virginia, the Carolinas, and Georgia. It was a nomadic existence, and there were low points, but in the overall it was an exhilarating experience for a young man with a craving to sample from life's offerings.

This was, however, a dangerous time for a Northerner to be in the South. Emotions ran hot over the issue of slavery, and Southerners were threatening secession. I had acquired a staunch abolition-

ist philosophy from my father, but giving public voice to my beliefs would have been inadvisable. As a means of self-protection, I often used the Southern accent of my on-stage character during my social interactions.

When our troupe reached Atlanta, we were afflicted by weariness and illness, our funds were nearly exhausted, and our nerves stood on edge from the South's enflamed passions. It seemed a propitious moment to say our farewells and set our separate courses. My course was north through Tennessee, Kentucky, West Virginia, and home to Pittsburgh.

After a period of rest and reacquaintance with my parents and siblings, I felt an increased maturity and seriousness about life. My father suggested, as he had before my travels, a position at the iron factory, but this prospect was not appealing. Instead I took a clerk's position in my uncle's Pittsburgh law office and found the work to be quite interesting.

In 1861, events many had feared came to pass. South Carolina, then Mississippi, Florida, Alabama, Georgia, Louisiana, and Texas seceded from the Union. Virginia, Arkansas, Tennessee, and North Carolina would eventually do the same. The seceding states created a Confederate government in Montgomery, Alabama, with Jefferson Davis as President, and began to seize federal forts in the South. In April of 1861, Confederate militia fired on Fort Sumter in Charleston, South Carolina. The war had begun.

I yearned to help the Union cause, but a hunting accident had left me with a limp that prevented my serving as a foot soldier. My frustration grew as months went by, and my uncle took notice. He was acquainted with Edwin Stanton, the nation's Attorney General, who had practiced law in Pittsburgh before going to Washington, D.C. When President Lincoln appointed Stanton Secretary of War in 1862, my uncle arranged for me to take a clerkship in the new Secretary's office.

From the outset, I throve on my job and on life in the nation's capital. There was much excitement, turmoil, and intrigue. Many military officers and civilians who had been working in Washington at the outbreak of the war were from the South, and most had departed to join the Confederacy. Within the Lincoln government *there was suspicion of Southerners who remained, and suspicion even of some Northerners thought to have Confederate sympathies.*

When Secretary Stanton warned me to trust no one, for Confederate agents were everywhere, I told him of my acting experience in the South, saying I knew the Southern culture well, and could speak the dialect. I meant this as a joke, but the Secretary's interest was piqued. He suggested I associate with Southerners in the capital and attempt to uncover spies. This I did with some success, which earned me the Secretary's respect, and increasingly important duties.

One day in the summer of 1863, Secretary Stanton summoned me to his office. He said that a submersible torpedo boat constructed in Mobile, Alabama, had been sent to Charleston, South Carolina. It was believed that the Confederates would use the torpedo boat to attempt to sink Union ships blockading Charleston harbor.

The Secretary asked if my acting troupe had visited Charleston. I told him we had visited but not performed. Restiveness among the populace over possible abolition of slavery and secession had militated against Northerners appearing in public. However, using my stage name of Nathaniel Clary and my acquired Southern accent, I had circulated around the city and found it beautiful and enjoyable.

My reply pleased Secretary Stanton. He directed me to travel to Charleston on an espionage assignment of the utmost importance. In case anyone there remembered me, I was to use my stage name as I had before, and, of course, I would speak in my Southern dialect. I would tell Charlestonians that I had been wounded in battle and forced to leave my Confederate regiment, thus explaining the limp from my hunting accident. My mission: to learn all I could about this submersible Confederate fish-boat called the Hunley, and sabotage its efforts to sink Union ships.

Chapter Ten

In my dream *I was ocean swimming. Francie Giordano, my Newport detective lieutenant, now Newport police chief, rowed alongside, brown shoulders rippling with muscle. We'd been out for hours, and Francie's black curls, pink shorts and sleeveless white top were sopped with sweat and salt water. I churned through the waves, dove on instinct and asked sea creatures if they had seen my mother. Sharks, eels, seals, dolphins, rays all told me no. Each time I surfaced, Francie leaned over the side of the boat with a hopeful expression. Each time I shook my head and the corners of her full lips curved down glumly.*

This time when I dove I came across a sunken pirate ship. A skeleton with an eye patch, peg leg and hook for a left hand stood on the deck. I described my mother. He'd seen her, and he pointed in the direction she'd gone. I surfaced to tell Francie, but she was frowning, preoccupied. "We need to get out of this weather, Russell," she said.

I stared up at her, wondering if she was suffering from sun stroke. The azure sky was cloudless. "Hail," she told me.

I saw nothing—at first. Then a round pellet struck the boat, followed by a second and a third. "One more dive," I pleaded. "Mom's close."

"No," Francie said. "We have to go now or the hail will punch holes in the boat and sink us."

"One more dive," I repeated and dove.

I spotted mother resting on a rock sipping tea. She waved, but a sudden, powerful rip tide pushed me away. I fought, but the tide was too strong. I decided to go back up and have Francie row me to a point where I could dive straight down. I was deeper than I real-

ized though, and the climb seemed interminable. I heard the muffled thump of hail above me, but I couldn't reach the surface. I was nearly out of air, struggling to keep my mouth closed ...

My eyes snapped open. My breathing was ragged, my mouth dry, but I wasn't drowning. I'd fallen asleep on the family room couch reading the diary entries left behind by my late night visitor. I still heard hail, though. Strange sounding hail. A hard thump on the roof, interval of silence, thump, interval of silence ... as if God were dropping stones on the house. What sins had I committed that were so egregious I deserved this personal attention? Four or five possibilities crossed my mind.

I stood slowly, grimaced at a stab of pain in my lower back, massaged my stiff neck and flexed my knees. When I felt mobile I shuffled to the sliding glass doors. Three men occupied the fourteenth fairway. One stood beside a golf bag, and a second dropped a ball in the grass. The third, holding a club, took a rhythmic, three quarters swing, and the ball arched over the trees and landed on my roof with a thump.

I put on shorts and shoes to supplement the boxers and teeshirt I'd slept in and went out the sliding glass doors and down the deck steps. I crossed the yard, exited through the gate, jumped the ditch to the golf course and approached the men. Two were massive, in the six-feet-three, two-hundred-and-fifty pound range. One had on tasseled loafers without socks, cream-colored slacks and a rust and green striped shirt. Oiled black hair ran back from his forehead. The other wore tan canvas slip-ons, navy slacks and a short-sleeved maroon linen shirt. He had a shaved head and brown goatee. They were power-lifters, arms packed with muscle, shoulders broad enough to park a car on. Maybe not the white SUV sitting nearby on the fairway, but a smaller sedan.

The third man leaned on his club, grinned and said, "Russell Q. How's the boy?" Arnie St. John was dressed in brown huarache sandals, khaki cargo shorts and a gold polo shirt. He was wearing a straw hat, sunglasses and a white golf glove.

"Life goes on, Arnie." We shook hands. Arnie was short, about five feet seven, but his long-fingered hands were powerful. He'd taken gymnastics lessons as a kid, and his body was still taut and well-developed. Being a boy gymnast had made him a target for ridicule and sexual slurs in high school. Until he'd beaten a linebacker senseless behind the buses one afternoon.

"Couple of things," I told him. "The practice range is over by the clubhouse, and I'm guessing the Club frowns on vehicles being parked in the fairway."

Arnie's grin expanded. In elementary school he'd fallen off his bike and broken several teeth, which had been jagged thereafter. Now they were perfectly shaped and spaced, and gleamed in the sunlight like polished ivory. "Not to worry," he said. "I bought the Club last month. Some of the old policies are being revised."

He swirled the nine iron above his head. "My short game's been erratic recently. This seemed like a good spot to work on it. You can keep the balls, they're new Maxflis. Any damage to your roof shingles, send me the bill care of the Club."

The sprinklers had watered earlier, and the toe of my running shoe stained green when I rubbed it in the wet grass. Beads of sweat pooled on my brow from the humidity and a surge of testosterone.

"Your message is too subtle for me, Arnie."

He cocked his head in perplexity. "Message? What message?"

"You're out here banging golf balls off my house before breakfast, and your caddies are New York muscle. It feels like you're trying to tell me something."

Arnie removed his sun glasses, wiped them on his shirt and put them in his cargo shorts. Then he stripped off his golf glove and flipped it to the gorilla with oiled black hair. The gorilla stowed the glove in a zippered pocket of a red golf bag supported by two metal legs. "We go way back, Q. You were always a stand-up guy who treated me right when others in our class spat on me. Truth of the matter is, you were always sort of a hero of mine. I kind of wanted to be like you. But that's ancient history. Now I don't want to be anyone but me."

"I'm happy your self-concept has improved," I said. "But I'm still not getting what this is about."

He took off the straw hat and scratched his head. His curly blond hair was tangled with perspiration. "A couple of nights ago you rumbled with some boys at the Griddle Grill. My step-son, DuBois, was one of them. Last night you went downtown to Cherisse's club and spent a lot of time with her behind closed doors. My messages are several." He squeezed the grip of the nine-iron, and sinews rippled in his forearm. "Message one: I've known retired cops who acted like they weren't retired, and life turned ugly on them. I'd hate to see that happen to you, so be cautious about your involvements. Message two: If you're looking for a job, I've got something that won't turn out badly for you. Message three: Cherisse and I are married now. Stay the hell away from her."

On the other side of the fairway a woman jogged along the cart path with a leashed golden retriever. A dog in a fenced yard barked as the retriever passed. Blood rushing to my head muffled the barking. By reputation Charleston was one of the most civil and friendly cities in the United States. So far I wasn't seeing it. In the last few days I'd scuffled with local punks, been harassed by a redneck cop, exchanged hostilities with a detective who once was my friend, been assaulted by a mystery man who broke into my house, and now was being threatened by an old high school buddy. A convention of Islamic terrorists would have been friendlier.

Arnie was lightly balanced on the balls of his feet, knees bent, nine iron ready to use as a weapon in case I took enough umbrage at his messages to deliver a message of my own. The gorillas had subtly shifted position to cover me from the sides. Their shirt tails hung loose, and guns were probably tucked in holsters clipped to their rear waistbands.

"There's nothing happening between Cherisse and me," I told Arnie.

"Not yet anyway," he said. "What did the two of you talk about?"

"This and that."

He nodded as if I'd revealed something enlightening. "Any of the this or that have to do with your helping find DuBois?"

"The subject came up."

"And ... ?"

"And no decision was reached."

Arnie took a practice swing with the iron. The blade dug up a divot of grass and dirt that sailed by my shoulder. I tensed and sensed the gorillas bracing to respond if I took the flying divot as an affront requiring payback. I brushed dirt specks off my shirt.

"Stay out, Russ," Arnie said. "It's complicated, plenty of local twists and turns. You've been away too long to know the lay of the land. I'm watching out for DuBois; he'll be all right—unless too many cooks stir the broth. If you want to cook, sign on with me."

"What do you think, Gino?" I asked. "Would employment with Arnie be a good career fit for me? Offer a nice benefit package and opportunities for advancement?"

The shaved-headed, goateed gorilla chuckled, a noise like a lawn mower with a bad spark plug. "Told Mr. St. John you'd remember, Captain."

Gino had been working for one of the New York families when our paths crossed about six years ago. He'd come to Newport on personal business involving his nephew, Tony, left fatherless when Gino's brother was killed by a rival family. Tony began to run wild and his mother couldn't control him. Gino had an unmarried aunt who taught elementary school in Newport, and he shipped Tony off to live with her. All went well until the aunt was diagnosed with breast cancer. Tony couldn't deal with another potential loss and reverted to old bad habits. We had him on a felony drug charge when Gino called me. He'd been given my name by people we both knew. Could we meet?

We'd drunk coffee at a place on Thames Street while Gino gave me the background. Then he told me his plan. He wanted to send Tony to live with a relative in Ohio who was headmaster at a private school, which Tony would attend. To make that happen, Gino needed me to convince the prosecutor to recommend Tony for juvenile diversion. And he needed me to convince the diversion staff to let Tony complete his program requirements in Ohio. Who knows why I'd agreed? Maybe my normal job-induced cynicism took sabbatical that day and I was feeling optimistic about saving a young soul. Maybe I felt sorry for the hand Tony had been dealt and thought it was worth giving him another wild card to see if he could win the pot.

"How's Tony doing?" I asked.

Gino smiled. "Sophomore at Ohio State. No cop trouble since

he left Newport."

"I'm glad. Your aunt's cancer turned out okay too, I hear."

"Yeah, it was a happy story all around."

"What about your story? You change jobs?"

Gino glanced at Arnie and rolled his tongue around his mouth while he manufactured an answer. "Me an' Mikey ain't exactly regular employees of Mr. St. John. We're more like, whadda ya call it, on loan from our boss."

"I'm partnering with Gino and Mikey's employer on several business ventures," Arnie clarified. "Gino and Mikey are consultants." I stared at him. I'd never before heard Mafia hit men referred to as consultants.

A red mowing machine had begun to cut swaths in the fairway beginning at the tee box and moving in our direction toward the green. As the mower passed, the Mexican driver looked at the SUV and scowled. Mikey took a step toward the driver.

"Let it go," Arnie said. Mikey hesitated, then turned back around. Arnie tossed him the nine iron, which he deposited in the golf bag. "I'm very sorry about your father," Arnie told me. "I didn't realize it at the time, but according to my parents he was always a strong source of support to them when Charleston's stuffed shirt shitholes treated them like scum. I saw him not too long before he was killed and thanked him for that."

"I'm sure he appreciated it."

"He seemed to." Arnie tapped the knuckles of his left hand against the palm of his right in apparent accompaniment to music in his head. "Your dad and I had a common interest."

"What's that?"

"The *Hunley*."

"The *Hunley* was one of his passions," I said. "But from what I read in the paper, your interest in it is a little different than his. I doubt if he would have supported your reality show."

"He didn't support it."

"Why not drop the idea?" I suggested. "The mistreatment of your family happened a long time ago. Your parents moved to Greenville after you graduated from high school and enjoyed a good life up there."

Arnie stepped closer to me, eyes frigid, fists clenched. "But they never got over their humiliation in Charleston. You can't convince me that didn't contribute to my dad's fatal heart attack in his fifties."

"I won't try."

"There's going to be payback, Russ; there has to be," Arnie hissed. "Some of those pompous pricks from my dad's time are still alive and playing their cliquish power game. Dressing up in tuxes and gowns for the symphony and opera, projecting a phony aura of civility, and acting like benevolent rulers of the kingdom. Here's a news flash for them: their kingdom is about to come crashing down."

Arnie's voice rose as he ranted, face contorting like a hideous Halloween mask. "They want to worship at the altar of the *Hunley* and portray the sub and crew as a heroic example of Charleston's proud resistance during the War of Northern Aggression? Well I'm going to shove that bullshit up their collective asses and show the *Hunley* for what it really was, a cross between the boats and crews from McHale's Navy and Gilligan's Island. A bunch of buffoons who sank the *Housatonic* in water so shallow the masts didn't submerge." He chuckled harshly. "And what was the final tally? Eight *Hunley* crew compared with only five Union sailors dead. It takes a lot of spin to package that as a Confederate victory."

Diatribe done, Arnie took a deep breath and blew it out, cracks in the veneer of his face smoothing as his muscles relaxed.

"You ought to see someone about that anger," I said.

He willed warmth back into his eyes and grinned. "Nah, vengeance is a lot more fun than counseling. Question for you. Did your father ever mention a diary about the *Hunley*?"

"Nope."

"Nothing about a diary in his church or home records?"

"Not that I've come across."

"Keep me in mind if you find anything, will you."

"Why?" I asked

"If there is a diary, it might have information I could use for my show."

"What makes you think I want to help with your show?"

He expanded his grin and shook his head. "Like father like son."

"I'll take that as a compliment."

"That's the way it was intended." He removed his straw hat and spun it on an index finger. "Any chance you've come across a man named Moze Cheddar?" He asked casually, but his pale blue eyes were keen as he watched my face.

"Who's Moze Cheddar?"

"Just a guy I might want to do business with, but I'm having trouble tracking him down. If you happen to run into him, maybe you'll let me know."

"Why would I run into him?"

"It's a small world," Arnie said.

He sailed the straw hat high in the air, did a back flip into a hand stand, and used his left foot to hook the hat as it floated down. Then he walked away on his hands.

Chapter Eleven

I blended raisins and almonds in a cup of non-fat yogurt, poured a glass of tomato juice and ate at the kitchen counter looking out the windows. Arnie St. John, Gino and Mikey had vacated the fairway, and the red mower continued to cut as if it were attempting to excise all traces of my conversation with Arnie. But I recalled from high school that avoiding entanglement with Arnie's enterprises wasn't quite so simple as mentally consigning them to a state of indifference.

A cardinal landed on the bird feeder and flitted away in disappointment. Apparently he hadn't heard about my parents' passing. They'd cared for all manner of creatures: birds, stray dogs, the homeless, abused women, alienated teenagers, Gary Nagle, Ellen Talley, even Arnie St. John's parents. I hoped no one was expecting me to assume the role of nurturer. I couldn't even keep seed in a feeder.

My neighbor's head bobbed above his fence, and he came through the side gate to check his pool controls. He was wearing a gray suit, white shirt and burgundy striped tie. On his way to work. I remembered having a place to go in grown-up clothes every morning. Now I was retired and playing a character in a random series of skits with unclear connections.

I microwaved a cup of green tea and carried the cup and the note and diary entry Moze Cheddar had left out to a chair by the pool. My muscles were heavy with fatigue, as if they'd been injected with liquid cement. Retirement was going to be exhausting if people kept disrupting my sleep by breaking into my house and rat-a-tat-tatting golf balls off my roof.

I summoned a burst of energy, lifted the note and pages and reviewed them. My father's interest in the *Hunley* had led him to Moze, who'd told dad about a diary kept by Moze's ancestor, Ezra, a Union spy sent to Charleston to sabotage the *Hunley*. Then my father had gone home and gotten killed.

Arnie St. John was making a reality show about the *Hunley*, and according to the *Post and Courier* article I'd read at the Griddle Grill the other night, there were rumors that Arnie was pursuing a secret diary about the submarine. A short time ago on the golf course, Arnie had asked me whether my dad had known about a *Hunley* diary. Arnie had also asked if I'd come across Moze Cheddar, with whom Arnie wanted to transact business.

It was easy to draw a fast conclusion. Arnie had learned of the existence of a *Hunley* diary and had reason to believe my father knew something about it. Arnie had approached Dad, Dad had refused to tell him anything because he opposed Arnie's reality show, and Arnie had killed Dad so he could comb through his records for diary information. If that was what had happened, Arnie's combing had clearly been unsuccessful, because he'd asked me if I'd come across anything about the diary in Dad's files. Was Arnie's Plan B to try to acquire the diary directly from Moze Cheddar, and did Arnie figure that, since Moze and my dad had been acquainted, Moze and I would connect at some point?

Another question occurred to me. Gary Nagle had said last night at Denmark Vesey that a guy who had something somebody was after was going to come to see me, a guy named Moze Cheddar. How had Gary known that Moze would pay me a visit?

Why speculate? Why not ask Gary? I dialed his number, got voice mail and left a message. I could have driven to his house in Old Village and beaten his door down, but that seemed like a lot of work.

Mental exertion having reached a dead end, I decided to get physical and carried my father's dumbbells and ankle weights down from the attic to the pool deck. After forty minutes of lifting and leg exercises, sweat dripped from my body like rain dribbling off plant leaves in a tropical forest. My shoulder ached, and I'd tweaked a hamstring. But that was okay, exercise made the body stronger, I was certain I'd read that somewhere. I cooled off with laps in the pool, showered and took a nap.

Later in the morning I went to the garage and unwrapped a memorial stone with the inscription: Kam Lim, Missing in Search of The Path. I'd had the stone carved when Lim vanished in Cambodia, and I'd put it in a garden behind our Newport cottage. The cottage we'd called Gautama, the true name of the original Buddha. In Search of The Path referred to The Noble Eightfold Path, Gautama's principles for understanding truth and ending suffering.

The stone had been carved by Lim's uncle, Pran Chea, another of those who had fled Cambodia to the United States. I had helped him buy a small motel, where he lived in an apartment behind the office. Pran and I had bonded closely after Lim's disappearance, and I missed his company and guidance. I also owed him a phone call.

I carried Lim's memorial stone to the back yard and set it in a spot visible from the kitchen windows and sliding glass doors. After I chose a permanent location I'd construct a rock and flower garden around the stone like the garden in Newport. Not for the first time I wondered how Lim would react if she knew I'd left the Gautama cottage. I felt guilty and disloyal to her memory, as if I'd abandoned our life. Of course, Lim had abandoned our life first. And I hadn't sold Gautama, I was renting it to Francie Giordano's daughter, Trina.

Francie Giordano … somebody else for me to feel guilty about. My former detective lieutenant, now Newport's Chief of Police. The job that should have been mine. Except I'd claimed disinterest, convinced Francie to apply, ardently advocated for her, then gone away mad when she was selected instead of me. Francie deserved a phone call too.

The phone rang. I had the kitchen portable in the pocket of my shorts, and the up-close, sudden, harsh jangle made me flinch. Possibly Pran or Francie tired of waiting for me to call. I dug the phone out of my pocket, pushed the talk button and said hello.

"Russ Berard?" It wasn't Pran or Francie.

"Yes."

"This is DuBois Dane. I talked to my mother a little while ago. She thinks you might be able to help Ronnie and me."

"What sort of help do you need?"

"Not on the phone. Can we meet?"

I thought about it. There were multiple reasons not to. But I'd settled into a nice little routine of doing the wrong thing at the wrong time. Why quit now? "Where and when?"

"I don't want to say on the phone."

"Okay. You want to try smoke signals, mental telepathy, Morse code, carrier pigeons?"

"I'm talking to you as a favor to my mother, asshole. I can hang up."

"Go ahead."

He hung up. But first he said, "Somebody will be in touch about meeting."

I dialed Gary's number, got voice mail again and didn't bother to leave another message. Then I bent, kissed Lim's memorial stone and went back in the house.

The oak stairs to the second floor loomed in the front hallway like Jack's beanstalk to a disquieting world. I climbed five steps to the landing that faced the street. Just outside the tall windows, the bottlebrush tree's long-stamened red flowers glistened like bloody spikes. I climbed the remaining five steps, steeled myself, and stepped through the door into the master bedroom for the first time since I'd returned. Externally most everything was as I remembered. Four-poster bed, bureau with a mirror, dresser with a TV. Arm chair with designs in orange, brown and gold that had caused my dad to call it the turkey chair. Matching ottoman. Doors to the closet and bathroom. Cathedral ceiling with a skylight. Wall-to-wall windows with blinds.

I opened the blinds and sat on the ottoman, the sun warm against my back. The room smelled of my father's woodsy aftershave and my mother's mango perfume. I closed my eyes and imagined them here. Mom dressing in front of the mirror, Dad fresh out of the shower with a towel around his waist telling a silly joke. Mom laughing. Tears ran down my cheeks …

I stood, wiped my eyes and noticed my father's favorite old Bible on a bedside table, black cover coming loose, pages dog-eared. I carried it downstairs for no good reason. I'd grown up in Presbyterian churches where Dad had preached, and I'd studied Buddhism under Lim's tutelage, but these days agnosticism seemed more compelling than either of those belief systems.

I was organizing laundry when the telephone intruded again. Possibly DuBois Dane calling back to say he'd decided he didn't want my help after all. That would get me off the hook with Cherisse and uncomplicate my life. "Russell Berard?" a raspy non-DuBois voice asked.

"Yes?"

"I have information of interest to you."

"I'm listening."

"Not on the phone."

Just what DuBois had said. Why didn't anyone trust telephones anymore? "Let me guess, you want to meet."

"You know the Pepsi machine near the fifteenth tee down the street from your house?"

"We're meeting there?"

"There's an envelope behind the machine, smart ass. Go get it."

"Let's slow down," I said. "Who are you, and what's this information about?"

"The note will tell you."

"How about a preview?"

"Go get the note, Berard. If your phone's tapped, someone might beat you to it."

"Why would my phone be tapped?"

"A lot of people appear interested in you."

Chapter Twelve

The cart path to the fifteenth tee curled off Casseque several houses down on the left. A small building with bathrooms squatted just before the tee, and outside the building were a drinking fountain and a blue Pepsi machine. I used a stick to slide a sealed envelope out from behind the machine. Two golfers carrying their bags and chattering about a missed putt on fourteen strolled past, glanced my way and nodded. A blue jay crinkled leaves in the limbs above my head. A child playing in a yard across the street tripped and began to cry. Everyday life proceeded apace in the easy summer calm of suburbia, and I was extracting mystery messages from behind a soft drink machine.

I walked the sealed note home, sat on a stool at the kitchen island counter and slit open the envelope with a knife blade. The note was computer generated, crisp and to the point.

I'm Leonard Alcott, retired FBI. I attended your father's church, got to know him a little, and he told me you were a Rhode Island police detective. I've heard from others in the church that you retired and moved down here after your father was killed and your mother died. I've got a situation on my hands and could use your help. As a quid pro quo I can pass along information about your father's murder. I'll call back to be sure you got this note. If you can see me tomorrow, tell me a time that's four hours later than the actual time you want to meet based on a twenty-four hour clock. I'm at the AllNight Inn. I'll give you a number when I call. Subtract nineteen from it to get my room number. Don't use my name on the phone, and be sure you're not followed if you come tomorrow.

It sounded like FBI deviousness, but a little Internet research on my mother's office computer wouldn't hurt. After reading material from old newspaper articles, federal reports, press releases and other sources, I'd learned that Leonard Alcott's FBI career had been moderately illustrious with some high profile experiences during his tour with the Atlanta field office in the 1980s. He'd participated in the investigation of killings of black children in a case referred to as the Child Murders. He'd been involved in a shootout with a gunman who forced his way into the Atlanta FBI office and took hostages. And he'd helped contend with the Siege of Atlanta, Operation Rescue's four month anti-abortion protest.

Alcott had also been the lead agent in the 1987 investigation and arrest of three prominent Atlanta blacks who'd done serious prison time for conspiring to send mail bombs and poisoned letters to leaders of white supremacist groups including the Ku Klux Klan, Nationalist Movement, White Patriot Party and Aryan Nations. The mail bomb and poisoned letter plot had been hatched following disruption by white supremacists of a January 1987 march against racial intolerance by 20,000 people in Forsyth County, Georgia.

Alcott had retired to the Charleston area ten years ago, and there wasn't much about him on the Internet after that. His name did appear in the context of activities involving my father's church. Capital fund development committee, nursing home outreach, fellowship committee, church security advisor after my father received hate mail—that was interesting ...

The damn phone interrupted for a third time. I made a mental note to cut the lines.

"Did you get the envelope?" the raspy voice asked.

"I did."

"Still sealed?"

"Yes."

"And?"

"Fourteen," I told him.

"Fifty-five," he said and hung up.

I wondered if Alcott's codes would work. I'd said fourteen for 2:00PM, which, according to his instructions, meant 10:00AM tomorrow. And subtracting nineteen from his fifty-five should mean he'd be in room 36 at the AllNight Inn. But given the way my attempts at collaboration with the FBI had gone when I was a cop, Alcott might be expecting me at 10:00 tonight in room 63 of the Holiday Inn Express.

Gary Nagle hadn't returned my call by one o'clock, so I phoned a third time, got his voice mail a third time and left a second message. I had a hunch he had a hunch I wanted to talk about Moze Cheddar and was ducking me. I ate half a cheese sandwich, a carrot and a quarter of a green apple with a glass of tap water. I paced the house while I ate, feeling caged and edgy.

A Mt. Pleasant patrol car passed the house twice while I paced. After the second pass the car parked in Covenant Square near my driveway.

The patrol car was still there when I went out to do errands, and it followed. After a mile its lights flashed and I pulled over. Through my side view mirror I watched a slim, uniformed officer with a toothpick in his mouth step from the cruiser and walk toward me. He crouched at my open window, looked in and feigned surprise. "I'll be a tar baby's uncle if it ain't Russell Q. Berard in living color. Didn't recognize your car, bo."

"Come across a lot of Avalons with Rhode Island plates, Officer Pritchard?"

"Yours is one too many, and the Rhode Island plates is why I pulled you over. Move here from another state you got forty-five days to register your vehicle in South Carolina. You lived here more than forty-five days?"

"No."

"Really? Seems to me I recall newspaper stories four months ago where you was down here running your mouth about your daddy's killing. Pictures of you too. Bet I could check the archives of the *Post and Courier* and *Moultrie News*, dig those stories out."

Pritchard was balanced on the balls of his feet. His face was freshly shaved, sideburns cut precisely at mid ear. His beady eyes glittered with ill will. "I was living in Rhode Island then," I said. "I came down to help my mother and attend to my father's affairs."

Pritchard turned his head, spat and turned back to face me. "Attend to your daddy's affairs and mess in police business. You got evidence of when you moved here?"

"I have notarized statements from three neighbors, a proclamation from the governor and a video documentary of my move. I can send you copies."

Prichard leaned nearer. His breath smelled of spicy peppers and sausage, and his teeth were sharp and caffeine-stained. "Advice I gave you the other night about being safer in Rhode Island still holds. You hang around here and run your mouth, there's bad things could happen."

"Is that a threat?"

Pritchard's glare converted to a disingenuous grin. He put his right palm on his heart and tilted backward at the waist. "You got me all wrong, bo. I'm an officer of the law. I'll do my best to protect you, but I can't be covering your back 24/7."

"Is that why you've been driving past my house, to cover my back?"

"It surely is. I'm concerned about your well-being."

"I can't tell you how much safer that makes me feel."

"Knew it would," he said. He rubbed nail-chewed fingers across the top edge of the lowered window and furrowed his brow. "One particular thing worrying me in regard to your well-being is Ronnie Hodge. He don't take kindly to getting his ass kicked. He's gonna want payback for what you did to him the other night. He hasn't come by your house has he, or maybe called to say he's planning to do you harm?"

"Nope."

"Well you hear from him or find out where he is, let me know. We're interested in having a chat with him."

"Who's we?" I asked.

"Law enforcement."

"I didn't realize you're involved in the Jason Grimes murder investigation."

"I ain't just another pretty face on patrol. Got me a military intelligence background, and I like to help the detectives when I can. Then too, I know Ronnie better than others do. He might open up to me."

I resisted an urge to take Pritchard's intelligence background as a straight line. I couldn't give him a pass on his entire comment though. "I bet Captain Talley appreciates your assistance."

He chuckled as if at a private joke. "Captain Talley, yeah. It's real nice having a girl in charge of investigations. Course there's those don't think so, think maybe she won't hold the job much longer. But I'm all for her. You be sure and let her know that when you see her."

"Putting in a good word is the least I can do considering all the attention you've paid to me. Covering my back must be taking you away from other duties."

He flexed his knees and pushed up to a standing position. His polished belt buckle gleamed, and I could smell the sun-heated leather of his holster. His voice carried down to me from above. "Don't worry yourself about that, bo. I don't sleep much, I'm always out there watching and listening, taking appropriate actions as I see fit. Good thing for you to remember, that I'm out there watching, listening and taking appropriate actions. You remember that, maybe you'll keep your nose out of things that don't concern you."

He smacked his palm against the Avalon's roof, spit against my front tire, then glided along the pavement toward his cruiser.

Chapter Thirteen

Pritchard followed me down the drive connecting Snee Farm with Route 17, the front bumper of his patrol car three feet from my tail. Out on 17, I pulled into the left turn lane for the Isle of Palms connector, and Pritchard continued straight, honking and waving as he went by.

I turned onto the IOP connector, turned right at the first light onto Hungry Neck Boulevard, turned off Hungry Neck into Towne Centre and blundered into a vacant parking space. Towne Centre was a strip mall on steroids: an uncountable number of stores and eateries arranged in no discernible pattern or order. The interior roads and parking lots were bizarre mazes with fiendishly illogical turns and dead ends. Each time I came in I wondered if I'd be able to navigate my way back out. It wasn't difficult to imagine riding around forever, like the Kingston Trio's mythical Charlie, who'd boarded a Boston subway car and couldn't get off.

I bought coffee at Atlanta Bread Company, took it outside, sat at a shaded table and watched the world go by. Couples of various ages strolling past on their way to the Palmetto Grande movie theaters, kids coming from Old Navy and Gap, adults with Barnes & Noble bags. One adult in particular caught my eye: Ellen Talley exiting Atlanta Bread with a carry-out sandwich sack. She saw me, and her face cycled through various unpleasant expressions before deciding on repugnance. Or possibly I was misreading. She set her chin in resolve, approached my table and spoke, "Russ."

I said, "Ellen."

She showed a tiny smile. It was a pretty smile that could distract me if I became careless. "Same beginning as at your house the other day."

"That went downhill fast," I said. "Maybe we should quit while we're ahead."

"You think we're ahead?"

"That depends on what starting point we use."

She glanced away, looked back and blinked. Her eyes were the purplish-blue of a passion flower. "May I sit and eat my sandwich?"

"There are other tables empty."

She arched her shoulders and blew out an exasperated sigh. "I'm trying to play nicely, but I could use some help."

It was fun behaving liking a petulant brat, but she had a point. "Please sit."

She placed the sandwich sack on the table, hung her powder blue linen jacket over the back of a chair and sat. A heart-shaped copper pendant dangled over her white blouse from a leather cord looped around her throat.

"What are the ground rules?" I said. "Can I ask police questions, or are we just going to talk about good books we've read recently, your favorite chili recipe, South Carolina's football team, that sort of thing?"

She unwrapped her sandwich, a turkey club on multi-grain bread. Her hands were square with short fingers. "It's always too much," she said of the sandwich. "I'll take half home for dinner." She extracted a bottle of water from her handbag and unscrewed the top. "You can ask me any question you want, as long as you understand that there are some things I can't tell you. And it wouldn't hurt if you treated me with respect."

"With all due respect, you know what I want to ask about."

"I do, and I don't have any new answers about your dad's killing," she said. "Just the same problem, no witnesses. It was late when he went back to the church to do paperwork, nobody else except the person who shot him was there, and no one in the neighborhood admits to having seen or heard anything. The popular theory is that he surprised a thief in his office."

"But nothing obvious appears to have been stolen from the church."

"Indeed," she said. "Although the intruder might have arrived just before your father got there, shot him, panicked and fled without taking anything."

"You sound lukewarm."

She spread a paper napkin on her lap and shrugged. "We've been pushing informants hard, grilling the usual suspects and hangers-on, but everything comes back empty."

"Any whispers that Dad may have had information about a secret *Hunley* diary that somebody was after?"

She cocked her head. "A secret *Hunley* diary? You mean this alleged diary that the *Post and Courier* claims Arnie St. John wants?"

"Possibly."

Her eyes narrowed. "Don't give me possibly. You didn't pull that question out of thin air. What prompted it?"

"It does pretty much come out of thin air," I said, wondering why I was saying that instead of telling Ellen about Moze Cheddar's visit and the note and diary pages he'd left. Possibly I had the egotistical notion that I could make better use of the information than the Mt. Pleasant Police Department.

"I'm grasping at straws like you," I added. "Dad was a *Hunley* buff, and I have a vague recollection that he mentioned something about a diary during a phone conversation not long before he died." That last was untrue, but as long as I was withholding information from Ellen, why not prevaricate too?

She stared at me suspiciously, but I'd interviewed enough suspects in my day to be able to replicate their guileless expressions. "If you're holding out, Russ, so help me I'll land on your head like three tons of bricks. But no, the *Hunley* diary angle hasn't come up."

"Do you think there's any chance Dad was intentionally killed?" I asked, wanting to get away from the diary topic before my guileless expression wore off. I could already feel my facial muscles straining.

"I can't rule it out."

"Motive?"

"Possibly gay rights," Ellen said. "Your father was never shy about taking vocal positions on unpopular social justice issues, and gay rights was the most recent. He was chairing a committee planning a big event, and he was getting hate mail and threats. He turned the letters over to us as they arrived, but we could never trace them."

"Are you acquainted with a retired FBI agent named Leonard Alcott who provided security assistance to Dad at the church as a result of the hate mail?"

"Where did you hear about Alcott?" Ellen asked.

"From notes in Dad's office files," I lied. I should have told her about Alcott contacting me and claiming to have information pertaining to Dad's murder, should have told her about my subsequent Internet research of Alcott, should have told her about my scheduled meeting with Alcott tomorrow morning. But having been deceitful about Moze Cheddar and the *Hunley* diary, why switch tactics now?

"Alcott and I had some contact about the threats your dad received," Ellen said.

"What kind of a guy is he?"

"He seems okay; he knew what he was doing."

"But he wasn't at the church the night Dad died?"

"Alcott was volunteer part-time help, not a full-time bodyguard."

"He didn't have any insight into the killing?"

Ellen shook her head, swinging her caramel hair. "Not that he shared with us."

I sipped lukewarm coffee and watched a gaggle of babbly teenagers with ice cream flit past. The boys preened and strutted to impress the lithe, leggy girls. Just as I'd preened and strutted in high school to impress Cherisse Dane, and if I were honest, to impress a too-young Ellen Talley.

"Any luck locating DuBois Dane?" I asked.

She dunked a corner of her sandwich in honey mustard dipping sauce, nibbled on the corner and wiped her lips. "I'd like to be friends again," she said. "But that doesn't mean I can tell you everything about everything. And I still don't want you poking around in Jason Grimes' murder. Which includes not getting in our way looking for DuBois."

That should have been my entrée to let her know about DuBois' phone call, but deception was fun once you got into it. "Durrell Pritchard and I had a little chat earlier," I said as a substitute for disclosing DuBois' call.

Ellen scowled. "Where did you see Pritchard?"

"He pulled me over in Snee Farm."

"What was he doing in Snee Farm? That's not his patrol sector."

"He was looking out for my well-being. He's worried someone might do me harm."

She got a bottle of Tylenol out of her handbag. "It's been a long morning, Russ, and it's going to be a longer afternoon. Please don't speak in tongues."

"Pritchard's excuse for pulling me over was concern I might be in violation of the South Carolina statute requiring that a car be registered here within forty-five days of relocation. But he didn't waste much energy on that. His real agenda was talking about Ronnie Hodge and not so subtly warning me to mind my own business."

"Warning you to mind your own business I totally understand, but I don't get the Ronnie Hodge part."

"Pritchard wanted to know if I've seen or heard from Ronnie, which I haven't. If Ronnie does contact me, Pritchard would appreciate being the first to know." I grinned. "Pritchard says he likes to help you and your detectives with your cases."

Ellen groaned, unscrewed the top of the Tylenol bottle and tapped two capsules into her palm. She put the capsules in her mouth and washed them down with water. "That's just what I need, Durrell Pritchard helping with my cases. Any idea what he's up to?"

"Not a clue. Is he dirty, possibly involved with Ronnie in something felonious?"

She opened her mouth to speak, apparently thought better of it and closed her mouth.

"Right," I said. "An internal department matter, and I'm just a member of the public." I tried to keep my tone free of rancor.

"I gave forewarning that I can't tell you everything. But you're playing that way too, aren't you? I understand there was some weirdness on the Snee Farm golf course this morning."

"Somebody with a swing as bad as mine?"

"Somebody parked an SUV on the fourteenth fairway and hit golf balls toward a house," she said. "The SUV is registered to Arnie St. John. The description of the golf ball hitter matches Arnie. And speaking of hitters, descriptions of the two men with Arnie sound like a couple of Mafia goons Arnie's been keeping company with."

"That is weird."

"There's more," she said. "A fourth man was out on the fairway for awhile talking to Arnie. About six-feet-two, a hundred-and-eighty pounds, short reddish-brown hair."

"He sounds devilishly handsome."

Ellen leaned across the table, her face as hard and pale as white granite, her eyes frozen purple marbles. "Don't jerk me around, Russ. What was going on?"

"Arnie wanted to talk to me about a few things. And you know Arnie, he always likes to make a show-stopping entrance. Somebody complain?"

"Course maintenance staff. But the Club manager called back to cancel the complaint. Turns out Arnie bought the Club recently, so he can park eighteen SUVs in the fairways if his little heart so desires. And I mean little heart literally. What did he want to talk to you about?"

"Curiously enough his agenda was similar to yours," I said. "Don't get involved looking for DuBois, and stay the hell away from Cherisse."

Ellen fiddled with the edges of the sandwich sack. "So have you stayed the hell away from Cherisse or signed on to try and find DuBois?"

"If I've signed on, it would violate professional ethics to talk about a client."

"Client?" Ellen said. "That's a cute way to describe your relationship with Cherisse." She squeezed the sandwich sack more tightly, as if it were my throat. "Okay," she said when she was through squeezing. "Let's quit while our discourse is still moderately polite and I haven't had to arrest you for impeding an investigation. And while I can still pretend that you had the good judgment to say no if Cherisse did attempt to hire you."

She stood, slipped on her blue suit jacket, capped the water bottle and returned it to her handbag. She took a small tube of lotion from the handbag and rubbed some on her hands. The lotion had a sandalwood scent. Thunder rumbled in the darkening sky, and Kenny Chesney sang out the open window of a passing pickup truck.

"Watch yourself with Arnie," Ellen said. "He's supposedly in deep with these New York goons. And he's taking heavy fire over this screwball *Hunley* reality show idea. He may have finally gotten too clever for himself. And when guys like Arnie go down, they take others with them. Especially others they think are sleeping with their wives."

Chapter Fourteen

Rain slashed at Moze Cheddar's truck windows and drummed the roof and hood. He was at peace, though. He'd growed up tracking and hunting in downpours, then done a different kind of tracking and hunting for the military in jungle monsoons. Rain gave a man cover like friendly artillery, swung the odds to the daring and quick. When others was water-blinded and mud-bogged, Moze slipped through the torrents keen-eyed and nimble-limbed.

But at this present moment there wasn't no need to slip through the torrents. Moze was parked and hunkered down dry in the I'On development. Goddawful ugly place. Houses big as office buildings on strips of property not much larger than a slice of bread. Made no sense to Moze why folks would spend a trailer load of money to jam their selves close enough to hear a neighbor sneeze. Could take that money upstate, buy a little place and several acres of quiet and have plenty left over.

Moze wasn't in I'On on account of shopping for real estate though. He'd followed a fella here trying to find out who'd wrote the anonymous letter that showed up at the cabin right before he left home. Letter had included in it a phone number for contact if Moze wanted to talk about selling his diary. Moze didn't have no intention of selling the diary, but there was other things he wanted to talk to the letter writer about. So Moze had called the number this morning and told the sleepy sounding fella who answered that he had some pages from the diary might be of interest to the letter writer. Sleepy sounding fella told Moze to deliver the papers in an envelope to a bartender name of Purvis in a joint called Salty's on Coleman Boulevard.

Moze had attached a radio frequency identification chip not much larger than a hair to the back of one of the sheets, sealed the pages inside a manila envelope, and drove to a gym and paid for a one day pass. He'd used free weights and a treadmill, showered and ate lunch at a sandwich shop. Afterwards he'd gone to Salty's Bar and handed his envelope to the bartender name of Purvis.

After the dropoff he'd sat in his truck close by Salty's and waited. Folks came and went, and eventually Moze's receiver picked up a signal from the RFIP chip indicating a fella who'd just left Salty's was carrying the manila envelope. Fella got in a dirty crapheap of a red pickup and pulled away. Moze followed. Followed to where he was parked now in I'On watching a house had a driveway with the red pickup in it. Long, tall charcoal-shingled house, three levels, first story wings extending at angles, upstairs porches, palmetto and oak trees, flower beds ...

House wasn't strange to Moze, he knew who lived here. Fella name of Arnold St. John who was making a reality show about the *Hunley*. This was the house Moze had followed the boys in the silver SUV to the other night before they'd ended up at the Griddle Grill restaurant and then at that Etiwan Pointe place.

Matters appeared to be clearing theirselves up nicely. Arnold St. John had somehow learned about Moze and the diary from the Gavin Berard minister fella, maybe killed the minister. Then he'd sent the four boys to Moze's cabin to steal the diary. When that didn't work, he'd wrote Moze a letter offering to buy the diary. Could be that all Moze needed to do to set things straight was take the St. John fella somewhere private and explain a few facts to him.

Thunder boomed, and jagged lightning flashed above the rooftops. Rain pounded down, creating narrow cascades between street and curb. Shiny pools formed in low stretches of pavement. Moze drank from a bottle of cranberry juice and thought about the Russell Berard fella. Wondered if Berard had read the diary section Moze left him. Moze liked the way Berard had handled hisself last night when they'd tussled: clean fighting, no panic at Moze's attack. Moze believed you could tell a lot about a man from how he reacted to such surprises, how he fought. So Moze had been having good feelings about Berard, been thinking he might be trusted. Now though, Moze felt concern. Anonymous letter was what had suggested Moze get in contact with Berard. But if St. John had wrote the letter, was Berard tied up with St. John?

Rain began to ease, and Moze lowered his window. Air smelled sweet from wet grass and flowers. Water dribbled in the window, and he opened the glove compartment for a rag. Noticed the Powerball ticket he'd bought the other morning. Drawing was tonight. Have to remember to check his numbers tomorrow. Pot was forty or fifty million. Couldn't imagine what he'd do with money like that. Didn't really have no needs. Fix up the dock, buy a bigger boat and a new tent. Donate money to the group trying to keep the lake clean. Be nice to give money to families of fellas fought in the jungles but never came back. Trouble was, the military didn't want no one to know about such fellas, wouldn't provide Moze with names and addresses.

Front door of the charcoal-shingled house opened, and the fella who drove the crap-heap of a red pickup walked out. Moze hadn't got a chance to take much of a look at the fella back at Salty's. He used his scope for a once-over now. Big fella, mid-to-late forties Moze guessed. Going to fat but powerful build. Brownish blond hair retreated from the front, growed long in the back and rubber banded in a pony tail. Moze grimaced. Didn't care for a man with a pony tail. Fella had on blue jean shorts and a faded black tee-shirt with a slogan that read: *If you want to live in the past, don't wake up tomorrow.*

Woman stepped out on the porch with the big fella, and Moze got more interested. Kind of life Moze led, relations with women had been mostly him paying for services. They'd been all shapes, sizes, colors and nationalities, and Moze didn't have no more illusions, didn't put none of them on a pedestal. He knew it was prob'ly wrong to think women was just there to be used, to meet a man's needs, but that's the way things had been for Moze.

This one standing on the porch, she was a whole different kind. Black woman, not young, forties somewhere, but with taut skin and body. Breasts thrusting against a pink tee-shirt, rounded hips and butt wrapped snug in tight, white shorts. She had brown eyes slanted a little like Asian girls, and there was knowing in those eyes and in her temptress smile.

She was standing close to the big fella talking, head cocked, fingers on his forearm. When she was done she stepped back, and the big fella nodded, made a reply and wandered off the porch into the drizzle. The woman went back into the house and shut the door.

RFIP signal was still coming from the house, so the envelope had been left there. If it had been left for Arnold St. John, then Moze wondered who the black woman was to St. John. But Moze could find that out later. Question now was whether to watch the house or trail the big fella. Parking too long in this neighborhood risked somebody calling the police, and the house wasn't going nowhere. Moze'd be able to find it again when he needed to. Seemed best to learn more about the big blond fella.

The red pickup reversed out of the driveway and headed down the road. Moze gave it a minute, U-turned and took the same route.

Red pickup swung left out the I'On entrance to Mathis Ferry Road. Moze let a couple of cars coming along Mathis Ferry get inbetween before he turned. He wasn't worried about losing the big fella. Had took a chance, stuck a tracer under the pickup while it was parked in the black woman's driveway.

Past the 526 overpass the red pickup and one of the cars behind moved into the left turn lane approaching a light. Moze did the same. Left turn put them on Whipple, and up a ways the red pickup's right signal flashed. Moze cozied into the right turn a careful distance behind, read Welcome to Snee Farm on the white stone entrance, thought, *Well what do you know.* Hung back as the red pickup drove Law Lane to Liberty Circle, looped the circle to Governor's, took a right on Casseque Province.

Moze smiled coldly. Could see where this was heading. Red pickup swung left at Covenant Square and into the Berard fella's driveway.

Chapter Fifteen

I sat beside a pile of file folders in my parents' home office on an area rug striped with reds, blues, browns and golds. Ebbing rain trickled beyond tall windows framing the gunmetal gray file cabinet. The portable phone I'd just turned off also sat on the carpet. My head throbbed from the torturous conversation with Cherisse Dane.

Had DuBois contacted me? I told her yes. Had DuBois said a third party would be in touch to arrange a meeting? I told her yes, wondering why my tone sounded so prickly. Maybe I was trying to assert dominance in at least one of my relationships. Maybe I was trying to convince Cherisse, and me, that any aid I provided was a humanitarian gesture devoid of emotion and lust. My tone made Cherisse sniffle. She wished I understood how much stress she was under and how desperately she needed my help and understanding. I said a number of people were professing a desire for my help and understanding, but none of them seemed inclined to tell me what the hell I was supposed to be helping with. The sniffles became more teary, and she pleaded with me to be patient and not forsake her.

Had Arnie been by to see me? I told her yes. What did he want? The opposite of what she wanted, I said. What did I mean? I told her I meant Arnie wanted me to stay away from her and DuBois. He has no right, she bristled. It's none of his business. Were those New York gangsters with him? I said yes. Had Arnie and the gangsters threatened me? I said not in so many words. Please meet with DuBois, she begged in conclusion. He needs you. I need you.

Now as I sat listening to the rain, I pondered the tension in Cherisse's voice, her sniffles and tears, the pleading whine. Out of character for smooth, calm, cool, collected Cherisse. I wondered what she'd gotten into. And I wondered whether I ought to be getting into it with her. Getting into something with Cherisse was romantic, also foolhardy. I was out on a lot of limbs considering that folks like Arnie St. John and Ellen Talley were standing by with chain saws.

Besides, I had work to do, sorting my parents' file folders, for instance. Most of the folders were my mother's: home repairs, bills, household purchases, warrantees, bank statements, volunteer activities, swimming material and mom's poetry. Those folders were meticulously organized and free of fluff. My father's folders were a different story. Organizational skills hadn't been one of his strong suits. He'd kept some folders in his church office and some in the home office. Mom had joked that she couldn't have an affair because she never knew when Dad would appear to retrieve a folder required at church. Both home and church folders were a mess, full of misfiled pages, duplicative material and barely decipherable notes. Dad had a habit of jotting down thoughts, ideas and experiences on scraps of paper and stuffing the scraps in the nearest folder. Frequently there was no relationship between what was written on the scrap and the folder topic.

The folder in my lap was typical. The overarching theme was the gay rights event Dad had been planning, but the folder also contained an old grocery list, an article about military spending and Dad's predictions of last year's NCAA basketball tournament games. Relevant to the gay rights event was an Excel spreadsheet with data about volunteers. One of the names was Leonard Alcott, the retired FBI agent. I thumbed on through the file and found half a sheet of lined yellow paper between the pages of a draft of the gay rights event brochure. My father's ballpoint scrawl ran sideways on the sheet: *Learned disturbing news today regarding Leonard's past and current activities. Not sure what I should or can do with the knowledge. Confidentiality issues involved.*

Presumably *Leonard* was Alcott. *Confidentiality issues involved* could mean Dad had thought that what he'd learned was protected by clergy-penitent privilege. I'd encountered clergy-penitent privilege as a Newport detective. Generally speaking, communications to ministers were confidential if the minister was acting in a professional capacity as a spiritual advisor, and if the circumstances of the revelation indicated that the confessor wanted the communication to remain secret. So someone had told Dad something disturbing about Alcott, and because the revelation was confidential, Dad couldn't go to the police if criminal activity was involved. But who had disclosed the information? If it was Alcott himself, had he regretted talking to Dad and killed him to ensure his silence? If someone else, why hadn't the person come forward after Dad's murder?

I should turn the note over to Ellen Talley, but I'd lost the knack for doing the right thing. I decided to see what transpired tomorrow with Alcott. Maybe after that I'd share my father's note with Ellen. If I were still alive. This business about Alcott providing me with information pertaining to Dad's death could just be a ruse. Alcott might be worried that sooner or later I'd discover what Dad had learned about him, in which case I could be next on the hit list if indeed Alcott had killed Dad.

I took Dad's note from the file, closed the folder and stood. Sopping tree limbs were bowed low, and lights from neighboring houses twinkled in the late afternoon murk. A clap of thunder announced the arrival of a red pickup. Gary Nagle stepped onto the driveway, saw me at the window, grinned and danced a jig. He turned his face up to the rain, swallowed water, coughed, shook himself like a wet dog and headed up the front walk. Rain made Gary happy and childlike. That was nice. I'd feel better about things if he were in a good mood when I killed him. I put my father's note in a desk drawer beneath other papers and shut the drawer.

Gary wasn't one to bother with conventions such as knocking. He ambled on in and gave a sloppy left-handed salute as I came out of the office. "What up, Q? Got your messages and made it quick as I could."

"No kidding," I said. "Quick as you could. Where did you come from, Mogadishu?"

He chuckled, chock full of good will toward man, not to be dragged under by the likes of me. "Been busy. Lina Pinheiro spent the night. We had quality time, slept in, then had more quality time." He chuckled again. I decided that if he chuckled a third time I'd shoot him.

"I couldn't be happier for you," I said. "And I'm more than a little impressed that you're not too proud to take Viagra."

"To hell with that noise. What Lina got was all natural."

"She must have been bitterly disappointed."

"Up yours." He ran his hands through his wet hair. "There a towel around?"

"Under the sink in the half bath."

I was sitting at the kitchen table reading the paper when he returned. He pulled a Dr. Pepper from the refrigerator and joined me. "Man gets dehydrated during quality time," he said.

I muttered sounds that didn't quite add up to words.

"Okay," he said. "What are we bein' pissy about?"

"While you and Lina were having quality time, so was I."

He tilted his head and curved the corners of his mouth high in a broad smile. "Damn, don't tell me the Hardy Boys both got lucky on the same night?"

"Not exactly," I said. "My quality time wasn't spent with someone soft and curvy and delicious. It was spent with a guy made of leather and steel who fought like Bruce Lee. He broke into the house without my hearing him, removed a gun from a drawer in my bedside table without my hearing him and toyed with me during a little hand-to-hand combat. My skills may have deteriorated, but that's pretty impressive work."

Gary's smile shriveled.

"Which brings us to why I called and left messages for you," I told him. "Last night at the Denmark Vesey you said a guy named Moze Cheddar might come to see me. But you neglected to mention that Cheddar was going to drop by after normal visiting hours, bypass the front door to get in and toss me around the family room like a stuffed doll. You also neglected to mention how you knew Cheddar was going to drop by. Maybe you'd like to explain all that now."

Gary looked down at the table top. "How sure are you this guy was Moze Cheddar?"

"Very sure. Who is he?"

Gary raised his head and met my stare. "Guy who lives upstate. Ex-military and ex-government something. Even more secret than what you and me did. He's a tough dude."

"No kidding he's a tough dude. What's the rest of it?"

"The rest of what?" he asked, trying for a wide-eyed innocent expression. He needed more practice. He reminded me of an oil company executive being questioned by Congress about excess profits.

"Knock it off," I said. "We're supposed to be friends. I want to know everything you know about Cheddar and how you knew he was coming here."

"You gotta give me room, Q. I'm in the middle of this shit."

"No, I'm in the middle. While you and Lina were cuddling and spooning last night, I had Cheddar, who's apparently a cross between Jason Bourne and Davy Crockett, breaking into my house. Then bright and early this morning I had Arnie St. John banging golf balls off my roof with the help of two Mafia hit men so he could wake me up and ask if I'm acquainted with Cheddar. You'll excuse me if I find all this a wee bit disconcerting."

Gary chewed on his lip and stared out the sliding glass doors, where shards of lightning crackled in the gray-black sky. The rain cascaded harder now, rolling off the gutterless roof like a waterfall. I imagined my mother swimming far out at sea fighting the storm and wished her safe travel.

"You're my best friend, Q, always have been, always will be," Gary said. "But this is complicated. There's other people involved I made promises to. You wanna call me an asshole for making the promises, maybe you'd be right. Doesn't change the fact that others are counting on me to keep my word."

"You're not doing dirty work for Arnie are you?"

Gary's face reddened. I could beat on him for only so long before guilt and regret turned into belligerence. "I said I can't tell you! Let it goddamn go!"

I wanted to scream at him that I'd happily let it go if people would let me go. But screaming at Gary would be slightly less productive than pounding my head against the wall.

The air conditioning clicked off, and the house was suddenly still. Aromas reminiscent of my mother's Thanksgiving turkey and my father's garlic tomato sauce swirled like ghostly vapors. I knew how to purge the house of my parents' clothes and other tangible goods, but I didn't know what to do about scents, sounds and sights associated with their shared life here.

Gary swallowed Dr. Pepper and wiped his lips. "So what did Cheddar want?"

"If you think I'm going to tell you anything about Cheddar's visit without information in return, your cerebral processes are confused," I said.

He grinned. "Figured it was worth a try." You couldn't keep Gary down for long.

"I need a glass of wine," I said. "Lots of glasses of wine." I stood to retrieve a bottle from the wine rack in the dining room.

"Your mom kept Girl Scout cookies in the freezer," Gary said. "How 'bout grabbing me a sleeve of Thin Mints. But go easy on the wine. We're taking a ride in a little while."

"Excuse me?"

"We gotta go for a ride."

"This isn't the right time to be clever or inscrutable," I said. "What the hell are you talking about?"

"DuBois Dane wants to see you tonight."

Chapter Sixteen

Gary drove us to the sitdown with DuBois Dane. He knew where we were going; I hoped he knew what he was doing. Gary had a habit of leaping off the high board without checking the water level in the pool, and his secretive entanglements with DuBois and Moze Cheddar could result in a head first landing. Of course, I was becoming entangled with DuBois and Cheddar too, but I never landed on my head. Rarely landed on my head. Had a flattened skull from frequent head landings.

We took the Mark Clark Expressway west. For all his other crazed behavior, Gary drove cautiously, sticking to the right hand lane and keeping the pickup under sixty. But that didn't make for a stress-free ride. Eighteen wheelers barreled up behind like runaway locomotives, then pounded past churning torrents of road water against the pickup's windshield. We crossed the Wando River, went by upscale Daniel Island and its tennis and soccer stadiums, mounted the high bridge over the Cooper River and inhaled noxious fumes from the paper mill plant.

Gary lit a cigarette, adding to the noxious fumes. "You gonna sulk the whole trip?"

"How long is the trip?"

He lowered his window six inches to evacuate cigarette smoke and residual mill fumes. "Whadda you want, Q? You want me to apologize for knowing DuBois, for DuBois knowing I know you, for DuBois asking me to bring you to see him? I thought I was doing you a favor. If I got it wrong I'm sorry."

"You didn't get it wrong," I told him. "I'm just wondering how many thumbs you have. They seem to be in a lot of pies."

"Just covering your back like always."

I grunted.

Beyond Rivers Avenue Gary ended our engagement with the Mark Clark and swung northwest onto Route 26 toward Columbia. The rain had ceased, but the pickup's wipers continued to swish away spray from passing cars. Gary tapped cigarette ash into the pullout tray and clicked on the radio. Neil Young was singing "Helpless."

"Couple of folks phoned me the last few days," Gary said

"It's nice you have other friends."

"These were your Newport friends, Francie Giordano and Pran Chea."

I toyed with the idea of jumping from the car. But if the fall didn't kill me, the traffic would. "Pran I can see, but you and Francie hate each other. Why would she call you?"

"Same reason as Pran. They're both worried about you."

I leaned back in the seat and folded my arms across my chest. The pickup's headlights cut bright holes in the blackness, and Gary's cigarette winked like an interior beacon. The night air slipping through Gary's window smelled of auto exhaust and ozone. His fingers tapped the steering wheel in accompaniment to Neil Young's squeaky singing about going to a place where all of his changes had been.

A lot of my changes had been here, and when I'd decided to return I'd thought this was my place to go. But a lot of my other changes had occurred in Newport. "How's Pran?" I asked.

"Holding his own. Summer in Newport, things are hopping. His motel's full most every night. Sounds lonely though. Misses you, misses sharing memories about Lim."

So here we were, back deep in the past. "He's an old man, Q," Gary said. "His only family left was you and Lim. After Lim … after she … you're all he's got now."

I shut my eyes and opened my heart to a flood of misery. "You think I should go back?"

"I don't know, man, it just seems wrong, Pran being up there all alone."

Gary was right. I'd run away from a lot of responsibilities when I left Newport in a self-centered fury. "I wonder if I could talk him into selling his motel and moving down here. He could live with me if he wanted."

"Worth checking out," Gary said. "Another idea I had is to take a trip up there, spend some time with Pran myself. Always liked Newport in the summer and fall."

"How are you going to make that work with your band gigs and this thing developing between you and Lina?"

He shrugged. "You make things work however you can. Pran's like family to me too. Times I ran away from trouble in Charleston and went to Newport, he gave me advice, money, food and lodging when I pissed you off and you tossed me out. Music'll always be here when I get back. And I'm thinking Lina might go to Newport with me. I know a few musicians up there, bet we could do a little performing if we wanted, earn a few bucks."

I shook my head. Pran was my absent wife's uncle, and I'd deserted him. Gary wasn't related to Pran, but he might put his life on hold and travel a thousand miles to lend support. We must have fallen into a parallel universe. In the real universe I was the good one, not Gary.

We exited Route 26 near Summerville and wended west on a two lane road. Gray clouds now emptied of rain blew east toward the ocean, briefly exposing a pale yellow crescent moon. Gary fiddled with the radio dial and locked in on a country and western station. "You realize somebody's following us," he said.

"I do."

"You weren't going to say nothing?"

"I don't like to tell you how to do your job."

He snorted. "Since when? I'm gonna lose him."

"Or her," I suggested, uncertain why I suggested it. Ellen Talley? Cherisse?

"Whatever," Gary said. He mildly accelerated so our follower wouldn't be immediately aware and we'd gain distance. Around a curve he hit the gas hard and built our lead. Just after the next curve was a dirt trail turnoff. Gary spun the steering wheel left, and the pickup careened across the two lane and skidded onto the dirt. Gary switched off the ignition and headlights. We coasted along, the trail faintly illuminated by the shrouded moon.

I looked over my shoulder and saw bright beams on the two lane, then a car racing by. A sedan, but no chance of glimpsing the driver.

"Got any idea who it is?" Gary asked.

"No, but whoever it is, he'll figure out fast that we turned off somewhere."

"Or she," Gary said. He clicked on the headlights and reversed the pickup. At the two lane he headed us back the way we'd come.

"Giving up?" I asked.

"Gonna take a different route."

Several turns later we were bouncing over narrow, pot-holed roads through isolated, wooded country with scattered houses, a mobile home park and occasional ramshackle stores selling groceries, bait, gasoline, hardware and ice cream.

"Cooler's behind you," Gary said. "Got Dr. Pepper, those Girl Scout Thin Mints from your house and cherry tomatoes. Pull me a soda and a cookie and help yourself."

I popped the tab of a Dr. Pepper, handed it to Gary with a Thin Mint and scooped cherry tomatoes from a zip-lock bag. The radio station crackled with static, and the pickup's tires slapped the pavement in monotonous, torpid cadence. The air slipping through Gary's window was fragrantly scented of wet pine. "Let's get it all on the table," I said. "What did Francie tell you?"

He chewed on the cookie and took his time swallowing. "What you said before ain't true, about Francie and me hating each other."

"That might have been an exaggeration."

"It was bullshit. I like Francie fine. I think she likes me okay too, except she thinks I'm a bad influence on you."

"I stand corrected. What did she say when she phoned?"

"She wants you to come back to Newport and be captain of detectives again. She's holding the job open. If you don't wanna be captain of detectives you can be police chief."

"She's the chief."

"She says the job should have gone to you and she don't like it anyhow. You come back and be chief and she'll slide into your old job. That'll still be a promotion for her from when she was your lieutenant."

The conversation I didn't want to have. Or did I? I bit into a cherry tomato and felt the juice squirt around my mouth. We passed a strip mall with darkened dentist, realtor and lawyer's offices, signaling a return to some semblance of civilization.

"If the chief's job should have gone to me it would have," I said. "And Francie has the power to resign, but she doesn't have the power to decide who replaces her. Never mind how stupid it would be for her to take a backward step by quitting the chief's position and heading up detectives." Debating this with Gary would be a piece of cake. I'd been marshaling my arguments for weeks. It would be good practice for the real debate with Francie.

"What Francie says she don't understand, you convinced her to apply for chief. She didn't want to, wasn't going to. She liked working for you. She figured you'd make chief, she'd be detective captain. Everybody'd be happy. But you badgered her into applying. Told her there was no guarantee you'd get the job, told her it might be time for Newport to hire a woman chief, especially a black woman. She asked how you'd feel if she got the job over you. You said no problem, you'd be happy to work for her. So she got the job over you, and you said the hell with it, I quit. Then you did this thing you've been doing all your life when your feelings get hurt. You go into a shell, won't talk to nobody, won't let nobody reason with you."

So maybe my arguments needed more marshaling. If Gary could chop them into kindling, Francie would burn them to ashes. Which, if I were honest, was the reason I hadn't talked to her. "I didn't quit because my feelings were hurt when Francie got the chief's job. In fact I didn't really quit, I retired. And I retired because both my parents died, which shook the hell out of me, and I had an impulse to come back home."

"Your parents dying might have had something to do with you quitting and leaving Newport," Gary said. "But you're full of shit if you don't think Francie getting the chief's job over you had something to do with it too."

"I'll defer to your superior wisdom."

"Be an asshole about it if you want, but you know I'm right."

"I said I'd defer to your superior wisdom."

"Go to hell."

I chewed tomatoes, looked out my side window and watched the night sweep irrevocably behind us like youthful dreams perishing in the past. Inky fog dimmed the pickup's headlight beams, and on the static-cleared radio the Animals sang "Don't Le Me Be Misunderstood."

Chapter Seventeen

Moze Cheddar's truck tires crackled across the crushed gravel parking lot of the place out to hell and gone where Berard and the big fella had stopped. Good thing he'd stuck a tracer under the big fella's pickup while it was parked at the I'On house, Moze thought. Otherwise it would have been real hard to follow these boys without them realizing he was behind. Seemed like maybe somebody else had tried that and gotten theirselves dusted.

Moze had been hanging back a good distance when the tracer showed the pickup pulled off the two lane and halted. Berard and the big fella had reached their destination was what Moze had assumed first. But then the pickup returned to the two lane and headed back toward him. Caused Moze a moment of concern, but the pickup went on by, and Moze reversed his direction and resumed the chase. Only thing he'd been able to figure, Berard and the big fella must have noticed another car tailing and took countermeasures.

Gravel parking lot was rutted, and Moze's truck bounced to a halt beside an orange Mustang in the rear. Big fella's pickup was rows away but within direct sight. Place was an old juke joint named Little Minnie's Big Blues. Rickety wood rectangle with bright painted pictures on the outside. One of the pictures was a black female mouse wearing white gloves and a short, low cut red dress displaying big breasts. Could be Minnie Mouse for the Little Minnie in the juke joint's name. At the left of the building was an old rotted trailer. Moze guessed hookers used to take men out there for a little extra fun. Near the trailer was a two-story dog house, but Moze didn't see no dog. AME church neighbored the place on one side, and a nail and hair cutting shop had set up operations on the other side. Piney woods grew thick behind the property.

Moze rolled down his window, drank from a water bottle and tried to reason things out. How was the big fella who drove the pickup connected to Berard? Did Berard have hisself any link to the black woman at Arnold St. John's house in I'On? Was Berard and Arnold St. John working together? Didn't seem to be no way to answer those questions except by asking the parties involved. And Moze had been trained by the government how to ask questions so the answers came back true.

What else Moze was wondering, why had Berard and the big fella drove all the way out here to the middle of damn nowhere? Was they here to listen to music? Or was there some other reason had to do with Moze's diary? Maybe he should go inside, see what was what. Didn't seem like there was much risk of being recognized. He'd been wearing a mask during his tussle with Berard the other night, and there was a nice crowd in Minnie's judging by the cars. Moze oughta blend right in, be able to observe Berard and the big fella without them knowing.

He stepped out, locked the truck and pulled the black baseball cap low on his forehead. Good thing he'd brung extra caps. Stupid damn mistake losing the other one at Berard's. It didn't have no markings, but losing it had been a mistake just the same. He crunched across the gravel toward the juke joint's door, resolving that the next mistake weren't gonna be made by him.

Chapter Eighteen

Gary and I sat against Little Minnie's rear wall at a round table covered by a plastic sheet with a purple and green floral motif. A cork coaster jammed under one leg imperfectly steadied the table's wobble. White menu boards on the walls showed tonight's specials scrawled in semi-legible red marker. We'd ordered fried catfish, okra and sweet potato casserole, and the Carolina Panthers' defensive line would have struggled to finish our portions.

Minnie's was ramshackle atmosphere pieced together by whatever wood had been scroungeable during different phases of construction. The ceiling sagged and the dance floor sloped. Strings of Christmas tree lights dangled on wall nails above ancient license plates, posters of 1930s and '40s blues performers and beer ads. Window air conditioners futilely fought the humidity, body odor, perfume, cigarette smoke and reek of frying lard.

Business was booming. Nearly all the wooden bar stools and blue velvet benches were occupied, and an overflow of players ringed the pool tables. The Band's "The Weight" boomed from the jukebox, which seemed about right. I'd begun to think I was wearing a sign on my back encouraging people to lay their load right on me.

"That's Little Minnie," Gary said, nodding toward a short, fat, black woman of indeterminate age circulating through the crowd. "She and her sisters grew up around here singing gospel. Her daddy was the preacher at the AME church next door. Minnie could sing like Mavis Staples, branched out to blues, worked Chicago, New York and LA before she came back home. This place was a shut-down, dilapidated hot pillow joint. Minnie bought it and fixed it up, but not too much. She's still got enough contacts to attract quality musicians. I've played here now and again."

I was watching the front door for DuBois Dane. People came in, people went out. Most looked happy. Cheap booze, food, and conversation massaged the aches of their daily grind and made it easier to get up tomorrow and do it all again. Mostly blue collar types I figured. Construction, landscaping, auto repair, warehouse loading, furniture delivery, telephone linesmen. They kept their lives basic, didn't bring the work home, had extended family and tight friends, knew how to go off the clock and enjoy. They were light years ahead of me.

I ate the last of my okra and dropped the plastic fork on the paper plate. "We have an arrival time for DuBois?"

"He'll be here," Gary said. "Keep the faith."

"I'll take that as a no."

The person feeding money into the jukebox was a fan of The Band. "It Don't Make No Difference" played now. The door opened and three men and two women came through. Something about one of the men … His face was turned, but something about the way he moved. The five melded quickly with folks mingling near the bar, and I ran my eyes over everyone but saw nobody familiar. I considered moving around the room for a closer look, but Little Minnie maneuvered to our table and rested a hefty forearm on Gary's shoulder.

"Gary Nagle! Lawdy, lawdy, been ages since you come up this way! Doing your thing at Cherisse Dane's I hear tell. You fancy, hoity-toity downtown now, too good for Little Minnie's?"

"Come on, Minnie. You know you're the only woman for me," Gary said.

Minnie giggled. "In my day, sugar, in my day. But I put on a pound here and there." She patted her ample middle. "And that Cherisse a fine looking thing." She batted her eyelashes at me. "Speaking of fine looking things …"

"Russell Q. Berard," Gary said. "Whitest of the white knights. He'll goddamn ride to the rescue anytime, anywhere, anyhow."

Minnie squeezed my hand. Her palm was moist and charged with sexual energy. The small eyes in her fleshy face glittered rapaciously. "Usually I like me a black knight, Mr. Russell Q., but I ain't one to be prejudiced if something nice from a different color come along."

"You'd kill him, Minnie," Gary said. "He's out of shape."

She cocked her head and gave me a speculative once-over. "I bet he handle himself real sweet. But if not he at least gonna die happy."

"What time do you get off work?" I asked.

She giggled again. "Sugar, that trailer out back wasn't rotted out, there wouldn't be no need to wait."

"Use my truck if you want," Gary said. "Soft seats, strong suspension."

Minnie squeezed his arm. "You kind to offer, but this fat ol' body of mine like some creature comforts. An' anyway, y'all got folks waiting to talk. Go through the kitchen, out the back door, they be along."

She moved on toward another table, and I looked at Gary. "DuBois set this up through Minnie?"

"Makes sense," Gary said. "Word is DuBois feels more comfortable in joints like this than in Cherisse's club. He can kick up his heels, spit on the floor. And nobody here, including Minnie, gives a damn about the law. Bunch of 'em probably got warrants waiting, bunch of 'em probably spent a night or more on the wrong side of jail bars. Live and let live is how they see things. Come in here, have a little fun, don't kill anybody, you're welcome anytime."

"You fit right in."

He grinned and stood. "And you don't. But there's hope for you if you're doing shit like this. Let's go."

Lung-searing heat permeated the cramped kitchen. We wove between ovens, cutting blocks, grill tops and refrigerators and pressed through dense, fishy, fryolator haze. The rusty hinges of the rear door screeched when Gary pushed it open, and the door banged hard behind us. We stood on a concrete apron surrounded by empty produce crates, a dumpster, crushed beer cartons, cigarette butts and corn husks. Garbage stench fouled the air. Lightning flashed low over the pine trees, and a coyote wailed from deep in the dark.

Gary and I waited. Eventually the headlights of a navy blue van parked near the edge of the woods blinked once. We walked through wet grass toward the van. "You're carrying aren't you?" Gary asked.

"No."

"Why the hell not?"

"It would send the wrong message."

"What message? That we're hoping to stay alive?"

"That we're here to help. Why would DuBois want trouble?"

"DuBois is cool. But Ronnie's got a real short fuse."

The driver's side door of the van opened and Ronnie stepped out. He was wearing baggy, knee-length black nylon shorts, a sleeveless white mesh tee-shirt and high-top black basketball shoes. His shoulders were sinewy with muscle, and his biceps bulged like half-grapefruits. His lips spread in a mean smile. "Good to see you again, bud. Missed your rib-tickling humor."

"I've been working up some new material," I told him.

"Can't wait to hear it. But first y'all raise your hands, stroll on over here and assume the position against the van." The gun in his left hand made his request all the more compelling.

"This is bullshit, Ronnie," Gary said. "We came up here to help you guys."

"Yeah, maybe, but I'm real cautious when it comes to cops. Goes double for dipshit, Yankee ex-cops."

Gary and I leaned against the van while Ronnie ran his hands over us in semi-thorough fashion. "Gotta admit I expected to find a piece on you, bud. How 'bout you give me that blade in the holder on your belt, Nagle, and we'll go indoors."

Gary swore under his breath, handed Ronnie his fishing knife, and Ronnie slid back the van door. "You sit in back with Dub, bud. Nagle, you ride shotgun. I'll go around, slide in behind the wheel. They're not carryin', Dub."

The van smelled of tobacco, marijuana and barbecue. There were crumpled fast food sacks on the floor and a cooler, baseball bat, water bottles and wadded clothes in the rear. DuBois Dane sat behind the driver's seat smoking a cigarette. He had on jeans, running shoes and a gold tee-shirt, and he was using a Diet Sprite can as an ashtray. I sat down beside him. He waited until Gary and Ronnie were in up front before speaking. "I'm only talking to you because my mother asked me to."

"You mentioned that on the phone," I said. "Same for me."

"Yeah, you banged my mother in high school, and you want to bang her again, so you'll do whatever she tells you."

I stared at him.

"It's okay. Everybody does what my mother asks because they want to bang her." His voice pulsated with bitterness.

"You're being a little hard on her, aren't you?"

He laughed harshly. "You're right, I should be more compassionate. She conceived me with a white racist son-of-a-bitch, and as a joke on him she gave me a black civil rights leader's name. After my so-called father took off because it made him nauseous to look at his mulatto child, my mother focused on sleeping with men who could do something good for her, regardless of whether that was good for me. And now she's disappointed that I haven't followed in the footsteps of my namesake, W.E.B. DuBois, or otherwise amounted to jack shit. I apologize for being so hard on her."

Whew, I thought, this kid needs a team of Vienna psychiatrists. "We're off topic aren't we?"

"And on topic would be …?"

"What happened the other night when Jason Grimes was killed. Why you and Ronnie are hiding out."

He scratched a sideburn with an index finger. "Why should I tell you anything?"

"Because you need help."

"Why should I have any confidence you can provide it?"

"I'm not a consultant submitting a bid, DuBois. You're familiar with my background. If you want to talk, fine. If you don't, Gary and I can shove off."

"My vote's for them shoving off," Ronnie said. "I don't trust this prick."

DuBois looked down at his shoes, rubbed his heel on the floorboard carpet, looked back up. "There wasn't supposed to be any killing …"

"Dub—" Ronnie began.

DuBois shut him off curtly. "I heard you. I don't agree."

Ronnie bit back a reply. He might be mostly brawn, but he appeared to have enough sense to step away when the occasion required brains.

"After the Griddle Grill, we went to meet a guy named Alcott," DuBois said.

Chapter Nineteen

Moze focused the night vision scope from the front seat of his truck and saw four in the van. In front was a blond boy and the big fella who'd come with Berard, and in back was Berard and a dark-haired boy. The four was doing a lot of talking, looked like they'd dug theirselves in for a spell. Moze had been nervous he'd lose Berard and the big fella when they'd snuck out through Little Minnie's kitchen. He'd slapped down money on the bar to pay for his sweet tea and gone through the front door and around the side of the building to have a look-see. When Berard and the big fella got in the van, Moze had quick-footed to his truck, worried the van would hightail. Hadn't been no need to rush though. Didn't appear the van was going no place soon.

Blond boy and the dark-haired boy was two of the three Moze had seen at the Griddle Grill, then followed to the Etiwan townhouses, which meant they was also two of the ones who'd broke into Moze's cabin after the diary. So why was Berard talking to these boys? Had he joined up with 'em? Moze stretched his brain searching out answers. Didn't come up with no firm ones though. Nothing to do but watch and wait. And it helped to have a friend while you watched and waited. He took the Galil sniping rifle from a hidden compartment and caressed the folding wooden buttstock. Rifle had a two stage trigger, adjustable cheek pad and telescopic sights. Best kind of friend there was.

Chapter Twenty

"**This Alcott** you went to meet," I said to DuBois. "Not Leonard Alcott, retired FBI?"

"You know him?"

Until this morning I'd never heard of Leonard Alcott. Now his specter was omnipresent. "Just his name," I said. "Why were you meeting him?"

"To buy something."

"Buy what? Macadamia nuts, oranges, paper towels, a little red wagon?"

"There's that asshole humor," Ronnie said from the front. "Just can't get enough of it."

DuBois shifted position on the seat, and a spring squeaked. "The situation is complex. Alcott has material someone wants, they agreed on a price, and we were asked to deliver the payment and pick up the material."

I rubbed my chin and mulled.

"Doesn't sound complex," Gary said. "Alcott's blackmailing somebody, and you guys were making the payoff." Gary wasn't much for mulling.

"Draw whatever conclusions you'd like," DuBois told him.

"Jason Grimes' body was found at the Etiwan Pointe townhouses," I said. "Is that where you met Alcott?"

DuBois nodded.

"Alcott picked the spot?"

"Yes."

"Good choice," I said. "I took a ride out there. One road that dead ends at the townhouses. Doesn't look like many of the places have been sold, very little traffic, especially at that time of night. Easy for Alcott to monitor. What's the rest of the story?"

"There's a clubhouse near the front. We were supposed to leave the money on the porch, drive away, come back in ten minutes, and the stuff we were buying would be on the porch."

"Taking a risk, weren't you?" Gary said. "Y'all might have come back in ten minutes and found zilch: no money, no blackmail records."

"No shit," Ronnie muttered, crinkling open a bag of pretzels.

"We didn't like the setup," DuBois said. "But that's what the person we were representing agreed to. Alcott had considerable leverage to call the shots."

"What went wrong?" I asked.

DuBois sighed. The tip of his cigarette twinkled orange like a tiny shooting star as he swung it from his mouth and tapped ash into the Diet Sprite can. "We got a little too clever. I dropped Ronnie and Jason off out of sight before the townhouses. Then I went ahead and left the money on the clubhouse porch and drove away. The idea was for Ronnie and Jason to sneak up near the clubhouse and watch to be sure Alcott left the material."

DuBois stared at Ronnie's profile and clicked his teeth. Ronnie twisted in his seat to face us, cheeks flushed, lips pinched in a pale curve. "I didn't do nothin' wrong! Jason and I moved real careful and saw Dub make the drop and drive away. While we was waiting for Alcott we heard a noise in the woods. I told Jason I'd check it out, but it was too dark to see a damn thing. Then wham, somebody cracked my skull from behind and I went down for the count. When I came to I scrambled out to the road just as Dub was pulling up. He can tell the other parts better'n me."

I looked at DuBois.

"After I dropped off the money, I drove back down Wando Park Boulevard," he said. "There was a dark green truck pulled off the side of the road that I didn't remember from a few minutes before when we came in. Nobody in it. I didn't like that. I wanted to warn Ronnie and Jason that something might be going on, but I'd made them give me their cell phones so there was no chance they'd have the phones on and Alcott would hear them ring. I went around a curve, killed my lights, turned back and parked where I could see the truck. A couple of minutes later I heard gunfire and hauled ass toward the townhouses. When I got close I saw somebody holding a gun and standing over a body near the clubhouse. Whoever it was bolted into the woods when my lights shined on them. Then Ronnie staggered out of the woods from a different place. He got into the Cherokee, and we drove up to the body and discovered it was Jason."

"Dead?" I asked.

"Dead," DuBois said. "Shot in the chest. We should have put him in the Cherokee, but we panicked and took off. That's two we've left behind now. The dark green truck was still parked off the road when we went by. I wanted to wait and see if anyone came out of the woods and got in, but hanging around was too risky."

A couple wobbled across the parking lot sidestepping puddles of rain water that looked like shiny tar pools in the foggy light. Our windows were down, and we heard the couple chuckle as the man squeezed the woman's rump and whispered in her ear. My eyes ran past the couple and around the lot. I thought I saw a face in a dark colored truck parked in the rear. "What did you mean when you said that's two you've left behind?"

Dubois jerked his eyes away from me, blew a smoke ring and watched it rise. "Nothing to do with Jason. It's a different matter."

"Where's Dewey Welch been?" Gary asked. "Haven't seen him for awhile."

"What the hell do you care about Dewey?" Ronnie said.

Gary met Ronnie's glare impassively. "Didn't say I cared. I'm just wondering. Dewey and Jason were roommates, always together. But Dewey hasn't been around lately, and he wasn't with you three the other night when you went to Etiwan to deal with Alcott. Makes me curious about where he's at."

"Where he's at ain't none of your goddamn business," Ronnie said.

"Okay," I said. "Let's forget about Dewey. What do you think happened at Etiwan?"

Ronnie sneered. "You ain't got it figured out, Mr. Detective? Alcott drove in behind us, parked his truck, and was on his way up to the clubhouse through the woods when I heard him. He hit me from behind, came out on the road, shot Jason and grabbed the money. Ran back into the woods when he saw Dub's car lights, waited for us to leave, then scrammed with the cash and the stuff he was supposed to leave for us."

Dubois shook his head. "Alcott doesn't own a green truck. I checked that out afterward."

"He could have borrowed the truck from somebody," Ronnie said.

I had the impression they'd been arguing about this ad nauseam. Thunder rumbled to the north, and I stared again at the dark truck in the rear and inhaled the aroma of wet tree bark carried through the windows by a gusty breeze.

"Or …" Dubois said.

"Ah hell, man, don't start with that Cheddar shit again," Ronnie said.

"Who's Cheddar?" I asked, wondering how many Cheddars there could be interjecting themselves into my life.

"Guy named Moze Cheddar from upstate," Ronnie said.

"What's his role in this?"

"We were involved in a transaction with Cheddar that didn't go smoothly," Dubois said. "It's possible he's pissed off about that and down here wanting payback. I thought someone might have been following us before we went to the Griddle Grill the other night when we ran into you. And after that shit in the parking lot with you, it felt like someone could have been following us again."

"Did you see the license plate of the truck parked at Etiwan?" I asked.

Dubois shook his head. "The plate was mud splattered. I couldn't read it from a distance, and I didn't want to get too close."

"Who sent you to meet with Alcott?"

"That's irrelevant."

"It could have something to do with what happened."

"It doesn't. Either Alcott or Cheddar killed Jason."

I sucked in my frustration. "Okay, what was your transaction with Cheddar?"

"Again not relevant," Dubois told me.

"Knowing his motive could help determine whether he killed Jason."

"His motive is that he has something we tried to obtain, and he didn't appreciate the way we tried to obtain it, so he'd like to forcefully express his displeasure."

"Was the 'it' you tried to get a diary?"

"Damn!" Ronnie said. "I knew we shouldn't be talking to this guy!"

"Who sent you to get the diary from Cheddar?" I asked. "Arnie?"

"Get out, Berard," Dubois said in a cold, mean voice. "This conversation is over."

"Listen Dubois …"

"Get out of the damn van!"

"You heard him, bud," Ronnie said. "Get the hell out." The gun he'd used to convince us to enter the van was on display again. We got out.

Ronnie backed the van away from us, and a clap of thunder boomed. But this thunder was man made. A bullet slammed into the side of the van. Ronnie accelerated with a screech, and the van took a second bullet before squealing from the lot. The fun wasn't over yet though. Two more bullets kicked up gravel a few yards from Gary and me.

"Shit!" Gary said as we ducked for cover behind an old Volvo wagon. "Out of the frying pan into the fire. Great to be working with you again, Q."

Chapter Twenty-One

A bullet nicked the Volvo, then long silence. I rose just high enough to look over the hood in the direction of the shots. I didn't see anything, didn't die. My eyes roamed the lot. The dark colored truck that had been parked in the rear was gone.

Little Minnie bounced out the kitchen exit and waddled across the grass, arms in the air, hands waving. "Oh damn hell!" she shrieked. "Oh damn hell! What happen out here, Gary Nagle? What happen out here, Mr. Russell Q?" The bartender and several others crowded behind her.

Gary wiped his face with his shirt sleeve. "Just a little gunfire, Minnie. Not the first time for that at your place."

"No, but it always be a pain in the ass. We having a real good night, now folks gonna scatter knowing the po-lice will come. Dubois and Ronnie shoot at you?"

"No," I said. "Somebody else shot at them and us. We're sorry about this."

Minnie patted my hand. "That okay, sugar. People who go home now gonna come back tomorrow. You and Gary Nagle need to go home too. Po-lice just ask you a lot of foolish questions, keep you busy all night if you stay."

"We might as well take our medicine now," I said. "If we leave they'll track us down and be nastier when they ask their questions."

Minnie giggled. "You so precious, Mr. Russell Q. Ain't nobody gonna remember you two was here tonight. Ain't nobody tell your names to the po-lice or describe your fine selves."

"She's right, Q," Gary said. "That's the way it works at Minnie's. Let's ride."

Gary took the truck to the main road, where we heard sirens approaching from the right. He turned left. "It's funny how fast you can forget you were a cop for most of your professional life and violate all the principles you stood for," I said. "It's as if I joined a new team with a whole different code of conduct."

"Relax," Gary said. "Our team has way more fun than the cops, and we need a good quarterback. But say the word, I'll drop you off, you can hang around and chat with Dorchester County's finest."

I didn't say the word.

Gary stopped at a diner off Route 26. Gray fog sprites swirled below the lights, and the nearby interstate traffic whooshed and rumbled. The narrow trunks of two young palmettos flanking the front door of the diner swayed in the breeze. Pungent odors of tomato sauce, pepperoni and onion from a pizza place next door seasoned the night.

Gary appeared super-charged by the encounter with Dubois and Ronnie and the bullet-ridden post-script. His step was springy, his nose twitched, his eyes sparkled, and his torso rocked in cadence to internal music. He'd always thrived on the edge.

Inside we ferreted out an empty booth. The ferreting wasn't much challenge; there were only three other customers. I ordered coffee from the orange-curled waitress. Gary ordered a Dr. Pepper and pecan pie, winked at the waitress and drummed his spoon on the placemat.

"DuBois has some real issues with Cherisse, doesn't he?" I said.

"Yeah, he's a sensitive kid, and he and Cherisse have been through their good times and bad," Gary said. "Going through a shitty patch now, that's for sure. Part of it is that Cherisse and Arnie are near to exchanging gunfire, and as wacked out as Arnie is, he's treated Dub real well, prob'ly been the closest thing to a father the kid's ever had. So it's rough for Dub to see Cherisse and Arnie splitting up."

"Maybe Cherisse and Arnie won't split up."

Gary snorted. "Don't bet your pension on it. You like the story Dub and Ronnie told?"

"Who knows what to like and not like," I said. "Money left on a porch to buy something from this ex-FBI agent, Alcott. Ronnie conked in the woods and not seeing who shot Jason Grimes. A mysterious truck parked off the side of the road, maybe Moze Cheddar's. It sounds like the script for a bad TV movie."

"You noticed a truck parked in the rear of Minnie's, then gone after the gunfire?"

I smiled and shook my head. "I never give you enough credit, do I?"

He shrugged. "Can't get our military training out of my system."

The waitress delivered our food and drink, and Gary winked at her again. I thought she blushed, but it could have been the lighting.

"Do you know anything about Leonard Alcott?" I asked.

Gary inserted a forkful of pie in his mouth, chewed slowly and swallowed. Which was a convenient excuse for delaying an answer. "Never heard of the guy," he said eventually.

"My father never mentioned him to you?"

"Your dad? The hell would your dad mention Alcott?"

"Alcott attended Dad's church and was providing him with security help."

"First I've heard of it."

"What were Dubois, Ronnie and Jason trying to buy from Alcott?"

"Couldn't say."

"Did Arnie send them to make the buy?"

Gary banged his fork on the table top. "Damnit it, Q, ease back! What part of 'couldn't say' isn't getting through your thick head?"

"'Couldn't say' is a careful choice of words."

"Go to hell."

"Why is it that more and more of our conversations end like this?" I asked.

"Cause you're an asshole," he said.

"I knew you'd have a simple explanation."

"I'm declaring a cone of silence till I finish my pie."

Cones of silence went back to our school days. We'd declared them to avoid escalating disputes into fistfights. Cones of silence seemed childish now that we were mature adults. At least I was a mature adult. At least I aspired to be a mature adult. But if Gary wanted to play by childish rules, to hell with him. I'd been planning to tell him about my meeting tomorrow with Leonard Alcott and ask him to cover my back, but not now. That might cost me my life, but there was a principle involved. I couldn't think of what the principle was, but it would come to me.

I paid the bill and went outside. The crescent moon was a vague outline in the misty sky, and the stars were low voltage pin pricks. Gary appeared, yanked cigarettes from his jeans, studied them, decided no and stuffed the pack back in his pocket. "Let's go home," he said.

He drove us east on 26 and picked up 526 toward Mt. Pleasant. The oldies radio station played Dylan's "Forever Young." The last thing I was feeling tonight was young.

"You think that truck parked at Minnie's was Moze Cheddar's and he's the one fired the shots?" Gary asked.

"It's possible, but I have a hunch Cheddar doesn't miss when he shoots."

"Kind of a coincidence the truck was gone after the shooting ended."

"Yeah, there is that," I said.

"Could be Cheddar was firing warning shots, not shooting to kill."

"A warning about what?"

"Keep our noses out of his business."

"I don't know," I said. "Cheddar's visit to my house last night seemed to be an invitation to get actively involved in his business. And I'm not sure who those shots were aimed at. The first volley struck the van when we were out of it, which suggests Dubois and Ronnie were the targets. But the last few were toward us after the van left."

"Maybe Cheddar fired a few rounds to pin us down, then went after Dub and Ronnie."

I arched my neck and yawned. "Too many maybes, too many hypotheticals. One of us, let's call him the genius, could probably figure this all out before breakfast if the other one, let's call him the fathead, wasn't holding back information."

"Fathead's a little strong," Gary said. "Don't be so hard on yourself. But it's nice you're finally realizing I'm a genius."

Chapter Twenty-Two

Gary dropped me off in my driveway. The house rose placidly in the shadowy calm, and inside was quiet. Quiet felt good after the din at Little Minnie's, the contentious conversation with DuBois and Ronnie and the gunfire. But the quiet didn't last long. It never does.

"Crazy damn night, weren't it?" the voice said from the dark of the family room.

My hand was on the kitchen light switch, but I didn't click it. "Moze?"

"Yessir."

"Weapon trained on me?"

"Yessir. S&W 686 revolver. I saw out the window that big blond fella drives the red truck dropped you off. Ain't coming back is he?"

"No."

"You're later than I expected," he said. "Starting to worry you was detained by law enforcement at Little Minnie's."

"We stopped for coffee. How do you feel about my turning on the kitchen light?"

"Reckon we'll leave the lights off for now. You come in here, take a seat."

I stepped down from the kitchen, saw Cheddar crouched in the sun room doorway pointing the revolver. His body swiveled to follow me as I settled on the sofa. "You got a head start on us from Minnie's," I said.

"Didn't have no more interest than you in speaking with law enforcement. You armed?"

"No."

"Guess I oughta check on that," he said. "No offense against your word intended."

"None taken."

"Have to ask you to stand, come around the coffee table, assume the position. Apologize for the inconvenience. I should have did this before you sat."

"Not a problem," I said. The frisk was professional; Moze's probing hands didn't miss any spots where a weapon could be secreted. His body odor and the musty smell of his clothes hung heavy in the air like the barracks' scent of unwashed soldiers.

"Huh," Cheddar said. "You told the truth. Don't know as I like that. You can take your seat back now, turn on a light."

I returned to the sofa, reached out slowly with my left hand and switched on a table lamp. Cheddar pulled an ottoman near the coffee table and sat with the revolver in his lap.

"You don't like it that I told you the truth about not carrying a gun?" I said.

He shook his head. "Like the truth just fine. Don't so much like it that you ain't armed."

"Because?"

"Makes me wonder," he said. "I got the idea them two boys you talked to in that van at Minnie's are my enemy. Fact you went into the van without a weapon gives the impression you're friendly with the boys. If you're friendly with them, could be you're my enemy."

"Or it could be I'm neutral."

His lips curled down, souring the expression on his seamed, nut brown face. "Neutral's sometimes just another word for gutless, and you don't seem to be a gutless fella, Mr. Berard."

"Maybe I just haven't chosen sides yet."

"Fella takes too long to choose, others put him on a side. Then they treat him according to the side where they put him."

"Why don't we stop talking in riddles, Moze. What's this all about? Did you fire those shots at Minnie's?"

He rubbed a palm across his bald crown. "You think I did?"

"Every way I add things up leads to you, but for some reason I don't think you did it."

"That's on account of you having good instincts."

"Or being stupid," I said. "If you didn't fire the shots, who did?"

"Don't know. Shots come from the woods off to the side of where I was parked, but the shooter was pretty well hid."

"Did you follow us to Minnie's, or did you follow the boys in the van?"

"Followed you," he said.

"See anybody else tailing us?"

"Saw you take countermeasures like you'd noticed somebody. But I was pretty far behind, didn't actually see nobody."

I looked at him quizzically. "You were following us, but you were far behind … A tracer. You put a tracer on Gary's truck?"

He shrugged.

I shook my head. "This is beginning to feel like a James Bond movie."

"You look at those diary pages I left last night?" he asked.

"I did."

"What do you think?"

"It's an interesting story, your ancestor, Ezra, a Union spy in Charleston during the Civil War, sent to sabotage the *Hunley*. Are those the pages you showed to my father?"

"Same exact ones."

"But he didn't take any pages with him?"

"No sir, I wouldn't allow that."

"You think my father told someone here about the diary, or someone found out some other way and killed Dad trying to obtain more information?" I asked.

"Don't rightly know who killed your daddy or why, but I can't see no way around the fact that he must have told somebody about the diary. Wasn't nobody else who knew about it, and now it's being talked about in your Charleston newspaper. Riles me up on account of your daddy promising me he'd keep the diary a secret. Thought I could trust him, but now I ain't so sure that was a smart thing to do."

I felt my face flush. "Are you accusing my father of lying to you?"

Moze shrugged. "Don't know as I'd use the word lying, least not yet. But it sure don't look like he kept the diary secret."

I drew and released calming yoga breaths. They weren't all that calming, but they did prevent me from springing across the room at Moze and either getting my ass kicked or being shot dead. The trouble was, I couldn't fault his logic. "You mentioned the newspaper," I said. "You saw the article about Arnie St. John and his reality show and his interest in the diary?"

"Yessir, I surely did."

"Have you had contact with Arnie?"

Moze narrowed his eyes and brushed a forefinger across his chin. "That ain't such an easy question to answer as you might think. You talk about this St. John fella like you're acquainted. That so?"

"It is. We went to high school together, and I saw him this morning."

He shook his head. "I just can't get myself a good handle on you, Mr. Berard. Instincts tell me you're a fella to be trusted, but you got yourself an entanglement with this St. John who wants my diary, and earlier tonight you was having a friendly conversation in that van at Little Minnie's with two of the four boys who broke into my cabin awhile back to steal the diary. Boys who might could have been sent by the St. John fella."

That clicked a couple of puzzle pieces into place. DuBois and Ronnie had kicked Gary and me out of the van when I'd asked if it had been a diary they'd tried to obtain from Moze, and before that Ronnie had been annoyed when Gary asked about one of their friends. "Any chance that one of the four who came to your cabin didn't make the return trip?" I asked. "A kid named Dewey Welch?"

Moze leaned toward me, eyes glinting with menace. "I ain't a killer, Mr. Berard. Least ways not a killer in civilian life. But I'll do what's needed to protect what's mine."

I couldn't see any percentage in lecturing Moze about not taking the law into his own hands. Who knew what he'd faced when the boys appeared at his cabin? And Moze was accustomed to casualties. I'd done his kind of work years before in the Marine Corps, and I understood the hard-hearted mind-set toward death that develops. People on your team die, people on their team die, and those still living go on. Besides, I wasn't the best person to be lecturing about cooperation with law enforcement, considering that I'd been withholding information and obstructing justice to a fare-thee-well.

"Point taken," I said. "What do you want from me?"

He wrinkled his forehead and stared over my shoulder at the cream-painted wall. "I got a strong feeling my problem and yours has theirselves a connection. If so, we're gonna need to work together. If we're gonna work together, there's gotta be trust."

"Makes sense," I said. "But I'm not the one holding the gun."

He chuckled and slid his pistol into a pocket of his black nylon pants. "Reckon you got me on that one."

"My problem is solving my father's murder," I said. "What's your problem exactly? Trying to keep your diary private?"

He chewed on his lip for a moment, then nodded. "Guess that's a fair way to put it. The diary tells a story I ain't proud of, but your daddy part-way convinced me it might be used for good. Maybe I'll give that a try, but if I do, it's gonna be on account of I decide so, not on account of somebody taking the diary and revealing its contents. So what I came down here for is to find out who's trying to steal the diary and convince 'em to stop."

He paused, and when he resumed his voice was as cold and sharp as a knife blade. "Convince 'em to stop the easy way or the hard way, whichever's required."

"Okay," I said. "Message received. If you're worried that I'm conspiring against you with the two boys I was talking to in the van at Little Minnie's, you don't need to be."

"What was you talking to them about?"

"Events at Etiwan Pointe two nights ago. Are you familiar with what happened there?"

"Read something in the paper. A boy was shot dead wasn't he?"

"Jason Grimes, a friend of the two in the van and a friend of Dewey Welch. The two in the van were at Etiwan also."

Moze shook his head. "Those boys is pulling a mountain of shit down on their heads."

"I wouldn't argue with that."

"You know what they was doing at this Etiwan place?"

"They claim that what they were doing didn't have anything to do with your diary. But maybe you think differently."

"What would I know of it?"

"The boys saw a truck at Etiwan Pointe that sounds like the truck I saw at Minnie's tonight … the truck I'm guessing you drive."

"There's lots of trucks the style and color of mine. Them boys get the plate number?"

"No."

"Too bad."

"You know a man named Leonard Alcott?" I asked.

He shook his head. "Ain't never heard of him."

I had the feeling he was telling the truth about Alcott.

"So what do we do next?" I asked.

"You read more from the diary," he said. "Learn yourself more about the story I'm trying to protect. Meantime both of us'll study on whether we think we can put faith in the other. Then we'll have us another conversation." He stood, went into the sun room and returned with a black knapsack.

"One other thing," he said, rummaging through the knapsack. "How well you know that big blond fella?"

"We grew up together. He's my best friend."

"You got trust in him?"

"I do," I said. "Why?"

"Note I left you the other night said a letter came to me from somebody who wants to buy my diary but didn't give no name. Note did give a phone number though. This morning I called the phone number on account of being curious about who wrote the letter. Told a fella who answered that I had diary pages might be of interest to the letter writer. Fella told me to take the pages to a place and leave 'em with a bartender. I left a few pages that don't say much, and I put a tracer chip on the back of one of the pages."

He paused, tugged a manila envelope out of his knapsack, tossed it to me, closed the knapsack, looped the straps over his shoulders and continued. "When a fella picked up the pages from the bar, I followed him to a house in a place nearby here called I'On. Arnold St. John's house. Only it wasn't St. John the fella brung the pages to, it was a black woman. And the delivery fella was your big blond friend."

Chapter Twenty-Three

Moze departed, and I sat deliberating in the family room gloom. It didn't come as a shock that Gary would be helping Cherisse. She could manipulate him as easily as she could any other male. If Cherisse had sent the letter to Moze, and Gary was aiding and abetting her, that would explain how Gary had known Moze might come to see me. But why would Cherisse have sent a letter to Moze offering to buy the diary? Was she trying to obtain it for herself for some reason, or acting as an agent for Arnie? Then too there was the still unanswered question of how Cherisse and Arnie had learned about Moze and his diary. Had Dad told one or both of them?

I cerebrated and ruminated and cerebrated some more, but my brain was fried and enlightenment elusive. Eventually I surrendered to unenlightenment, rose and turned on more lights, poured a glass of vegetable juice, and settled back down with part two of the diary of Ezra Cheddar, Union spy. On a mission for Secretary of War Edwin Stanton and operating with a Southern accent as Nathaniel Clary, Cheddar told the following tale.

I reached Charleston in September of 1863 and found parts of the city in ruin. I was saddened by the devastation that had occurred since my pre-war visit, even while recognizing that much of the damage resulted from Federal bombardment in pursuit of goals I cherished: an end to the vile and immoral practice of slavery and preservation of the Union. The bombardment had commenced nearly a month earlier, and the barrage of mortar fire continued without abatement. As if this were not enough, Charleston had also been ravaged by a fire in December, 1861, that destroyed six hundred or so homes and buildings over 540 acres. One might despair that this Holy City of churches had been inexplicably abandoned by God, though in my view it was the citizens of Charleston who had abandoned God by their unwillingness to support abolition of slavery.

After securing accommodations, I initiated my quest for information about the submersible torpedo boat. Confederate soldiers were everywhere. I roamed through the camps of military tents stretching up from Battery Ramsay at White Point, and I frequented bars such as the one at the Mills House. I listened carefully, ingratiated myself into conversations, and read news reports in the Charleston Mercury. I learned the following:

The boat, named the H.L. Hunley *after Horace Hunley, one of the investors and designers, had been sent from Mobile to Charleston in August at the behest of General P.G.T. Beauregard, Commander of Confederate forces in Charleston. The base of operations was Sullivan's Island, across the Cooper River. The fish-boat, as she was sometimes called, could submerge and be propelled underwater by a hand crank connected to the propeller. A metal spar pole attached to the bow carried a torpedo. The plan was to propel the boat underwater and ram her torpedo into Union ships blockading Charleston Harbor. After ramming a ship and embedding the torpedo, the fish-boat would back away until a rope connecting her to the torpedo trigger stretched tightly, detonating the torpedo and sinking the ship. It was thought that by the time of detonation, the fish-boat would be far enough away to avoid damage.

Several weeks after the boat's arrival in Charleston, an accident had occurred that caused her to capsize. Of the crew of nine, four escaped and five drowned. The boat was raised, but pessimism was growing among such Confederate military leaders as General Beauregard about the value of the undertaking.

Horace Hunley had come to Charleston from Mobile and proposed that he be placed in charge. Hunley promised to bring an experienced crew from Mobile to assist with the boat's operation. Just before my arrival in Charleston, General Beauregard had accepted Hunley's offer. However, lacking confidence in Hunley's experience, Beauregard and the Navy Department had determined that the boat's commander would be Lt. George Dixon, commander of the boat during her trials in Mobile. *The new crew was now being assembled and trained for an attack on the Union blockade fleet at the earliest favorable moment.*

My task was clear. I must insinuate myself into the company of Hunley, Dixon, and others in the crew, observe the fish-boat's activities, and avail myself of any opportunity to undermine the Confederate plans.

I took a room on Sullivan's Island and spent much time at the dock where the boat was being readied. The design interested me greatly. The hull had been constructed of iron, with an interior less than four feet high and forty feet long. Two fins controlled diving, and ballast tanks were flooded to submerge and pumped out to surface. Two pipes could be raised from just below the surface to provide air. The crew, normally consisting of the captain plus eight others, entered through two small hatches with glass windows that permitted viewing when the boat was partially submerged.

In addition to my surveillance at the fish-boat's dock, I ate and drank at establishments patronized by the crew members and engaged in amiable discourse with them. I told the cover story Secretary Stanton and I had prepared. My name was Nathaniel Clary; I had been wounded in battle against Union soldiers, thus explaining the limp from my hunting accident in Pennsylvania; and as a result of my wounds I was forced to leave my Confederate regiment. I purported to be greatly frustrated by my inability to continue with the infantry, and desirous of assisting the Confederate cause in other ways. I said that I had acquired considerable experience with boats as a youth, which was true, and that I would gladly lend support to the fish-boat's undertaking.

I was soon able to strike up a friendship with George Dixon, the lieutenant selected to captain the Hunley. *George was in his twenties, a handsome fellow with fair hair, and nearly six feet tall. He came from a family of some means, spoke and dressed well, and appreciated the finer things in life. He was an engaging conversationalist with a quick wit. When George heard the story of my 'battlefield wound,' he laughed and told me we had that much in common. He had fought in the Battle of Shiloh in April of 1862, and been shot in the left thigh. However, the bullet had struck a coin in his pocket, a twenty dollar gold piece given to him by his Mobile sweetheart,*

Queenie Bennett, when he went off to war. Thus, George's injury had been minor; whereas without the buffer of the coin, his leg might have required amputation. He showed me the gold piece, which had been bent in the shape of a bell by the force of the bullet, and said he carried it with him always for good luck.

The crew members rigorously prepared for their assignment, familiarizing themselves with operation of the Hunley's *diving planes, ballast tank pumps, and sea valves. Dives were frequently practiced under the Confederate ship Indian Chief. George Dixon captained the Hunley during most of her training runs, but on occasion Horace Hunley would take command.*

As George Dixon and I became better acquainted, he would often invite me to substitute when one of the regular crew members was incapacitated. I possessed uncommon strength in my arms and hands and thus could ably assist with turning of the propulsion crank. However, my injured leg proved to be a handicap when entering and exiting the Hunley, *and sitting in the cramped interior quarters. The experience of being packed into such a small area and diving beneath the sea was extraordinary, inspiring feelings of excitement and dread. The only one who seemed never to be afraid was George. He would laugh and make jokes, which I suspected had the purpose of allaying any fears plaguing his crew.*

During my occasions on board, I paid close attention to the physical characteristics of the fish-boat, and to the means by which she was maneuvered. Eventually, my observations gave rise to an idea about how I might disable her. I would frequently stroll along the sand in the nighttime hours, planning the details of my subversion. Living conditions on Sullivan's Island were far from the best, but I took great pleasure in the beauty of the wide sweeping beaches and the panoramic views. From Fort Moultrie on Sullivan's Island, it was barely more than one mile across the water to Fort Sumter, where the War had begun.

My stratagem to scuttle the Hunley *at last firm with regard to all particulars, there was one obstacle to be addressed before the plan could be executed. I must find a way to remove George Dixon. Most importantly, this was because of George's keen eye. There was little likelihood that he would overlook the sabotage I intended. It seemed* certain that during his pre-training inspection, he would see what I had done. Although George would doubtless attribute the defect to slovenly crew work rather than to sabotage, he would nonetheless correct the problem before putting out to sea.

There was a second reason for my wanting George to be unavailable for the fateful training run. Though we were enemies in this War, he had become my best friend. I did not want him to be a casualty of my actions.

The evening before my intended treachery, I mashed juice from holly berries and added the concoction to a bottle of wine. Later I served the wine to George and, unbeknownst to him, filled my glass from a different bottle. In the morning when I went to George's room, he told me that he had become ill with an intestinal disorder during the night. I replied that I had suffered some of the same symptoms and was feeling a bit better, though still weak and slightly nauseated. George asked me to advise Horace Hunley that he should command the boat on today's outing. I silently rejoiced, having accomplished my objective.

When I explained George's sickness to Hunley, he immediately agreed to lead the training run. He enjoyed such opportunities, having taken offense at the judgment by General Beauregard and the Navy Department that George should captain the fish-boat, because Hunley lacked experience. Hunley asked if I might like to join the crew for the day, but I begged off, telling him that I too was ill.

When Hunley and other crew members were away from the boat, I tampered with the bolts for the hatches so that they could not be securely sealed. I also jammed the forward sea valve so that it could not be closed and water would fill the ballast tank. As the crew made ready to depart, I felt a sudden wave of nausea, which was due not to last night's liquor, but rather to the cold realization that if my plan succeeded, I would be a killer. Men on that boat who might die were men I had eaten with, drunk with, laughed with. They were men I liked and respected. My spying was no longer a romantic adventure, but rather an undertaking with life-or-death consequences. Much different this from impersonal battlefield killing. I told myself that the men on the boat had chosen a particular set of principles to fight for, and I had chosen a contrary set, and there could be no turning back until one side or the other prevailed. This reasoning gave me but shallow comfort.

The fish-boat pushed off as usual, and in due time dived under the Indian Chief. Observing closely, I saw air bubbles rise to the surface, which indicated that my tampering had worked, and the hatches had not properly closed. When the boat failed to surface, I and others set out to search for survivors, but there were none to be found. And because of the depth of the water and the poor weather, there was no immediate opportunity for a rescue dive attempt. Eventually, I delivered the sad news to George, who was inconsolable. He paced his room in a frenzy, tearing at his hair and blaming himself for succumbing to illness and shirking his responsibilities. This was so difficult for me to watch that I nearly shouted out that blame rested on my shoulders, not his.

Three days later, the boat was raised. It had been discovered with its bow buried in mud and the hull sticking up at a thirty-five degree angle. Horace Hunley and the first officer had apparently been asphyxiated as they tried to push open the hatches. The others had drowned. My plan had succeeded. The boat was towed to nearby Mt. Pleasant and hoisted on a wharf for removal of the bodies. I watched the corpses come out. Then I purchased whiskey, returned to my room, and drank myself into a stupor.

Chapter Twenty-Four

In my dream *I was a child watching from the dock as the* Hunley *embarked. My mother, in command, waved as she lowered through the hatch. I waved back, buffeted by raw wind swirls that reeked of sweet pipe tobacco, wet sand and washed-up rotting fish. The boat set off, and harsh, roiling waves jounced it up toward gray-black clouds drooping in a sunless sky. Arnie St. John stood beside me wrapped in a wool overcoat, his cheeks and nose reddened by cold and whiskey. He puffed on a cigar, eyes sparkling with secret knowledge of alternative truths.*

"Watch this, kid," he said. He snapped his fingers and the fishboat exploded: a booming ball of flames that hung briefly above the horizon in the form of a fiery low setting sun, then disintegrated into glowing shards of metal that settled atop the water like smidgens of burning ash flicked from Arnie's cigar.

I ran from the dock to my father's church, where a wedding was in progress. Gary Nagle and Moze Cheddar, dressed in tuxedoes, ushered me down the aisle to the front. The bride facing my father turned: Ellen Talley. There was no groom. Little Minnie stood with the church choir singing "The Night They Drove Old Dixie Down."

"It's mother!" I cried. "The boat blew up! She's dead! They're all dead!"

My father blinked and shook his head. "What?" he said dully. "What?"

Behind me there were footsteps. Gary and Moze parted and an androgynous figure masked by a hood stepped between them. The hooded figure held a gun. Ellen screamed. The gun fired. My father fell ...

I jerked awake. *Hunley* diary pages were strewn on the floor beside the sofa where I'd fallen asleep. I swung my legs off the sofa, sat up, rolled my shoulders and rubbed my eyes. There was a bitter taste in my mouth from last night's catfish and okra at Little Minnie's, and from the coffee I'd drunk at the diner with Gary Nagle after we'd talked to DuBois and Ronnie and been shot at. I glanced at the clock: 5:15. Slate-hued light filtered through the glass doors as night lifted. A motorcycle muffler popped out front, and my neighbor's wheelbarrow rattled along the driveway transporting trash.

I bent, picked up the diary pages I'd read and paper-clipped them to the unread pages. It occurred to me that I ought to find a hiding place for the diary. Moze Cheddar had demonstrated that breaking into my home was slightly less difficult than picking the door lock of a doll house. That meant Arnie St. John or anyone else after the diary wouldn't encounter much challenge.

I hobbled stiff-kneed to the office where piles of my parents' unsorted file folders lay on the carpet. In the middle of a pile was one of my father's folders labeled "Summer 2007 Children's Church Literacy Program." I slid the diary pages between sheets in the folder and stuck the folder back in the middle of the pile. Then I changed into running clothes, ate half a banana coated with peanut butter, drank a glass of water and gimped out through the garage to purge my body of evil spirits.

Rivulets of cool air palliated the humidity, and reddish gold streaks supercharged the powder blue sky. I loosened with gentle squats and stretches and sprinted out of the driveway. At least I thought I was sprinting. But two turtles, a ninety-five year old woman in a leg cast, and a man pushing a marble with his nose surged past. It had been a longish spell between my runs. At the golf course cart path crossing I turned right toward the fourteenth green. By the time I cleared the fourteenth tee and climbed the slight rise to the thirteenth green I'd established a comfortable rhythm. The cart path ended, and sodden turf softened the impact of my footfalls.

I heard a motor behind, figured course maintenance staff, and drifted farther left. An electric red golf cart with a cream canopy pulled up beside me driven by Gino, Arnie St. John's rented mafioso. "What shakes, Cap?" he said. His head was freshly shaved with a pink nick above his left ear. He wore a short-sleeved yellow linen shirt with the tail out over lime green slacks, and a lump beneath the shirt shouted holstered gun. A Rolex watch encircled a sunburned wrist the size and color of a brick.

"Easing into the day, Gino," I said. "Yourself?"

He flicked sweat off his face. "Always this goddamn hot so early in the morning?"

"Gets hot in New York in August."

"Sure, but you know, them guys I work for up there, they mostly stay inside with AC. Mr. St. John, he's an outdoor guy."

"Where is outdoor Arnie?"

Gino motioned backward with his thumb. I looked over my shoulder and saw a fast approaching runner. Trailing the runner was another golf cart. Presumably Gino's power-lifting partner, Mikey.

Arnie glided alongside, stride fluid and relaxed. Gino drove ahead. "Top o' the morning to you, Q," Arnie said.

"Not hitting practice balls today?" I said.

He raised his arms to the sky. "Beautiful dawn like this, what better to do than scamper a few miles, spark the brain waves." He was shirtless, wearing orange shorts, running sandals with no socks, sunglasses and a white visor. His abs were ridges of muscle.

"Cherisse ever run with you? She was greased lightning in high school track."

Arnie's chuckle was hollow-shelled. "Running is on the list of things Cherisse and I never do together. Theater, concerts, breakfast, lunch, dinner, conversation, sex, they're on the list too. Helps keep our marriage strong."

We crossed Plantation Lane to the twelfth green and accelerated downhill on the cart path. Out to the left white birds fluttered above the marshland. Beyond the marshes commuter traffic whizzed on Long Point Road. The fairways were overlaid with webs of dew, and moss swung on oak branches like white-furred monkeys. The air was scented with the spicy fragrance of Oriental lilies blooming in a back yard garden. In another back yard a beagle howled, and ducks on the water between the tee and fairway flapped their wings and squawked.

"Speaking of Cherisse," Arnie said. "I'm receiving vibes that despite our little chat the other day, you're helping her help DuBois."

"You're not tapping phones are you, Arnie? That's a federal offense."

"The problem here is that you're thinking with your cock," he told me. "I'm not the bad guy. I'd like to pull DuBois out of the shit he's in. But your muddling around will only confuse matters. Come to work for me and everything will be a lot simpler—and safer."

"Come to work for you doing what?"

"Security, a little of this, a little of that."

"I thought Gino and Mikey were your security."

"They're more like personal bodyguards. I've been getting threats."

"From whom?"

"A sweet little group called Guardians of the Confederate Truth. Ever heard of it?"

"I saw something in the paper that said the Guardians are less than thrilled with your *Hunley* reality show concept. The article quoted Jubal Jeff Longstreet as the Guardians' president. Not our old high school history teacher?"

"The very same," Arnie said. "Jubal Jeff's a lawyer now. He decided to use his oratorical skills for more financially rewarding purposes than education. What you saw in the paper is the tip of the iceberg. The private statements he's making are a whole lot uglier."

"Even so, you don't need to recruit bodyguards from the Mafia."

Arnie braked, stepped off the cart path, and did jumping jacks in the grass. His liftoff was explosive; at five feet seven he'd been able to dunk a basketball in high school. Round biceps pressed against his ears as his arms stretched high and his hands came together in a triangle.

He stopped, caught his breath, filled two paper cups from the water tap near the eleventh tee and handed a cup to me. "I made my first million before I turned thirty, Q, and I haven't looked back since. One lesson I learned early on was to feather my risk by bringing in partners to shoulder some of the load. Mikey and

Gino's employers are partnering for the *Hunley* show, and they sent the boys along to help remove any obstacles that may arise."

He dropped parallel to the ground, balanced on his palms and the tips of his toes, did twenty pushups, bounced back up, and began running in place and shadow boxing. "Remember the regional baseball championship game our senior year?"

The game had gone into extra innings. In the top of the tenth Arnie beat out a bunt and stole second. I hit a long fly ball, and the right fielder made an off balance catch and banged into the fence. Arnie tagged and tried to score all the way from second, running through the third base coach's stop signal. The throw to the plate beat him, but he blasted the catcher, who outweighed him by thirty pounds. The catcher dropped the ball and Arnie scored, giving us a one run lead. In the bottom of the tenth, with runners on first and third and two outs, their catcher hit a line drive to center field. Arnie could have played it on a bounce, letting the tying run score but only advancing the winning run to second. Instead he attempted a diving, game ending catch. The ball tipped off the edge of his glove, both runners scored, and we lost.

"I remember," I said.

He threw a left jab in my direction. "I still have nightmares about that play."

"Nobody blamed you."

"No, but plenty of people were happy I failed. And nothing's changed. I still go for broke on every play, business or personal, and most of the time I succeed. But when the ball gets by me, folks are lined up three deep cheering silently. Not you though. You were the best of us then and you're the best of us now. That's why when I warn you to stay away from Cherisse, I'm not sure if I'm telling you that for my benefit or yours. But it doesn't really matter."

He danced close, lips smiling, eyes cold. "This is your final warning, Russ. Keep your hands off Cherisse. I won't allow you to steal her from me. I'll probably lose her for other reasons or cut her loose, but you're not stealing her. People don't steal from me with impunity."

He jabbed at my jaw. Maybe he intended to stop the punch

short, maybe he didn't. I caught his wrist and held it. We had a brief staring contest, then he yanked his arm backward out of my grasp and let his smile spread to his eyes.

"What's your interest in the *Hunley* diary?" I asked.

Arnie's smile escalated to a mocking laugh. "Don't tell me you were prevaricating the other morning when you denied knowing anything about a *Hunley* diary or Moze Cheddar? It couldn't be that you and Moze have been conversing could it? I have to tell you, Q, I'm shocked, shocked and appalled. Next you'll confess to chopping down a cherry tree."

"You don't need whatever's in the diary," I said. "You're not making a documentary, you're making a reality show. You can have things happen however you want regardless of the contents of the diary."

He shook his head and made a tsk-tsking noise. "You're thinking too small, you've got to think Big Concept. That's what it's all about. Making fools out of stiff-backed Charleston ass-wipes is just the beginning. That will draw national attention, which will provide opportunities for a multi-media platform about the *Hunley*. The diary could be dynamite. I might be able to turn it into a film, a TV movie and/or a book. I've got the right contacts. There's another thing too. I want to know what the diary says before I finalize the reality show, because if there's a large disconnect I'm going to need to revise my plans for the show. I can find a role for you in all this, my man, just say the word."

"I'm a simple country boy, Arnie," I told him. "The worlds of entertainment and high finance are way beyond me."

"Don't sell yourself short, Q, give my offer thought." He waved at Gino to bring the golf cart. "I've gotta go, but one last thing. When you see Moze Cheddar again, be sure to tell him I have a keen interest in his diary. And emphasize that no isn't an answer, it's a serious misjudgment of my resolve and capabilities."

Chapter Twenty-Five

The AllNight Inn was in a complex of short and long-term motels/hotels off Johnnie Dodds just before the Ravenel Bridge to downtown Charleston. I came in from the rear off Wingo Way and drove around to reconnoiter. There were two levels with approximately a hundred rooms in total and exterior motel-style entrances to each room. The honey-colored building was U-shaped with the office at the bottom and an outdoor pool between the two wings. Room 36 was on the second level. Nothing looked suspicious, but short of snipers on the roof and a mine field in the parking lot, I wasn't sure what would look suspicious.

I parked in a visitor's spot in back and walked toward a set of stairs. It was a few minutes before 10:00AM, Leonard Alcott's appointed hour for our tête-a-tête. The neon blue sky radiated heat, and I realized for the fifty-third time that I needed a Southern wardrobe. My traditional cotton polo shirt couldn't cope with the steam. Of course, buying a Southern wardrobe would represent a commitment to staying.

A brunette mom in a one piece bathing suit stood on the pool deck talking on a cell phone while she watched two squealing kiddos bob in donut tubes. Non-stop traffic hummed along Johnnie Dodds, and Sheryl Crow sang from the radio of a truck parked at a convenience store gas pump. The aroma of grilling beef from a fast food restaurant across the highway reminded me that I'd missed breakfast. But it was early for lunch, and Leonard Alcott awaited.

I climbed the concrete steps, turned right, found room 36 and knocked. No response. I knocked again. No response. A middle-aged Hispanic woman pushed a housekeeping cart out of a room two doors away and glanced at me. "Have you cleaned this room yet, ma'am?" I asked.

She shook her head.

"It's my father's room," I told her, the lie rolling smoothly off my tongue. "I was supposed to pick him up at ten o'clock, but he's not answering. He has health problems, and I'm wondering if you could go in and see if he's there and okay. I'll stay out here."

She weighed the pros and cons, nodded and came to the chocolate painted door with her passkey. She knocked sharply, called, "Housekeeping!"

We waited, but there was no reply. She inserted the key, clicked the lock, pushed back the door so it stayed open and went in. I watched her walk down the short, narrow entrance passage, saw her hand go to her mouth. She swung her head toward me. "He is here," she said. "On the bed. On his back. He look funny, very stiff."

I entered fast and moved by her. The man on the bed appeared to be mid-sixties. He also appeared to be dead. He had a lean face, thin lips, thick eyebrows and short curly gray hair. He was lying on top of the flowery green bedspread, no pillow beneath his head. There was a crumpled pillow on the carpet and two other pillows strewn out of place on the bed. Rigor mortis had definitely set in, but I took his pulse, checked for breathing and raised his eyelids.

The housekeeper stared at me wide-eyed. "Is … is he …?"

"I'm afraid so," I said. "Could you go down to the office and tell the manager there's a man in room 36 who appears to be dead. Tell him he should call 911 and let the police know that a retired police officer is with the body."

The housekeeper left, and I had a yen to search the room before the police arrived. But my circumstances were going to be dire enough when Ellen Talley learned that I was associated with a dead body, and learned that I'd discovered the body by lying to the housekeeper. If my fingerprints were found in the room, Ellen would use rendition to send me to a prison in Iran.

I went down to the parking lot and waited. And reflected. All the murky streams I splashed through seemed to feed into the same cesspool. Leonard Alcott had said he knew something about my father's murder. Later I'd discovered a note in my father's files indicating that Dad had learned something disturbing about Alcott. Then I'd found out that DuBois Dane and Ronnie Hodge had been involved in some sort of payoff to Alcott, possibly on behalf of Arnie St. John. But the transaction had gone sour and Jason Grimes was killed. Now Alcott was dead, presumably murdered.

Did DuBois and Ronnie track down Alcott and kill him in retaliation for Jason Grimes' death? Or did Arnie deploy Gino and Mikey to snuff out Alcott after the payoff went bad and Alcott absconded with Arnie's money and whatever Arnie was trying to buy? And what was Arnie trying to buy? Had Alcott been blackmailing him or peddling something to do with the *Hunley* that Arnie wanted?

Which raised the question of Moze Cheddar. If Alcott had been shopping material pertaining to the *Hunley* diary, Moze would have been very interested. Possibly interested enough to trace Alcott to the AllNight Inn, kill him and take the material. I didn't think Moze was a killer, but he'd told me, I'll do what's needed to protect what's mine. How would Alcott have obtained material about the diary though? He'd assisted with security in my dad's church and would have had access to Dad's files. But Moze said he hadn't given Dad any diary pages, so what could have been in the files?

This rumination was a nice intellectual exercise, but I'd come to talk to Alcott because he'd told me he had information about my father's murder. If there was a relationship between my father's death and Alcott's dealings with DuBois, Ronnie, Arnie, or Moze, I wasn't astute enough to see it. But I didn't have to be very astute to see that with Alcott dead, the odds of solving my father's murder were longer than ever.

My musings were interrupted by a Mt. Pleasant patrol car. The cruiser pulled into a slot near where I was standing, and two officers stepped out. They regarded me cold-eyed, leaving their doors open for cover, shoulders tense, hands on their gun butts.

"I'm Russell Berard, a retired Rhode Island police detective," I told them. "I had a ten-o'clock appointment with Leonard Alcott in room 36. When he didn't answer, a housekeeper entered the room and discovered a man on the bed. I checked his pulse and breathing; he's dead. No blood or obvious signs of violence. It's possible he was smothered with a pillow."

The cops frowned and thought it over. The older one, late thirties, said, "You that Berard? The one whose daddy was murdered?"

I nodded.

He stroked his chin with his thumb and fingers. "Interesting. Dead man's Alcott?

"I don't know; this would have been my first time to meet Alcott."

He pondered some more. "Okay, guess we ought to do this close to the way the book reads. Mr. Berard, no disrespect intended, but I'd like you to assume the position on the hood of our car. Jimmy, you want to look at his ID, see if he's carrying."

Until the past few days I hadn't assumed the position since Gary and I were Marines and a melee with MPs broke out in a bar. Then last night Ronnie had spread eagled Gary and me before we entered the van to talk to DuBois. And later Moze Cheddar had spread eagled me in my family room. Now this. I was beginning to get a persecution complex. Jimmy, the younger cop, wasn't quite as thorough as Moze, but he wasn't bad. "ID says Russell Berard. Photo matches. No weapon, Mike."

"Good as gold then," Mike said.

I resumed a more natural position and noticed the housekeeper who'd discovered the body with me standing outside the office with a scarecrow-like man. Probably the manager. They were staring our way.

Mike noticed them too. "Natives are restless. That the woman found the body with you?"

"Yes."

"Go talk to 'em, Jimmy," Mike said. "See if the housekeeper's version of events is the same as Mr. Berard's. Tell her to hang around for awhile. I'll go upstairs, take a look at the body. Maybe you'll come with me, Mr. Berard, wait outside the room in case I've got questions." Meaning he wasn't letting me out of his sight, but he wasn't letting me back into the room either.

Mike took his look, came out of the room and stood beside me at the railing. He rolled a stick of gum, plopped it in his mouth and held the pack out to me. I shook my head. "What gives you the idea he might have been smothered?" Mike asked.

"Bloodshot eyes, abrasions around his mouth. Check his ID?"

Mike's expression soured. "Detectives don't care for patrol officers touching anything. Maybe you remember that from when you were a detective."

Jimmy came up the stairs two at a time and joined us. "Housekeeper lays it out the way Mr. Berard did. He asked her to unlock the door and go into the room. She did, saw the body, advised him it looked stiff. He came in, examined vital signs, said the man was dead, asked her to go to the office and tell the manager to phone 911."

Mike tugged on his ear. "Okay then. I'm gonna take Mr. Berard down to the car, call in what we know, tell them we need detectives. Stay up here and watch the room, Jimmy."

I waited in the parking lot while Mike used the patrol car radio. The lemony yellow sun was swollen with heat, and jet exhaust trailed between feathery white clouds. One piece bathing suit mom and her kiddos had fled the pool, and the water lay still like a rectangular blue mirror. Beyond the pool fence, palm trees ringed a grassy grove containing a picnic table and gas grill. A gull laid claim to a plastic meat wrapper on the ground beside a trash can in the grove. A workman's drill whirred shrilly to life, making my teeth ache.

Mike walked toward me suppressing a grin. "You and Captain Talley had dealings before, Mr. Berard?"

"You bet."

The grin broke through. "What she told me was, if you even look like you're thinking of leaving the scene before she arrives, I should blast you with my stun gun, smash you in the balls with my baton, shoot you in both knee caps, and then chain you to the bumper of my car."

"She must be in a good mood today."

"Sounded like it to me," Mike agreed.

Chapter Twenty-Six

By the time Ellen Talley arrived, detectives, forensics specialists and the coroner were at work in and around room 36. Ellen parked her sedan beside my car. Probably coincidence, I thought. The odds were against it being a symbolic gesture of support and unity, the two of us against the world.

Ellen strode across the parking lot and caught sight of me sitting in a metal chair at a glass-topped table on the pool deck reading the *Charleston Post and Courier*. She paused, pushed her sun glasses up into her caramel hair and glared. I decided I wouldn't tell her that Jimmy the patrolman had given me the newspaper. She might construe that as coddling the enemy and assign Jimmy to scrubbing police department toilets with a toothbrush. She pulled the sunglasses back down over her eyes and resumed her purposeful stride toward the death room.

She was gone awhile, and when she came down from room 36 she went to the office. Eventually she came for me, arms swinging at her sides, shoes clacking against the concrete. She halted near the pool fence, crooked her left index finger and wagged it in a "come hither" command. Not a sexual come hither. More like come hither so I can remove your fingernails with pliers. As I pushed through the gate and exited the pool area, she said "Follow me," and turned and walked away quickly. She wore navy blue slacks and a sleeveless silver blouse, and she carried a gray blazer over her right forearm and a blue handbag over her left shoulder.

She led me to a room on the first level, inserted an electronic key and viciously shoved the door inward as if it and not I was the source of her vexation. She marched across the room, yanked open the drapes, sat in a chair at a small round table and pointed to the other chair.

"What in heaven's name am I going to do with you?" she said after I sat.

"Thank me," I suggested.

"Thank you? For what?"

"Discovering a possible homicide and immediately reporting it to the police. I don't see what you're mad about."

"You don't see? In other countries people are executed at sunrise for less crap than you've been pulling. First of all, you didn't report the dead body. You sent the housekeeper to tell the hotel manager to report it, which conveniently left you alone in the room."

"I didn't touch anything in the room."

"Maybe, maybe not." She lifted her shoulders, blew out a slow breath and massaged her temples with her fingertips. "Why were you here looking for Leonard Alcott?"

"Is the dead man Alcott?"

She hesitated, clearly not in a mood to tell me much of anything, including last night's baseball scores, the temperature in Dubuque, or what she'd eaten for breakfast. But not telling me whether the dead man was Alcott would limit her line of questioning. "Yes," she said.

"He called and asked me to meet with him." I didn't see any point in boring her with the details of the note Alcott had left behind the Pepsi machine near the fifteenth tee. That would just complicate her life. Mine too.

"Why?"

"Why did he want to meet with me?"

She crossed her arms beneath her breasts, swelling her triceps. "Don't stall, Russ, I'm not in the mood. You've done this line of questioning a million times, you know where I'm going with it. I should just be sitting here listening to you tell the whole truth and nothing but the truth. Pretend you're in court, which is where you may end up, possibly as a defendant in leg irons."

"Alcott said he knew something about my father's murder," I said. Which was true, but didn't quite comply with her admonition to tell the whole truth. There was the little matter of Alcott's note also saying that he had a situation on his hands and wanted my help. It seemed likely that the situation was Jason Grimes getting killed during the drop off of money to Alcott. But if I disclosed that to Ellen, she'd want to know how I knew. If I told her about my meeting at Little Minnie's with Dubois and Ronnie, she'd call in a team of cops to shackle me with her aforementioned leg irons. And leg irons would wrinkle my pants and bruise my skin.

"When did Alcott call you to arrange this meeting?"

I'd been afraid she'd ask me that. "Yesterday morning."

She smiled coldly. "Yesterday morning. Well. That would explain why, when I saw you at Towne Centre yesterday afternoon, you asked if I knew anything about Alcott. But I don't remember your mentioning that Alcott had phoned to arrange a meeting to provide information about your father's murder."

"I guess it slipped my mind. I've been under a lot of stress lately."

She pushed back her chair, stood and stared down at me inscrutably. The air was stuffy with odors of mold and carpet shampoo, and beads of perspiration pooled at her hairline. She wrinkled her nose, turned and stared out through the glass doors. The doors led to a tiny patio with two bronze colored metal chairs. The patio was bordered by green shrubs, and a narrow expanse of sun-seared grass ran from the shrubs to pine trees separating the AllNight from a neighboring motel.

"Why didn't you tell me Alcott had phoned you?" Ellen asked.

"If he wanted to talk to the police about my father's murder, he would have already done it. He probably would have gone mute if a bunch of cops barged in on him. I thought it made more sense for me to find out what he knew, tell you, and let you do follow-up questioning."

She turned away from the doors to face me, lips curled scornfully. "There are three things wrong with that. First, I have a little more finesse than to send a bunch of cops to barge in on someone. Second, if you'd told me about Alcott yesterday afternoon and we'd contacted him then, we might have saved his life. And third, your answer is total bullshit." Her voice was flat and icy. "You're giving me a rationalization for your behavior, not the truth. The truth is that you don't trust me and don't have confidence in my ability to solve your father's murder, and you want to play detective yourself."

"Ellen—"

"Shut up!" she said. "Just shut up! I don't want to hear any more bullshit!"

She brushed back thick hair with her palms and sat on the edge of the blue and gold bedspread. Her breasts rose and fell as she steadied her breathing and calmed her emotions. "Okay," she said. "Let's see if we can get through this without my strangling you."

I took it as a negative that her threats had escalated from leg irons to strangulation.

"So you came to see Alcott at the appointed time, rapped on the door and got no answer?" she said.

"Yes."

"Then you lied to the housekeeper about Alcott being your father to persuade her to check the room?"

"Yes."

"Why?"

"I was afraid something might have happened to him."

"Why would you think that?"

"Because he picked the time and the place. I expected him to be here."

"It didn't occur to you that he might have gone out for coffee or cash from an ATM machine and was late returning?"

"I don't know what to tell you, Ellen. I reacted impulsively. Maybe it was a cop's instinct that something was wrong."

She pressed her knees together and pursed her lips. "Ex-cop's instinct you mean. Here's my cop's instinct. You already knew Alcott was dead and wanted to put on a show of having someone else discover the body."

"How could I have known Alcott was dead?"

"Because your meeting with Alcott was actually earlier, and you found him dead and left without being seen. Or, and is this the theory I really like, you knew he was dead because you'd killed him earlier."

I couldn't read her expression or tone, but it was difficult to believe she was serious. It felt more like she was seizing the opportunity to beat on me with every spiked club in her armament. "That's ridiculous," I said. "And it's unprofessional to like a theory just because you want it to be true."

"How about this, then? Alcott was alive, possibly sleeping, when you and the housekeeper entered the room. You told the housekeeper he was dead, sent her down to the office and smothered him with a pillow."

"You're going from ridiculous to insane. Alcott's been dead for at least twelve hours, you saw the rigor mortis. Besides, what motive would I have to kill him?"

She stood and gathered her handbag and gray blazer. There were fatigue lines around her eyes and mouth. Through her features I saw the little girl from years ago who'd tagged along behind her brother and me. The little girl who'd turned into a big girl when I came home on summer break after my freshman year in college. My relationship with Cherisse had blown up, and I'd looked at Ellen and thought wow! But she was only a high school sophomore then …

"Why are you staring at me?" she asked. She asked in a softer, more feminine tone than she'd been using, as if she sensed the nature of my thoughts.

I felt my face flush. "I don't … I mean I wasn't … I'm sorry, I didn't mean to stare."

She studied me for a few more moments and sighed. "Damn it, Russ. Just when I reach the point where I believe I can hate you, you do or say something, or I think of something …"

Memories circled through the awkward silence like goldfish in a bowl. I heard our laughter on the creek banks where I'd taught Ellen to bait a hook and cast a line, felt the slippery scales of the trout we'd hooked, and tasted the bologna and mustard sandwiches she'd packed in a cooler.

She regained equilibrium first, glanced at her watch and pushed up from the bed. "I have to go."

I stood clumsily and captured a whiff of her perfume, which reminded me of the cherry popsicles I'd bought us on the way home from fishing.

"Ever heard of a place in Dorchester County called Little Minnie's?" Ellen asked.

It was interesting being on the other side of police questioning. Going from one lie to another until you couldn't remember what lie you'd told five minutes ago. It was interesting being on this side, but it wasn't much fun. "I think Gary Nagle mentioned it to me," I said. "Some kind of juke joint?"

"Some kind is right," Ellen said. "Last night the sheriff's department responded to reports of gunfire in the parking lot. Minnie's patrons tend to become afflicted with amnesia when law enforcement arrives, but there are indications that DuBois Dane and Ronnie Hodge were there talking to a couple of other men in a van when the gunfire started."

She paused and waited. I didn't respond. She nodded sadly as if my silence was the answer to a question she hadn't asked. "I guess you're trying to help Cherisse, but she's trouble with a capital T. You better get your mind off her body and wake up fast. Your present behavior is a disappointment and a disgrace, and I've just about lost all respect for you."

So much for reveries about idyllic summer days fishing together from creek banks.

I gave Ellen time, and her car was gone when I came out of the room. But that didn't mean I was free from the oppressive yoke of law enforcement. Durrell Pritchard leaned against the passenger side of my car wearing pressed jeans, a red and white striped polo shirt and boating moccasins. His gun holster was hooked on a wide brown belt with a silver buckle. The black stubble of his freshly razored hair glistened as if he'd rubbed tonic on his scalp. The tip of his nose was sunburned, and a toothpick jutted from the corner of his mouth.

He withdrew a quarter from his pocket, snapped it in the air with his thumb, caught the quarter in his palm and slapped it down on his forearm. He chuckled and said, "Tails. Is that what you was doing cozied up in there with the Captain, bo? Getting some tail?"

Under other circumstances I might have let it go, but Pritchard was the wrong man in the wrong place at the wrong time. He read the intention in my eyes and began to bring up his fists and drop into a crouch. But he wasn't quick enough. I got my shoulder behind a right hook that plowed into his solar plexus and doubled him over. I slammed a left jab against his jaw, his eyes glazed, and he dropped to the pavement on all fours. Shaking his head groggily he grasped the door handle of my car, pulled himself to his feet and turned to face me on shaky legs.

He touched his jaw and winced. "That there's a mean hard punch you throw."

I watched his right hand hover near his gun. "You're not going to get that out of the holster before I knock you on your ass again," I said.

He grinned, moved his hand away from the gun and wiped his palms on his jeans. "You got yourself a violent streak don't you, bo? And you got yourself a big problem if I choose to make one for you. Assault on a police officer, even an off-duty officer, that's serious business. Lucky for you none of the crime scene detectives was out here to see it. And lucky for you I don't rely on the badge to square injuries done to me."

His grin vanished as if it had been a mirage created by the reflection of light rays in the sweltering air. He squinted his eyes into close-set. venomous dots and exposed his teeth. "I'll square things with you another time, bo, when you ain't expecting me." He spat on the pavement and wobbled away.

Chapter Twenty-Seven

Sun streaks sliced through tree cover in the grove where Moze Cheddar's truck hid. Grove sat across the road from a fish camp where the two boys who'd talked to Berard and the big blond fella at Little Minnie's might be secluding theirselves. Moze had wrote down the license plate number of the boys' van last night at Little Minnie's and run it through the government database in his truck. That had gave Moze the name of a fella who was serving with the army in Afghanistan. Moze had done more research and learned that the soldier had hisself a fish camp on a lake in Dorchester County and a cousin name of Ronnie Hodge. Cousin turned out to be the same Ronnie Hodge who owned the silver SUV Moze had followed before.

So here now was Moze at the fish camp belonged to the soldier in Afghanistan, waiting to see would this Ronnie Hodge fella and the other boy from Little Minnie's show up in the van. Moze wanted a conversation with them boys about the break-in at his cabin, about his diary and about who the boys was working for.

Earlier Moze had snuck through the woods and down the dirt lane to the camp, which was a trailer on a wood platform at the lake's edge. Through windows he'd seen plates in the sink, unmade beds, scattered clothes and beer cans strewn about. Wasn't no van around, but there was fresh tire tracks in the mud from a good-sized vehicle.

Moze drank from a bottle of milk and wiped his mouth with the back of his hand. Truck window was open, and he breathed air flavored by fragrances of pine and purple gladioli spikes. Vegetation was colored by pink begonias, yellow lilies and red and white striped dahlias. Breeze puffed holes in the tree canopy, revealing azure patches of sky. A mockingbird prodded pokeweed berries and a blue warbler trilled a tune.

Peacefulness of the grove calmed Moze's angry soul. Tempting to lay his head back and close his eyes. But calm didn't mean fool-headed. Fall asleep, he might wake up to one of them boys pressing a gun barrel against his skull. Moze unscrewed a thermos, poured coffee in the lid and added milk from the bottle.

Chapter Twenty-Eight

Cherisse Dane kept a condominium south of Broad in downtown Charleston. Kept it, she told me, for the convenience of not having to go home to Mt. Pleasant when she stayed very late at her club. But her Mt. Pleasant home wasn't so far, and I wondered if occasional separation from marital interactions with Arnie might be the condo's primary purpose. Whatever the condo's purposes, Cherisse suggested we meet there, where she'd supply drinks and I'd supply details of last night's meeting with DuBois. Going to her condo was so replete with possibilities I knew it was a terrible idea. In the end we agreed to meet at a tavern.

I parked in a public garage on Queen Street. The sun hovered below the horizon, and copper-colored smears stained the faint blue sky. A couple ahead of me turned at the entrance for Poogan's Porch, and I thought I saw Poogan peering between the white porch posts and wagging his tail. But it was an illusion produced by dancing shadows. Poogan had been dead for nearly thirty years: a neighborhood dog who begged for food scraps when workmen converted the Victorian house to a restaurant in 1976, stayed on to welcome diners and became such a fixture that the restaurant took his name.

I crossed King and Meeting Streets and turned right at the intersection of Queen and Church. The only remaining independent French Huguenot church in America loomed ponderously on the corner, gothic revival style arches and iron spires towering in the twilight. I was in the heart of the French Quarter: cobblestone streets, gas lit alleys, art galleries, theaters, Georgian houses, piazzas, courtyard gardens and graveyards. The air was dense and stagnant, and Zs of heat lightning crackled to the west above the Ashley River.

On a side lane off Church Street I swung open the tavern door of a salmon colored building and stepped into the 1700s, when Blackbeard, Stede Bonnet and other pirates marauded in Charleston's waters. A caged parrot in the foyer squawked an unintelligible welcome. The tavern had plank flooring and a heart-pine bar with a tender wearing an eyepatch, bandana and toy flintlock pistols. The walls were decorated with telescopes, grappling hooks, skull and crossbone flags and paintings of masted ships being pillaged by buccaneers.

Cherisse Dane was modern day in a sleeveless white dress with a slit skirt and high heels. She rose like undulating smoke to greet me, and male tavern chatter lulled and other women glowered. Cherisse touched my wrist, and the press of her fingertips joggled my nerve endings. We sat and she passed a drinks menu with a treasure map on the cover. "I'm having this delightful rum concoction," she said. Then she giggled. "I arrived a little early, and I may have had too much too fast. I hope you won't take advantage." The giggle sounded contrived.

A silky blond waitress came, costumed in a black skirt, puffy sleeved blouse with a deep V, cuffed boots and tri-cornered velvet hat. I ordered a beer.

Cherisse watched the girl's hip rolling departure with distaste. "That was quite a cleavage show, not that you seemed to object. Apparently you lust after young blonds just like Arnie."

"I thought Arnie lusted after you."

She snorted. "Arnie lusts after the idea of thinking he possesses me, which he doesn't. Nobody ever has or ever will. You know why I like coming here?"

"Obviously, not because of the waitresses."

"They have an Anne Bonny night for women every week. You remember Anne Bonny?"

"The pirate you had a girl crush on in high school?"

"Feminist pirate," Cherisse said. "She grew up around here, married a pirate named James Bonny, went to Nassau with him, then took up with another pirate named Calico Jack Rackham.

When Rackham's ship was attacked, Anne fought while most of the crew hid. Supposedly that made her so angry she shot and wounded Rackham and some of the others. She was fearless, and she didn't play second fiddle to men."

Which described the Cherisse I'd known. "It's funny though," she said. "I can be fearless about me, but not about DuBois. I'm terrified for him, even though he's named after another of my heroes, W.E.B. DuBois. You know who he was, don't you?"

"An early civil rights leader," I said, recalling DuBois' tirade in the van, which had included reference to himself as a mulatto, and reference to Cherisse naming him after a black civil rights leader as a joke on DuBois' "white racist son-of-a-bitch" father.

"Co-founder of the NAACP," Cherisse said. "He had some radical ideas and didn't always play nicely with others, but he was brilliant and highly principled. I thought naming a child after him would be inspirational. It hasn't worked out that way though. DuBois is smart enough, and he has W.E.B.'s independent streak, but he's not channeling his energies in a positive way. And the irony is that he's always hated his name. His friends just call him Dub. Dub … Where's the historical, cultural and racial significance in that? I might as well have named him Chuck."

"You can't blame DuBois' name for the trouble he's in, Cherry," I said.

She stared into the rum morosely, as if revelations swirled in the depths. "Okay, I've put off asking the question long enough, haven't I? What did DuBois tell you he's into?"

"He told me what happened at Etiwan Pointe when Jason Grimes was killed. DuBois, Grimes, and Ronnie Hodge went there on behalf of someone to buy something from a retired FBI agent named Leonard Alcott. It sounds like a blackmail payoff, but whatever it was, the deal blew up, and Grimes was shot. DuBois and Ronnie claim they didn't see who did the shooting. Possibly Alcott, possibly somebody else."

Cherisse's eyes widened. "Not the Leonard Alcott who helped with security at your father's church?"

"Yes, do you know him?"

"I wouldn't say I know him; he and I had casual contact when I came to your father's church to work on social justice projects. But blackmail? DuBois and those other boys have been doing jobs for Arnie. Do you think Alcott was blackmailing Arnie?"

"DuBois wouldn't tell me who sent them," I said. "But the story gets worse. Leonard Alcott was found murdered in a Mt. Pleasant motel this morning. I'm the one who discovered the body. Alcott had called and asked me to meet him."

She pressed a hand against her throat. "You don't think DuBois ..?"

"I don't know."

Cherisse drank more rum and set the glass down, arm trembling. "I can't believe DuBois would kill anyone, although Arnie's such a horrible influence … These New York gangsters he's hanging around with … But I'm not aware of any connection between Arnie and Leonard Alcott. What would Alcott have been blackmailing Arnie about?"

"I don't know that either."

"Why did Alcott want to meet with you?" she asked.

"He said he was in trouble and wanted my help, and in return he'd give me information about my father's murder."

"What would he have known about your father's murder?"

"I have no idea. Maybe something occurred to him about the death threats Dad received. Or maybe he didn't really know anything about Dad's killing and was trying to use the possibility that he did as a lure to get me to help him out of the jam he'd gotten into at Etiwan Pointe."

Cherisse shook her head, her hair oscillating and shimmering in the flickering light of the table candle. "This is just so … It all sounds so crazy. None of it makes sense to me."

"Join the club," I said. "And there's another complication, not that another is needed."

"What's that?"

"A man named Moze Cheddar."

"Who in the world is Moze Cheddar?"

I looked at her with feigned surprise. "He's the man you sent an anonymous letter offering to buy the *Hunley* diary. The letter that suggested Moze contact me for help."

She blinked, swallowed and licked her lips. "I don't … I have no idea what you're talking about."

"It's no good, Cherry. Moze is a smart guy. He put a tracer on the diary pages he left at the bar, and he followed Gary Nagle when Gary picked up the pages and delivered them to you."

Cherisse stared at me for a moment. Then she stood abruptly, banging her knee against the table. She lifted her handbag and looped the strap over her shoulder, but her movements were herky-jerky, and the strap slipped loose. "I'm sorry," she said, clutching the handbag with both hands. "I'm woozy from the rum. Please take me for a walk so I can clear my head." She tottered toward the door without waiting for an answer.

Chapter Twenty-Nine

I settled the bill and caught up with Cherisse on the sidewalk. A fleeting downpour had puddled the streets while we were in the tavern, and steamy breeze circulated clammy odors of drenched cobblestone and soggy palmetto fronds. A car sloshed by, rap music booming, and a passenger shouted, "Hey foxy momma!"

Cherisse's eyes followed the car, then turned to me. "Let's walk."

I nodded. She led me up Church Street in the direction of the Market, but at Cumberland she turned left. "Where are we going?" I asked.

"White Point Gardens," she said. "I changed my mind."

We turned left on Meeting Street and headed toward the tip of the peninsula, passing the Gibbes Museum of Art and the pink Mills House Hotel. Approaching City Hall and the County and Federal Courthouses on opposite corners of Broad, the silence became deafening. "Is your head clearer now?" I asked.

She hooked her arm around my elbow and expelled a breath. "Obviously, you're right. I did send that letter to Moze Cheddar offering to buy his diary."

"Why?"

"I … I'm embarrassed to tell you."

"Tell me anyway."

She sighed. "I made some bad investments, and I need money. If I get hold of the diary, I'm sure Arnie will pay quite a bit for it."

That was consistent with what Gary had told me about Cherisse having financial difficulties. "How did you learn about the diary?" I asked.

"I … I eavesdropped on Arnie talking to those two disgusting mafia cretins and heard him say he'd sent … people … to the home of someone named Moze Cheddar to steal a diary about the *Hunley*. The theft wasn't successful, and Arnie intended to try again using the Mafia men. After I heard that, I found Moze Cheddar's address and sent him the letter."

"The people Arnie sent the first time were DuBois, Ronnie Hodge, Jason Grimes and Dewey Welch?"

Cherisse nodded. "And Dewey hasn't been seen since, but DuBois won't talk to me about it."

"Moze says the letter suggested that he contact me. Why did you tell him that?"

She pressed closer, skirt swishing against my pants leg. "I thought you might help convince Moze to sell me the diary."

"Why would I do that? For old times sake?"

"Heavens no," she said, laughing girlishly. "For new times sake."

We were South of Broad, the preferred downtown residential address, where opulent homes with manicured gardens, Georgian gables, Greek parapets, Italian arches and Victorian turrets hid behind fences and walls. George Washington, Robert E. Lee and Teddy Roosevelt had all been here. If you stood still and cocked your head, you could hear money breathing. You might also hear your instincts suggest that you were being followed.

The velvet night sky was flecked with silver, and golden glow from street lamps pooled on the slate sidewalks. I listened for the footsteps I'd heard behind us earlier, but oak leaves and palm fronds rustling in the breeze masked other sounds. Probably the footsteps had been someone who'd turned into a house. Probably …

"I'm going to file for divorce," Cherisse said. "I can't live this way any longer. Arnie has no idea what being a husband means. All his interactions are about power. He uses leverage, threats and bribery to get what he wants, whether it's a business deal or a personal relationship."

It was a nice diatribe, easy to swallow if you knew Arnie. But I recalled Cherisse telling me at Denmark Vesey that all three of her marriages, including the one to Arnie, had been for financial and social gain. It might be a poor racial pun to say that Cherisse's self-serving speech was a case of the pot calling the kettle black, but presumably she'd had her eyes wide open when she walked down the aisle. If matrimony was a business arrangement for her as well as for Arnie, it was difficult to muster much sympathy for either one of them.

"Maybe this was meant to be, Russ," she said. "Both of us back here. I still think of you as the great love of my life."

"Not counting Duncan Hamlin?"

She yanked her arm away, stopped sharply and turned to face me. "That's a hateful thing to say!"

"You can't revise history to jibe with a fantasy, Cherry."

"Your being the great love of my life isn't a fantasy, damn you! I was eighteen, my head got turned by a sophisticated older man with money who showed me things I'd never seen. I left you for him, and it was a huge mistake. I've regretted it ever since. I'm sorry, I'll always be sorry. Do you want me to get down on my hands and knees and grovel? Will that satisfy you?"

The truth was that I had no idea what would satisfy me. So I shut up and kept walking. Cherisse stomped along beside, but she didn't take my arm. At the end of Meeting Street we crossed South Battery into White Point Gardens on the tip of the peninsula. Charleston Harbor stretched out to the east, fed by the Cooper and Ashley Rivers. Fort Sumter sat in the near center of the harbor between Sullivan's Island and James Island.

White Point was a picture of serenity: drooping oaks, sun bleached oyster shell paths, large gazebo. But the monuments and decorative cannons memorialized more violent days when the grassy expanse was a primary point of defense against first the British and later the Union. This was also the place where the pirate Stede Bonnet had been hanged in the early 1700s. Pirates had been encouraged to lay over in Charleston and boost the local economy by spending their ill gotten gains, but Bonnet had a habit of departing with a prominent citizen, whom he'd hold for ransom. Tiring of this game, the authorities tracked down Bonnet and his crew, brought them back to Charleston and strung them up in White Point Gardens.

Cherisse wrapped her arm around my waist and snuggled against my shoulder. Her skin gleamed like black marble in the moonlight. "I don't want to fight, Russ. I know we can't step back into high school. Too many years have passed. But I want to try. I hope you do too."

I wasn't sure what she wanted to try, wasn't sure I wanted to find out.

Chapter Thirty

Cherisse and I walked to the bottom of the park, where palm trees lined Murray Boulevard and waves sloshed against the concrete wall partitioning Murray from Charleston Harbor. The air smelled of sodden tree bark and wet grass, and moss swaying from gnarled oak limbs dribbled water on the green-slatted benches.

"Someone shot at DuBois, Ronnie, Gary and me last night," I said.

Cherisse gasped. "Why didn't you tell me before? Was DuBois hurt?"

"I don't think so, but I'm not sure. You haven't talked to him?"

"No, we … our relationship is tense right now. Who shot at you?"

"I don't know."

A mosquito buzzed near Cherisse's face, and she waved her hand at it like a fan. "Well you can bet it's someone who was sent by Arnie."

"Why would Arnie have somebody shoot at DuBois and Ronnie?"

"I was thinking the shots were fired at you"

Wind ruffled the grass and blew a plastic cup lid along the sidewalk like a shuffleboard puck. Rotating beacons from the Sullivan's Island Lighthouse illuminated the harbor, and the moon showed hazily behind diaphanous cloud cover. The driver's door of a white SUV parked on Murray Boulevard opened, and a big man with oiled black hair stepped out.

I grabbed Cherisse's forearm, said, "Let's go," and turned her toward the top of the park.

But I'd been stupid, forgotten the footsteps behind us on Meeting Street. Another big man stepped out from behind a thick oak. A man with a shaved head, a brown goatee and a gun. "Sorry,

Cap," Gino said. "Mikey and me, we gotta ask you to hang around for a few minutes, have a conversation with us."

Mikey came up close behind. I could smell his cloying aftershave. "Mr. St. John, he's disappointed you don't listen, don't take his message serious," Mikey said. "Maybe the way Gino and me will explain it, you'll catch on faster." He pounded a ham-sized fist into my kidney.

Bile burbled up through my throat into my mouth from the punch. I sagged, and Mikey clubbed the back of my head with clasped hands. I fell in the grass, ears ringing, vision blurry.

"No!" Cherisse shrieked. "Leave him alone!" She tried to shove Mikey away from me, but he clamped a hand over her mouth and twisted her arm behind her back.

"Easy," Gino told him. "We ain't supposed to hurt her." He touched the back of my neck with his gun barrel. "How 'bout you get up, Cap. We oughta move this conversation away from the street. Keep it private between friends."

I stood, winced and wobbled forward. Mikey released Cherisse and gave her a shove that brought her up beside me. "Have to ask you not to scream, Mrs. St. John," Gino said. "Ain't no reason to be concerned. The Captain here understands how it is. We gotta rough him up a little, make him think twice. Nothing personal in it, just professional work. Cap's stand up, he'll take it like a man, move on without no real harm done."

Cherisse whirled to face him, hands on her hips. "Make him think twice about what?" she hissed. "Being with me? This is America, where people are free to choose their friends. You go back and tell Arnie to expect a police visit, felony charges and front page newspaper stories."

"All due respect," Gino said. "Mr. St. John don't think you'll wanna call the cops. You talk to the cops, he'll talk to the cops, won't do nobody no good."

Resolve drained from Cherisse's face. "You tell him he's not going to get away with this," she said weakly.

"I'll tell him that for sure," Gino said.

We were midway into the park now, concealed from passersby and car riders. Gino was correct that I understood the situation. He and Mikey were going to smack me around, leave me somewhat bloodied, but no serious injuries. I could take it like a man or make them earn their money. If they had to earn their money they'd deliver Arnie's message far more forcefully, but there was a line they weren't supposed to cross.

Cherisse under control, the big men turned to refocus on me. As they were turning I was pivoting on my right foot and raising and bending my left leg. I slammed the sole of my shoe into Mikey's kneecap, planted my left foot and kicked him in the groin with my right. He groaned and sagged. But there were two of them. Gino cuffed the side of my face with his gun barrel. While I was engrossed in the stars bursting before my eyes, he hooked me in the stomach and hammered the gun against my skull.

I collapsed on the oyster shell path, arms and legs splayed. "Stay down, Cap," Gino suggested. "It'll go easier that way."

I struggled to my feet. Mikey was bent over holding his groin with one hand and his knee with the other. Cherisse was sobbing. Gino pointed the gun at me and said, "No." But I was absolutely certain he wouldn't fire. Well I was reasonably certain he wouldn't fire. I charged, buried my shoulder in his gut and drove him backward into an oak. He thumped hard against the trunk and tried to slash me with the gun, but he couldn't gain any momentum for the blows. I stomped his instep. He swore, dropped the gun, seized my shoulders and threw me sideways.

I staggered, bumped into a bench and fought for balance. Gino was coming for me, face flushed and fists balled. I had a hunch he was through playing good goon to Mikey's bad. I steadied myself to defend against the onslaught, and Cherisse cried, "Russ!" Her warning was too late. Mikey, recovered from my knee and groin kicks, bear-hugged me from behind. I writhed and banged my head against his face. He grunted but didn't loosen his squeeze.

Gino approached, face registering disappointment at my lack of cooperation. I lifted my foot and smashed it into his chest, disappointing him further. Pain reverberated through my leg as if I'd kicked a stone wall. He stumbled backward a few steps. "Damn, Cap!" he said, brushing off his pullover with a palm. "This is a new shirt. You got mud on it from your shoe." He hit me twice in the midriff, punches so hard it felt like my belly button had been driven into my spine.

Mikey released me as I bent forward, and Gino kneed the point of my chin. Nerves went dead all over my body, and I fell on my side. Mikey stomped my ribs.

"Stop it!" Cherisse screeched. "Stop it now!" She'd picked up Gino's gun and was gripping it with both hands in a crouched shooter's position.

"Come on, Mrs. St. John," Gino soothed. "Like I told you before, there ain't nothing too bad gonna happen. No call for nobody to get shot." He took a step in her direction.

"Halt right there or I'll put a bullet in your brain!" Cherisse warned. "And my name is Ms. Dane, not Mrs. St. John!"

Gino halted.

"Now both of you get the hell out of here!" Cherisse said.

Gino licked his lips. "My gun." He looked down at me.

I struggled into a sitting position. "Give him the gun," I told Cherisse.

She stared at me as if the beating I'd been administered had caused dementia. "What?"

"We're finished here aren't we?" I asked Gino.

"Far as I'm concerned we are. We all got in some good swings."

"It'll be embarrassing for Gino to leave here without his gun," I said to Cherisse. "Besides, the gun might have an ugly history; you don't want it found in your possession."

"I think you're out of your mind," she said. But she clicked on the safety and threw the gun into the night. It landed in the grass and bounced.

Gino extended his arm and pulled me to my feet. "No hard feelings, Cap? I ain't gonna forget I still owe you for helping my nephew. Just wasn't the right night for returning the favor."

"No hard feelings toward you," I said. "But tell Arnie I'll be by for a private chat."

Gino tugged on his cauliflower ear. "You unnerstant that part of my job is to make sure Mr. St. John don't have none of them kind of private chats?"

"I understand."

He nodded. "Long as we're clear."

Gino collected his gun, and he and Mikey sauntered toward their SUV on Murray Boulevard, moving with the thick-legged sway of power lifters. Gino waved and honked the horn as he pulled out from the curb. It gave me a warm feeling to know we were still good buddies.

Chapter Thirty-One

"*Are you* all right?" Cherisse asked, putting her hand on my shoulder.

I arched my back and groaned. "Define all right."

"Your face is bleeding." She took a handkerchief from her handbag and wiped my cheek where Gino's gun barrel had cut the skin. I grimaced at the stinging sensation. "You might need stitches, and you should get X-rays to be sure there isn't any internal damage."

"Which will require a hospital emergency room visit, which could lead to a police report. And from the byplay between you and Gino, I gather you don't want police."

She frowned. "Your health comes first." Her tone suggested that whatever was second had lost in a photo finish.

"I don't think the cheek wound is that deep," I said. "And Gino and Mikey pulverize people for a living. They know just how far to go without damaging organs or causing internal bleeding. I'll be sore for awhile, but I don't need medical attention."

"Then you're coming to my condo; it's only a few blocks from here. I have all kinds of pain pills and disinfectant for your cheek. You can clean up and ice your injuries too."

"Cherisse—"

"It's either that or I dial 911."

I knew that her calling 911 was an empty threat, but I felt like I'd been trampled by stampeding elephants. The prospect of trekking to the parking garage and driving home didn't have much appeal. On the other hand, the idea of being nursed had considerable appeal. After all, I'd put on a macho performance for Cherisse, she owed me a little coddling. Well, okay, I'd gotten my butt kicked and she'd bailed me out by grabbing the gun, but why split hairs?

We walked up King Street, or rather Cherisse walked and I shuffled. At times like these I missed being a cop. Cops assaulted mafiosos, not the other way around. There ought to be a grace period during which retired cops could beat hell out of anybody for any reason. Joining the general citizenry without transition strained the psyche.

A cat meowed from a veranda, moonlight painted formless shadows on night surfaces, and our footfalls echoed in unsynchronized cadence. Hazy human shapes moved past brightened windows in the hulking house fronts. Breeze fluttered tendrils of Cherisse's hair, a tic pulsed in her cheek, and her eyes squinted in thought.

We turned onto Tradd Street. "What does Arnie have on you that made him so certain he could pull a stunt like this without your going to the police?" I asked.

"It's complicated," she said. "Let's not talk about it now. I want to get you to the condo and medicated."

Clearly a dodge, but I played along. My body felt like a giant migraine, and I wasn't much in the mood for talking either.

Cherisse's condo was in a three-story gray stucco building with black shutters. She had a second floor unit, and in better circumstances I would have climbed the winding stairwell, but tonight we elevatored up. The unit was one bedroom, one bath with high ceilings, Brazilian cherry floors, mahogany bookshelves around a gas log fireplace and granite kitchen countertops. While Cherisse searched the bathroom for meds, I looked out tall windows at a ground level courtyard containing flower beds, fountains and wrought iron furniture. Gas pole lamps edging the stone walkways flickered eerily.

Cherisse bustled out of the bathroom with a pill vial, tube of disinfectant, wash cloth, cotton swabs, gauze pads and tape. "You're prepared," I said. "Do you set men up to be human punching bags and then bring them here for treatment on a regular basis?"

"You're the first," she said chirpily. "I wanted to pilot test the idea before expanding."

My remark had been flippant, but in the dark recesses of my suspicious mind I wondered if Cherisse might have led us to White Point Gardens so Gino and Mikey could batter me around. I was fuzzy on possible motive, though. Then there was the question of why Gino and Mikey would do a job for Cherisse and pretend to be doing it for Arnie. Not to mention the fact that Gino and Mikey weren't the sharpest knives in the drawer. How much disingenuousness were they capable of? Or had Cherisse set it up in such a way that Gino and Mikey thought they were doing it for Arnie? And why was I giving Arnie the benefit of the doubt?

Cherisse cupped my elbow in her palm and walked me to the sectional sofa. "Sit your derriere down and let Nurse Cherry do her thing," she said. "You're out on your feet, honey pie."

Honey pie … that sounded cozy, intimate. I settled back against the cream-colored microsuede cushions and let Nurse Cherry do her thing. She cleaned my cheek wound, applied disinfectant, taped a gauze pad over the wound and ran the tip of her forefinger along the tape in a way that made me shiver. Then she handed me two capsules and a glass of liquid. The liquid was brandy, and it had a kick going down.

Cherisse had dimmed the lights, and her almond eyes were huge and luminous. She nestled close and kissed me. Her lipstick tasted like fresh strawberries. The kiss went on and on. After we broke it off she nestled her head against my shoulder. "Tell me this isn't meant to be," she murmured, voice thick with textured emotions. "I dare you to tell me that now."

Chapter Thirty-Two

Well past dark, Moze Cheddar watched a navy blue van turn down the dirt lane toward the fish camp across the road from where he was hid behind tree cover in the grove. Same van had been drove by the two boys Berard and the big blond fella had talked to at Little Minnie's. Van that was registered to an army fella serving in Afghanistan who had a cousin name of Ronnie Hodge.

Moze had long ago finished his coffee, eaten a cucumber and tomato sandwich, relieved hisself in the woods, and did pushups in the grass and pullups from a tree limb. Put him in good spirits to see the van; he'd worried the boys wasn't coming back to the camp. He rolled up the truck window, stepped out the door and strapped on his knapsack. Knapsack held the tools he'd need to get truthful answers.

Moze walked direct toward the fish camp on the dirt lane. Stepped off the lane before he got to the cabin, circled into the woods and saw the boys drinking beer at the end of a dock. They faced the cabin leaning against dock railings, and they'd see him before he got too close. He knitted his brow and scratched his chin. Could wait till they came off the dock. If only one came, that might be for the best. Be easier to manage one than two. And the one taken might be more likely to talk if he was facing pain and misfortune alone. Also, if these boys was working for the Arnold St. John fella, the boy who didn't get taken would maybe go running to St. John. Could be that would throw panic into St. John, cause him to do something foolish.

Moze settled down in a bushy area that gave a good view of the dock. He was wearing camouflage green, didn't expect the boys would see him, especially the way they was going through the beer bottles in their cooler. Moze rubbed odorless bug spray on his face, hands and shirt, but it didn't do no good. Mosquitoes swarmed around like they was wolves hadn't eaten for days and he was choice sirloin. A hooty owl screeched, a small critter scurried through the brush, and bass popped the lake surface. Lake smelled slimy and rank from fish spawning on the rock banks. Clouds in the gunmetal black sky poked around the moon.

Boys on the dock continued their work of getting shit-faced. Buzzes of conversation floated Moze's way, and he recognized the voice he'd been waiting to hear again. Voice of the leader of them that had come to his cabin. Strong, deep, confident-sounding voice with authority in it. Voice came from the dark complexioned boy, who baited a fishing line and cast it over the dock rail. Other boy, the blond one, had the fidgets, shuffling around and waving his arms.

Moze wanted the dark complexioned boy with the voice, but he judged the blond boy to be his best bet for answers. Seemed like the sort of fella who wore a lot of surface bluster, but cut into that surface and you wouldn't need to go too deep to find his yellow belly. Dark complexioned boy had hisself an appearance of grit that matched with his voice. Might require a good deal of time and effort to break him, and Moze didn't have a good deal of time.

Blond boy was the one came to shore first. Staggered along the creaking dock planks, belched and went inside. Squeaky screen door banged behind him. Darker complexioned boy turned and looked out over the lake, backside to the cabin. Moze took the opportunity to slip from his hiding spot and flatten hisself against the cabin around the corner from the screen door.

Couple of minutes later the door squeaked again and the blond boy stepped out. Carried a six pack of beer and a bag of chips. In several quick strides Moze was alongside, pressing the barrel of the S&W 686 to the boy's cheek. The boy stiffened, his fingers twitched and the beer carton and chips slipped free. Beer carton hit a rock, two bottles broke, and liquid fizzed and foamed. Dark complexioned boy heard the commotion, turned to look from the dock.

"Go, Dub!" the blond boy yelled, then tried to twist his body and grab Moze's gun arm. Stupid, awkward-assed move had no chance of working and would've got the boy dead if Moze chose to fire. But the boy did have more cojones than Moze had credited to him. Moze spread his thumb away from the fingers of his left hand and slammed the V into the boy's throat. Boy clutched at his throat, gurgling and gasping.

Moze glanced at the dock, saw the dark complexioned boy vault the rail into the rowboat. You an' me'll dance another time, Moze thought. We've had us a date since you brung those others to my cabin an' did me wrong.

Meantime Moze and the blond boy would get theirselves acquainted. Moze gripped the boy's hair and banged his head against the cabin wall. Then he jabbed stiffened fingers into the boy's gut and chopped his neck. The boy sank to his hands and knees, and Moze jammed the barrel of the revolver against the back of his head. "This here's an execution position, asshole," he said. "Don't try to fool with me again. We're gonna have us a talk might take till morning."

Chapter Thirty-Three

Sleep was feverish. I had departed Cherisse's condo with my long period of celibacy uncompromised. I was a man of steely self-control and high moral principles who couldn't be seduced by a married temptress with suspect motives and intentions. Also, the night manager at Cherisse's club had phoned with a mini-crisis that required her immediate attention, and she'd dropped me off at my car on her way to the club.

I awoke hung over from the fray with Gino and Mikey in White Point Gardens, choked by a claustrophobic sensation of confinement within a mausoleum that served as my ghostly parents' tomb. I dressed fast, fled the house and drove out of Snee Farm and across the Isle of Palms connector. A thin sheen of fog blurred the marshland, and from the connector's crest the Atlantic looked like gray vapor in the cloudy, sunless dawn.

I parked and bought coffee, then walked out a long boardwalk to the beach, sat near the dunes and unholstered my cell phone. Making a long overdue and now awkward call is like entering frigid water. You don't think about it, you plunge. I dialed a number.

"Giordano," the familiar husky voice said.

"Where's my barber's chair?" I asked.

When Tony "The Scissors" Salerno shut down his Newport barber shop and backroom bookie racket and retired to West Palm, he'd offered me the chair gratis. In The Scissor's words: "A watchamacallit? A memento. Yeah, that's what it is, Berard, a memento. You know, of all the good times we had. You busting my operation, me beating the charges." Followed by Tony's cackling laughter.

To avoid the appearance of impropriety, I'd paid him a hundred dollars for the chair.

"Russell?" Francie Giordano said.

"What did you do with my barber's chair?" I asked again.

There was short silence, then: "I moved it from your office to mine. Want to know why?"

"Not necessarily."

"So you'll have it when you come back to Newport and take this frigging chief's job off my hands and let me return to being a detective."

"Having fun are you?"

"A laugh a minute. I just stepped out of an hysterical budget meeting."

An image flashed in my mind of Francie sitting at a conference table drinking coffee from her powder blue mug with the gold-lettered slogan: *If God Had Wanted Men To Rule The World, She Wouldn't Have Built Them Stupid.*

"That's a shame," I said. "I'm sitting on the beach enjoying the sunrise."

"Imagine me uttering an unladylike obscenity."

"I can't imagine you ever uttering anything unladylike."

"Then you better get a new imagination, because your old one is shot to hell."

"I apologize."

"What?"

"I called to apologize for the way I behaved when I left."

"You mean for acting like a pouty, self-absorbed brat who turned his back on people who love him?"

"That's what I meant, yes," I said. "Thanks for spelling it out."

"My pleasure. I swear, Russell, getting along with you is more stressful than bobbing for apples with a piranha. And apparently I'm not the only female police officer who feels that way."

Uh oh, I thought. "I guess you better spell that out too."

"I had a call from a Mt. Pleasant detective captain named Ellen Talley wanting to know if you had a mental breakdown before you left Newport. Talley says you're messing up about eleventy-three investigations down there."

"She must have me confused with someone else. I'm just a law-abiding citizen enjoying retirement. Shuffleboard, canasta, that sort of thing."

"Well you better get the identity confusion straightened out fast, because Talley was throwing around terms like electric chair and guillotine."

"She has a dry sense of humor."

"She sounded serious to me. She also sounded like she might be a little sweet on you. God knows why. Do the two of you have a history?"

"She's the obnoxious kid sister of an old friend of mine. We can barely stand each other."

"Right," Francie said. "She's not one of those perky-breasted, pale-skinned blonds you go all ga ga over, is she?"

"She's a broad-shouldered redhead. Reminds me of you."

"Except for her not being black, you mean."

"Except for that."

"Russell …"

"Yes?"

"I miss you so much it makes my bones ache."

I swallowed around the lump in my throat. "I miss you too."

"You better answer when I phone from now on," she told me. "If you don't, I'll dummy up a warrant, fax it to Talley, have you brought back here. Don't think I won't either."

"I never take your warnings lightly."

"Good. I've got to get back to the budget meeting, but we'll talk soon. You understand that's a statement, not a question."

"I understand." I hung up feeling lonely and dispirited. The coffee I'd bought tasted acrid. I poured out the remainder, tossed the Styrofoam cup in a trash barrel, and began walking toward the fiery sun climbing the sky at the eastward end of the island. To my left beyond the dunes, multi-million dollar homes rose on stilts like a boxy mountain range.

Strolling toward me was a gangly, familiar-looking man with gray hair and beard. He was tossing a tennis ball into the water for retrieval by a black Labrador. "Russell?" he said. "Russell Berard?"

"Mr. Longstreet?"

His rumbly chuckle stirred remembrances of American history classes. "Let's dispense with the formality of Mister. It's been decades since you were in high school and quite awhile since I taught. I practice law now. Call me Jubal Jeff."

We shook hands. His grip was floppy, his fingers long and bony. "I'm surprised you recognized me," I said.

"I saw you at your father's funeral, but I didn't find the opportunity to have a word." He must have read something in my eyes. "It confounds you that I attended the service. Your daddy and I didn't see eye-to-eye on many matters, but I had high regard for his character."

"How did my father feel about your Guardians of the Confederate Truth?"

Jubal Jeff smiled; he'd always been a charming man. "He was ill-disposed toward the Guardians I'm afraid. He was inclined to regard us as racists, bigots and homophobes."

"Are you?"

"There may be a few of that ilk, but in the majority we're fair-minded folk with firm beliefs about certain social, historical and political issues."

The black Lab returned with the sopping green tennis ball, dropped it in the sand and shook water out of her coat. Jubal bent at the knees, scooped the ball and lobed it in a high arc toward the ocean. The dog sprinted after the ball, back legs kicking high and churning sand.

"It's propitious that we've run into each other," Jubal Jeff said. "I'm concerned about one of your high school classmates, Arnold St. John. You're aware that he intends to produce a television program that could besmirch the *Hunley* crew, and that he possesses or is in pursuit of a secret *Hunley* diary?"

"I've heard those rumors."

Jubal Jeff clicked his teeth, narrowed his eyes and stared past me toward the pier. His bushy eyebrows were snowy white, his large teeth nicotine-stained. "The mission of the Guardians is to protect the true story of the Confederacy, continue to honor those who served, and vigorously oppose any effort to shame or distort the Confederate cause. Our work is legal and peaceful, but we have a few hot-tempered members. I try to prevent violence, of course, but there's a limit to what I can do, and I'm apprehensive that harm may befall Arnold. As I recollect, the two of you were close in high school, so perhaps he'll take your advice. If so, it might be wise for you to counsel him to cease and desist and return to New York."

"Is that a threat?"

He shifted his gaze to meet mine. "Just information provided out of concern for a former student. Do with it as you wish."

"Any particular members of the Guardians with Arnie in their sights?" I asked.

Jubal Jeff rubbed his palm against the leg of his baggy shorts and frowned. "There is one member about whom I have especial concern."

"Who would that be?"

He shook his head. "I'm afraid I can't disclose that. I don't have knowledge of a crime or potential crime, only foreboding. It would be inappropriate for me to reveal the name of one of our members based on skimpy intuition." He patted my arm. "It's been good seeing you, Russell."

"Jubal Jeff!" I said as he started away. He halted and looked over his shoulder. "Did one of your members, maybe the one who's after Arnie, kill my father? Is that why you attended his funeral? Guilt? The two of you despised each other."

He shook his head and adopted a sad-eyed expression. "I'm sorry grief is causing you to lash out like this, Russell. Perhaps we can talk another time when you're in better control of your emotions." He scratched the Lab's ears and shuffled off toward the pier.

Chapter Thirty-Four

I drove home, carried my mother's yoga mat into the back yard and meditated beside Kam Lim's memorial stone. But I couldn't focus my breathing or calm my emotions. Eventually I gave up, rolled the yoga mat, kissed Lim's stone and walked to the rear fence. Breeze fluttered a rope swing beyond the fence, and cars flashed between houses on Plantation Drive across the golf course. The air smelled of wood mildew and clammy growth blocked from light by overhanging oaks.

A canary-colored golf cart motored down the edge of the fairway and stopped. A broad-shouldered woman with caramel-shaded hair stepped out of the passenger side and walked around to the back of the cart. She was wearing an almond visor, orange and cream striped shirt and tan skirt. She drew a wood club from her bag, removed the cover, appeared to glimpse me out of the corner of her eye and said something to her partner. He drove the cart under the oaks and began to walk the tree line, swinging a mid-iron.

"This side!" I called.

He looked at me, and I pointed to a ball in the grass beyond my fence. "Shit," he said and jumped the ditch. He was about five feet nine with glossy black hair and a pretty boy face. Cranberry shorts and a white polo shirt hung loosely on his lean frame. He bent to check the ball, said "Shit" again, picked up the ball and stood.

"Thanks," he said.

"Not a problem," I told him.

He turned toward the ditch, hesitated and turned back to face me. "You're Russell Berard?"

"I am."

He stuck out a pointy jaw, pushed back his shoulders and stretched up on skinny white legs. "I'm Grant Wilbraham, Assistant Solicitor for Charleston County. My girlfriend tells me you've been sticking your nose into criminal investigations."

"Your girlfriend?"

He crooked his elbow and pointed his thumb over his shoulder. "Captain Ellen Talley of the Mt. Pleasant Police Department."

This snooty prick was Ellen's boyfriend? And I'd thought she was pining away for me.

"Consider this to be an official warning," Wilbraham said. "Stay out of law enforcement matters. Otherwise I'll use the full powers of the prosecutor's office to chop you into little pieces and feed the pieces through a meat grinder." He punctuated his warning with what I supposed was his courtroom glower, pivoted and started back to the course.

I allowed him to take seven steps before I called, "Wilbraham!"

He pivoted back to face me. He was good at pivoting, possibly an ex-military lawyer.

"I'm sorry if Ellen's thoughts drift to me during pillow talk," I said.

He flushed, and his face contorted in ugly wrinkles. "You son-of-a-bitch! I ought to come over there and kick your ass!"

I propped my forearms on the fence top and waited.

His shoulders tensed, he raised the golf iron like a battle club, and I thought he might come. He held the threatening posture for a few moments, then rage seeped from his body or good judgment seeped in. "You son-of-a-bitch," he repeated with a low hiss. "If I weren't an officer of the court I'd be continuing this discussion in your face. But don't think we're done."

He tramped back to the ditch, jumped, stumbled and fell to his knees. Struggling to his feet he hurled the golf club. It clanged against the side of the cart and dropped to the ground. He picked it up, broke the shaft across his knee and threw the pieces in my direction. Then he got into the cart and screeched it around in a ninety degree turn, spinning the tires on pine needles, and bumped out to the fairway where Ellen was standing, mouth wide open.

Wilbraham hopped down from the cart and commenced an

animated conversation with Ellen, gesturing at me and waving his arms as if he were making an impassioned closing argument in a criminal trial. When Wilbraham's words petered out, Ellen jammed her fairway wood in her bag and stomped a direct path toward me. If a tree had been in her way she would have flattened it. Her feet were moving so quickly she didn't so much jump the drainage ditch as walk through the air above it.

She approached the fence, trembling with fury. "Who the hell do you think you are making comments regarding my personal life! Referring to what I think about during pillow talk! Of all the inappropriate and despicable things you've done recently, this takes the cake!"

"As long as we're reviewing inappropriate things people have done recently, how would you classify the conversations you've had with your boyfriend about me?"

Her face registered bewilderment. "My boyfriend? What are you talking about?"

"Wilbraham said you're his girlfriend and you've been telling him that I'm interfering with police investigations. Then he threatened to use his office to feed me through a meat grinder. That's a cozy arrangement. Someone makes you mad, you run to your boyfriend, and he eliminates the problem."

She tilted her head and stared at me. Her expression suggested that she was listening to a man stoned on dope speak gibberish. "Grant is not my boyfriend!"

"But you're dating?"

"What business is it of yours who I date?"

"I'm just wondering if the two of you had these conversations about me in a social or professional setting."

She rubbed her palms across her cheeks, then used her fingertips to tug her perspiration-stained shirt loose from her breasts. "Grant's a solicitor. We talked shop at dinner one night and your name came up among other things. We weren't having a specific conversation about you."

"Did you eat out or cook him dinner at your place?"

"Go to hell," she said. "And don't try to change the subject. This isn't about me, it's about you. I want an apology for your disgusting behavior."

"Here's what my behavior consisted of," I said. "I meditated in the back yard beside my missing wife's memorial stone. Then I walked to the fence and looked out at the golf course. You and Wilbraham came along, and you pointed me out to him. He swaggered over here and told me you told him I'm lousing up police investigations. Then he threatened me. If you want an apology, you're looking in the wrong direction."

Ellen kicked at the piece of broken golf club Wilbraham had thrown. The sheen on her tanned, muscular leg gleamed in the sunlight. "I hate men," she said. "I hate every goddamned one of you."

She strode toward the drainage ditch, crossed it and homed in on Wilbraham. He was sitting sideways on the golf cart seat holding a can of diet soda. Ellen planted her feet in front of him and began to talk. It was lively talk. Her head bobbed and her finger jabbed at his chest. I couldn't hear her words, but I could read the picture. She was explaining that her universal hatred of men included Wilbraham. He shook his head, extended his arms and turned his palms up in supplication.

But Ellen wasn't in a merciful mood. She went to the rear of the cart, lifted out her bag and strapped it on her back. Wilbraham followed, prattling and gesturing. Ellen ignored him and began walking toward the fourteenth tee. It was a long way to the clubhouse, but this was a martyrdom march. Wilbraham got in the golf cart, slammed his foot down on the gas pedal and angled in my direction. As he sped by he made an obscene gesture with his middle finger.

Later, I drove to the Harris Teeter on Long Point Road and bought orange juice, peanut butter, salmon steaks, wheat bread, cereal, chocolate, beer, vegetables and fruit. When I came out, Arnie St. John was standing by my Avalon, two grocery bags at his feet. He was juggling three white eggs from a carton open on my car hood. The eggs rose hypnotically in the brilliant sunlight, then plunged like gulls diving for fish.

"Sorry about last night's object lesson at White Point," Arnie said. "But you're not taking me seriously. The Russell and Cherisse days are over. And what you don't appreciate is that I'm doing you a favor by taking a hard line on this. Cherisse is damaged goods."

I put my groceries in the trunk and came around to the driver's door. Arnie swiveled to face me, still juggling effortlessly. "Where are Gino and Mikey?" I asked. "On a rooftop with rifles in case things get nasty out here?"

He grinned. "Enjoying some time off. They said they were going to the opera. I'm flying solo if you want to take a pop at me as payback for last night."

Arnie had dressed beach casual: tan bathing suit, New York City Marathon tee-shirt and unlaced black high-top cross-training shoes. Beard stubble splotched his face, and his eyes were red-rimmed and glassy. His gold wedding band and silver earring sparkled in the sun. I smelled tanning lotion and marijuana. Most likely he'd been mellowing out beside his pool before the supermarket trip.

"Guess who I saw a little while ago?" I said.

"Don't keep me in suspense." He caught the eggs one at a time in his left hand and transferred them to his right as they were caught. Then he cupped his left palm over the three eggs as if he were protecting baby chicks.

"Jubal Jeff Longstreet."

The corners of Arnie's mouth curved high in feigned enthusiasm, but the hollowness of his smile made him look as spiritless as a jack-o-lantern with an extinguished candle. "Jubal Jeff? No kidding. Remember in high school how girls who saw him in the flesh called him Mr. Longdong? What did the old horndog have to say?"

"He wants you to drop the idea of a *Hunley* reality show."

Contempt flickered in Arnie's eyes. "Old news, my man. I told you the other day when we were running on the golf course that the Jubester and his Guardians of the Confederate Truth have been making veiled threats."

"He unveiled this threat. Apparently there's an enraged member of his otherwise peaceful flock who may be planning to scramble your eggs. Jubal Jeff suggests you head back north."

Arnie reinserted the three juggled eggs in their carton and sealed the lid. Then he put a hand to his ear and cocked his head.

"Hear that rumbling, Q? The volcano's about to erupt, and lava's going to flow hot, fast and furious and do a crapload of damage."

"It's not too late to put a cork in the volcano," I said.

His eyes became deep blue pools that saw things beyond my ken. "That's my intention, but there are still going to be casualties." He balanced the egg carton on top of his head, bent at the knees and grasped one bag of groceries in each hand. "You happy to be back here?"

"It's had its ups and downs."

"Things will get better. Charleston's a great place."

"I thought you hated it."

"Just some of the people," he said. "The city rocks. I have another office in Atlanta, but that area's a little too sprawling for me. You spend any time in Atlanta?"

"Not for decades."

"Cherisse was there in the late 1980s, but you two had broken up by then hadn't you?"

"We had."

He nodded. "Crazy times for her in Atlanta from what I understand, crazy times." He straightened, winked at me and walked away.

Chapter Thirty-Five

The ambiguity of Arnie's volcano metaphor occupied my thoughts during the short drive home. I wondered if the impending eruption referred to his marriage or to acquisition of Moze Cheddar's *Hunley* diary. Regardless, Arnie looked and acted like a man who's bet the farm on a horse trailing by ten lengths down the stretch. The swagger was still there, and the egg juggling shtick had a certain flair. But the haunted smile and marijuana reek suggested that fear had taken up residence deep in his gut and begun to gnaw away at his nerve endings. I could imagine him checking into the Francis Marion Hotel and firing an assault rifle out his room window at a Marion Square festival crowd until a SWAT team arrived and punched his ticket to the afterlife. I might be underestimating Arnie, though. He'd always had the resilience of a rubber man attached to a concrete base. Whack him with a baseball bat and he'd smack the ground and bounce back up.

I'd bought the *Post and Courier* at Harris Teeter, and when I got home and scanned the headlines I saw a story about the restoration of the *Hunley*. Which reminded me that I'd never finished reading the diary sections left by Moze Cheddar the other night. I rummaged through the pile of folders in the office and located the one with the diary pages I'd hidden. I carried the folder out to the deck and conjured an image of Ezra Cheddar/Nathaniel Clary in his Sullivan's Island room recording diary entries by candle light …

With two Hunley *crews now drowned, the second because of my sabotage, I thought it certain that the submarine's threat to Union boats blockading Charleston Harbor was at an end. Indeed, General Beauregard expressed grave concern about the* Hunley's *capabilities* and at first refused to consider another undertaking. But neither the General nor I reckoned on the resolve of George Dixon. George was convinced that had illness not prevented him from commanding the Hunley, the second crew would still be alive. Of course, he did not realize that the cause of the illness was holly berry juice I had mixed in his wine. Racked with guilt, George was determined to seek vindication for the Hunley and those men who had perished in her service. Eventually his pleas wore Beauregard down, for the General agreed to allow George to overhaul the submarine and try again to take her into battle.

Repairs completed and a new crew found, George began to make practice expeditions and await his opportunity. As he had done before the second crew perished, George frequently asked me to assist because I had more experience than did the new crew. Nearly always I accepted, so that I could keep a close eye on developments. Obstacles frustrated George. We were deep in the winter months, and harsh winds hampered our efforts. In addition, deserters had taken descriptions of the Hunley to captains of the blockading Union vessels, who were now anchoring their vessels farther off shore, where the fish-boat would have greater difficulty reaching them.

In February of 1864, George cast his eye on a new and inviting target, the USS Housatonic. The Housatonic was one of the most formidable sloops of war in the blockading Union squadron, and I took secret pleasure in stories I heard of her exploits. She had helped capture a number of blockade-running ships attempting to deliver war materials and other supplies to Charleston. She had helped repulse the Confederate ironclads Chicora and Palmetto State after they rammed and crippled other Union vessels. And she had landed raiding parties to attack Charleston's outer defenses.

The Housatonic now anchored in the evenings off Rattlesnake Shoal, much nearer than other Union vessels to Breach Inlet on Sullivan's Island, where we of the Hunley crew were engaged in preparations. In addition to being a more accessible target, the Housatonic had particular appeal to George because of the havoc she had wrought to the Confederate cause. George believed sinking the Housatonic would carry a special cachet, and that such an accomplishment would do much to restore the Hunley's reputation.

I was distraught. On the one hand, I could not stomach the

thought of subversive actions that would result in the death of my good friend George Dixon, not to mention the deaths of another Hunley *crew. On the other hand, I would fail in my mission and disgrace myself if I allowed such a valuable Union resource as the* Housatonic *to be sunk by the fish-boat. As a practical matter, sabotage would be a far more difficult task than had been the case before. George was meticulous about inspections whenever the* Hunley *went out, and the boat was watched closely at night by Confederate troops from Battery Marshall. Should I strike upon a way to sink the* Hunley *again, I could not feasibly incapacitate George to keep him safe, as I had done previously. He would not permit the submarine to leave the dock without him.*

I could think of but one possibility. Before my departure from Washington, Secretary of War Stanton had given me the name of a man in Charleston who was assisting the Union cause by passing information about Confederate defenses and strategies to the ships of the Union blockade. Stanton had warned me to avoid contact with this man unless absolutely necessary. It was best, Stanton believed, to keep intelligence operations separate, so that if one agent was captured he would not be able to compromise another. Nevertheless, I now considered my situation delicate enough to require the help of the other spy. To carry out the plan I had formulated, I needed to get a note to Admiral John Dahlgren, Commander of the Union blockade squadron.

The man whose aid I sought was named Josiah Murray. One evening, I took a boat from Sullivan's Island to Charleston and walked to King Street, where Murray's apothecary shop was located. I was watching from the other side of the street when Murray locked the door of his shop and started home. I crossed and caught up with him at the corner. "Mr. Murray?" I asked. "Mr. Josiah Murray?"

He turned his head to appraise me. He was quite tall, well over six feet, wrapped in an overcoat with the collar turned up. He had a curly black beard, thin lips, a hawk-like nose, and dark piercing eyes beneath bushy brows. The right sleeve of his coat hung empty against his side. "I am Murray," he said in a rumbling voice. "And who might you be?"

"My name is Nathaniel Clary," I told him. "We have a mutual friend who suggested that I look you up should I be in need of assistance."

"And who is this mutual friend?"

"It might be wise for us to have our conversation in private," I said.

He chuckled. "In private. I think not. I know nothing about you, Mr. Clary, except that you have been watching my shop. It is quite probable you intend to rob me or otherwise do me harm. I think my wisest course of action is to keep to the main streets and make haste."

Murray accelerated his long stride, and try as I might to keep up, my damaged leg prevented me from matching his pace. The distance between us grew quickly. "'Ol' Bess!" I called to his back.

He halted abruptly and spun on his heel. "What was that you said?" His voice was taut and harsh now, and as I drew close I saw threat in his icy-eyed glare.

"'Ol' Bess,'" I repeated. "Our mutual friend recommended I use that as an introduction to establish my bona fides."

He stroked his beard and wrinkled his forehead. His cheeks were red from the bitter February wind. "I see. Perhaps then I was wrong, and we should have our conversation in private. At the end of this alley lies a public house where I am known. We can use the back room."

Murray started down the alley without awaiting my reply. Something in his manner caused me trepidation, but I had no choice except to follow. A half dozen steps along the narrow, dank passage, my trepidation proved to be well-founded. Murray turned with a pistol in his hand. Instinctively I backed up, but bumped into a body that felt as large and solid as a stone wall. Before I could react, the cutting blade of a knife was pressed against my throat.

"Nicely done, Rufus," Murray said. "Bring Mr. Clary down this way and search him for weapons, if you will."

Rufus did as instructed and told Murray I was unarmed.

"Very good," Murray said. "Now then, Mr. Clary, who exactly are you, and what is the purpose of this encounter?"

"I'm like you," I told him. "A Union spy."

He stepped nearer and jabbed his pistol into my ribs. "Spying is not a matter to be joked about."

"Indeed it isn't," I agreed.

"What leads you to believe I'm a spy?"

"Our mutual friend told me you are," I said. "In addition, he told me you have been informed that should someone approach and say 'Ol' Bess, you are to infer that this person is also a Union agent."

Murray chewed his bottom lip, eyes cloudy with thought. "Did the individual you claim is our mutual friend explain the significance of 'Ol' Bess?"

"Yes, he said that when the two of you were classmates at Kenyon College, you waded into a mob intent on hanging a Negro woman called Ol' Bess. She was alleged to have committed theft from a white family whom she served as a maid. You saved her life, but in doing so, you sustained wounds that required the amputation of your right arm."

Murray withdrew his pistol from my ribs and took a step backward. "That is quite a tale, Mr. Clary. Quite a tale. But you're taking an enormous risk, are you not? If I am a loyal son of the Confederacy, you have signed your death warrant."

My stomach churned, and I felt perspiration on my brow despite the cold. "That is a risk I am compelled to accept."

"Why?"

"You know of the submarine boat called the Hunley?" I asked.

"Of course," Murray said.

"Well, one night soon she will go out into the harbor to sink the Housatonic."

Murray and the man he called Rufus laughed in unison. "That boat is a fiasco," Murray said. "She has sunk twice and lost two crews. I don't believe the Union has anything to fear from her escapades."

"You are mistaken," I told him. "I have infiltrated the crew and observed the Hunley's capabilities. There is no doubt in my mind that the submarine can succeed—especially under the command of George Dixon."

Murray rubbed the metal of the pistol barrel against his cheek as gently as a woman's caress. "Assuming that what you say is true, what do you expect me to do about it?"

"I intend to be on the crew when the Hunley goes to attack the Housatonic, and I have a plan to scuttle the mission. But I must get a note to Admiral Dahlgren so the blockading squadron will be prepared."

"And exactly what is your plan?" Murray asked.

"The explanatory note to Admiral Dahlgren is in an unsealed envelope in my left coat pocket," I told him. "If I may be permitted?"

Murray nodded and put away his pistol. I withdrew the envelope, removed and unfolded the note, and handed it to him.

"Watch the street, Rufus," Murray said, as I struck a match for reading light. "Let's see what we have here, Mr. Clary. When weather permits, the Hunley will slip out into the harbor and attempt to ram a spar torpedo into the hull of the Housatonic, and you will be aboard. You will take control of the Hunley at gunpoint before the ramming occurs, open the hatch, and flash a signal light to the Housatonic, which must be vigilant every night, because the night of the attack is unknown. Having received your signal, the Housatonic is to send lifeboats, which will evacuate you and take the Hunley crew as prisoners. The Hunley may either be sunk or towed somewhere safe, such as Morris Island."

Murray studied me, a smile flitting at the corners of his lips. "My heavens, Mr. Clary, that is quite an ambitious undertaking."

"I know," I said. And I did know. There were many details still to be determined.

"Well then," Murray said, surrendering the note and envelope to me. "Are you willing to gamble that a complete stranger who doubts the efficacy of the Hunley will risk life and limb to convey this note to Admiral Dahlgren?"

"I am," I said. refolding and reinserting the note in the envelope.

Murray began to speak, but a stone bounced suddenly near our feet, calling our attention to Rufus, who approached rapidly from the intersection of the alley and the main street, where he had moved. "Confederate patrol," he mouthed, rolling his eyes and tilting his head in a clear signal: Heading this way.

I shoved the note at Murray with a whispered plea.

Murray slipped the pistol and note into his pocket. "It would never do to be caught with your missive in my possession, would it, Mr. Clary?" He tipped his hat. "Good luck to you, sir. Perhaps we'll cross paths again."

Murray and Rufus set off in swift strides toward the end of the alley opposite where the Confederate soldiers were approaching. I hobbled after them, having no guarantee that Murray would make an effort to transmit my note to Admiral Dahlgren.

Chapter Thirty-Six

I finished the diary pages and wished Moze Cheddar had left the remainder. Eight bodies, not nine, were inside the *Hunley* when she was raised off the ocean floor; all the bodies had been identified, and Ezra Cheddar/Nathaniel Clary hadn't been among them. If Cheddar/Clary had made it onto the *Hunley* the night the sub attacked the *Housatonic*, he'd apparently failed in his efforts to capture the crew. And if he'd been a ninth crew member, how had he avoided the fate of the other eight? Of course, all these questions assumed that the diary was authentic.

I slid the pages back in the folder, stood and massaged my neck. Birds hidden in the leafy branches of trees beyond the deck warbled, and a gas-powered hedge trimmer gurrrred to life in a nearby yard in response.

Later I'd put a salmon steak and sliced potatoes on the grill, drink beer in the dark and allow contemplations of my father's murder, my mother's suicide, Cherisse Dane's sexual voltage, Arnie St. John's shenanigans, Moze Cheddar's *Hunley* diary and Ellen Talley's wrath to temporarily slide from my mind like water off a duck's back.

Then I noticed the man. He staggered across the fairway, stumbled through pine needles, fell across the ditch, struggled to his feet, lurched forward, and draped his arms over the top of my fence. Ronnie Hodge with a glazed expression and a blood-stained tee-shirt. I opened the gate, looped one of his arms over my shoulders, took his weight against my side and half dragged him across the yard, up the deck steps and into the house. I settled him down in a chair at the kitchen table, and he slumped back and groaned. "I'm shot bad, bud."

I cut away his shirt with scissors and revealed a bullet wound in his right shoulder. The bleeding had stopped, and there didn't appear to be arterial damage. "How long ago?" I asked.

"Fifteen … twenty minutes. Happened in my apartment parking lot. Decided to drive here, but I turned wrong, ended up on Plantation, ran out of gas." His chuckle emerged as a raspy gurgle. "Can you believe that shit? Ran out of gas. Had to walk up a driveway and across the golf course."

"Why didn't you drive to the hospital?"

"That woulda got me cops."

"You're getting cops anyway," I told him as I dialed 911.

When I hung up I sprayed disinfectant on Ronnie's wound, packed gauze pads over it and wrapped it with a gauze bandage. Then I ran tap water in a glass and added bourbon. Ronnie took a swig and shivered as the liquid went down.

"Who did it?" I asked.

"Goddamn Cheddar."

"Moze Cheddar?"

"Didn't see the shooter, but I'm guessing it's him. Cocksucker found Dub and me last night at the fish camp where we was holed up. Dub got away, but Cheddar grabbed me, took me someplace in his truck."

Ronnie swallowed more bourbon and water and coughed. His face was pasty, his eyes glassy, and he was sweating heavily. Going into shock, I realized. "Let's get you stretched out until the medics arrive," I said.

I helped him out of the chair and over to the couch in the family room. He sank down and I got his head flat. I raised his legs and propped his feet on the arm of the couch.

"What did Cheddar want?" I asked.

"Wanted to know a bunch of shit, like who … sent us to his cabin to steal the *Hunley* diary."

I was pretty sure he'd lost a lot more blood than was good for him. I wasn't sure how long he'd remain coherent. "Did you tell him?"

"Told him … something …"

"How about telling me what you told him, along with the truth, if that's different from what you told Moze."

"How about … you kiss my ass."

I contemplated shooting Ronnie three or four more times, but ballistics analysis would reveal that the wounds were from different weapons. "How did you get away?"

"Son-of-a-bitch finally let me go, up in Summerville this morning. I called Dub … he … came an' got me—" Ronnie gagged, rested his cheek on the cushion for a moment, forced his eyes open. I gave him a hit of bourbon straight from the bottle, and he gagged again. "What Dub and me decided, we need to be out of South Carolina for awhile. Things've … got too frigging crazy. I went to my place, Dub went to his. We were gonna … pack, meet up later … take a road trip. But when I came out of my place, somebody—cut loose on me."

"If Cheddar released you earlier, why would he try to kill you now?"

"Don't know, bud. Guy ain't carryin' a full set of crayons, you ask me … I ain't thinkin' too clear myself … red lights flashin' in front of my eyes. Lemme take a little nap … You … call Dub … warn him. Whoever shot me … prob'ly goin' after him. Dropped my damn phone in th' parkin' lot … when I got hit." He mumbled DuBois' number, put his head down and closed his eyes.

I dialed, and DuBois picked up after two rings. "Yes?"

"It's Berard."

"What do you want, and how did you get this number?"

"Ronnie gave it to me. He just went unconscious on my couch. Somebody shot him at his apartment building."

"Shit! How bad is he?"

"Bad enough, but I don't think fatal," I said. "Emergency rescue is on the way. Ronnie wanted me to warn you that whoever took him down may be headed in your direction."

"Did he see who did it?"

"No, he thinks it might have been Moze Cheddar, but that doesn't make sense to me."

"It wasn't Cheddar," DuBois said. "It was probably the same person who fired on us at Little Minnie's."

"Arnie's Mafia boys, Gino and Mikey?"

DuBois snorted. "You really don't have a clue what's going on, do you?"

"Explain it to me."

"Figure it out for yourself, you're a detective. And don't trust certain cops."

After medics had hauled Ronnie away, Ellen Talley paced my family room with her hands clasped behind her back. Her eyes looked down, but I knew she wasn't studying the Oriental carpet design. There were enough furrows in her brow to plant corn. She was wearing jeans, a pink tee-shirt and sandals. She had small, wide feet with round toes, and her nails were painted pink. "I should take a vacation," she said. "Immediately. Like tomorrow. The Caribbean's too hot this time of year. I'm thinking southern France. Rent a small villa, sleep late, read all those books that have been piling up. And maybe, just maybe, when I return you'll be gone. Poof, vanished. And this crime wave that's churning around you will have ceased."

"You're right," I said. "The next time someone shows up at my door with bullet wounds, I'll let him expire and bury him in the back yard so you won't be troubled."

I was sitting at the pine table in the chair Ronnie had used before I put him on the couch. I'd told the responding police my story, and I'd told the story again to Ellen. But, as had become the norm for my interactions with her, I'd skipped a few details. Ronnie's mention of being kidnapped and questioned by Moze Cheddar. DuBois' reference to the gunfire at Little Minnie's. DuBois' advice not to trust certain cops.

Ellen quit pacing, came to the table and sat across from me. The bottle of bourbon Ronnie had used for medicinal purposes was still on the table, and I pushed it toward Ellen. "Don't tempt me," she said.

Her hair was pulled back in a pony tail showing delicately shaped ears that protruded from her skull. She was without jewelry and looked girlish. But she didn't talk girlish. "So DuBois Dane told you he thinks he knows who shot Ronnie, and you promptly advised him to leave the state? Does the term accessory after the fact mean anything to you? I've heard rumors you used to be in law enforcement, though I'm finding that increasingly difficult to believe."

"Accessory after the fact would only be an issue if I knew DuBois had committed a crime and I helped him avoid arrest," I said. "I don't think DuBois shot Ronnie, and neither do you. Besides, I didn't advise DuBois to leave the state, I just warned him that he might be in danger."

"You should have advised him to contact the police for protection."

"He wouldn't have done that."

Her purple eyes flamed. "He wouldn't have done it because he wouldn't like the questions we'd ask. Such as what went down at Etiwan Pointe the other night when Jason Grimes was killed. Such as why DuBois and Ronnie have been hiding out ever since. But we have Ronnie now, and when his condition is stabilized, we'll ask him."

"Good luck with that," I said.

Ellen leaned toward me. There was a red blemish below the left corner of her mouth and a small brown mole just above the collar of her tee-shirt. "You know what else I want to ask Ronnie? Why he came to your house when he was shot."

"I told you I asked him that and he said he came here because he was afraid if he went to the hospital they'd call the police."

"Isn't it interesting that Ronnie thought you'd protect him from the police."

"If he thought that, he was wrong, wasn't he?"

Her lips curled scornfully. "Big deal, you finally drew the line somewhere. But Ronnie also trusted you to contact DuBois, and he wasn't wrong about that. You seem to have an awfully cozy relationship with those two. Which makes me wonder if you're helping them with something. Possibly something Cherisse asked you to help them with."

"What does Cherisse have to do with this?"

"You tell me."

I turned my head sideways and looked out the sliding glass doors. Gusty wind whipped bushes beyond the rear fence, and clumps of dark storm clouds were pushing in from the west.

"Are you suggesting that I'm involved in criminal activity with Ronnie, DuBois and Cherisse?" I asked.

"I'm suggesting that you're withholding information and interfering with police investigations," Ellen said. "And it wouldn't be difficult to bring charges against you."

"Why don't you, then?"

Emotions flashed briefly in her eyes, then she set her jaw, and the eyes turned cold and pitiless. "Because, on a personal level, you're someone I used to venerate and care about, and on a professional level, charging you wouldn't do any good; you still wouldn't talk. But I have a feeling your rope is nearly played out, and very soon I'm going to be forced to take you down hard, or somebody else is going to take you off the board permanently."

After the front door slammed and the house quit shaking, I went out to the deck and brought in the folder with the *Hunley* pages.

Chapter Thirty-Seven

Moze Cheddar's truck was parked in the shade of a shopping center. He'd followed the black woman, who'd drove from her I'On house in a white Jaguar convertible and was at present inside a nail salon located between an ice cream parlor and a store where doll clothes and children's toys was sold. Moze had bought hisself a butterscotch cone and was eating it on a bench facing the nail parlor. Prickly wind rustled nearby palmetto trees, and the darkening sky prepared to spit and snarl. Moze wasn't a man normally saw symbols in the world around him, but his skin itched with the feeling that it wasn't just a storm soon to break loose, but all hell too. Such forebodings used to come to him in the military, and usually they'd turned out true.

Moze was watching the woman on account of what was told to him by Ronnie Hodge, the boy Moze had took from the fish camp last night. Ronnie was the shy type, didn't talk easy. Eventually though, Moze had come across the proper persuasion, and Ronnie had spilled certain facts. Said that when the boys broke into Moze's cabin after the diary, they was working for the black woman, not Arnold St. John. 'Course, an interrogator never believed what was first told to him, and could be Ronnie's story weren't nothing but a pile of cow dung. Seemed possible Ronnie and the others had truly been working for St. John, and Ronnie was now trying to pass blame along to the woman.

Next step for an interrogator was to get more serious with questioning, find out was the same story or a different one told the second time. Which was where Moze had discovered a curious thing. He didn't no longer have an appetite for serious questioning. Screams of men and women he'd seriously questioned in the military still rang in his ears. Memories of blood-streaked faces and bruised bodies took away his sleep. Looking at Ronnie strapped to a tree, knees sagging, head drooping, drool running off his chin, Moze had realized he couldn't go no further, and he'd turned the boy loose.

On account of turning Ronnie loose without more serious questioning, the only way to test the boy's story was for Moze to take hisself a closer look at the black woman. So here Moze sat on the bench eating his ice cream cone and wondering would the woman lead him anyplace better than a nail salon.

There was another reason too why Moze was taking hisself a closer look at the woman. According to Ronnie, her name was Cherisse Dane, and the dark complexioned boy with the leader's voice was her young 'un, DuBois. Which put Moze in a pickle, 'cause on the one hand the black woman and the dark complexioned boy had been behaving like they was Moze's enemies, but on the other hand, if they was named Cherisse Dane and DuBois Dane, they was also Moze's relatives.

Chapter Thirty-Eight

Ronnie and Ellen Talley had departed my domicile differently, Ronnie in an ambulance, and Ellen in a rage, but they'd departed nonetheless. With my unexpected company gone, I could now re-focus on the plan I'd been formulating when Ronnie showed up at my back fence. The plan where I'd put a salmon steak and sliced potatoes on the grill, drink beer in the dark, and allow contemplations of matters such as my father's murder and Moze Cheddar's *Hunley* diary to temporarily slide from my mind like water off a duck's back.

Except I couldn't. The events of the last couple of hours had jazzed me up, and I felt as frenzied as Arnie St. John had looked and acted during our earlier encounter in the supermarket parking lot. Thinking of Arnie pricked recall of a remark he'd made that hovered in the back reaches of my consciousness like the muted drip of a faucet. A remark about Cherisse's crazy times in Atlanta in the late 1980s. I had the feeling Arnie had been telling me something without actually telling me. Cherisse and I were long over by then; I was discharged from the Marines, married to Kam Lim and beginning my law enforcement career in Rhode Island. I knew Cherisse had done undergraduate and graduate work at the University of Georgia, but I had no idea where life had taken her next.

It took some Internet searching to find out. Most of what I turned up about Cherisse was of relatively recent vintage. Social events she'd attended with and without Arnie in New York, Atlanta and Charleston. Human service agencies and charities she'd served as a board member or volunteer. Involvement with the ACLU, Southern Christian Leadership Conference and Southern Poverty Law Center. Alumni mention from UGA. Road racing results in Charleston. Articles about her club, Denmark Vesey. Talk about her running for Charleston County Council.

By tracing fragments of information from link to link I moved back in time to 1987, when Cherisse had worked for an Atlanta-based civil rights organization called All Shall Be Free while she was a grad student at Emory University. She'd been one of the demonstrators injured by rocks and bottles during the March for Brotherhood in Forsyth County in January 1987. A week afterward, Cherisse and 20,000 others, including Coretta Scott King, had marched through winter slush to the Forsyth County courthouse. Along the way they'd been harassed by white supremacists shouting racial slurs and waving posters that read: *James Earl Ray–American Hero,* and *The Future Is Red Necks, White Skin And Blue Collars.*

A few months later, several black leaders from All Shall Be Free, the civil rights organization where Cherisse worked, had attempted retaliation against the white supremacists with mail bombs and poisoned letters. But they'd been arrested before the plan could be implemented, convicted in federal court and given stiff prison sentences. I'd read part of this story before when I was researching Leonard Alcott. Alcott had been the lead FBI agent responsible for the arrests of the black leaders.

Had Arnie been cryptically pointing me toward the possibility of an old tie between Cherisse and Alcott? No information I found about the arrest and conviction of the All Shall Be Free leaders mentioned Cherisse's name as conspirator or witness. Years later, Cherisse and Alcott had both ended up in Charleston, but it was hard to read that as anything other than coincidence. Alcott retired here, and Cherisse was from the area originally. If her return was related to Alcott's presence, I couldn't see the connection.

I shook my head. Attempting to reason this through without more information was hopeless. I needed answers straight from a horse's mouth. One of the horses, Alcott, was dead. That left Cherisse and Arnie. I called Cherisse's cell phone and left a voice mail. I called her home number and left a voice mail. Then I called her club and talked to a real live person, who said Cherisse hadn't been in but he'd leave a message for her.

Nothing to do but wait for her to receive one of my messages and return my call. But I wasn't in a waiting mood. My muscles twitched and pulsated as if I'd overdosed on caffeine. If I couldn't locate Cherisse, maybe I'd have better luck finding Arnie. I was still troubled by his enigmatic statement in the shopping center parking lot that a volcano was ready to erupt and cause casualties. It was time to seek clarification. I clipped the holster with my .38 Special to my belt, thinking it might facilitate the clarification process, especially if Gino and Mikey were with Arnie.

No one answered the bell at Arnie and Cherisse's house in I'On, and no one was around back by the pool. Frustrating. Witnesses, informants and suspects on television are always home when the detective knocks on their door, and the investigation speeds right along. But people in real life have real lives and never seem to be where a detective wants them to be when the detective wants them to be there.

I dialed a number on my cell phone and finally reached someone I wanted. Gary Nagle said, "Hullo."

"Where would Arnie St. John be on a Saturday evening?"

"What? That you, Q?"

"Where would Arnie St. John be on a Saturday evening?" I repeated.

"Is this some kind of riddle? How the hell would I know where Arnie is? Home?"

"Not home."

I heard a yawn. "Christ, man, I was taking a nap. We're playing tonight at the Vesey." I heard a feminine voice, then Gary whispering.

"Is the rest of the band napping with you?"

He chuckled. "Not the entire band."

A man in bed with a good looking woman invariably has a cheerful outlook on life. At least that's what I vaguely recalled. "Do you have any idea where Arnie hangs out on weekends?"

"Damn, you've been high maintenance since you moved back here," Gary grumbled. "Arnie and I don't exactly travel in the same social circles you know. There's a place where he plays cards, but that's late night shit. Otherwise … otherwise … I guess he might be hitting softballs."

"Hitting softballs?"

"Yeah, he was playing in a fast pitch league, but it was all pretty civilized and polite, and you know Arnie, he plays rough. Cleated a couple of guys in their family jewels, deliberately drilled a guy in the face with a throw, ran over a catcher at home plate, who got a dislocated shoulder. They finally tossed Arnie out of the league."

"So why would he be hitting softballs?"

"He told the league to go screw itself, bought a piece of property off Route 41 and built a regulation softball field with lights, seats and a concession stand. Claims he's gonna start his own league. Hasn't done that yet, but word is he jacks himself up on dope or booze, goes to the field and hits balls for hours. There's a pitching machine."

"Where's the field exactly?"

"What's wrong with your voice?" Gary said. "You sound weird, all wired up."

"I drank too much coffee earlier."

"You're not gonna brace Arnie alone are you? Not with those Mafia guys living in his back pockets."

"I'm out of patience," I said. "I need to make something happen."

"That's crazy. You're talking like me. And you got me giving advice like you."

"Role reversal is a wondrous thing."

"I like the old roles better," he said. "Why not swim a few laps in the pool to take the edge off, turn in early with a good book, and call me in the morning."

"Why not give me directions to Arnie's field and finish your nap with Lina."

There was female murmuring in the background and a muttered response from Gary. "Ah hell," he said to me. "Lina thinks I oughta go along. Where are you?"

"At Cherisse and Arnie's."

"Go back to your place. I'll come by for you in ten minutes."

Chapter Thirty-Nine

Moze finished his butterscotch ice cream cone, scowled and shook his head. Cherisse Dane woman still hadn't come out of the nail parlor. Made no kind of damn sense to Moze how women could waste time and money getting their nails painted. He had hisself an urge to barge into the parlor and drag the Dane woman out by the scruff of her neck. His nerves was fraying and his patience thinning, but there wasn't nothing to do but wait.

He wiped his lips with a napkin, dropped the napkin in a trash barrel and went back to his truck. He rolled down the windows and opened a bottle of water he took from his cooler. He'd drunk a third of the bottle when the Dane woman did finally come out. She paused on the curb, reminding Moze of girls he'd seen in Asian clubs stop to draw a breath before they put their slinky bodies on display so men could choose. She was wearing high heeled sandals, yellow shorts and a blue top.

She stepped down off the curb, halted, dipped her hand in a handbag, brought out a cell phone, raised it to her ear. She listened, talked, listened, talked, listened. Moze couldn't hear none of it, but her body stiffened and fury lines scrunched her face. She spoke last words, snapped shut the phone, dropped it in her handbag and clicked the high heels to her white Jaguar. She lowered the convertible top, screeched partway out of the parking space, braked hard to a stop, re-raised the top. Then she just sat there for a spell. Calming her nerves Moze guessed. She's riled. Moze drank more water waiting for her to budge. He'd finished another third of the bottle before she backed the Jag totally free of its space and squealed away fast.

Moze followed. Followed her to Route 17 where she turned north. She was in a hurrying mood, but traffic boxed her, like a race horse trapped in the pack. She switched from lane to lane trying to break free, but it didn't help her none. Just caused frustration judging by the flashing brake lights. Wasn't no trouble for Moze to keep her in view. She held her course steady up Route 17. Passed by Towne Centre. Passed the intersect where Route 517 shot east like an arrow across marshes and the Inland Waterway to Isle of Palms. Turned her Jaguar right eventually on a road called Hamlin. Went by a school, come to a four way stop and swung left at Rifle Range Road. Moze dawdled at the stop sign, let a car traveling on Rifle Range get between him and the Jag. The Dane woman turned right onto Boston Grill, and the car inbetween turned there too, continuing to give Moze cover. Small tidy houses sat along the slim road, black faces in front yards. Felt like an area where blacks had settled before property near the water grew more expensive than gold bullion.

Car in front of Moze swung into a driveway, and the Dane woman drove to the bottom of Boston Grill, where newer houses stood. Moze figured that if you lived up the block, you'd look down the street at the new houses, understand what was coming and begin to think about where you was gonna move when big money forced you out.

A dirt lane continued to the right of where a Road Ends sign sat, and the Jaguar bumped along the lane. Moze braked short of the sign and studied the situation. Dirt lane twisted through tall grass to a cedar shingled cottage built up on wood posts. Cottage looked fresh painted, had flower boxes, curtains and a satellite dish. Marshland spread from the cottage to the water. The Dane woman parked her Jag in front of the cottage and got out, hair fluttery in the wind.

Moze gave it thought. Didn't care much for the setup. Couldn't drive down the dirt lane. Terrain was wide open, and the Dane woman would see the truck for sure. Couldn't park here on the side of the road and watch. Somebody from the big money house across the road would call the police, report a suspicious vehicle. Couldn't park a distance away and walk back, 'cause he'd need the truck handy should the Dane woman leave.

Moze U-turned, headed up Boston Grill searching for a solution. Found one before he'd traveled far, a narrow strip of pavement curling into the woods. Moze followed the pavement to where it ended at a rotting, tottery garage. He parked behind the garage and made his preparations. Put on rain gear, pocketed the Sig Sauer automatic pistol and nestled the Kalashnikov assault rifle in its weatherproof carrier. Dane woman was family of a sort, but that didn't mean she wasn't his foe.

Moze looped the carrier strap over his shoulder, set off on foot and reached the edge of the woods, from where he could see the cottage real clear. The first droplets of rain pattered against his parka. He grinned. Man wanting answers always held the high cards in the rain.

Chapter Forty

Gary Nagle drove us up Route 17 and onto Route 41. Eventually 41 would reach and cross the Wando River, but I doubted we were traveling that far. The windows were rolled down, and incoming air gushed thick and sticky with odors of exhaust fumes, heated pavement and approaching rain.

Gary steered with one hand and lit a cigarette with the other. He was wearing a floral-patterned aloha shirt brightly colored in purple, gold, pink and white. His jowls and goatee drooped above the shirt's open neck. Skin was peeling off his nose from sunburn, and his dirty blond hair was covered by a navy blue cap with a red marlin above the bill. "Why do you wanna see Arnie?" he asked.

"My puzzle is full of blanks; I want Arnie to fill some of them in. You can help too."

"Don't start that crap again, Q. I'll help you try and find Arnie, but I'm not playing twenty questions about other shit."

"Here's a funny story," I said. "Guess who was waiting at my house when you dropped me off after we came back from Little Minnie's the other night?"

"Ellen Talley in a negligee?"

"Moze Cheddar."

"No kidding," Gary said. "He tell you why he shot at us in Minnie's parking lot?"

"I don't think he was the shooter, but he did tell me something else interesting."

"Yeah, what's that?"

"You picked up *Hunley* diary pages that Cheddar left at a bar on Coleman and delivered them to Cherisse. You forgot to mention that to me, but Cheddar put a tracer on the pages and followed you."

Gary dragged on his cigarette, blew smoke toward the window and licked at a spec of tobacco on his front teeth. "Whatta you want me to say here, Q? So I did a favor for Cherisse. Big deal."

"Cherisse is playing some kind of deep, dark game, and she appears to be playing against Arnie. I want to know what the game is and why she's playing it."

"Ask her."

"I did. Her explanation is smooth on top but soggy underneath, like an undercooked cake disguised by a layer of frosting."

Gary turned his truck off Route 41. We bounced along a narrow, potholed road with a centered yellow stripe so faint it might have been there since Francis Marion fought the British in the swamps. "Cherisse's game is complicated," Gary said. "I'm just a part-time player, and I don't understand all her goddamn rules."

Gary parked us outside a fence that ran along the left field line of Arnie St. John's softball field. The scene made me think of Field of Dreams, stadium lights shining on a ballpark in the middle of nowhere. But "build it and they will come" wasn't working for Arnie tonight. No Shoeless Joe Jackson materializing from between tall corn stalks, no long line of cars approaching with spectators to fill the grandstands.

Action on the field was surreal, though. Arnie crouched barefoot in the right hand hitter's box wiggling a red aluminum bat. He wore black tuxedo pants, a frilly white dress shirt with gold cuff links and black tie and a navy blue Charleston RiverDogs baseball cap. His shoes and folded tuxedo jacket lay in the grass near the on-deck circle. The pitching machine rifled a softball toward home plate, and Arnie slashed at it. The bat connected with a poing, and the ball rocketed between the center and left fielders, Gino and Mikey.

Gino trotted after the ball, retrieved it near the outfield fence, trotted toward the infield and lobbed the ball in the general direction of the pitching machine. He was dressed in white linen slacks, a yellow short sleeve button down shirt and brown alligator shoes.

He looked like he'd run through a sprinkler, sweat dripping from his shaved head and saturating his clothes.

Arnie ripped the next pitch down the left field line. Mikey backhanded the ball on two hops, pivoted and threw. A sizzling frozen rope of a throw that bounced once and came up just where a second baseman would want it to make a sweeping tag. Mikey jogged back to his position in stocking feet, pounding his fist in the pocket of his glove. There were grass stains on his taupe silk pants and dirt splotches on his pink dress shirt. His brown and white loafers sat by the foul pole near two blue blazers and two shoulder holsters hanging on the outfield fence.

"Q and the Nag!" Arnie said, as if our arrival made his evening complete. "Gives us a third of our starting high school lineup. Entrez-vous, gents, have a libation and take a little batting practice for old times' sake." The pitching machine fired another round, and Arnie caught the softball in his bare hand. He took a remote control from his pants pocket and clicked it, deactivating the machine. Then he tossed the ball he was holding in the air and swung the bat with one arm. There was another poing, and the ball arced up into the darkening sky. Mikey scurried backward with surprising agility and caught the ball in front of the fence. "Damn!" Arnie swore and hurled the bat into a dugout along the first base line.

Gary and I entered the field through a gate along the third base line. Gino ambled toward us, and Mikey slid his stocking feet into his loafers, lifted the blazers and shoulder holsters off the fence and followed.

"Overdressed for softball aren't you, Arnie?" Gary said.

"There's a function tonight at the Aquarium. I had good intentions …" Voice trailing off, he sat in the dirt, opened a cooler and spooned cracked ice into a Styrofoam cup. Over the ice he poured Wild Turkey, orange juice and lime juice. "A Louisville Chill without the powdered sugar," he said. "Goes down way smoother than Mint Juleps. I've got a luxury box at Churchill Downs. Next year the three of us will make a road trip to the Derby. I ought to be divorced by then, free and loose like you studs. We can do some serious catting around." He held up a palm as if Gary or I were about to interrupt. "Yeah, I know, if I'm divorced, that means Cherisse will be available, which means Russ will be all over her. But by April he will have learned what I've learned—what he learned in high school and forgot. Cherisse hasn't changed, never will. Yeah, by April Russ will be back in the land of the unattached, ready to boogie with us, Nag. It'll be good." He raised the cup and ingested a substantial portion of its contents.

Gino and Mikey meandered closer. They'd strapped on their shoulder holsters. "Easy," I said to Gino. "This isn't about last night at White Point Gardens. I'm in a conversational mood. It doesn't have to get any louder than that."

Gino smiled ruefully. "All due respect, Cap, I been to a lot of sit-downs where things didn't need to get loud, but still they did more often than not."

"Lighten up, Gino," Arnie said. "There's no hostility in the air. All good buddies here. We'll get comfy around the campfire, gobble Wild Turkey, tell ghost stories."

Gino frowned. His eyes said he knew Arnie was going over the falls in a barrel.

"Help me roll the train out of the station, Nag," Arnie rambled on. "There's beer on ice if bourbon doesn't toot your whistle."

"I got a little thing going with AA," Gary told him. "I'll take orange juice straight."

Arnie poured OJ in a cup and handed the cup to Gary, who sat. "Q?" Arnie asked.

"What kind of beer?" I asked.

"Sam Adams. Direct from Boston. Just the ticket for a former New England boy like you. Should bring back sweet memories of the Sox and Patriots."

"What do you have for a Mets and Buffalo Bills fan?" I asked.

Arnie grinned. "Arsenic and prune juice."

"Beer," I said, settling beside Gary.

Arnie passed me a bottle and an opener. Then he fished in the cooler for two Diet Cokes, flipped them to Gino and Mikey and motioned for them to sit. So there the five of us huddled in a cozy semi-circle. Maybe we'd toast marshmallows later.

Arnie jerked off his tie, tossed it over his shoulder, gripped the collar of his sopping shirt with both hands and yanked. Buttons popped and the shirt front ripped open, exposing curly blond tufts of chest hair. "It's going to rain like a son-of-a-bitch," he said. "Remember that game in Beaufort County when we were juniors? Went extra innings and began to pour. They brought in that skinny jug-eared dweeb with coke bottle glasses who threw like Nolan Ryan. No way to pick up the ball in that weather. But Nag timed one and hammered it to Savannah, and we went home happy."

"Somebody shot Ronnie Hodge this afternoon," I said.

Arnie's eyes widened. "Ronnie? Jesus! Is he okay?"

"I don't know."

"Who did it?"

"Ronnie didn't see the shooter. It happened in the parking lot at his apartment."

Arnie took off his RiverDogs cap and studied the insignia of a dog holding a bat. "You know a lot about it."

"Ronnie came to my house after he caught the bullet."

"No kidding. Did he get confused and mistake your house for a hospital?"

"He'd had a rough day. Moze Cheddar kidnapped him last night."

Arnie swallowed more Louisville Chill, hand trembling slightly, a tic pulsing in his cheek. The rain drops had paused, but humidity dribbled off vegetation surrounding the field, and the air was thick as liquid oxygen. Mikey scratched his side and kept his hand near the gun in his shoulder holster. Gino finished his Diet Coke and squeezed the can until it imploded. Gary yawned and brushed at a buzzing mosquito.

"Mikey and I'll play you and Gary three innings," Arnie said. "Gino can be permanent pitcher. Team at the plate has to hit between second and third. Team in the field has a shortstop and left fielder. Anything caught in the air is an out, any ground ball the shortstop gets is an out. Ground ball that makes the outfield or fly ball that drops is a single. Ball over the fielder's head is a double. Ball that hits the fence on the fly is a triple. Ball over the fence is a home run."

"I'm not here to play, Arnie."

"Sure you are. But you're playing a different game. The one

where you accuse me of shooting Ronnie."

"I'm here to find out what the hell is going on."

Arnie finished his drink and licked his lips. "Moze Cheddar's shown you his diary?"

"Some of it," I said.

"And you're working for Cherisse? Giving the material to her?"

"No."

He raised his head and compressed his eyes. "Bullshit. I know she got pages of the diary from Gary. I have an arrangement with our housekeeper. She tells me things, and I pay her for what she tells me and don't call immigration."

"Gary's working his own side of the street," I said.

"That's straight, Arnie," Gary affirmed. "What I gave Cherry didn't come from Q."

Arnie scratched a cross in the dirt with his forefinger. "I misspoke before. About the team at the plate needing to hit between second and third. Nag's a lefty. When he bats, Mikey and I'll shift to the right side. In fact I think I'll hit lefty and you two can shift for me."

"You sent DuBois, Ronnie, Jason Grimes and Dewey Welch to Cheddar's cabin to steal the diary," I said. "But Cheddar caught them at it and killed Welch. Cherisse found out, probably from DuBois, and tipped off Cheddar that you were the one behind the attempted theft. Now Cheddar's down here after you."

The sky had dulled to black and gray, and swollen storm clouds sagged like low hovering blimps. Gusty wind jiggled tree limbs as if they were puppet arms tugged by invisible strings, and hard-edged thunder reverberated ominously. Arnie stuffed his hand in his pocket, withdrew a pill bottle, unscrewed the top, tapped a capsule into his palm, plopped the capsule in his mouth and washed it down with a slug of Wild Turkey. "You have your head up your ass, Q. But let's quit talking about this shit and play some ball. We'll be lucky to finish an inning before we're washed out."

"Are you saying you didn't send the boys to Cheddar's cabin?" I asked.

"That's what I'm saying."

"Who then?"

"The dutiful wife, my man. When in doubt, cherchez la femme."

"Why would Cherisse want to steal the *Hunley* diary?"

"Leverage against me," Arnie said. "She wants out of our marriage, and she wants to take a healthy share of my money with her." He tipped back his head, turned the Wild Turkey bottle upside down, guzzled and gagged. His cheeks were flushed, his eyes bloodshot and burning with malice and irrationality.

"Cherisse is a crappy businesswoman," he continued raspily. "She's got bigtime money problems, and I'd been helping, but I shut off the cash flow when things turned nasty between us. We've got a prenup, and I told Cherisse that if she wants to walk away from the marriage, walk, but walk with empty pockets. She heard about the possible existence of a *Hunley* diary and approached me with a proposition. If there actually was a diary and she got hold of it, would I be interested in taking it off her hands for a price. I said I'd be very interested for the reasons I gave you on the golf course the other day. The diary could impact the way I develop the reality show, and it could open the door for a large and lucrative *Hunley*-related media platform."

That was consistent with what Cherisse had told me when we were walking to White Point Gardens. She'd sent the anonymous letter to Moze Cheddar offering to buy the *Hunley* diary because she thought she could re-sell it to Arnie for enough to take care of her financial woes.

"You could have decided to skip the middle woman and go right to the source for the diary," I said.

"I did decide that," Arnie said. "Cherisse wouldn't tell me the source, so I had Gino and Mikey follow her around. I realized she was spending a lot of time at your father's church, knew your dad had a fixation on the *Hunley*, and guessed that was where Cherisse heard about the diary. I went to see your dad and tried to pump him for information, but that got me nowhere."

"Then how did you learn about Moze Cheddar?"

He grinned. "Plan B. Used a listening device that picked up Cherisse mentioning Cheddar to DuBois."

"Possibly," I said. "Or possibly you dialed up the pressure on my dad. Maybe you sent Gino and Mikey to have a chat with him, and he gave up Cheddar's name, and then he died."

"Hey, Cap, come on now!" Gino said and Mikey began to rise.

Arnie put up his palm in a stop gesture. "I'll give you that one, Russ and call it even for the battering you took from Gino and Mikey at White Point Gardens." His voice turned to ice. "But don't say anything like that to me again ever. I admired the hell out of your dad. Besides, Gino, Mikey and I were in New York when your dad was killed."

"Where was Cherisse?"

"In Europe."

At an international civil rights conference. I remembered her telling me that was the reason she hadn't been able to attend Dad's funeral.

Arnie popped to his feet. "I can't sit around like this all night. Let's shake, rattle and roll." He tap-danced barefoot on home plate as he polished off the bourbon. Then he took three quick steps, sprang in the air and released the bottle as if he were shooting a basketball. The bottle banged off the fence and dropped into a green trash barrel. "Yes!" he said. "Yes!"

He ripped off the remnants of his shirt, tossed it toward Mikey and sprinted down the first base line. He rounded the bag with perfect technique and continued toward second, shouting, "Inside the park round tripper, sports fans! Inside the park!" Approaching third base he hollered, "Coach is waving me in! Oh yeah, he's waving me in!" Sprinting toward home, arms and legs pumping and a maniacal gleam in his eye, he lurched suddenly and belly flopped in the dirt with his hands extended. His fingertips came to a rest a foot short of home plate. A head-first slide miscalculated I thought. Then I saw the blood on his back.

Chapter Forty-One

Mikey sprang up clawing the gun from his shoulder holster. "Not on my watch!" he screamed. "No goddamn way!"

"Get down, Mikey!" Gino yelled. "Get down!"

Mikey ignored him, crouched, fired two rounds at no particular target and started toward Arnie's body. He didn't make it. A bullet slammed into his chest, and he grunted, staggered, dropped his gun and fell.

Gino said "Shit!" and took a step toward Mikey. I wrapped my arms around Gino's chest and wrestled him to the ground. It wasn't much more difficult than ripping a building off its foundation. A bullet passed with a loud crack, and we rolled close to the backstop out of the line of fire. Gary was already there lying flat. "Shooter's behind my truck," he said.

"See who it is?" I asked.

"Nope. Only thing showing was a rifle barrel."

We waited and listened to silence. Eventually I put Gary's navy blue cap on the head of the softball bat and extended the bat. Nothing. We poked our heads up and glimpsed a figure entering the woods. "I'm going after him," I said to Gary. "Call 911, then see if there's anything you can do for Arnie and Mikey."

"A road beyond those trees intersects this road we're on just before Route 41," Gary said. "Rifleman probably parked over there. Take my truck, see if you can cut the son-of-a-bitch off." He tossed me the truck keys.

I stood and looked at Gino. "This is going to bring a lot of cops. You can ride with me."

He shook his head. "Thanks, Cap, but I ain't got no current

warrants. Even if I did I'd have to stay. Boss'll want to know the situation with Mr. St. John, and Mikey's my cousin."

I ran for Gary's red pickup, and Gary and Gino went to aid the fallen. Arnie showed signs of life, but Mikey wasn't moving.

I squealed the truck out of the ballpark lot and rattled down the potholed lane, jouncing in the seat. A couple of hundred yards ahead a black motorcycle appeared from the intersecting road and veered right onto Route 41. I followed. The helmeted biker was bent forward and too far ahead for me to identify. A dark substance smeared on the license plate made it unreadable. At Route 17 the cycle roared through a yellow light and went left. The light was red when I arrived. I couldn't run it because of thick traffic on 17, so I waited.

When the light changed I crossed Route 17's southbound lanes and accelerated north. I didn't like my chances, though. The biker had a lengthy lead, and there were plenty of places where he—or she—could have exited 17. Eventually I gave up the chase and U-turned south. I'd go back to the ballpark, see what condition Arnie and Mikey were in and talk to the police.

If I were really unlucky, Ellen Talley would be at the scene. It had only been a few hours since she'd stomped out of my house after questioning me about Ronnie's shooting. She'd be thrilled to see me associated with more gunplay, and even more thrilled that I'd chased and lost the motorcyclist instead of notifying the police. Possibly she'd nominate me for a citizen's award. Or slice off my testicles with a rusty hacksaw. I seemed to remember her threatening disembowelment during one of our previous verbal skirmishes.

My cell phone rang. Ellen, or possibly Gary. It was neither. "Mr. Berard?"

It took me a moment to adjust my frame of reference. "Moze?"

"Yessir. Got a funny kind of a situation I don't hardly understand. Thought you might lend a helping hand."

"I've got myself a situation too," I told him. "What's yours?"

"Had me a little chat with that Ronnie Hodge fella last night—"

"I heard about your chat," I said. "Somebody shot Ronnie this afternoon."

I heard Moze inhale, briefly hold the breath and expel it. "I'm real sorry to hear that news," he said. "I don't pretend to care nothing about the boy, but it always saddens me when there's shooting."

"It's been a day for shooting. Arnie St. John and one of his bodyguards were cut down a short time ago."

There was a pause, then: "Maybe we got us a bad connection, but your voice sounds full of suspicion, Mr. Berard. You think I did these shootings?"

"The possibility crossed my mind. You came down here for payback against Arnie because you thought he tried to steal your diary."

"Things has changed some," Moze said. "Ain't so sure I got a bone to pick with Arnold St. John after all. Ronnie Hodge told me it wasn't St. John sent them boys to my cabin after the diary, it was the Cherisse Dane woman."

Which was what Arnie had told me at the ball field.

"Been taking an interest in the Dane woman's movements," Moze continued. "Followed her to a place and had in mind that I'd announce myself at the door, have a heart-to-heart. But just now a fella arrived on a motorcycle and went inside. Complicates matters a little."

That was an understatement. I wondered what the chances were that the motorcyclist at Cherisse's was someone different than the person I'd chased. "Where are you exactly?" I asked.

"Off a road name of Boston Grill. You know its whereabouts?"

"I do. Is Cherisse at a cottage in the grassy marshland at the end of the road?"

Another pause before Moze said, "Yes sir, she is."

"Where will I find you?"

"Down near where the road quits there's pavement runs into the woods. That'll lead you to a garage could fall apart in a harsh wind. I'll be there. What's your vehicle?"

"Red pickup truck."

"Truck belongs to the big blond fella?"

"Yes."

"Okay then, I'll be watching for you."

I wondered if he'd be watching with a rifle. There was a possibility Moze had shot Arnie and Mikey, guessed I was the one chasing when he escaped on the motorcycle and decided to reel me in with the story about Cherisse and this anonymous motorcyclist and remove me from the equation.

I turned off Route 17 onto Porchers Bluff at the Super Walmart shopping center, took a right on Rifle Range and then a left on Boston Grill. It had been a lot of years since I was here. A lot of years since Cherisse and I experimented with sex in her family's getaway cottage. At least I was experimenting. Cherisse had already earned several merit badges.

Near the bottom of Boston Grill I entered the woods where Moze had instructed. He was standing by the rickety garage wearing camouflage rain gear, a waterproof rifle carrier looped over his shoulder. I wasn't quite as well prepared. There was a yellow rain slicker behind the driver's seat of Gary's truck. I put it on, tied the hood and transferred my .38 Special from the belt holster to a pocket of the slicker.

"Appreciate you coming," Moze said.

"Why did you invite me?"

"Need your brain. I don't have me the damnedest idea what's going on. These people all act like they got screws loose and darkness in their souls. I'm hoping you can make sense of it."

"I chased the person who shot Arnie St. John," I said. "I didn't see him clearly, and I lost him on Route 17, but he was riding a motorcycle."

Moze tapped a knuckle against his chin. "Fella just arrived here to see the Dane woman you figure?"

"It's possible."

"Think we oughta see what's going on in that cottage?"

"I think we should," I told him. "Lead the way."

We paused at the edge of the woods. A Jaguar convertible was parked in front of the cottage. "Where's the motorcycle?" I asked Moze.

"Fella took it around the rear."

"There's an overhang in back," I said "He probably parked under it to keep the bike dry."

Moze twisted his head and stared at me. His eyes were cold

gray pebbles. "Sounds like you been here before, Mr. Berard."

"I have, but not for a very long time."

"Cottage belong to the Dane woman?"

"It was her family's 'way back when."

"Something between you and the Dane woman?"

"There used to be."

"Now?" he asked.

"I don't know."

He rubbed a forefinger across the tip of his nose. "I'm wondering about your loyalties, whether I can trust you."

I met his stare. "You can trust me to do the right thing."

"Right thing ain't always crystal clear though, is it? Men like us been to battle learn that real fast. Guess you and me'll learn a fact or two more about each other before the night's done." He adjusted his rifle carrier and stepped out of the woods.

We moved toward the cottage, staying out of sight of the front windows, where light shone behind drawn curtains. Rain splattered our parkas, and sopping knee-high marsh grass prickled my bare legs. I struggled to recall the cottage layout. Front door opened into the living room. Hallway off the living room led to three bedrooms and two baths. Kitchen, dining area and utility room in the rear through the living room. Screened porch on the back. I'd lost my virginity to Cherisse on the porch. She'd lost hers much earlier to a Sullivan's Island lifeguard.

Moze and I halted at the rear corner of the cottage. A black motorcycle sat under the overhang extending from the screened porch. "Bike you was chasing?" Moze asked.

"Looks like it," I said.

"Figure the biker shot St. John for the Dane woman?"

"Who knows?" I said. "Maybe the biker shot Arnie and is here to kill Cherisse."

"Got an idea in mind for finding out what's what?" Moze asked.

"I do. I'm going inside. You're going to stay out here and call the police."

Moze squinted at the marsh running flat to Hamlin Sound. Gray-green chop sloshed in the wind and rain. Off to the right the Isle of Palms Connector was a vague curve in the mist. "Don't know as I care for that idea," he told me.

"If the person inside is the one who shot Arnie, there's bound to be more shooting if we both barge in," I said. "If only one of us is going in, I ought to do it, because the person inside probably knows me and is less likely to start firing than if he or she sees you."

Moze pursed his lips. "Makes sense the way you explain it. But I got a suspicious nature, Mr. Berard. Anything you do smells funny, I'll take appropriate measures." He hesitated, then said, "Another thing you oughta know, the Dane woman's my cousin-in-law."

I stared at him open-mouthed. "What?"

"Don't expect there's time to explain it right now," he said. "Just figured it was information worth telling so you wouldn't think you was the only one with a personal stake in what happens here. Somebody particular with the police you want me to call?"

I gave him Ellen Talley's name and number.

Chapter Forty-Two

***T*he unlighted** rear of the house seemed like the best entry point. I flicked up the hook on the screen porch door with a credit card, then used the card to click back the loose deadbolt on the kitchen door. From the kitchen I heard two voices arguing on the other side of swinging doors leading to the family room. I recognized both voices: Cherisse and Durrell Pritchard. I dug my .38 out of a rain slicker pocket, stepped to the doors and listened.

"Shooting Arnie was crazy!" Cherisse said shrilly.

"You wanted him gone," Pritchard answered.

"I wanted a divorce!"

"Shooting's quicker," Pritchard said. "Besides, a shitbird like St. John don't deserve to live. Went north and took on Yankee ways, then came home to make a laughingstock of eight boys who died fighting the unjust hand of federal government. I can't understand why you married him in the first place. Whoring for money I suppose."

The sound of a slap was followed by Cherisse's voice: "Don't you ever talk to me like that!"—followed by a feminine groan.

"You're done giving me orders like I'm the nigger," Pritchard said. "The horses is running wild, and it's time for me to take the reins. St. John knew too much. Ronnie and DuBois too. I didn't get good shots at them the other night at Little Minnie's, but I put Ronnie down today, and I'll catch up with DuBois in due time."

"No, not DuBois. Please, Durrell—"

"Doesn't matter he's your son. He's a danger to us. And it's us against all others now."

Feet scraping on the floor, a thump, glass shattering. "Nigger whore!" Pritchard swore. "You wanna play rough and tumble, I'm your boy."

A feminine gurgle …

I pushed through the doors. Pritchard was behind Cherisse, elbow locked around her throat as he twisted her arm up her back. He saw me, released Cherisse's arm, and produced a pistol with his now free hand. "Welcome to the party, bo," he said, holding the gun barrel beneath Cherisse's chin. "No need for that firearm though. Just drop it on the rug."

They were several yards away, Cherisse between Pritchard and me. She twisted her neck against his elbow lock, eyes pinched with fear. Pritchard's eyes blazed with testosterone.

"I'll hang onto the gun," I said. "It might go off if I drop it. The safety's a little touchy."

"You don't drop it, I'll shoot her."

"Then I'll shoot you."

We stood in limbo. Pritchard's back was to a pink faux marble mantel with tall candlesticks. Fragments of a clear glass vase littered the floor at his feet, probably what I'd heard crash during the struggle between Pritchard and Cherisse. Rain tapped drearily on the closed chimney flue, and table lamps beneath the front windows glowed with ironic warmth.

Cherisse scratched at Pritchard's arm until he loosened his hold. Her hair drooped limply, her makeup was smeared, and one of her high-heeled sandals had come off her foot. "He's insane, Russ!" she gasped. "I hired him to do some work for me, but he's totally out of control! Forcing me to cover up for him!"

"How can he force you?" I asked.

"He … he knows things about me," she said.

"What things?"

Pritchard laughed, a grating, odious noise. "Go ahead and tell him what I know. Tell him how you sold out those nigger leaders in Atlanta to that FBI dickhead, Alcott, in exchange for him not pressing drug charges against you. How Alcott kept records, and when he found out you was living here he decided to shake you down. How you had me kill him to get his records after DuBois, Ronnie and Jason Grimes screwed up the payoff."

"No!" Cherisse shrieked. "I don't care what you do to me! I

can't take these lies anymore!" She clawed at Pritchard's gun hand.

"Bitch!" Pritchard said and shoved her. Cherisse lurched forward, arms spread. I had no shot at Pritchard around her body. She crashed against my chest, the momentum driving me backward. Our legs tangled, and we fell with Cherisse on top. I rolled free, expecting gunfire from Pritchard, but he was gone.

The front door squeaked open, and Moze Cheddar darted in low and fast, two-handed grip on his automatic pistol, eyes sweeping the room.

Pritchard's bike roared to life out back, sputtered and died. "I want him," I said. "Stay with your cousin-in-law." Cherisse lay on the floor in a fetal position, sobbing.

The bike roared again, quit again. "That Captain Talley woman's on her way," Moze told me. "Don't seem to like you much, though. Made threats as to what she'll do to your person if you're not here when she arrives."

"Tell her I'll be back or dead," I said. "She ought to be happy either way."

I shouldered through the swinging doors into the kitchen. The door to the screened porch stood open. Pritchard's engine gurgled a third time but didn't catch. I grabbed two coffee mugs off the counter, tossed one out on the porch, heard it bang against a metal-framed chair and ducked behind the refrigerator. Pritchard's gun erupted, and bullets ripped through the porch screens and slammed into the door frame. I waited a minute, crawled near the doorway and flipped the second mug out to the porch. It shattered on the concrete slab, but there was no answering gunfire.

I crawled onto the porch, raised to my knees, saw the bike but not Pritchard. I went out the screen door in a crouch, .38 in my hand and scanned the area. The rain and lowering curtain of nightfall shrouded the marsh in an opaque haze. No sign of Pritchard. I blinked, refocused, scanned again. Picked him up this time. A lean shape running through the reeds toward a dock where a small power boat was tied and bobbing in Hamlin Sound. I sprinted in pursuit and yelled, "Pritchard!"

He looked back, fired a pair of wild shots over his shoulder and continued toward the boat. I didn't want to shoot him; there were unanswered questions. And even if I'd wanted to shoot, hitting him in low visibility at that distance with both of us moving would be about as likely as impaling a gnat with a hurled spear. But I needed to reach Pritchard quickly. If the outboard started manually, he wouldn't need a key to disappear in the dark.

I lengthened my stride, stepped in a hole and tripped. I landed hard on my side, and the impact knocked the .38 from my hand. On my knees I combed the tall grass. No luck, and Pritchard was clattering down the dock. I swore, gave up on the gun, snatched a rock and ran. Rocks were good. David had used a rock and slingshot to defeat Goliath. Of course, Goliath hadn't been equipped with an automatic pistol.

I'd twisted my ankle stepping in the hole, and my run was more of a grimacing stagger. I hobbled along the dock as the outboard engine varoomed. Pritchard saw me and jerked the pistol from his belt holster. I hurled the rock at him. He sidestepped to avoid the rock, stumbled and smacked against the steering wheel. The pistol sailed out of his hand and splashed in the water. Now we were even.

I hopped into the boat as it motored away from the dock and landed on my injured foot. Wincing at the pain I instinctively grabbed for my ankle. Which allowed Pritchard to slip behind me, loop a piece of rope around my throat and jerk the loop tight. I gurgled, resisted the impulse to fight the rope and slammed my elbow into Pritchard's ribs. He grunted but kept his grip. I stabbed my index fingers back past my ears. One connected, possibly with an eye, and he yelped. I hammered his ribs again, and the loop loosened slightly. I stomped on his instep, got my hands around the rope and propelled us sideways. We crashed into the rail and went over. As we hit the water I yanked the rope forward and ducked my head away from it.

Pritchard and I surfaced a few yards apart, treading water and fighting to maintain balance against the swift current. Pritchard's hand darted below the surface and reappeared with a hunting knife drawn from a sheath on his belt. You had to give him high marks for preparation. I wondered if his pockets were full of hand grenades. His lips peeled back from his teeth in a ghoulish grin.

"Final showdown, bo."

He pedaled toward me and jabbed with the knife. I leaned away, he jabbed again, and I grabbed his wrist. He yanked his arm back, and my fingers slipped off his wet skin. I tipped forward, and Pritchard raised his knife hand and chopped. I submerged, but the blade followed, slicing my shoulder. I knew there'd be another strike. I rolled on my back underwater and snap-kicked both legs against his chest, pushing him away.

I emerged and Pritchard attacked with the knife held high. I grasped his forearm and smashed his nose with the palm of my free hand. That was my wounded arm, and I groaned at the contact. Blood flowed from his nose, and he gritted his teeth and punched at my face. I blocked the punch with my elbow and squeezed his knife arm with both hands. I wanted to force him to drop the knife, but it was near impossible to get leverage treading water.

We grappled silently, pummeled by the current. Eventually I got Pritchard's arms extended above his head and attempted to topple him sideways. But a jolt of pain coursed through my damaged shoulder, weakening my grip. Pritchard grunted and tried to chop the knife down toward my chest. I twisted his wrists, turning the knife inward as it descended, and the blade embedded in his neck.

Pritchard's mouth opened wide, his eyes rolled back in his head, and he jerked the blade part way out. Blood spurted from the wound, and he pushed the blade back in, yelping. Bad, I thought, very bad.

Pritchard knew, too. He blinked and licked his lips. "Guess this is where we part company, bo."

"We'll get you into shore and patch that up," I said.

"Don't think so." He leaned close, and I could smell death. "Maybe you think you laughed the last laugh, but here's the punchline. I killed your daddy."

He braced his palms against my chest and shoved us apart. Then he blew me a kiss and sank. I went under after him, grabbed at his leg and clung to his jeans with one hand. But he kicked me in the face, breaking my tenuous hold and floated away in the dark.

I surfaced, wheezing and clutching my wounded shoulder. Rain splattered on my head and pattered in the water. The lingering odor of gas fumes from the departed outboard blended with residual sour odors from the departed Pritchard. Exhaustion filmed my eyes, and fog hung like thin black cotton. I'd drifted far out in the Sound, and lights from Cherisse's cottage winked faintly. Shore seemed a hundred miles away. Maybe I'd follow Pritchard's lead and float off and leave the rest to chance.

Then I heard an engine, and a yellow beam sliced through the inky night and captured me like a theater spotlight. The engine slowed to a purr, and the boat sidled close. Standing at the rail, Ellen Talley peered down at me.

Chapter Forty-Three

A virginal sun lit the morning sky with rose-tinted brilliance, promising a fresh start and forgiveness of yesterday's sins and errors. But the promise didn't extend to Durrell Pritchard or Mikey the Mafioso, who wouldn't awaken in this world today. Arnie St. John and Ronnie Hodge had been more fortunate. They'd drawn long straws from fate or chance or God and survived Pritchard's bullets.

I had survived Pritchard's knifing, and now I sat on my deck trying to decide which of the actions I'd taken yesterday were sins and which were errors. From around the back of the house came a person who most likely intended to provide clarification.

Ellen Talley wore a gray suit and white blouse, and she carried a take-out coffee cup and a brown leather briefcase. "You didn't answer the front bell," she said, pausing at the bottom of the deck steps.

"I didn't hear it."

"Yes, you did." She came up the steps and took a chair across from me. Her red-rimmed eyes suggested that any sleep she'd managed was even less than mine. But she was required to investigate Pritchard's life and death. I'd only had to kill him.

She reached in her briefcase, produced a sealed plastic bag containing a pistol and laid the bag on a black wrought iron table beside her chair. "Crime scene investigators found it in the marsh grass where you lost it chasing Pritchard."

I nodded.

"You're welcome," she said. "How's your shoulder?"

"Fine."

"You should have stayed in the hospital."

"You mentioned that last night … among other things."

Ellen chewed on her lip and scraped a fingernail along the plastic top of her coffee container. "I was a little agitated."

"No kidding? I didn't notice."

"For Christ sake, Russ, you were a half step ahead of a trail of bodies all afternoon and night. Of course I was upset. When you checked out of the hospital against the ER doctor's advice, I could have hauled you over to the police department and questioned you until the cows came home and went back out again."

"I gave you a written statement."

She harrumphed.

A breeze blew cool against my cheek, and the sun soothed my throbbing shoulder. A redbird ate from one of the feeders I'd filled this morning with seed my mother had stored in the garage. I sipped tea and stared at Kam Lim's memorial stone in the yard. Lim would want me to calm myself and find peace now that all was done. I should draw deep breaths and allow the purified air to push tension out through my fingers and toes. But my soul was black, and I felt as if an untreatable cancer were ravaging my heart. I'd killed the man who'd murdered my father, and all that had gotten me was another bloody scar on my conscience. No sign of my father returning, or my mother either.

I finished the tea, stood and hurled the cup against the side fence. It shattered, and shards fell into moss that had dropped from oak trees. I sat back down.

"Feel better?" Ellen asked.

"Yes," I said.

"Feel well enough to tell me about Moze Cheddar?"

"What makes you think I know anything about him?"

Ellen pealed the plastic lid from her coffee container and gazed into the milky brown depths, as if explanations for my various character defects and personality disorders would swirl to the surface. "I ran Cheddar's name through law enforcement databases, and the skimpy bio I got back adds up to a quasi-military spook whose background is buried under deep security. He told me he's retired and down here fishing and hunting. He told me he happened to be traipsing around the marsh near Cherisse's, heard commotion at the cottage, went to check it out, ran into you, and you asked him to call me while you chased Pritchard. What would you like to tell me?"

I watched a tiny gecko skitter across the cedar shingles and plaster itself against the glass doors to the sun room. I knew I should have a smooth answer to Ellen's question, a clever lie or obfuscation. But the pain pills fogged my mind, and my thoughts broke up and shot off disconnectedly, as if my brain were a computer hard drive in desperate need of defragmentation. Or maybe I was just depleted of lies and obfuscations.

"Moze has a family diary about the *Hunley*," I said. "He thought Arnie St. John was trying to steal it, and he came down here to find out. He contacted me because he'd told my dad about the diary and thought that might have been the reason Dad was killed. In the process of poking around, Moze got the idea Cherisse might be involved, so he started paying attention to her as well as to Arnie. Yesterday afternoon Moze followed Cherisse to her cottage planning to have a chat with her, but a motorcyclist showed up, and Moze called me thinking he might need help. His call came a couple of minutes after I lost the motorcyclist I chased from the ball field where Arnie and Mikey were shot. When I arrived at Cherisse's and saw the motorcycle, I was pretty sure it was the one I'd been chasing. I told Moze to stay outside and phone you while I went in. You know the rest."

Ellen blistered me with her glare. "Like hell I do. There are enough details missing from that yarn to fill in Charleston Harbor."

She was right, of course. One detail I'd omitted was Moze's startling statement just before I'd entered the cottage that Cherisse was his cousin-in-law. I hadn't seen either Moze or Cherisse after I'd been pulled from the water and taken to the hospital, and I had no idea whether their relationship, whatevever it was exactly, had played a role in recent events. But I wanted to find out for myself before I broadcast Moze's revelation.

"That's the condensed version," I said. "I'm too tired to tell the entire story."

"Well when you feel better, you're going to provide the unexpurgated version and clear up all the inconsistencies and omissions. For instance, in your written statement last night you left out the part about being at the cottage because of a call from Cheddar. You implied that you'd followed Pritchard to the cottage from the ball field after he shot Arnie and Mikey."

"I didn't see anything to be gained by pulling Moze in."

Ellen smoothed her skirt, studied the lettering on the gas grill and pursed her lips. "I'm going to do my level best to remain calm while I tell you this," she said. "You don't have the right to decide who's going to be pulled into criminal investigations and who isn't. Your responsibility is to pass along what you know and let law enforcement decide what to do with the information. With your background as a police detective, I can't believe it's even necessary to have this conversation, yet I feel like we have it every five minutes."

I could tell her that my background was the reason for my behavior. The workings of the criminal justice system reminded me of the old football joke about the defensive lineman who, when asked how he knew which offensive player to tackle, said he grabbed everybody in the backfield and discarded them one by one until he found the person with the ball. Similarly, the CJ system tended to suck in everybody who might have the remotest connection to the crime of concern and spit people back out until somebody was found who could be charged. Along the way, folks were needlessly traumatized and their lives sent spinning in a downward spiral as a result of pointless entanglement in criminal proceedings. I'd spent a lot of years as an agent of the system pointlessly entangling and inflicting trauma, but no more. From now on I intended to err on the side of keeping people out of the system, and if that resulted in my being misleading and evasive with law enforcement, I'd roll the dice on the consequences.

I could tell Ellen all that, but then she'd lose her calm, excoriate me and go away mad again. That was a tired routine. Better to shift the topic of conversation.

"Has Pritchard's body turned up?" I asked.

"Nope," she said. "How certain are you that he died in the water after he floated away?"

"If the knife perforated his carotid artery, it's hard to see how he could have survived."

"And he didn't say why he killed your father?"

"No."

"Could it have been because of this *Hunley* diary?"

"I can't figure why Pritchard would have been interested in the diary," I said. "And anyway, Dad didn't have the diary, didn't even have pages from it. I think Pritchard was a far right nutcase, probably a member of Jubal Jeff Longstreet's Guardians of the Confederate Truth. When Pritchard and I had that encounter in the Griddle Grill parking lot, he used a lot of slurs to describe my father, referred to him as the preacher man who loved queers, niggers and spics."

"So you think it was a hate crime?"

"Could have been," I said.

"I don't know," Ellen said. "That doesn't feel right; it's too simple and convenient."

I couldn't argue with her; it didn't feel right to me either. I drew a long breath and smelled putrid water in a statuary bird bath and wet rubber from a porch mat drenched by last night's rain. I saw a squirrel scamper along the top of the wood pile my father had neatly layered near the back fence. Beyond the fence I saw a towheaded child kick a beachball across the drainage ditch onto the golf course. There were other things I didn't see.

"What are Arnie and Cherisse saying?" I asked.

"Next to nothing," Ellen said. "They both have million-dollar-an-hour lawyers who are advising them that silence is golden. In Cherisse's case that's especially wise counsel; she has a bunch of problems. According to your statement, she sent DuBois, Ronnie Hodge and Jason Grimes to Etiwan Pointe to make a blackmail payoff to Leonard Alcott. That didn't work out and Grimes died, so Cherisse sent Pritchard to kill Alcott and take the blackmail material."

"My statement said that's what Pritchard alleged, but Cherisse denied it."

"Uh-huh," Ellen said with no more interest in my clarification than if I'd told her potato should be pronounced potahto.

"Cherisse hasn't told you anything at all?"

"She admits Alcott was blackmailing her," Ellen said. "When Alcott was an FBI agent in Atlanta, he wanted to take down the leaders of the civil rights organization Cherisse worked for. He got Cherisse cold on drug charges and coerced her into secretly providing evidence about mail bombs and poisoned letters that Cherisse's bosses were planning to send to white supremacists. When Alcott retired here and Cherisse came back, he saw an opportunity to supplement his pension. Cherisse paid him because she was afraid he'd go public and destroy her reputation and her future."

"Have you charged her with anything?"

"Not yet," Ellen said. "Ronnie Hodge is playing dumb about what happened at Etiwan, Arnie is stonewalling us on all topics, we can't locate DuBois, and of course, Pritchard is dead. One thing we think we do know is that Leonard Alcott killed Jason Grimes at Etiwan. We found the murder weapon in Alcott's motel room, a gun registered to him."

"Maybe you should consider the possibility that Cherisse isn't guilty of anything," I said.

Ellen gave me a withering look. "Right, and maybe I should also consider the possibility that Elvis is alive and well and working behind the bar at Red's Ice House."

She rose and stared down at me. "Here's something for you to consider. People connected to Cherisse seem to have unusually high mortality rates."

Chapter Forty-Four

A woman *with a veiled face lay down beside me in the dark, exuding a strawberry scent. She spoke in a throaty purr, telling a tale of perfidy, but using words my brain could not assimilate. Characters in her tale sounded familiar, though their names eluded me. A second veiled woman entered and offered pills for my pain. I swallowed the pills, and the strawberry scent putrefied to the odor of rotting fruit.*

I broke from my dream, stumbled to the bathroom and vomited. I was getting comfortable on the bathroom rug, thinking I'd make it my base of operations for the remainder of the day, when I heard footsteps. I hoped it wasn't someone with a gun, knife, or softball bat.

"Holy shit, Q!" Gary Nagle said, appearing in the doorway. "Are you okay?"

"In mint condition," I told him.

"Yeah, it looks like it. Guess I picked a hell of a time to bring Lina by to meet you."

"It's a swell time. Invite her back here."

"Don't think so. You make a crappy enough first impression as it is. Curled on the floor next to the toilet won't help." He extended a hand and pulled me up.

Lina Pinheiro was in the kitchen. She wore red nylon shorts and a James Island road race tee-shirt that did nice things for her breasts.

"Lina, meet Russell Quentin Berard," Gary announced.

"Hello, Russell Quentin," she said. "We brought lunch." She waggled an Arby's sack.

"Q just tossed his cookies," Gary told her. "He never could handle meds."

"I'll make toast," I said. "You two go ahead."

Lina opened the sack and removed roast beef sandwiches and curly fries. Gary took a bottle of ketchup and two cans of Dr. Pepper from the refrigerator. I put bread in the toaster oven and drank a glass of hot tap water.

"Pran knows you got stabbed," Gary said.

"Who's Pran?" Lina asked.

"Pran Chea," Gary said. "Uncle of Kam Lim, Q's missing wife."

"Dead wife," I said.

"Usually you call Lim missing, now you want to call her dead. So you're in a shitty mood and acting like a prick. But since you killed a guy and nearly got killed yourself, we'll let it go."

"How does Pran know I was knifed?"

Gary bit off a chunk of sandwich, masticated slowly and regarded me amiably. "He reads the *Post and Courier* online. He saw the article about you and called me. You oughta phone him, let him hear first hand that you're all right."

"Maybe later when I'm feeling better."

"Why not do it now?"

"I said later."

"What's a different way to tell Q he's acting like a prick, Lina?" Gary asked.

Lina narrowed her smoky eyes in thought and tapped a chubby index finger against her chin. "You could say he's failing to heed your sagacious advice and trying to pass off contumelious remarks as wry humor."

I stared at her, and she smiled. "Undergrad degree from Muhlenberg, grad school at NYU. And you thought I was just a night club bimbo."

"In my defense, you are with Gary," I said.

She laughed.

"Asshole," Gary muttered.

I spread blueberry jam on my toast and took a can of Coke from the refrigerator.

"We stopped off at Cherisse's before we came here," Gary said.

"A little band business."

I looked out the window at a sky shimmering like polished chrome. Breeze ruffled the gum tree above the deck, and a leaf fluttered free and settled on the chair Ellen Talley had occupied earlier. "You think I can get into a fantasy football league?" I said. "Or is it too late for this season?"

"Cherry wants to see you," Gary said. "She and Arnie are breaking up. She says it's just a matter of who files the divorce papers first. She told me to let you know that."

"Arnie took a bullet last night. Maybe divorce plans should wait awhile."

"He's okay, checked himself out of the hospital this morning. Didn't go home though, went to a hotel. I think he and Cherisse are honest-to-God done. You've got clear sailing, and Cherisse will be waiting at the dock."

Near the base of an oak tree, fallen acorns lay in patches of dirt ringed by thin grass that looked like fringes of side hair. "Is somebody paying you a commission based on the number of times I see Cherisse, or based on the number of people killed or wounded as a result of my seeing her?" I asked.

"Damnit, Q—"

"Step away and give him room," Lina said. "It's not your business."

Gary glowered and rose. "Screw it," he said. "To hell with both of you. I'm trying to help a couple of old friends get back together, but what do I know? I'll wait in the car."

Lina watched him tromp down the hall, looked at me and shrugged. "His heart's in the right place."

"His brain's sort of in the right place too," I said. "Cherisse and I do have matters to resolve."

Chapter Forty-Five

Mid-afternoon I went out back and swept up ceramic fragments from the mug I'd hurled against the side fence during Ellen Talley's morning visit. Then I made a cup of green tea in another mug and sat with it in a lawn chair beside Lim's monument stone. My neighbors' child pedaled a toy car around their pool perimeter, wheels clack-clacketing against the concrete. The air was as still as a hurricane's eye, sun-broiled and enfeebling, and steam rising from my honey-sweetened tea smelled like sugar candy.

I watched a white SUV roll along the fourteenth fairway and halt. Arnie St. John stepped down from the front passenger door. He wore blue denim shorts, a maroon tee-shirt, wraparound sunglasses and a tan visor. A white bandage was visible above the neckline of the tee-shirt. Gino appeared at the rear of the SUV, opened the hatch and lifted out a bistro table. His biceps bulged like melons against the sleeves of his green-striped shirt, and khaki shorts exposed skinny bowlegs. Arnie pointed to a spot and Gino shuffled toward it. He deposited the table, returned to the SUV, dragged out a pole with a Cinzano umbrella and inserted the pole through the table's center hole. Next he brought three chairs. Two people, three chairs. I counted again and arrived at the same totals.

Arnie waved his straw hat in my direction. So I was chair number three, the guest at the fairway party. At least Arnie hadn't rapped golf balls off my roof by way of invitation this time. I gimped out the rear gate on the ankle I'd sprained chasing Durrell Pritchard last night and crossed over the drainage ditch on my neighbor's golf cart bridge. A frog spooked by my passage hopped from pine needles and splashed in the ditch water.

"Come on in and make yourself to home, Q," Arnie said. He was sitting at the table twirling his sunglasses and grinning, but the grin seemed mostly for show. His eyes were red-rimmed and dulled by pain, his skin sallow.

"Course closed this afternoon?" I asked.

"Just this hole."

"Leaving one out will be a problem for calculating handicaps won't it?"

"They mentioned that at the pro shop. I told them to let people play a hole of their choice twice. I'll be an absentee owner pretty soon, and they can return to business as usual."

"Taking a trip?" I asked.

He jerked his thumb at Gino, who was removing a gallon of low-fat chocolate milk and three chilled glasses from a cooler. "Have to jet up to New York and explain the current state of affairs to my business partners, Gino's bosses."

"What's the current state of affairs?"

"I'm putting the *Hunley* reality show on hold. You can tell your pal Cheddar that his diary's safe from me. I'm going to work out of my Manhattan office for awhile. I need to be away from here. Coming back home hasn't turned out the way I'd hoped. Bring it on, Gino."

Gino poured chocolate milk in the glasses, returned the carton to the cooler and sat down. "Sorry about Mikey," I told him.

He nodded. "Appreciate it, Cap. Lost a brother, two uncles and now three cousins doing this shit. Drills deep holes in you."

"Gino and I thank you for erasing Pritchard's number from the speed dial," Arnie said. "I'll remember that son-of-a-bitch every time my back throbs in cold weather."

"We'll all have ugly memories. I'll remember him slipping away from me in the current."

"Well I say death to the bad guys." Arnie lifted his glass, clinked it against Gino's, and swung his raised glass toward me. I sat with my arms crossed. Arnie frowned. "Is there a problem here, Russ?"

"Maybe we should clarify the definition of bad guys."

He cocked his head and looked perplexed. "You think I'm dirty? I'm one of the victims."

"You've been a lot of things in your life, Arnie, but victim isn't one of them. And I'm still trying to interpret some of the subtext."

He grinned. "Riddles and puzzles and enigmas. Life is a mystery indeed. But that's why I invited you out here, my man. To provide answers, or at least clues. You bring whipped cream?" he asked Gino. "Not that Cool Whip crap, the real thing."

"Got it," Gino said. "He opened the cooler, fished inside, produced an aerosol can of whipped cream and flipped it to Arnie.

Arnie shook the can, snapped off the plastic top and sprayed a curling ribbon of cream on his chocolate milk. He extended the can toward me, and I shook my head. He shrugged and drank from his glass. When he put the glass down, there was whipped cream on his chin. He wiped it off with a paper napkin.

"I had Mikey follow Cherisse from time to time," Arnie said. "She and Pritchard were meeting regularly at the cottage where you found them last night, so Mikey and Gino installed hidden recording equipment. The routine we picked up was usually the same. Cherisse gave Pritchard instructions about something she wanted him to do, or Pritchard reported back about something he'd done. Then Cherisse paid him, probably with money embezzled from her club, since she was nearly broke. A couple of times she screwed Pritchard, maybe because she didn't have any cash."

"Arnie—"

He held up a palm. "Hang with me, Q. This is more than bitter ravings of a cuckolded husband. There's something in it for you. Sip a little chocolate milk and lend me an ear."

I sighed and sipped, and Arnie continued.

"After the ex-FBI agent Alcott was murdered, Cherisse told Pritchard it was time to quit their business relationship," Arnie said. "With all the investigating going on by the police, you and Moze Cheddar, she was afraid they were going to get caught."

"Get caught doing what?"

Arnie curled his lips sardonically. "Just the usual sort of stuff: trying to grab Cheddar's *Hunley* diary, causing people to die."

"Causing what people to die?"

"I'll get to that," Arnie said. "Pritchard argued that they couldn't break things off because there were too many loose ends that needed to be tied. Cherisse said she wasn't asking for Pritchard's opinion, she was telling him they were done. Pritchard laughed and told her she better think again. He'd used his digital voice recorder to preserve a prior conversation of theirs about your father's death, and he was sure Cherisse wouldn't want the police to hear that."

I looked past Arnie and watched a caravan of four men in three golf carts zip along the cart path toward the fifteenth tee. They stared at us, undoubtedly wondering why the Club had shut down the fourteenth hole so three people could sit under an umbrella and laze away the afternoon. Beyond the cart path a gray-haired woman watered flowers in her back yard with a red garden hose. A tiny terrier beside the woman yapped at the motoring golfers. Sun slid off the edges of our protective umbrella and sketched black shadows in the sparkling green fairway. One of the shadows resembled Cherisse's profile. The air smelled of medicinal ointment from the bandage beneath Arnie's shirt.

"And?" I said.

"And Cherisse turned conciliatory fast when Pritchard mentioned the recording."

"And?" I repeated.

"And they didn't discuss the exact contents of the conversation, and I don't have Pritchard's recorder."

I gripped the arms of the chair and pushed to my feet. "Thanks for the chocolate milk, Arnie. Give me a call the next time you're in Charleston."

"Come on, Q, I'm not just talking to hear the sound of my voice. Sit your ass back down. There's more."

I hesitated, but there was no point pretending lack of interest. I sat my ass back down.

"The question is, what did Pritchard do with the voice recorder?" Arnie said.

"It might have been in his pocket last night when he drowned," I suggested.

"Might have been," Arnie agreed. "In which case all you can do is wait and see. Another possibility is that Pritchard hid the recorder in his apartment, in which case you can talk to your friend

Ellen Talley and see if the police have found it."

"Are we going to consider a limitless array of possibilities?" I asked. "Bus station lockers, safe deposit boxes, secret compartments, holes in the backyard. Because if we are, I'm going to need to take a bathroom break pretty soon."

Arnie chuckled, then winced, groaned and reached to his wounded back with his fingers.

"Come on, Mr. St. John, let me drive you to the hospital," Gino said.

"You're a good man, Gino, but shut the hell up about the hospital," Arnie told him. "Here's something we learned from following Pritchard that the police and Cherisse may not know yet. He spent time at the Shemside Apartments off Coleman Boulevard. At first we assumed it was a girlfriend's place, but not so. Pritchard's parents died a long time ago, and there was an old maid family friend who was like a second mother to him. Filomena Berducci. He called her Aunt Fil. The apartment off Coleman was hers."

"And you think Pritchard gave her the voice recorder to hold for him?"

"Not exactly. Aunt Fil passed away earlier this summer."

"You're making my brain hurt, Arnie."

He shook his head in a tsk-tsk gesture of rebuke. "Don't be so impatient. Take more interest in the richness and subtleties of the story. Show more professional appreciation for Gino and Mikey's investigative work. Am I right, Gino?"

Gino tugged on his ear with sausage-sized fingers and grunted.

I wondered how many pain pills Arnie had consumed and what beverage he'd washed them down with.

"Pritchard took over the lease on Aunt Fil's apartment after she passed," Arnie said. "I ask myself why, and the best answer I come up with is that he wanted a hideaway. A place where he could lay low if need be and a place where he could store various items of value. Items like the digital voice recorder with the conversation about your father's death. We bring Oreos?" he asked Gino.

Gino withdrew a sleeve of Oreos from the cooler and passed it to Arnie. Arnie used the scissors on a Swiss army knife to neatly snip open the sleeve. He tapped out an Oreo, deftly separated it and bit off a piece of the section with vanilla filling.

"So Gino and Mikey broke into Aunt Fil's apartment and took the voice recorder?" I said.

Arnie shook his head. "You're not following along closely enough. I told you I don't have the recorder. We got hold of a key to Aunt Fil's and made copies, but we haven't had a chance to go into the apartment."

"How did you get a key?"

He shrugged. "Money greases wheels. Don't get bogged down in details." He looked at Gino, who dug a postcard-sized white envelope out of his pants pocket and dropped it on the table with a clink. Arnie pushed the envelope toward me as if he were dealing the final card in a high stakes poker game.

I let the envelope lie. "What's the rest?"

"What rest?" Arnie said.

"I think there's more."

He licked Oreo chocolate off his fingers and knitted his brow in make-believe thought. "More … more ..? Okay, there is one little thing, hardly worth mentioning. When I leave you I'm going to stop by my soon-to-be ex-house, tell this same story to my soon-to-be ex-spouse and give her a little white envelope with a key too."

"What's your end game, Arnie?"

He grinned. "Bringing you two love birds back together. Reversing the clock to the high school days of yesteryear, when you and Cherisse had life by the tail. It's my parting gift."

The envelope sat before me like a passport to a dark continent best left unexplored. But my choice was foreordained. I took the envelope.

"One other thing, Q," Arnie said. "Remember what Coach used to tell us? When you hit against a flame thrower, you need to expect a fast ball and adjust if it's off-speed, because there's no time to adjust if you expect off-speed and the thrower brings heat?"

I nodded.

"Well, Cherisse has a vicious heater. You get distracted by her curves and she'll drill you between the eyes."

Chapter Forty-Six

I parked behind a Thai restaurant at one end of a shopping plaza on Coleman Boulevard. Spicy aromas wafting from the restaurant's exhaust vents tempted me to go inside, savor a plate of Pad Thai and forget about voice recorders. But I resisted temptation and followed a narrow sidewalk along a street leading to the Shemside Apartments. The sidewalk was bowed and cracked by oak roots and cigarette butts littered the gutter. A helmetless pony-tailed man sputtered past on a motor bike, prompting a Doberman tied in a front yard to bark and strain at its line. The key Arnie had given me jingled against pocket coins, and the .38 felt lumpy stuffed in my other pocket.

    The apartment building was three stories of chipped red brick and dingy white wood. The key opened the outer door and admitted me to a tiny foyer facing a staircase and elevator. Hallways ran down both sides, with two apartments on each hallway. Aunt Fil's apartment was rear right. I stared into the peephole for a moment, wondering if Arnie had set me up. Then I clicked the lock and stepped inside, drawing the .38. Durrell Pritchard didn't charge me, but traces of his cologne did, musky sweet remnants in the musty air. I walked through the apartment to be sure there weren't other visitors. It was a quick walk-through. Living room separated from a galley kitchen by a counter with two stools. One bedroom with a petite bath. Inexpensive but attractive furniture, full bookcase, flat-screen TV, old-fashioned record player above a shelf with jazz albums, seascape prints on the walls. No digital voice recorder in plain sight.

    I rummaged through drawers and cabinets, looked under cushions, checked kitchen canisters, searched beneath the bed and mattress, then turned my attention to the bedroom closet. Pritchard had kept clothes there: police uniform, blue blazer, jeans and khaki pants, button down shirts, windbreaker, shoes. But no digital voice recorder in clothes pockets or shoes.

That led to the bathroom. The recorder wasn't in the wall cabinet, wasn't in the bottom of the Kleenex box on the counter, wasn't submerged in the back of the toilet in a waterproof bag. It was in a sleeve sewn between the folds of a towel stored beneath the sink.

I wandered into the kitchen, the pocket-sized recorder cold and deadly in my hand, like a poisonous reptile gripped by the jaws to immobilize its bite. I found a small bottle of apple juice in the refrigerator and took it, figuring that I was already on the hook for illegal entry, and juice theft wouldn't add much to my sentence. I sat on a blue and white striped armchair in the living room, set the recorder on the glass-top coffee table and waited to see if it would talk to me of its own volition. It wouldn't. I leaned forward to press the play button with my index finger, but the finger recoiled.

Sunlight suffused the room with a soft, golden glow, and I sensed Durrell Pritchard's ghostly presence in the shadowy corners. I wondered about the fullness of his being, the good Durrell I hadn't known. What he'd been like with Aunt Fil for instance. Driving her to doctor's appointments, doing handy man work. Coming for Sunday dinner with flowers and a box of chocolates, the two of them reminiscing about happy moments with his deceased parents. This was a weakness of mine, wanting to personalize people I killed. Better to think of them as one-dimensional evil. Well, maybe not better, but easier.

Two little boy voices squeaked in the outer hallway, their basketball slap-slapping against the floor. The rear door to the building opened and slammed shut, and quiet returned. Quiet except for drip dripping of the kitchen faucet. I considered shutting off the valve beneath the sink, but I was afraid Pritchard would emerge from the shadows and reclaim the voice recorder if I moved. I twisted the top off the apple juice bottle, raised the bottle to my mouth and drank.

There wasn't any guarantee Cherisse would come. Arnie could have been playing mind games when he told me he was going to tip her off about the possible location of the recorder and give her a key. Arnie's brain seemed to be operating on a psychedelic frequency with internal logic not comprehensible by normal man. And Arnie's guess that the recorder contained information incriminating Cherisse in my father's murder was just a guess, based on a few words of conversation between Cherisse and Pritchard captured on tape by Gino and Mikey. Although the fact that Pritchard had gone to such lengths to hide the recorder did suggest that it held information incriminating somebody in something. The trouble was, I no longer felt an obsession to know. Or possibly I feared knowing. I ought to walk up the Ravenel Bridge, toss the recorder over the railing and walk back down the bridge into the rest of my life.

I was mulling options when footsteps in the hallway stopped outside the door. A key turned the lock, and the door swung open. Cherisse halted as if she'd bumped into an invisible shield. Her eyes widened, her mouth gaped, and her hands clenched in fists. I'd wondered if Arnie would tell her that he'd given me a key. I had my answer.

"Russ!" she said. "What? I wasn't … Why are you here?"

"The same reason you are."

Composure quickly supplanted surprise. Her arms relaxed, her mouth closed, and emotion evanesced, leaving her eyes hooded and inscrutable. "I don't know what you mean."

"That's not going to work," I told her. "This isn't a chance meeting in the grocery store, Cherry. Arnie gave both of us keys."

She thought it over. "Arnie gave you a key and told you what?"

"That Pritchard had a voice recorder with a conversation between the two of you about my father's murder, and that the recorder might be here. It was here, hidden in a bathroom towel. And now it's here." I pointed to the glass-top table.

She thought some more. Then she moved across the room, skirt brushing my knee as she passed, and perched on the sofa cushion nearest to my chair. When she leaned forward her lily of the valley perfume swirled around me like a soporific spray. "There's a context to this that's impossible to explain," she said. "Pritchard had done things to me … Please don't listen to the conversation, Russ. Let me take the recorder and dispose of it." Her voice was low and throaty, and her body radiated heat.

I was struck by how easy it would be to agree. But I recalled my father's admonition that distinguishing right from wrong often meant determining the easiest course of action, then doing the opposite. And the recorded conversation was about him. "I can't," I said. "I'm sorry."

Her hand darted for the recorder. I caught her wrist and jerked her arm, pulling us close. She parted her lips and kissed me on the mouth. The kiss sent shock waves down to my toes. She slumped back on the sofa, drew her knees up on the cushion and regarded me through luminescent eyes. I slowed my breathing, lifted the recorder and pressed the play button.

"I didn't tell you to kill Gavin Berard!" Cherisse's voice said shrilly.

A nasty laugh I recognized as Durrell Pritchard's. "You sent me to his office to find information about the Hunley diary, and that's how he got dead. You ain't skating away and leaving me on the thin ice."

"I didn't tell you to kill him," Cherisse repeated.

"You know what's caused all this misery, you helping that left-wing, jerk-off minister with planning of his queer rights event. Queers are disgusting perverts, they ain't got any rights; the Bible tells us so. God brought his wrath down on the Reverend Berard, and he's bringing it down on you for helping the reverend. God's even bringing some wrath down on me for helping you. But the Lord knows I'm a fine Christian man, and I've repented, and soon as a few things are cleaned up, I'll be back in the Lord's good graces."

"This has nothing to do with the gay rights event!"

"Bullshit it don't," Pritchard said. "If you hadn't been at the church working with the reverend, you wouldn't have overheard him say he'd found out there was a diary that explained the sinking of the Hunley. *If you hadn't overheard that, you wouldn't have got the idea of selling the diary to your craphead husband for his reality show. 'Course, first you had to be in possession of the diary, and you didn't have the faintest damn idea where it was. So you asked good ol' Durrell to break into the church and have a look-see through the reverend's files."*

"That's exactly right," Cherisse said. "I asked you to search for information in Gavin's office, that's all I asked you to do."

"Which is what I was doing when the reverend strolled through the door. He knew who I was, he would have turned me in, and I would have rolled over on you. You think you would have liked that better?"

"You should have worn a mask so you wouldn't be recognized," Cherisse said. "I thought you were a professional."

"A professional law enforcement officer, not a burglar. And I did everything just the way you told me. You wanted to be extra careful about protecting your goody-two-shoes reputation in case the break-in got investigated and people like you who spent time in the church was looked at. So I waited to do it until you was at your liberal civil rights conference in Europe. And I broke in at a time of night when you told me nobody would be around. I didn't have no reason to believe there was need for a mask."

"And I didn't have any way of knowing Gavin would return to the church to catch up on paperwork. If you'd found the Hunley sheet of paper with Moze Cheddar's name and address a few minutes earlier, you would have been gone when Gavin arrived. It was just bad luck the way things happened."

"Like hell," Pritchard said. "It was God punishing you and the reverend for your immoral queer event, and I got caught in your wake."

"You're despicable," Cherisse said. "I don't know why I hired you."

"'Cause I'll kill for you, and ain't nobody else will do that. For sure not DuBois and Ronnie. Using those wet-behind-the-ears boys has been nothing but dumb. They botched the payoff to Alcott, and I had to kill him for you. And they messed things up at Cheddar's cabin trying to get the diary. You'd sent me like I suggested, I would have brought back the diary."

"And you probably would have killed Cheddar."

"So?" Pritchard said. "You told me I'm gonna have to kill him anyway if he gets too close to realizing you're his problem, not St. John. That was another stupid-ass mistake you made, sending Cheddar that letter offering to buy the diary. All it did was bring him down here poking his nose into things."

"I had no choice. I need that diary. And if you think I'm so stupid, why did you agree to work for me?"

"Money's real good," Pritchard said. "Sex ain't bad either."

The recording ended with a post-script from Pritchard stating the date and time.

Cherisse and I sat thinking private thoughts that possibly converged around regret. The sun had wandered west, fading the room's golden glow to a sallow dinge, like a lie whose apparent truth has been bled out by too many fabricated recitations. Television noise blared suddenly through the wall connecting to the next apartment, then abated as an unseen hand adjusted the volume.

Cherisse closed her eyes and shook her head as if she were attempting to dislodge a malignant memory and alter the past. Her eyes were damp when she opened them. "I can't ... I don't know what to say, Russ. Your father was an incredible man, I cared about him deeply. The last thing I wanted was for him to be killed. It wasn't my fault."

"You'll need a good attorney," I said. "The prosecutor will argue that if you hadn't sent Pritchard to break into to the church and steal from Dad's files, Dad wouldn't have been killed."

She chewed on her lower lip and crossed her legs, hiking the skirt up her thigh. My eyes disconnected from my brain and followed the motion of her legs. "Is there really a need for this to go to court?" she asked. "I mean do the authorities have to learn about the recording? I've made mistakes, I won't deny it. I've had enormous financial pressures that caused me to exercise bad judgment. I thought if I could get hold of the *Hunley* diary and sell it to Arnie ... All right, that's just an excuse, and I don't want to offer excuses. But I'm a good person, Russ, you know I am. I've worked so hard to correct societal injustices, and there's so much more I can do. What would be accomplished by imprisoning me?"

Here before me was the first big test case of the brand new Russell Q. Berard policy of functioning as a filter of evidence that did and didn't pass through to the police and screener of who was and wasn't punished. I'd been dissembling and withholding evidence at every turn, why stop now? My reservoir of rage over my father's murder had been emptied last night with Durrell Pritchard's death. I didn't believe Cherisse had wanted Dad to die. Participating as a witness in her trial would be agonizing, and her conviction, by no means certain, would bring me no additional peace.

But I had a problem ...

"There's too much here to ignore, Cherry," I said. "Dad's murder isn't the only issue. Pritchard said last night at your cottage and again on the recording that you had him kill Leonard Alcott to get the material Alcott was using to blackmail you. And according to the recording, you also told Pritchard he might have to kill Moze Cheddar."

She chewed on a finger nail and stared at the floor. "That recording might not be admissible evidence."

"I expect your attorney will make that argument," I said. "But I wouldn't count on it working. And the recording isn't the only evidence. The police are grilling Ronnie, and with his prior record, enough pressure will be applied that he'll reveal that he, DuBois and Jason Grimes went to Etiwan to pay off Alcott for you. He may also reveal that you sent him and the others to Moze Cheddar's cabin to steal the *Hunley* diary. And Ronnie and Pritchard seemed to know each other pretty well. Maybe Pritchard told Ronnie about killing my dad and Alcott for you, and maybe Ronnie will spill that to the police too."

Cherisse continued to stare at the floor for several moments. Then she looked up and smiled at me beseechingly. "If you change your statement about what Pritchard said at the cabin last night, and if you don't give the police this recording, I think I can manage. You won't consider a gigantic favor for your first love?"

I shook my head. "You said I know you're a good person, but I don't. Possibly you'll be able to beat any charges or bargain them down to something minimal. But I'm not making the decision to let you walk. I'm sorry."

She sighed and nodded. "You've always been an honorable man. It's such a shame." She reached into her handbag and withdrew a gun. "Take a final ride with me for old time's sake."

As I stared at the gun barrel, I thought belatedly of Arnie's warning to be ready for her fastball and not get distracted by her curves.

Chapter Forty-Seven

I drove Cherisse's Jaguar. She sat in back with the gun in her hand and Durrell Pritchard's recorder in her handbag. "Is this a one way ride to join my father?" I asked.

"Not if you do what I tell you." Her words clanged like cold hard steel. She'd discarded remorseful, beseeching Cherisse as if that persona was a worn out plastic mask.

"Which way?" I asked, approaching the light at Route 17.

"Left. We're going into Charleston to my club."

"For drinks?"

"Don't be flippant, Russ."

"It's a nervous reaction to someone pointing a gun at my back."

"Someone who loves you."

"I could say something really flippant about that."

"Don't."

I didn't.

It was past 7:00PM, traffic into Charleston moderate. I considered stomping the gas pedal and turning the Jaguar loose in hopes of attracting a police car. I didn't trust Cherisse's mental state though. She might put a bullet in my skull or fire indiscriminately at a pursuing cruiser. She obviously had a plan, so why not try to gum up the works after we were parked and out of the Jag?

We ascended the Ravenel Bridge toward a dove gray sky tinged with sunset reds and golds. Walkers, runners and bikers populated the sealed off recreational lane. Baby blue current from the Cooper River wrapped around Drum Island and flowed to the bottom of the peninsula to join the Ashley River. Wind jostled the Jaguar and blew odors of ocean salt and pluff mud through my open window. Ahead, a plumber's van cut in on a BMW, and the Beemer bleated in outrage. Through the rearview mirror I watched Cherisse flip open a cell phone and text message with her left hand, gun stable in her right.

I recalled traveling the Ravenel in the opposite direction five nights earlier and making what had seemed to be an innocuous stop at the Griddle Grill. Life since had been a bumpy, bruising express ride past graveyards full of bodies and memories. And wherever the ride terminated tonight with Cherisse, the conclusion would be joyless.

I exited onto Meeting Street and headed downtown toward Chalmers Street. As we approached the Denmark Vesey, Cherisse said, "Go around back." I did and parked in her owner's space.

"The club's closed on Sundays," Cherisse told me. "But somebody may be inside doing odds and ends. You'll lead the way through the rear door and along the hallway to my office. I'll be following with the gun. If we see anyone, you'll smile and nod and not say a word. Please don't test me."

The hallway was clear, no opportunity for testing and possibly dying. But I was certain there would soon be more opportunities for dying. Cherisse shut and locked the office door behind us. "Lie face down on the carpet with your arms extended above your head," she said.

The off-white Berber carpet smelled of spilled vodka, shoe leather and marijuana. I turned my head and watched Cherisse insert a key in a door and open it. A closet. She stepped inside and pulled out a black duffel suitcase on rollers.

"Getaway bag?" I asked.

"I've been planning this contingency for awhile," she said. "In addition to all my other problems, I'm facing an IRS audit that would be disastrous. I'd be charged with tax evasion, embezzlement, who knows what else. Matters just got completely out of hand. I took some risks that didn't pan out, and I borrowed money from one business to put into another and repeated that a few times, and the next thing I knew I'd perpetrated a Ponzi scheme on myself."

"Then where did the getaway money come from?"

"Some of it I siphoned off from the club," she said. "That's how

I paid Pritchard too." She chuckled. "And a lot of it is thanks to Arnie, though he doesn't know that. Until recently he was willing to help me by co-signing for loans and giving me money. He didn't realize that I diverted a healthy portion of his loans and cash to my rainy day fund."

More and more I was thinking that, if there had been a good guy in Cherisse and Arnie's marriage, it had been Arnie. "It's difficult to disappear," I said.

"Difficult but not impossible." Cherisse unzipped the suitcase, removed a large brown deerskin pouch and transferred the pouch to her handbag. "I have a new identity, and the rainy day fund is in offshore accounts."

"There was a career criminal in Newport named Donnie who committed a murder and vanished with a couple of million dollars," I said. "We worked with international law enforcement agencies trying to locate him. No luck though, and after a time it became a cold case. Then one morning a few years later Donnie was standing outside the police department smoking a cigarette when I arrived at work. His hands were shaking and he was twenty pounds thinner than I remembered. 'I can't do it no more, Berard,' he told me. 'Food tastes like crap, booze burns my stomach, I don't sleep for shit. A real prison's gotta be better than life on the run worrying all the time if I'm gonna be nabbed.'"

Cherisse shook her head. "Maybe I'll turn up on your doorstep someday, but don't hold your breath. I can't face going to prison."

"I've known a lot of people who thought they couldn't face going to prison, but they did go and managed the experience all right. Besides, you haven't been charged with anything. And if you are charged, who knows if you'll be convicted?"

"So says the man who'll be the star witness for the prosecution," she said. "The man who won't fudge his story to save an old love."

Out of words, we let silence settle in. Sorrowful silence weighted by foregone opportunities and unrealized dreams.

Eventually Cherisse's lips curved in a wistful smile. "Time for me to go, honey pie. You're going to crawl on your hands and knees to that open door, which leads into a bathroom. It's actually part bathroom, part sitting area. I designed it as a retreat from the noise and freneticism of the club, so it's sound-proofed. You can beat on the door until you collapse, but no one will hear you. And I have your cell phone, so you won't be able to call anybody. But you'll be comfortable. The sink has drinking water, and there's a mini-fridge with snacks. I'll call here in the morning from a safe phone and tell whoever answers to let you out."

"No," I told her.

"Excuse me?"

"I'm not going into the bathroom."

The arm with the gun attached had been hanging loosely. Now it stiffened, and the gun barrel pointed down at me. "You are. It's not negotiable."

"I'm not."

"I'll shoot you, Russ! So help me God I will!"

I didn't like the edge of hysteria in her voice. But I'd played my cards. There wasn't anything to do but wait and see how she played hers.

Her face contorted and her finger tightened on the trigger. I didn't move. An eternity passed, and still I remained motionless on the carpet, and still Cherisse stood pointing the gun and almost squeezing the trigger. But I could tell from her facial expression that she wasn't going to fire, and I exhaled.

And she squeezed and fired.

Chapter Forty-Eight

Cherisse had jerked her arm up first though, and the bullet slammed into the padded back of an arm chair. I rolled for cover in case a second bullet followed, but Cherisse ran for the door.

I clambered to my feet and went after her. In the hallway I saw her turn a corner toward the front of the club. It occurred to me that I was unarmed; Cherisse had taken my .38 back at the apartment. But an experienced detective like me could surely conjure up a means of dealing with her guns. I had no immediate idea what those means would be, but something brilliant would occur to me before I caught up with her. Sure it would.

I entered the Denmark Vesey's bar and lounge just as Cherisse reached the front door and discovered I had a more immediate problem than Cherisse's guns. Lewis the warehouse-sized bartender blocked my path. He looked at me regretfully and shook his head. "Ms. Cherisse say: Lewis, that Mr. Russ Berard fella who was in here the other night wants to do me harm. He just pull a gun and fire a shot at me in the office. Lucky the shot miss and I get away, but he going to come after me. You take hold of him while I go outside and call the police."

Lewis raised his left arm. "Ms. Cherisse give me this to use 'case I need it." My .38 Special, which Cherisse had appropriated at Aunt Fil's, was buried in his massive left hand like a miniature water pistol in the pocket of a catcher's mitt. He pointed toward a table. "We can sit right there, Mr. Russ, wait for Ms. Cherisse and the po-lice."

It would be a hell of a long wait, but I was an accommodating guy—up to a point. I pulled out a chair, whirled and slammed it into Lewis' chest. He stumbled backward and dropped the gun. I slammed him with the chair again, and he thudded against a table, lost balance and toppled. I scooped my .38 off the floor and headed for the door. The ankle I'd sprained chasing Durrell Pritchard last night throbbed, and swinging the chair at Lewis had aggravated the knife wound in my shoulder.

As I exited the Vesey, Cherisse was quick-stepping along Chalmers. Pulling the getaway suitcase slowed her, so that even on a bum ankle I made up ground. She peered over her shoulder through the lamp lit night, saw me narrowing the gap and took the gun from her handbag. I'd tucked my .38 in my pocket after retrieving it from the floor of the Vesey. So we both had guns; what was the likelihood we'd use them? Cherisse had given me a pass in her office and fired into a chair. But she was nearly cornered now. She might not be so generous a second time. And what was I prepared to do?

Cherisse swung left on State Street, then cut into an alley leading to East Bay Street. She looked over her shoulder again, saw I was closer and dropped her escape bag. A few more strides and she stopped, turned, and aimed her gun at my chest. I braked, .38 still in my pocket. No one else was in the alley, just the two of us playing out our last act. Cherisse's body twitched manically, and her eyes sparked in the darkness like short-circuiting hot wires.

She dropped her gun suddenly and darted toward East Bay. If she made it across the street she had an excellent chance of escaping. She'd been a track star, and freed from the burden of a suitcase, she'd be too quick for me and my sore ankle. Possibly she had a second car on the other side of East Bay that she could use, since I could describe the Jaguar to the police. If the pouch she'd transferred to her handbag at the Vesey held her new passport, other documents and money, she ought to be able to get by without the suitcase she was leaving behind.

This all turned out to be idle speculation. Cherisse didn't make it across East Bay.

A truck traveling south struck her with a sickening thump, flopping her body into the north-bound lane. A sedan screeching to a halt ran its front tires up on her legs and torso and backed off.

I reached her first and knelt. "Stay calm," I said. "Medics will be here soon."

"Chest … feels … crushed," she whispered. "Can't … get … air. Couldn't… shoot … you. Just … couldn't." She gripped my hand and squeezed. I returned the squeeze.

Someone knelt beside me, and Cherisse's gaze shifted.

"No!" DuBois said. "Please, mother, no!"

"I … I … love … you … sweetie," Cherisse said faintly. "It … will … be … all right. Don't …worry."

She made bubbling noises and shuddered, and her eyes widened as if new verities were being revealed. Her grip went limp, and I felt life leave her body and go on to wherever God intended.

"You bastard!" DuBois swore at me.

"DuBois—" I began, but he interrupted by slamming his left fist into my jaw. I toppled over, and he stood and ran.

A medical rescue siren shrieked impatiently in the distance, but Cherisse had all the time in another world. I got off the ground and stepped back rubbing my jaw as others surrounded the body. Two deaths in two nights I could take credit for. A record to be proud of. I raised my eyes to the sky, hoping to glimpse Cherisse's soul ascending. Then I remembered I was an agnostic. Lowering my eyes I noticed that her handbag had been thrown a short distance away. I picked it up. The flap was open, and Pritchard's voice recorder and my cell phone lay on top of the pouch Cherisse had taken from her getaway suitcase. All attention was focused on Cherisse with no one watching me, so I surreptitiously slipped the pouch into my side pocket next to the .38 and put the voice recorder and cell phone in the other pocket.

When I turned I saw Lewis the bartender on the sidewalk. I walked over to him.

"She dead, Mr. Russ?" Lewis asked, brow furrowed, eyes pinched in pain.

"She is," I said. "I'm sorry."

He sighed. "She seem awful troubled of late." We stood stoop-shouldered from heavy memories until Lewis spoke again. "She shoot at you in the office, not the other way around?"

I looked at him in surprise. "I ain't graduate high school, suh," he said. "But I learn two or three things about people along the path of life."

"She was the shooter," I said.

"Po-lice gonna ast me what happened in the Vesey 'fore Ms. Cherisse run out?"

"Yes."

"What you figure I oughta tell 'em?"

"We can tell it straight, or we can try to protect Cherisse, but we need to tell it the same way," I said.

"How I protect Ms. Cherisse?"

"You say that she and I were in the club for awhile and she seemed fine as far as you could tell. You didn't see us leave, so we must have gone out the rear door. You finished up your work, walked over to East Bay to get something to eat and discovered that she'd been killed. I'll say she was a little ahead of me and must have thought she could dodge traffic crossing East Bay and wait for me on the other side, but she apparently misjudged the speed of the truck that hit her. We'll leave out the parts about her having a suitcase and your holding a gun on me."

"You think the po-lice gonna believe that?"

"I don't think anybody saw me chasing Cherisse, so we can probably make it stick," I said. "If the police come up with a witness who saw me chasing her and saw her suitcase, I'll cover for you. I'll back up your story that Cherisse and I went out the rear of the Vesey, so you didn't see the suitcase and didn't know she was running away from me."

Lewis chewed his thick lower lip and squinted in deliberation. "Don't wanna say nothin' about pointin' no gun at you 'less I need to. Police got a sheet on me already. They hear 'bout me havin' a gun, they won't like it. One thing though. I see DuBois poke your jaw. He come in lookin' for his momma right after you and Ms. Cherisse take off from the club."

"What did you tell him?"

"That you an' Ms. Cherisse leave a couple of minutes earlier," Lewis said.

"You didn't say there'd been a gunshot and I was chasing Cherisse?"

"No suh. I didn't rightly know what was goin' on, an' I don't like to tell folks no more than I need to."

"That's an admirable trait," I said.

Lewis shrugged. "Jus' a good way to get by on the streets. Don't guess there's no need for me to say nothing 'bout seein' you remove things from Ms. Cherisse's handbag either."

"You're quite a guy, Lewis," I told him.

In the hubbub of arrival of a medical rescue van and police cars, I slipped into the alley through which I'd chased Cherisse. The alley was empty, and I picked up the gun Cherisse had dropped and collected the getaway bag she'd abandoned. A black wrought iron gate in a brick wall hung open. I pulled the bag through the gate and discovered several partially filled trash barrels. I wiped the gun, dropped it into one of the barrels and watched it sink out of sight. Then I removed Cherisse's pouch from my waistband, unzipped the getaway bag, dropped the pouch inside and re-zipped the bag. A blanket lay wadded on the ground. I used it to cover the bag.

Chapter Forty-Nine

Police were on the scene interviewing bystanders when I returned to East Bay Street. A uniformed officer approached me and said he understood I'd been the first to reach the body, appeared to know the deceased and had been punched by a young man who'd fled. I confirmed that all those things were true. The officer posed a few more questions and then asked if I had any objection to giving a written statement to a detective. I didn't have any objections I was willing to share, so a patrol car carried me over to police headquarters on Lockwood Avenue.

I relinquished my .38, made the acquaintance of a detective named Diego Mendoza, and told him that Ellen Talley from the Mt. Pleasant PD was interested in Cherisse Dane and might appreciate being part of our conversation. Mendoza knew Ellen and phoned her. She said she'd be along shortly. Possibly she asked Mendoza to have an extra set of brass knuckles ready so that she could fully participate in my interrogation. While we waited for Ellen, Mendoza got us coffee, showed me photos of his baby daughter and predicted that The Citadel's football team would go undefeated.

Ellen arrived, greeted Mendoza warmly and nodded at me with an expression that suggested I'd run over her dog the last time we'd been together. During Mendoza's questioning, she sat mute with a scowl fierce enough to wilt a petrified California redwood.

After I signed my statement and collected my .38, Ellen walked me outside and thawed slightly. "Want a lift somewhere?" she asked.

Sparse traffic ran along Lockwood, and breeze rustled tree leaves in Brittlebank Park across the avenue. The park's grassy banks swept down to the Ashley River, which spread like an ink spill below the star-dotted sky. If I accepted a ride, Ellen would chop up the story I'd told Mendoza with a meat cleaver. But that was going to happen sometime, why not get it over with? "I'd like to go back to the scene and deal with some emotions," I said.

During the trip across the city, Ellen didn't ask a question and didn't cut into my tall tale to Mendoza. When she dropped me at the corner of East Bay and Queen, just up from where Cherisse had died, she said, "If you want company, I'll be glad to hang around, buy you a drink or three."

"Thanks," I told her, "but *I want to be alone* for awhile. I'll grab a cab when I'm ready to go home."

"Okay," she said and touched my arm. "I realize this is a difficult time for you, Russ, and I'm sorry." I liked this kinder, gentler, solicitous Ellen. We might be able to get along after all.

I watched Ellen drive north on East Bay, feeling guilty about my deviousness. But the guilt wasn't strong enough to deter me from going back to the alley and collecting Cherisse's getaway suitcase from behind the brick wall where I'd hidden it. I pulled the suitcase over to State Street and dug the cell phone out of my pocket, intending to call Gary Nagle and ask him to pick me up.

But a dark sedan pulled up beside me before I dialed. "Get in," Ellen Talley said. She didn't sound like kinder, gentler, solicitous Ellen anymore.

I deposited the suitcase in the trunk and settled into the front passenger seat. "Nice detective work," I told her, buckling my seat belt.

Ellen snorted. "You didn't really think I believed that story you peddled to Mendoza, did you? From his limited perspective it's an okay story. But in view of all the other things that have happened, Cherisse accidentally dying crossing the street is a little hard to swallow. And then I want to be alone when I offered to buy you a drink? Was that supposed to be an imitation of Greta Garbo with a phony sob in your throat?"

"That's insulting," I told her. "I thought I got the sob just right."

"I suppose it's pointless for me to ask what's going on and expect an honest answer," Ellen said. "So why don't we drive back to the Charleston PD, turn that suitcase over to Mendoza and see what's inside."

I tried to think of a story that would dissuade Ellen from taking me back to the Charleston PD, but I had nothing ... nothing except the truth. What a revolting development it was to be forced to rely on the truth. On the other hand, I'd never tried the truth with Ellen. Possibly she'd go into shock and I could jump from the car and catch a slow boat to China.

"I discovered a recording of a conversation between Cherisse and Durrell Pritchard," I said. "The recording reveals that Cherisse overheard my father tell someone that he'd learned about the existence of the *Hunley* diary. Cherisse was in deep financial trouble and reached an agreement with Arnie that he'd pay her a lot of money if she obtained the diary and sold it to him. Cherisse sent Pritchard to break into my father's church and search his files for information about the diary, my dad showed up unexpectedly, and Pritchard killed him.

"Cherisse listened to the recording with me," I continued. "Then she pulled a gun and made me drive her to the Vesey, where she had her getaway suitcase. She tried to lock me in a bathroom, but I wouldn't cooperate, so she took off. I chased her, and she dropped the suitcase and ran into East Bay Street trying to escape from me."

Ellen emitted a series of guttural noises and curse words before her speech became intelligible. "You're ... You ... I don't know what to say about your behavior anymore. Where's the recording of the conversation between Cherisse and Pritchard?"

"In my pocket," I said.

"You walked into the Charleston PD with the recorder in your pocket?"

"I was a cooperating witness, not a suspect. They didn't have any reason to search me or a warrant to authorize a search."

Ellen wheeled the sedan away from the curb. "Where are we going?" I asked.

"Where the hell do you think we're going? To the Charleston Police Department."

"Why?"

"Is that a serious question? You just signed a false statement, and you've been concealing evidence: the suitcase and the recording of the Cherisse/Pritchard conversation. I don't want to think about what Mendoza will do to you, or what I'll do to you once Mendoza is through doing whatever he's going to do."

"What are you going to accomplish?" I said. "Cherisse probably paid Pritchard to kill Leonard Alcott, and she may be legally culpable for my father's death, because Dad died in the course of crimes that Cherisse instructed Pritchard to commit. But what difference does it make? Pritchard and Cherisse are both dead. You don't have anyone to prosecute for anything and neither does Mendoza. The only other homicide is Jason Grimes, and you told me you have evidence that Alcott killed Grimes."

Ellen pulled back to the curb and glowered. "Now you're asking me to help you conceal evidence and aid and abet your perjured statement to Mendoza."

"No," I said. "You're exercising police discretion. Cops do it every day. And do you really think Mendoza wants to dig into this? The only issue in his jurisdiction is Cherisse's death, and that was a traffic accident."

"I'm supposed to forget that Cherisse was probably responsible for two murders? Are you going to forget that your father was one of those murders?"

"Of course, I'm not going to forget, but what are we going to do, hold a press conference? Write a book?"

Ellen arched her neck and smacked her palms against the steering wheel. "Aargh! Lord you make me crazy. I can't believe I'm even considering this. Police don't exercise discretion by letting civilians destroy evidence. Which is what you want me to do, isn't it? Let you get rid of the voice recorder and the suitcase?"

"Yes," I admitted. There wasn't any way to sugar-coat that part.

She mulled. "What's in the suitcase?"

"I'm not sure. I'd guess fake passport, fake ID, clothes, maybe cash, maybe foreign bank account info. Want to check?"

"No!"

She deliberated awhile longer. Then she slammed the car into gear, screeched up State Street, swung right on Market and turned left on East Bay.

"Don't talk!" she said when I opened my mouth as we sped up the ramp to the Ravenel Bridge. "Not a word! I don't want to hear a sound out of your mouth, not a sound!"

Ten minutes later Ellen curled the sedan into my driveway. She kept the engine running and stared straight ahead through the windshield at my garage doors.

"Thank you," I said.

She turned to face me. Street lamp illumination cast her face in a soft halo that warmed her eyes and flushed her skin with a radiance that erased age and fatigue lines. I saw the young girl I'd fished with so many years ago. "Do you think the odds are at least 50-50 that we could have dinner together without exchanging gunfire?" she asked.

"I don't know if I'd go as high as 50-50," I said. "Possibly 30-70."

She wrinkled her brow and considered. "Those are better odds than I've had with other dates recently. Maybe I'll call you. In the meantime, get out of my car and take that damn suitcase I don't know anything about."

Chapter Fifty

I went inside, saw lights I hadn't left on and thought, *What now?*

"Moze?" I called.

"Yessir."

"You're not going to point a gun at me again, are you?"

"No sir. You and me has established trust. 'Course I can't speak for others."

I came around the corner of the hallway carrying Cherisse's getaway bag and saw what Moze meant by not being able to speak for others. He was sitting on one side of the kitchen table, and DuBois Dane was sitting at one end holding a gun.

"Take a seat, Berard," DuBois said. "You might as well be comfortable in your remaining moments." His voice was hoarse, his eyes red-rimmed and feral.

"I was sloppy in my work, Mr. Berard." Moze's lips twisted in a regretful, self-censuring expression. "Can't make no excuse for it. Didn't give thought to the chance of somebody else breaking into your house. Boy got the jump on me when I arrived."

"It's all right." I set down Cherisse's bag and took the chair across from Moze.

DuBois was between Moze and me, his chair pushed away from the table to provide room to react. He leaned forward, left hand gripping the pistol, left elbow propped on his thigh for stability. I could think of three ways to disarm him, which meant Moze could think of twelve. Which caused me to suspect that Moze had a plan. I hoped I wouldn't bollix it up.

"Let's hear your grievances against me, DuBois," I said.

"Grievances! You want to hear grievances!" The gun wavered

as his hand trembled, and I sucked in a breath. "How about this, asshole? You killed my mother!"

"According to the radio news, death of your momma was an accident," Moze said mildly.

"That's bullshit!" DuBois snapped. "Berard either pushed my mother into traffic or chased her into it trying to kill her."

"Why would I have wanted to kill your mother?" I asked.

"Because you think she was responsible for your father's murder."

"Why would I think that?"

"Stop asking me why questions, goddamnit!" DuBois said. "We both know my mother did some bad things."

"I don't know details of any bad things your momma done," Moze put in. "But from what I hear tell, she did plenty of good too. Mix of good and bad is the best that can be said for any of us. Reckon the Man Up Above has kept hisself a balance sheet and will make the necessary judgments."

"Screw the imaginary Man Up Above," DuBois said. "My mother caused people to die. You think that will hurt her balance sheet?"

"Seems likely," Moze said. "But I don't rightly see how you causing Mr. Berard to die will help the situation none."

DuBois blinked and swallowed. "You're not going to talk me out of this, old man," he insisted, but there was uncertainty in his tone now.

"Don't figure I need to," Moze said. "You're hurtin' bad inside on account of your momma dying, and you wanna blame somebody, so you're lashin' out at Mr. Berard, though you know he ain't responsible. In a minute or two you'll get yourself calmed down."

"Why don't you shut the hell up? This doesn't concern you. It's between Berard and me."

"Starts off that way," Moze said. "But after you shoot Mr. Berard, seems like it's gonna be between you and me. Besides, it'd disturb me greatly to see a fella like you who's got hisself plenty of potential throw his life down the crapper. Thought when I heard your voice instructing them other boys in the woods at my cabin that whoever the voice belonged to was a leader. Thought the same watching how you handled yourself since I came down here. Except for now. Right now you're acting like a jackass, but I'm willing to make allowances on account of your sorrow. Folks in our family always take the death of loved ones hard."

DuBois stared at him. "What do you mean, folks in our family?"

"You and me is related, son," Moze told him. "Been scratching my head for awhile now trying to recall who your voice sounds like. Then when I learned your name the other day, I knowed it was your daddy your voice reminds me of."

"My father? You and my father were related?"

Moze nodded. "'Fore I start my story of explanation, you mind laying that weapon down on the table? You're in a nervous, twitchy state of mind, which causes me concern that the trigger might get squeezed accidental-like. Then we'd have us a situation."

DuBois hesitated, then placed his pistol on the table, and my pulse dropped below eight hundred for the first time in ten minutes.

"Ain't much funny about what's been happening with folks trying to get their hands on the *Hunley* diary," Moze said to DuBois. "And I guess funny ain't exactly the right way to describe you being part of it, but there's coincidence or maybe fate involved. That diary was wrote by an ancestor of yours and mine, Ezra Cheddar, who was a Union spy during the Civil War, sent to Charleston to sabotage the *Hunley*."

"Why don't I know any of this?" DuBois asked.

"Your side of the family separated itself away from Ezra pretty far back," Moze said. "Ezra growed up in Pennsylvania, and he went home after the War. But he was ate up with guilt about some of the things he'd done as a spy, and he decided to move back to South Carolina. Figured if he became a Southerner and helped South Carolina rebuild, maybe he'd do his penance and be at peace. Settled upstate on account of being afraid that if he came to Charleston, there might be folks who'd remember him, and he'd been using a different name when he was a spy. He married an upstate girl, and they had theirselves a son and daughter. But Ezra never did find peace of mind. He had mental troubles, nightmares and such and turned to liquor for help. One day he put a gun in his mouth and pulled the trigger."

"Jesus Christ!" DuBois said, jerking away from the gun lying before him on the table as if it were a black viper about to strike.

"Real rough on the family members," Moze continued. "Been a lot of strain amongst them on account of Ezra's problems even before he shot hisself, but once he was dead things got worse. Ezra's daughter didn't get along with her momma or brother. In time she married and moved away and didn't never again have nothing to do with her relations. Split in the family just went on and on. I'm the last of those descended from Ezra's son, and your daddy, Bryson Capshaw, was my cousin descended from Ezra's daughter."

DuBois looked stunned. "I can't … I don't … My father deserted my mother and me when I was an infant, and he never had anything to do with my life. I don't know any of his family history."

"I can help with some of it," Moze said. "Got a few facts in my head and records back at the cabin. There's plenty we'd need to study on, though. Never was no family reunions or such, so none of us cousins ever got to know each other. My side of the family was always the poor relations, and your daddy's wealthy Capshaw side didn't have no desire to associate with the likes of us."

"Did my father know about the diary?" DuBois asked.

"He did," Moze said. "I found the diary hid in the walls when I fixed up Ezra's old cabin that hadn't nobody used for a real long while. Diary was wrapped up and preserved, and I unwrapped it and read what it had to say. Came as news to me. Ezra's spying wasn't never talked about, even on our side of the family. Shamed a South Carolina family to have a Yankee ancestor who'd done harm to the Southern cause. Anyhow, once I saw what Ezra had wrote, I thought your daddy might oughta see it too, 'cause he was the only living adult on that side of the family. He and I knowed each other existed, but that was about all, so he was real surprised to see me and what I'd brung."

"How did he react?" DuBois asked.

Moze sucked in his cheeks, and the skin around his eyes tightened. "Reckon that, though your daddy wasn't never really a father to you, you know something of his activities?"

"I know he was a right-wing racist who planned to run for governor until he got killed driving drunk with a black hooker in his car."

"That's a real clear way of putting it," Moze said. "Your daddy was also knowed for having a strong dislike for the North and for giving speeches saying the *Hunley* proved how much smarter Confederate boys was than Yankees. You ain't had a chance to see the diary yet, but when your daddy read it, he like to have a heart attack on account of learning that he was descended from a Yankee spy who had outsmarted all the Confederates in Charleston and sabotaged the *Hunley*. Your daddy was worried that if the public got wind of them facts, he'd be a laughingstock who couldn't get elected to no kind of office."

"And I bet he begged you not to reveal the contents of the diary," DuBois said disdainfully.

"He did a little begging, though it weren't necessary. I didn't have no intention of allowing others to see the diary anyhow. I growed up a South Carolina boy, and I don't feel too good about what Ezra done. Also, I like to live my life private, don't have no wish for the public to take note of my family history. Don't have no wish for newspaper and television reporters to show up at my cabin askin' for interviews either. I'm a simple man."

Moze paused and scratched his head, and a bemused expression crept into his eyes. "I said before there ain't nothing funny about this business, but it is a little funny how things has turned out. Ever since your daddy died, I been thinking I oughta contact you and tell you about the diary, 'cause you and me are the only ones left. But I knew how matters was between you and your daddy, and I didn't know the right way to make my approach. Then Mr. Berard's daddy came to see me at my cabin, and I told him about the diary, and that led to you trying to steal it, and that led to you and me sitting here now meeting each other in the house belonged to Mr. Berard's daddy."

I felt a lump in my throat. Moze might not be the most literate guy around, but he had a gift for articulating life's ironies.

DuBois gulped back his own emotions as he processed Moze's story. "So what do we do next?" he asked eventually in a voice that quivered despite his best efforts to hold it steady.

Relief and gladness showed on Moze's face, and I realized that he, like me, had half-expected DuBois to jump up from the table, grab his gun and bolt. I also realized that Moze was experiencing an intense connection to this kid and was discovering feelings for mankind that he had long suppressed on the world's battlefields.

"What I was thinking," Moze said to DuBois. "Mr. Berard has read all of the diary but the end. I could give him that part, and you and me could go out on his deck and finish this here talk. There's more I can tell you about our family, and maybe you got yourself questions I can try to answer. That is if Mr. Berard don't mind us making ourselves to home on his deck."

"I don't mind," I said.

DuBois looked down, rubbed his palms together, looked back up and nodded. "All right," he said. "Okay."

Moze stood, lifted his knapsack off the floor, set it on the table, reached inside, removed clamped pages and dropped them before me. DuBois stood also, and the two of them went through the glass doors to the deck.

I lifted the pages and began to read the last act of the *Hunley* drama featuring Ezra Cheddar as Nathaniel Clary, Union spy.

Chapter Fifty-One

During all my days in Charleston as a Union spy I had been anxious and fretful, tormented by fear of failure and discovery. But now as I made plans for my next sabotage of the Hunley fish-boat, sabotage which, successful or not, would surely be my last, I was near mad with apprehension. My hands palsied, my stomach churned, and my head pounded as if it would surely explode.

Key to my plan was advance warning of my intentions to Admiral John Dahlgren, Commander of the Union blockading squadron. Yet I had no way of knowing whether my letter to Admiral Dahlgren had been delivered by the Union agent in Charleston, Josiah Murray. When last I had seen Murray, he was running down an alley with my letter in his coat. Perhaps Murray had been caught and my letter found in his possession. If so, why had the Confederates not come for me? Perhaps they were lying in wait, desirous of capturing me in the act and making a public display of my failure in order to boost the spirits of their troops and citizenry.

I did my best to disguise my trepidations and continue to drill with the Hunley crew. But circumstances had changed. Previously, when George Dixon sought to persuade me to become a regular member of his crew, I demurred. Now in order to implement my plan it was essential that I be aboard when the fish-boat attacked the Union warship Housatonic. There were no positions open, however, and I could only hope that a vacancy would occur. So each day I went with the crew from Mount Pleasant to Battery Marshall on Sullivan's Island, where the Hunley was moored. We would practice night runs, then return to Mt. Pleasant. My damaged leg ached from the walking, but the exhausting exercise soothed my nerves.

Just when I concluded that I must take surreptitious action to *put a crew member out of commission to create a spot for myself, good fortune intervened. William Alexander, George Dixon's second in command, was ordered to return to Mobile, Alabama, for a new assignment. Fearing this might occur, George had been making some practice runs with Joseph Ridgaway in Alexander's aftmost position, and me filling the position of ninth man. With Alexander's departure now a certainty, this arrangement was made permanent.*

Winter winds and storms hindered our training, but more importantly, they prevented us from venturing far enough out into the Atlantic to torpedo the Housatonic. *Finally, on February 17, the sea lay calm and winds blew light, and George announced that we would attack. There was more moonlight than George liked, but he could not know when the weather conditions would again be so favorable. For my purposes, the moonlight was a blessing, because it would facilitate my signaling the* Housatonic, *once I seized control of the* Hunley *at gunpoint and halted the assault before the torpedo could be launched.*

The nine of us entered the fish-boat one at a time, arms extended over our heads to fit through the small hatchways. Once inside, we took our positions: George Dixon forward on the starboard Captain's bench beneath the conning tower; seven of us on the port-side crew bench at our cranking stations; and one to operate the bellows and pump. I was at the end of the bench nearest George. He had lit a candle, which provided flickering illumination as we settled in and bent forward. At shortly past 7:00 p.m., we began to crank in a steady, uniform cadence, and out into the sea moved the Hunley, *gears grinding. Save for the occasional nervous quip, we each remained quiet with our thoughts as our muscles strained. This was work we had performed countless times, and we did not lack confidence in our abilities. But in our minds, we contended with the uneasy realization that tonight this effort was authentic, and lives would most likely be lost, perhaps ours among them. I alone contended with the secret knowledge that my goal was in total opposition to the interests of the others.*

The currents from Breach Inlet were strong in our favor, and we rode them out, conserving energy for the return trip. By 8:00 p.m., George calculated that we were approximately halfway to our target. A quarter-hour later, we took a direct bearing on the Housatonic.

At 8:30, I drew my revolver, half-rose, and jabbed the gun barrel against George's side.

George's body stiffened, and a cold, knowing smile played on his face in the candlelight. "I've wondered about you, Nate. But I've enjoyed our friendship too much to act upon my concern."

The other crew members had stopped cranking and were staring at us. "I will shoot George, should anyone interfere," I warned them.

Tension filled the fish-boat like rising water, and I knew that an impetuous act by one of the crew could defeat my plan and throw us into turmoil. I counted on George's calm and reason, and I was not disappointed. "No reckless behavior for the moment, lads," he commanded. "I am prepared to die for the Confederacy, but only if doing so will bring some advantage. Keep cranking while we listen to Nate's intentions."

I breathed a sigh of relief. "First we must change positions," I told George. "You take my seat on the bench." This placed me under the hatch for easy egress to signal the *Housatonic*.

George complied, the two of us shifting awkwardly in the tight quarters. I sat down on the captain's bench across from George and the others and pointed my gun at them.

"We shall advance near to the *Housatonic* and halt, staying just above water," I said. "I shall exit and signal with our blue lamp. The captain of the *Housatonic* is expecting my signal." This I said with considerably more conviction than I felt. "Rescue boats will be sent from the *Housatonic* and all of you will be taken prisoner. At the conclusion of the war you will be released and allowed to return to the South as heroes, honored for your brave deeds."

There was silence as they considered. "And if we refuse to cooperate?" George asked. "You cannot hope to kill us all before you're overpowered."

"I shall kill you and kill or wound one or two others before I am overpowered," I said. "That should be sufficient to prevent ramming of the *Housatonic* with the torpedo. And overpowering me will not save those I fail to kill. If sailors on the *Housatonic* catch sight of the *Hunley* but not my signal, they will fire. Even if we are not sunk, I doubt those of the crew who survive my shooting will be able to navigate the opposing current and return to Sullivan's Island, especially without your direction. Most likely all will perish."

In the aftermath of this utterance I listened to my heart pound and the crank rattle as it turned. The fish-boat's dimensions seemed to be compressing, walls, ceiling, and deck squeezing ever tighter around me, causing my throat to constrict. Odors of damp metal, salt, sweat, and burning candle wax turned my stomach as I gasped for air.

"No," George said.

"What do you mean?" I asked. But I knew.

"The eight of us undertook this mission for the Confederacy knowing death to be a possibility," George said. "I cannot capitulate to your demands and surrender the boat because I fear dying. Shoot me if you must, but my men are steadfast and valiant. I have every confidence they will carry on without me, torpedo the Housatonic, and journey home to safety." This last appeared to be spoken to invigorate George's crew, whose disquiet was palpable.

"You are as fine a man as I have ever known," I told George. "Please, I have no wish to shoot you."

"War forces otherwise honorable men to commit heinous acts, Nate."

My muscles ached with strain, and I struggled to keep the gun steady. I was nearly out of time. If I were to stop the Hunley and signal the Housatonic, it must be now. If we drew much closer, we would be seen and fired upon.

"Order them to stop cranking!" I nearly shouted.

"I cannot," George said.

"Damn you, George! Damn you!" I squeezed the trigger with my mind but not my heart, and my finger answered to my heart and would not respond. "Damn you!" I cried out once more, my will broken. I lowered the gun and bowed my head.

George stood and unlatched the hatch so he could raise his head up in the conning tower and look out a view-port. He took a sighting, withdrew his head, and secured the latch. "Continue full speed ahead," he commanded. "The target is within our reach. Focus all your attention on the mission. Nate is no longer our concern. We shall deal with him later."

Bullets soon clanged against the fish-boat's exterior, but on we went. On and on until our iron spar struck the Housatonic with tremendous force. The impact shook the Hunley and threw all of us from our benches. My cheek struck something sharp, and I felt blood when I touched the injured area with my fingers. George was not moving, apparently knocked unconscious. Moans came from others.

I had one remaining hope. I stood up in the conning tower, unlocked the hatch, and clambered out. Icy wind blasted me, and I clung to the snorkel pipe as I struggled to remove my knife from its sheath. Tightly gripping the knife I mouthed a prayer, let go the snorkel pipe, and slid into the Atlantic. The frigid water brought tears to my eyes.

George and some of the others must have recovered, for the Hunley was backing away, yanking the spar loose from the Housatonic's wooden hull. The gunpowder torpedo was at the end of the spar, and if all worked as designed, saw-toothed corrugations would keep the torpedo within the hull as the spar came out. A lanyard attached to the torpedo trigger would draw taut as the Hunley reversed, eventually detonating the explosive.

I splashed through the water trying to ignore the cold, intent on slicing the lanyard before it could tighten and pull the trigger. A simple enough plan, and perhaps it would have been easy on land with a dry rope in warm weather. But I was bobbing in the ocean, left arm hooked over the line as I sawed with the knife clutched in my right hand. My fingers were numb, the lanyard hard and slick. Progress was slow, and slack in the line grew less as distance between the Hunley and the Housatonic increased. Frantically I cut faster … and lost my grip on the knife. It slipped from my hand and sank into the sea.

Now I had surely failed, with nothing to do but drown or hang onto the lanyard and hope for the best. Too much of a coward to drown, I chose the latter.

The line reached full extension, squeezed the torpedo trigger, and the device exploded, a booming blast that nearly shattered my ear drums and left me barely conscious. The Hunley's spar had embedded the torpedo in the Housatonic's magazine, and when the torpedo detonated, so too did the war ship's gunpowder. Pieces of the Housatonic's deck rose up in the dark sky, then plummeted down into the ocean.

I clung groggily to the lanyard, which had been separated from the torpedo by the explosion. A frigid wave doused me, paritally restoring my senses. My vision remained clouded, but the Hunley *appeared to have stalled, perhaps damaged by the blast.*

My situation was grave. Should the Hunley *resume motion, she would advance forward to turn, placing me in peril since I was in her way. And if I were not harmed during the turn, I should be dragged away as the crew made haste for Breach Inlet on Sullivan's Island.*

My only hope was launches from the Housatonic *that were rescuing sailors thrown into the water by the explosion. I released the lanyard and paddled toward the* Housatonic *with the aid of the current. I looked back occasionally, but in the darkness and numbed by cold I could not assess the* Hunley's *condition. Was the fish-boat now moving under her own power, or simply bobbing in the water? She seemed to be submerging, but was that an optical illusion created by buffeting waves, or was she actually sinking?*

I was concerned that if the Hunley *moved forward she would plow across the lanyard, which had curved unnaturally as a result of my extra weight. Very likely this would suck the lanyard into the propeller and wrap it around the screw, which would halt forward motion and almost certainly sink the fish-boat.*

Thoughts of the Hunley *submerging or sinking filled me with a new fear. Unless George had relocked the hatch after my escape, the boat would flood as she went down. But I was powerless to help unless I could summon assistance from the Union fleet.*

I reached a launch and was pulled aboard, my attire unnoticed in the chaos and darkness. Soon we encountered the Union sloop Canandaigua, *which had been informed of the torpedo attack by men from another of the* Housatonic's *launches, and was steaming toward her fellow ship to provide aid.*

Shivering on the deck of the Canandaigua *I saw that the* Hunley's *assault had achieved only limited success. The ocean was shallow here, and the* Housatonic's *masts had remained above water when the ship sank to the bottom. Many sailors had climbed the masts and were hanging onto the rigging awaiting rescue. Later I would learn that only five* Housatonic *crew members had died.*

Suddenly, a gun dug into my back and an officer said in a low voice: "Come along with me and explain to the captain why you do not wear a Union uniform. You have not come from the torpedo boat that wrought this havoc, have you? Wrap this blanket around you, and we shall be unobtrusive as we go. No need to alert others;

they might throw you overboard again."

This I considered a stroke of good fortune, for I wanted to speak with the captain as quickly as possible, identify myself, and beseech him to search for the Hunley and her crew.

The captain listened attentively to my story, then said: "Admiral Dahlgren did receive the letter you describe, Mr. Clary, and he showed its contents to those of us commanding blockading ships. Based on the letter, we were expecting you to seize control of the fish-boat and prevent the attack."

"A large wave struck the boat and threw me off balance," I lied. "The gun was bumped from my hand and retrieved by a crew member. I escaped, jumped into the water, and attempted to cut the lanyard attached to the trigger, but the waves, darkness, and cold proved too difficult to overcome."

The captain reflected. "Well. You have certainly performed courageously," he concluded. "We can regret that you were unable to prevent the torpedo from detonating, but it appears that your effort could not have been greater. However, I fear I cannot immediately honor your request to look for the fish-boat. Much as I should like to capture the murderous Confederate scoundrels who committed this outrage, my first priority must be assisting the crew of the Housatonic. I will have my lookouts scan the sea for any sign of the Hunley, but for the moment, at least, I can do no more than that."

My heart was heavy, but I could not quarrel with the captain's decision. In truth, I feared it might already be too late to save George Dixon and his men.

Respecting the secrecy of my mission, the captain issued me a Union uniform and refrained from revealing my identity to his sailors. He also arranged for my transport on a supply ship to New Bern, North Carolina, a Union stronghold. From there, I used various modes of transportation to reach Washington, where I reported to Secretary of War Edwin Stanton as Ezra Cheddar, and relinquished my rôle as Nathaniel Clary.

Chapter Fifty-Two

Moze and DuBois came inside from the deck, Moze's hand on DuBois' shoulder. Possibly something good would come of this night after all.

"Arnie texted me while we were out there," DuBois said. "I'm taking off now to meet him and make funeral arrangements for my mother."

I stood and extended my hand, and DuBois took it and shook.

"I don't know what your future plans are," I said. "But I'm planning to establish a detective business, and I could use some help."

"I don't know anything about that kind of work," he said.

"You know a few things about crime," I told him. "And I like your instincts. I'd provide training to help with what you don't know."

He chewed on it for a minute. "I might be interested," he said. "Mr. Cheddar has invited me to come up to his cabin after my mother's funeral to read the *Hunley* diary and look at other family records and pictures. Afterward I'll probably come back here and enroll at the College of Charleston to finish my degree. If I do that, I'll need a job to help pay for tuition and living expenses."

"It's a standing offer," I said. "Just keep in touch."

DuBois departed, and Moze picked up the diary pages I'd just read and dropped them in his knapsack. "What you planning to do with the other pages I gave you?" he asked.

"You can have them back. Or I could burn them."

"Burning's fine," he said.

"What happened to Ezra when he returned to Washington?" I asked.

"Secretary Stanton did all right by him," Moze said. "There hadn't been no trace found of the *Hunley*, so the way Stanton figured it, only five sailors from the *Housatonic* died compared to all eight Confederates from the fish-boat, which was in favor of the Union. Also, Ezra told Stanton the same lie he'd told to the captain of the Canandaigua, how a wave rocked the *Hunley*, causing him to drop his gun and lose control over the crew. Stanton couldn't put no blame on Ezra for that. Then there was the true part about Ezra jumping in the water and trying to cut the lanyard before the torpedo exploded. That was sure enough in his favor, especially since Ezra dressed it up a little, claimed he'd hung on to the lanyard till the last minute, hoping it'd get sucked into the *Hunley*'s propeller and sink the fish-boat if it didn't sink otherwise."

Moze's bald brown head looked like a wet acorn, glistening with sweat from his time on the deck. Through the glass doors behind him a silver stream from the brick corner post lamp lit my neighbor's wrought iron pool fence. I stretched my arms above my head and heard my joints crackle and pop.

"You believe the diary tells things the way they really happened?" Moze asked.

"I do," I said. "But why hasn't anyone ever come across records of what Ezra did?"

"There wasn't no records," Moze said. "Stanton got rid of the official file. Keeping secrets in Washington was like building a corral to trap air, and Stanton feared Ezra would be harmed if Confederate sympathizers got wind of what he'd done. That was okay with Ezra. He didn't take no pride in his actions, and others learning about his spy work didn't hold no appeal for him.

"Some days Ezra was tore up with regret that he hadn't shot George Dixon and stopped the *Hunley* from sinking the *Housatonic*. Other days he was tore up with regret that him escaping and leaving the hatch unlocked and hanging onto the lanyard might have caused Dixon and the others on the *Hunley* to die. Ezra wanted to put the whole business behind him and find a fresh life, but he never could get loose of his demons. That's why he put a gun in his mouth. Bothers me he ended things that way. I don't hold with suicide."

Moze wrinkled his forehead. "Guess that sounds like I'm ashamed of Ezra, think he was a coward. And maybe that is what I used to think. But today I went over to that Lasch Conservation place in North Charleston and took a look at the *Hunley* in that tank where they put it. When I saw how small that submarine boat is and gave thought to nine men being jammed inside and going out into the ocean, a shiver ran through my bones. I figure anybody brave enough to do what them men did deserves to be called a hero, including Ezra. His cause wasn't the same as the others', but he was willing to sacrifice his life just the same. Maybe you see things different."

"I see things the same way," I told him. "As for Ezra's suicide, you and I have been to war and know how that experience affects men. I think you should feel sadness about the way Ezra died, but not shame."

Moze cogitated, then blew out a breath as if he were attempting to expel an evil spirit. "Reckon I'll try to bring myself around to that point of view. If I can, might could be I'll be able to do what your daddy asked and use the diary for the good of the *Hunley* and its crew."

He lifted his knapsack and slipped the straps over his shoulders. "Guess I'll head on home. Need to take my suit of clothes out of mothballs and get it cleaned. Told DuBois I'd come back for his momma's funeral."

"I'll see you then," I said. "Maybe we can talk business."

"What sort of business?"

"Detective business. Hopefully DuBois will come in as a junior partner, and I'd also like to have a senior partner, somebody with experience available on as-needed basis."

Moze cocked his head and studied me. "Got a hunch that you hankering for the three of us to be in on something together ain't only about business. Whatever it's about, you can count on me."

Now I had junior and senior partners. If I could find any clients, my detective business would be a rousing success.

"Moze," I said, as he stepped around Cherisse's getaway bag on his way to the front hall.

He paused.

"That's your in-law's suitcase. Any chance you can dispose of it?"

"You don't think the boy oughta have it?"

I shook my head. "The bag has new identity documents. Cherisse was running away. I'd like to think she would have gotten in touch with DuBois once she was settled wherever she was going. But DuBois was rejected by his father; there's no need for him to know his mother was bailing out of his life too."

"Sure ain't," Moze agreed. "Boy's already got enough misery in his heart." He gave me a penetrating look. "Something else about this suitcase troubling you, Mr. Berard?"

"It's a raw reminder of what happened earlier," I told him. "DuBois accused me of killing Cherisse by chasing her into traffic, and it's hard to argue that he's wrong."

Moze narrowed his eyes as he weighed the possibilities. "Ain't that hard," he said. "Might be the Dane woman felt the world closing in on her and made a choice. Maybe you oughta try to bring yourself around to that point of view while I'm trying to bring myself around to the point of view that there wasn't nothing dishonorable about what Ezra did."

"Fair enough," I said, forcing a limp smile.

Moze lifted Cherisse's bag and nodded. "Reckon we both got ourselves work to do, then. I'll leave you to yours and go start in on mine."

Cherisse's suitcase swung like a pendulum oscillating back and forth in time as Moze carried it down the hall.

With DuBois and Moze gone, there was just me and my thoughts. I thought Gary Nagle and I would plan another trip to Cambodia to search for Kam Lim. I thought I'd drive up to Newport, make peace in person with Francie Giordano and invite Lim's uncle, Pran Chea, to relocate down here. I thought I'd say yes if Ellen Talley invited me to dinner.

I stuffed my hands in my pockets and discovered Durell Pritchard's voice recorder. I deleted the conversation between Durrell and Cherisse about my father's murder and microwaved the recorder in a bowl of water. Then I dropped the recorder in the garbage, discarding remnants of a past that no longer consumed me.

THE BEGINNING

Historical Notes

The Ninth Man is based in part on the Civil War story of the Confederate submarine *H.L. Hunley*, which was brought to Charleston, South Carolina, for the purpose of sinking Union ships blockading Charleston Harbor. Much of the information in *The Ninth Man* about the *Hunley* and her mission is true as best the author has been able to determine. This includes the physical description of the boat and her operations. References are made to actual crew members George Dixon, Horace Hunley and Joseph Ridgaway, but their characteristics and behavior in *The Ninth Man* are a blend of fact and fiction. The *Hunley* sank twice during training runs in Charleston, killing a portion of one crew and all of another. While *The Ninth Man* attributes one of these incidents to sabotage, the historical record indicates that both were accidents.

It is true as indicated in *The Ninth Man* that the *Hunley* vanished after attacking the Union warship *Housatonic* and was missing for one hundred thirty-six years until located at the bottom of Charleston Harbor and recovered. The *Hunley* was raised from the ocean near Sullivan's Island in 2000, and placed in a specially designed tank in what is now called the Warren Lasch Conservation Center on the old Navy base in North Charleston. Conservation efforts continue, and Friends of the *Hunley* sponsors weekend public tours. Friends of the *Hunley* is a nonprofit organization established by the South Carolina *Hunley* Commission to assist with fundraising for restoration and exhibition of the submarine.

It is hoped that restoration efforts will eventually solve the mystery of why the *Hunley* and her crew perished. However, the reasons for the boat's demise had not been determined at the time *The Ninth Man* was written, and the book's portrayal of circumstances that caused the *Hunley* to sink are fictional.

For many years prior to discovery of the *Hunley*, it was believed that the boat carried a crew of nine. However, only eight bodies were found when the *Hunley* was raised, and it is now assumed that the crew numbered just eight. *The Ninth Man* depicts a ninth crew member, but he is entirely fictional, as are all his actions including his role in sinking of the *Hunley*.

Factual information about the *Hunley* in *The Ninth Man* came from a number of sources. Most prominent among these are http://www.Hunley.org by Friends of the *Hunley*; *Raising the Hunley* by Brian Hicks and Schuyler Kropf; *The H.L. Hunley: The Secret Hope of the Confederacy* by Tom Chaffin; and http://www.theHunley.com by George W. Penington, particularly newsletter 33, which contains theories about sinking of the *Hunley*. Any inaccuracies about the *Hunley* in *The Ninth Man*, except intentionally fictional renderings, are the responsibility of the author.

The Ninth Man references other historical events in addition to the *Hunley*'s experiences. Edwin Stanton, for whom the Union spy works in *The Ninth Man*, was Abraham Lincoln's Secretary of War, and did practice law in Pittsburgh, Pennsylvania before going to Washington, D.C. The Child Murders case in Atlanta, the Siege of Atlanta anti-abortion protest and a gunman who forced his way into the Atlanta FBI office and took hostages, were real occurrences. Also real were the civil rights March for Brotherhood in Forsyth County, Georgia and a follow-up march. All of these Georgia events occurred in the late 1980s. The civil rights organization All Shall Be Free mentioned in *The Ninth Man* is fictional, as is the plot by leaders of that organization to send mail bombs and poisoned letters to white supremacist groups.

MEET THE AUTHOR:

Brad Crowther is a writer and consultant living in Mt. Pleasant, South Carolina with his wife, Chris, and their beagles, Hershey and Milo. Brad and Chris's son, Jon, is a business executive residing in Rhode Island. Prior to becoming a consultant, Brad was employed by Rhode Island's State criminal justice planning agency, first as a Law Enforcement Planner and then as Executive Director, a Governor-appointed position. Brad also served in the United States Coast Guard with assignments in California, New York, and Italy. Brad may be reached through his website:
http://www.bradcrowther.com.

Endorsements for *The Ninth Man* and for author, Brad Crowther:

Brad Crowther is winner of the 2010 Black Orchid Novella Award presented jointly by The Wolfe Pack and *Alfred Hitchcock Mystery Magazine*.

"Politics Makes Dead Bedfellows," our Black Orchid Novella Award-winning story, delivers an enigmatic whodunit that will please fans of classic detective stories, and gives us a fresh new crime-solving duo in the eccentric Edna Dugué and her sharp-tongued assistant Jerrelle Vesey —**Linda Landrigan**, Editor, *Alfred Hitchcock's Mystery Magazine*

"In a city as steeped in history as Charleston, S.C., the past isn't dead; it's not even past. Brad Crowther conveys its haunting power to perfection in *The Ninth Man*, a debut novel distinguished by pitch-perfect dialogue, a suspenseful plot, and a superb cast of characters. This fledgling series may do for Charleston what Laura Lippman is doing for Baltimore."—**Bruce DeSilva**, Edgar Award-nominated author of *Rogue Island*.

"For some, the legacy of the Civil War will never die. Told from the alternating perspectives of Russell Berard, wise-cracking retired detective, Moze Cheddar, an off-the-grid killer, and the diary entries of Ezra Cheddar, a Union spy who infiltrated the Hunley project, *The Ninth Man* is about three lives interwoven by espionage, murder, and conspiracy. Crowther's quick-witted dialogue and multi-layered plot make for a lively and intriguing read."
—**Carla Damron**, author of *Death in Zooville* and *Spider Blue*

"*The Ninth Man* blends a fast-paced story with a fascinating historical puzzle. Crowther has a keen insight into what still matters for people who cannot — or perhaps will not — let go of the past."
—**Albert A. Bell, Jr,** Award-winning author *Corpus Conundrum,* & the Pliny series of historical mysteries

"Was there a Yankee spy aboard the ill-fated Confederate submarine *Hunley*? Brad Crowther's new novel *The Ninth Man* stirs up the Lowcountry pluff mud with a thriller that brings that unsolved Charleston mystery into the mainstream of the Holy City today in a tale-twisting adventure." —**Ken Burger,** author of Swallow Savannah and Sister Santee.

"Brad Crowther has achieved a remarkable feat channeling Chandler and Shaara to combine my favorite genres in one fast paced mixture of history, mystery and suspense.

Crowther creates characters that leap both from the pages of history and those of my favorite authors. Russell Q. Berard could easily swap lines and punches with Philip Marlow, no small feat.

Charleston's history has yet to produce another character complicated and sharp witted like that of Detective Russell Q. Berard. At the end of *The Ninth Man*, a reader hopes that Berard returns to settle scores and mysteries from other centuries."
—**Batt Humphreys**, Award-winning author of *Dead Weight*

"The Ninth Man is an action-packed blend of history, mystery, romance, and suspense — I dare you to correctly identify the culprit."—**Vincent H. O'Neil**, Malice Award-winning author of *Death Troupe*

"The Ninth Man is rife with twists, turns and several interweaving sub-plots, remaining true to the classic style of 1950s detective novels sans the kitschy pulp one-liners." —**Kristin Hackler,***The Island Eye News*

CPSIA information can be obtained at www.ICGtesting.com
Printed in the USA
243686LV00002B/13/P